TIME WARPED

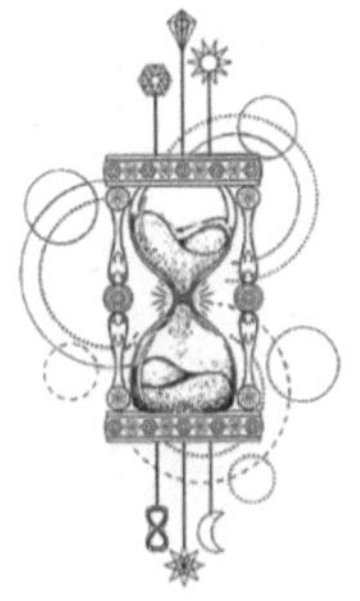

Micky O'Brady

Chapter One

"Welcome to the team, Lieutenant Thorburn." Admiral Grazer's perpetual scowl, visible even under his medical-grade face mask, deepens as he pins a little silver knob to my right collar. "May the wind be always at your back, may the sun shine warm upon your face, and, until we meet again, may fate watch over you and guide your every mission. The United Space Exploration Fleet is proud to call you one of ours. Congratulations." He extends a hand, and while he sounds even more grouchy than normal, I shake it.

"Thank you, sir. It's an honor to be promoted so early." As in, at seventeen *and* four weeks before graduating the academy. Pays to have worked my butt off, although to be honest, I still don't know how I ended up right here, right now. The last days have been a blur.

Grazer harrumphs, the deep sound bringing his considerable belly to a wobble. "An honor you'll have to thank Admiral Mashaule for. I would've—" He pauses and sighs, his grumpy expression softening the slightest bit. "Never mind, Lieutenant. I don't want you to get the wrong impression. You are the best of your year and have shown excellent progress since your admission to the academy. If anybody deserved that promotion, it was—is—you."

Music to my ears, especially if I choose to overhear the undertones of disapproval, but let's focus on the part where he finally acknowledged I'm the best of my year. It's taken me all my academy life for him to see that.

Grazer straightens his black uniform and points at mine. "How does it feel, Lieutenant?"

Lieutenant. Sounds good. Real good. I snap to attention, my self-sealing mask adjusting to the change in head position. Nice to know it's keeping me safe from breathing in virus-filled air. "Wonderful, sir. Fits." And I mean both, literally and proverbially. I've dreamed of becoming a member of Division Two since I was nine years old. And today, eight years later, I've made it. Granted, the uniform looks a bit different from what I remember and I'm missing the rainbow swirl patch, but oh, well. They probably changed the design in the last eight years.

The admiral nods. "Indeed, it fits you. Remember to take the uniform off once you leave here and to speak to nobody about this. I probably don't have to emphasize that for now your pre-termed promotion is highly classified and cannot be mentioned to anybody outside this room until you have officially graduated. You should consider yourself lucky we snatched you before official assignments for your year come out."

"I do. Thank you, sir. It came as a surprise, to be honest." But hey, I'll take it. This is Division Two, after all; the special forces group responsible for handling classified missions. Everything I've been working toward.

The admiral rolls his eyes. "To me too, believe me, but well… desperate times…" He sighs, and I'm pretty sure there's my reason: We've been at war with the Quaneez for over three decades, and the constant battle has taken its toll. We might be at a ceasefire currently—and have been for the last four months, thanks to the great work of our most awesome heads of OUTREACH and my mentors, Admirals Conolly and Upinga—but at this point, the academy is accepting recruits age sixteen and younger, which says all there is to say about our desperation to match the enemy in viciousness and numbers once they remember peace is not for them, but the annihilation of the human race is.

Ergo, the United Space Exploration Fleet is doing its best to crank out graduates who can fight the battle and turn the page, but if the Quaneez attacked right now, it wouldn't look good for us. Currently, we're working on three different agendas: we have battle cruisers out there, science vessels, and exploration ships… everything and anything that could give us the upper hand. So, either our battle cruisers beat them and we have peace, our science vessels reach an understanding with them and we have peace, or our exploration ships will find us a region of space suitable for peaceful living, relocate humanity there and hope the Quaneez are happy with that and leave us be. Voila, peace as well. I think I can speak for all humanity though when I say options number one and three suck. So yeah, most of us are rooting for understanding and peace.

The admiral sighs again and gives me a pat on the shoulder. "And those desperate times are exactly why I have your first mission for you." He turns to his desk and grabs an old-school manila folder from the top of the pile.

Excuse me, what? "A mission?" Already? I mean, I'm not complaining, I'm ready, but I'm not even official yet.

"Yes. A mission. The reason for your early promotion and the condition it is tied to."

"Condition?" It comes out as a squeak. What condition?

"Yes. Condition." The admiral wiggles the folder in his hand. "You still want to be a member of Division Two, don't you?"

Well, duh. Division Two has always, *always* been my goal. Insert Daddy's protest right here. "Of course, sir. But I—I thought that's what just happened." With my promotion. And the black uniform. And Grazer, the head of D-2, promoting me.

"Preliminary, Thorburn. Preliminary. If it goes well, I will turn it into a permanent assignment."

I barely suppress pulling on my collar. Feels tight all of a sudden, because this is nothing if not a hidden threat. Should've known. Grazer had years to evaluate me, and so far, he's never made a move to recruit me. This is Admiral Mashaule's support—not Grazer's love for me.

Grazer taps the folder in his hand. "When Admiral Mashaule brought up the idea for this mission, he had you in mind, Lieutenant. I guess you impressed him. He wouldn't consider anybody else, despite me urging him to do so—and here we are." He gives me a long, stern glance. "And if you handle this mission well, you'll have proven yourself and you're in, Thorburn."

A trial by fire, got it. Because this is still Grazer's Division, and even though Admiral Mashaule is the USEF's leading fleet admiral and president, he has no say over whom Grazer chooses for his team.

And unfortunately for me, Grazer has never been my biggest fan, although I might have to blame my dad for that.

"Now, as a disclaimer, Lieutenant, this mission is top secret, and when I say top secret, I mean less than three people know about it. Which means, it is also not cleared for *Admiral* Thorburn to know about. He isn't elected USEF president yet. You get what I'm saying?"

Mind reader. "Of course, sir. I will not talk to anybody about it, including my father." As an admiral's daughter, I'm used to secrets and need-to-know information, although up to now, I've only been on the receiving end of it. And honestly, keeping both, this mission and my early promotion quiet, will serve me well. I can hear the gossip already if the other students found out about either, and despite the fact that no instructor ever has given me any leeway because of who my father is, my classmates still think they must have, especially over the last year that Dad has announced his race for the USEF Presidency. Why else would the youngest in the year be leading the scoreboard? Must be because her father is an admiral. Never mind said admiral didn't want me in the academy or anywhere near Division Two in the first place, and never mind I had to work twice as hard for my grades compared to my classmates, because believe it or not, it's never easier as an admiral's daughter. Grazer is a prime example. There is a possibility he likes me, although he has been way stricter with me than with anybody else, as far as I can tell. Now, that could be because I'm wrong and he hates my guts—and today's spiel of this *preliminary promotion* plays into that—or it could be typical overcompensating so it doesn't look like he's favoring a colleague's daughter. Add being Admiral *Thorburn's* daughter, and I had my work cut out for me, but never mind all that. The rumors always stay.

Grazer opens the manila folder, then closes it again. "You know, all ambivalence about your promotion from my side apart, I must admit I'm sorry for you about the secrecy. You might be breaking an over thirty-year-old record here. Fastest mission out of the academy, if I'm not mistaken. Only Wildason was faster than you, but not by much."

My heart makes a silly little jump. Being mentioned in the same sentence—kind of—as Captain Kieran Wildason, the USEF's most famous and successful captain of all time, is a big, big deal… to me at least, but maybe because I'm biased. My mentors, Admiral Chase Conolly, former First Officer on Captain Wildason's *Pioneer*, and Admiral Zio Upinga, a Magellan and notably the first and only non-human in the USEF and also Wildason's former Medical Officer, handled a huge portion of my training. Thanks to them, I've heard all there is to hear about the famous captain who died in space way too young at the hands of the Quaneez. If push came to shove, I'd say besides Admirals Conolly and Upinga, I'm the one who knows most about Wildason. More than the history books, that's for sure, and those books are full of the *Pioneer*'s accomplishments. If it wasn't for those three officers, humanity would still be in the infancy of space exploration. I have to look up the exact numbers, but I would guess they discovered and connected humanity with at least two-thirds of the intelligent species we know today.

"Anyway, your mission: we need your help with the reptilian H12N3-Influenza pandemic on five out of our six out-of-solar system colonies."

I suck in a sharp breath. "The flu catastrophe?" What can *I* possibly do about that? It was declared a pandemic and humanitarian disaster over two months ago, which is when the USEF mobilized emergency reserves to help the victims and prevent spread. Still, it's nowhere near an improvement, despite all efforts to contain the disease. Face masks became mandatory on most colonies four months ago. Earth initiated pandemic protocol about eight weeks later, and while contact restrictions and masks work, not everybody complies with the mandate. Let's just say our numbers are going up, when they should be stagnating or improving. It doesn't look good.

"Correct, Lieutenant. The flu catastrophe. That virus…" His gaze loses focus for a moment. "I never thought we'd see another virus this aggressive or hard to control. Or that our containment measures would fail so spectacularly that it could spread like wildfire from one colonized planet to the next. Hundreds of thousands dead, several hundreds of thousands more infected… and absolutely no working treatment." His black facemask might be muffling his words, but the horror behind them remains unfiltered.

Chills run down my spine. The situation is getting worse by the day. The news said it was like during the Corona pandemic in the 21st century, or the plague in medieval times on those infected planets, and it's easy to see why they said so: lockdowns, people afraid to mingle, entrance doors marked when somebody got sick, hundreds of dead bodies burned or cremated every day, and in several instances, people killed their remaining family members out of fear of catching the illness. So far only one colony and Earth have not been lifted into official lock-down status—*so far*. Because the way that thing is spreading, it's only a matter of time, and then we're all doomed, no matter the travel restrictions, no matter the masks, and no matter our precautions.

Grazer holds up a finger. "But here's the kicker: we *had* no working treatment—until now. None of our mRNA-vaccine trials yielded any effect on the immune system. That virus…" He shakes his head. "It outsmarts us. Well, *outsmarted*, I hope. Our newest of the new deep space spectral analysis found evidence for a substance doctors think will help the immune system kill it, and said substance occurs in abundance in a nightshade-plant on an H-class planet about two maximum jumps away from here. You—"

"Help the immune system—like a vaccine?" I blurt. It would be a game changer!

Grazer smiles despite me speaking out of turn. Proof right there how the pandemic has changed us already. The last months haven't been easy on anybody, and it's not like the Quaneez made it easy on us before, but the threat of an invisible opponent has everybody on edge. Take any pre-pandemic day, and Grazer would've chewed me out for interrupting him, but not today.

He takes another paper, this one filled with the squiggles of a spectroscopy and points at it. "This is hot off the press. Admiral Mashaule himself sent it to me. These two spikes are what has us hoping we might be able to use the plants."

I whistle through my lips until I remember that might not be the most professional response for a newly minted lieutenant.

Professionalism, please. I clear my throat. "That sounds wonderful. I assume you'd like me to collect specimens?" What else would he need me for? Sounds easy-peasy, although this should go through Medical Services and their team. They could extract—and maybe even synthesize—whatever they need right there.

The admiral nods. "Indeed. Your mission is to jump to the planet, collect as many samples as you can, and bring them back to us for processing and replication, hopefully. If we can't stop this virus, it has the potential to… Well, let's put it like this—and that's also top secret, by the way, last thing we need is global panic—that if we don't stop the spread, it will take no longer than another two months and eighty percent of humanity is going to be infected. *Including* Earth. At this point, we're not talking about a death toll of hundreds of thousands, or even millions, we're talking about the extinction of the human race. We need those plants, and fast." He balls his hand into a fist.

Holy cow. My insides tighten. I had no clue it was *that* bad. Bad, yes—but doomsday bad, as in, we're counting our last months? Nope. I never imagined hearing those words in this context. The extinction of the human race—and not by the Quaneez. And they want *me* to take on a mission of this magnitude? *Me?* A cadet? Sorry… a new lieutenant?

I stand up straighter, my left leg aching as it always does when standing for too long. "S-sir, are you sure you want *me* to take on this mission? It could easily be one of the most important missions—"

Grazer smacks the folder onto his open palm. "Lieutenant, are you telling me you are refusing to follow an order?"

Oh, crap. "No, sir." I snap to attention.

"Or are you telling me neither the academy nor Conolly and the String Bean trained you well enough to jump a shuttle to pre-programmed coordinates, scan for plants and return with some *flowers*, of all things?"

A rush of hot anger sweeps over me. *String Bean.* Only years of academy training are to thank for keeping my reaction in check. I hate those thoughtless comments. I really do. Admiral Upinga is the USEF's most decorated medical officer and a great instructor. A great guy, period, no matter the species he belongs to.

Still, I keep my emotions in check. Helps to have a mask covering the lower half of my face. "No, sir. I can jump, scan, and retrieve samples. I apologize, Admiral." Sheesh.

Grazer's mouth snaps shut with a slight popping sound. He sighs heavily and shakes his head. "At ease, Lieutenant. No apologies needed, other than by me. The situation we're in has been quite stressful. And I know you can fulfill the tasks, they're not that difficult. But you were right questioning me. There's a catch."

Don't like the sound of that. I tilt my head. "Oh?"

The admiral opens the poor abused folder once more. Should've known this meant business when he brought out untraceable paper instead of a Personal Assistance Device. Nobody uses paper if a PAD will do.

"There is a reason why you were chosen, besides your skills. Here's the problem. The planet with those plants is located right here." He turns the top page around so I can see a map of the explored universe around our solar system. As always, our sun is in the middle of the map, with the USEF space outlined in red. It's shaped like the profile shot of a dog's head, Sol being the eye. A few irregular specks are marked around that, like the dog had shaken off some rain drops. Those are the territories of the other intelligent species we've encountered. But the biggie, literally, is bordering our space and looking more like an amorphous blob, as if the dog was looking right at it: the Quaneez's developed space.

And the planet Grazer marked, is smack dab in their territory.

Acid churns in my stomach. I cringe. "Ouch. That's… quite deep into their domain." An understatement. There's no way I could blame this on a navigational error if they found a USEF-officer this deep inside their space. It would be a violation of the treaty, and that would mean flare-up of the war.

Unless—

I look up at him. "That's the reason you're sending *me*, isn't it? Plausible deniability?"

Spot on. The admiral flinches. "Not the best phrasing, but yes. We need *you* for this, Lieutenant. For two reasons. One, you're excellent at what you do, and two, we specifically need you for this mission because you're not a graduate yet, which means we can sell it as a rogue human acting on her own. Seeing that you want to join D-2, might as well get used to the stealth mode."

His earlier words come back to me. I complete this mission, I'm an official member of Division Two. The problem dawning on me though is that the alternative is… I might not come back at all. I suppress a shiver.

"If you were caught—and I say *if*, not *when*, because I know you can and will get this done—the Fleet can deny all involvement."

And there we go. At least he said *if* I got caught, although deny it in front of whom? The Quaneez? Good luck trying to explain *that* to them. Would be the first successful communication in the history of the Quaneez Wars, hallelujah. And I doubt anybody else besides the Magellans would hold us accountable. We're the biggest space-faring power amidst all of them, and we're arrogant enough to not talk to them much, unfortunately. But anyway, appreciate the sentiment. Maybe he doesn't hate my guts after all.

I swallow hard. "Understood, sir." And *understood* means, I get it. Part of it. I succeed and bring the antidote to the killer-virus, I'm the hero. The unsung hero probably, because we don't want to broadcast we risked breaking the fragile ceasefire, but still a hero. But if I fail… Either I'm going to be killed in battle trying to escape, or I'm going to be captured, and we all know the Quaneez' preferred way to extract information and deal with prisoners of war. It ain't pretty.

The part I still don't get is why it's me. Send a retired, well-seasoned and experienced officer. The rogue human excuse works just the same for them. I'm honored I was chosen, but don't we want to maximize our chances? Lifting my chin, I give it one more try. "Sir, please don't get me wrong, but are we sure we want to send me instead of a senior officer with more overall experience?"

Grazer's jaw sets. "Apparently we are, Lieutenant. Not that I would've recommended you for that job, but again, you are a worthy choice."

Ouch. Glad the mask is hiding part of my flinch. Thanks for the diss.

A tickle of panic rises in my chest, one that brings the taste of bile with it. I pull my shoulders back, push my chin forward, and the rising anxiety down my throat. "You can count on me, sir. I'm not going to disappoint you." Or let humanity die. Even though he said it after a verbal jab, I *am* a worthy choice. I can get the job done. Plus, I've never backed down from a challenge since I was nine years old, and today is not the day to start.

Grazer gives me a crooked smile. "I hope not. Briefing tomorrow. My office. And please, do remember: not a word to anybody. Nobody can know. Not your mentors, not your father. *Especially* not your father. I can't emphasize enough how important secrecy is, in any outcome. The hope of those colonies and millions of people rests on you and your ability to keep a secret, Lieutenant. I trust in you. In two days, you will have the opportunity to save the human race." He pauses and gives me a look that burrows deep, into the bottom of my soul. "But do remember, peace is fragile. Please don't break it, or we're doomed, no matter what."

Chapter Two

". . . bringing the total of arrests up to one hundred and fifty in Iowa alone. But despite the magnitude of the arrest, Senator Morgan Vu, the head of Iowa's First Party, is optimistic he will have all his fellow party members released by the morning."

The image of the female newscaster is replaced by an older Asian man. *". . . we're not doing anything wrong. The opposite. We're fighting for the purity of the human race. It is our civic duty to prevent intentional harm and contamination, and we will not stop until Earth—and our space—is completely purely human again."*

The image blacks out and the newscaster is back. *"The exit polls during today's election show a slight increase for the First Party, with a majority passing Six and revoking Ten. Should this addendum come through as anticipated, the way is straightened out for Senator Vu and the First Party to restrict human-Magellan contact to off-world planets. And now, the weather forecast. Throughout Iowa, temperatures are going to drop—"*

Dad sighs and turns off the volume. "Should've bought that wine when I saw it in the store. The universe knows today is a day to take a sip. Restricting human-Magellan contact even more... damn them."

I look up from the silenced transmission and over my shoulder at my dad. He never drinks, because work could call him anytime. He rarely full-out curses either. "I assume it's even worse than I think it is?"

As an admiral with the USEF, Dad has more of an insight into politics than I do, watching the news or not.

My dad's lips press into a thin line. "People can be short-sighted, Nonie."

"Short-sighted?" I rock back and forth on the ginormous bean bag I've called my own since forever. I wouldn't be so kind and say it's short-sighted. Idiotic is more like it.

He shrugs. "Short-sighted. They can't see beyond what's right in front of their nose."

Duh. I roll my eyes. "I know what short-sighted means, thank you, Dad, and I was able to apply the metaphor to the current situation. I just wouldn't have chosen such tame wording."

He points at the transmission. "Believe me, I have kept the R-rated phrases to myself. You know, at the end of the day, these people are afraid. I try to keep that in mind to understand where they're coming from."

"Afraid of the Magellans." A people so peace-loving and gentle, most of their ships don't even carry weapons.

A faint smile pulls on the corners of his mouth. "Believe it or not, but yes. You're too young—"

"I'm almost fourteen, Dad."

"I know, but—"

"And I've aced my SATs last month."

He holds up a calming hand. "I know, Nonie, I know. But while you are smart, there are certain things in life you don't see yet."

"There you go again with your visual metaphors."

"Smart ass." My dad sticks his tongue out at me. "Anyway, point is people fear change. They fear to lose their footing in the natural hierarchy where humans like to consider themselves top of the evolution. In come the Magellans, and bring us technological advancements like the dematerializer, and instead of opening our arms and learning from them, we feel threatened. In fact, I'd go out on a limb and say those people fear the change that comes with embracing other cultures. And it becomes a Perpetuum Mobile, a never-ending story, the snake biting its own tail. They fear other cultures, but instead of getting to know and understand them, they push them away with all their might. Fear of the unknown."

I know that. Communication is key, as Dad always says. I quote him. "Most misunderstandings and conflicts happen from bad or nonexisting communication, right, Dad?"

He smiles. "Many of them. Not all, mind you, but good communication has never worsened any situation."

"You should come and teach at my school." I grunt and cross my arms in front of my chest.

Dad's face falls. "They're still bugging you?"

No need to clarify who *they* are. I shrug. "Not bugging me. I can deal with them."

"Which means they're still bugging you." He pinches the bridge of his nose with two fingers and sighs. "And here I was, thinking talking to the principal would help. Nonie, I don't know what to tell you besides what I've been telling you all your life. Ignore them. Don't listen to them. They—"

"They say I only passed my SATs already because you pulled strings." That one hurt, although I did my best not to show it. *Hold your head up high*, Dad says, and I did.

Dad rolls his eyes. "Idiots."

Oh, he hasn't even heard half of it. "And they said—" On second thought, never mind. I suck in my lower lip and bite it. Not a good topic.

"Said what?"

I drop my gaze to my lap. "Nothing."

"Nonie." Dad drums an annoying rhythm onto the couch's armrest. "What did they say?"

I suck in a deep breath and get the words out as fast as I can. "Thatyou'reatraitortothehumanracebecauseyou'reworkingwith*them*and *bringingtheenemytoEarth*." That one almost made me punch Stevie Beauchamps, and that's saying something.

Dad's fist comes crashing down onto the couch. "What the f—" He catches himself and clears his throat. "What the flickerbug, I mean. That was Stevie, right? His parents have always stood more right of the line than they should be comfortable with, so no surprise there."

Can't deny it. "Yeah. Stevie." And Tracy. Followed by Luna. Blake.

Fabrizio.

Dad gives me a critical once-over. "Who else? What else?" The way he emphasizes it it's clear what he's asking, but I'm not going there today.

I dig my nails into my palm. Must look unaffected. "Isn't that enough?"

"By all means it is, I just have little faith in humanity's common sense and decency these days."

And they have little faith in anything Magellan. I glide a palm over my left leg, a gesture that doesn't stay unnoticed.

"The leg?" Dad keeps his voice level, which is a victory for his self-control.

"Maybe." I shrug.

"For Heaven's sake." He sighs. "It's a biosynthetic leg. What's so hard to get over?"

I shrug again. Good question. Maybe the fact it was synthesized by the Magellans? That I'm the only human with a biosynthetic leg? That I still limp on that side, even though every MD I ever saw for the leg says it's *in my head*, because that leg is at a hundred percent? Doesn't really matter. If it wasn't the leg, they'd focus on my dad, and if it wasn't that… I'm sure they'd find something else.

Dad buries his face in his hands. A spike of guilt brings my stomach to a roil. Exactly what I didn't want—his guilt. Mentioning the leg will always bring on the guilt. I keep my eyes glued to my knee. "It's fine, Dad. I can handle it."

"It's not fine, Nonie," he growls from behind his hands, then drops them. "In a perfect world, your life wouldn't be affected by who I am, but…" Dad leans forward and supports his weight with his forearms on his knees. "But here's another life lesson, child. The leg and its origin aside, you're the daughter of a high-ranking USEF admiral, and said admiral takes a very strong pro-Mag stance, which comes with my job description as Ambassador to the Magellan people. I've ruffled feathers during my career, no doubt about it, and I can list at least five people in influential positions within the USEF who'd like nothing better than to see me and my stupid ideas for integration go up in smoke. Meaning, you're disliked by association. My name is stamped across your forehead, and while I wish being my daughter would make things easier for you, I'm afraid in this day and age the opposite is true."

A tiny flicker of pain crosses his face, gone as fast as it came, a remnant of *those days* a few years ago when being an admiral's daughter could have cost me my life.

I draw in my legs and wrap my arms around them. "You make me feel so much better, Dad."

Goal achieved: Dad chuckles, and it breaks the somber mood. He smacks me over the head. Lovingly, of course. "Shut up, premature thing, and listen. Nothing worth fighting for is easy, and if we want to thrive with the Magellans, we'll have to get through this xenophobia and have people look forward to what they're gaining, not fear what they might be losing. I'm doing all this because I believe to the bottom of my heart that peaceful cooperation is the way to go. Helps that I know Magellans, and that I can tell you I've yet to come across one who isn't a brilliant mind or downright decent being. I'm sorry my actions and my career are giving you trouble, but Nonie, you and I, we're not going to lower ourselves to throwing rocks at anyone, human or not. In fact, I'm going to go out on a limb and say people are going to come to you to make the world a better place one day."

Aww. "Thank you, but no pressure, huh, Dad?"

He ruffles my hair. "As you can tell, I have absolutely no expectations for you, child of mine. Be brilliant. Save the world."

Save the world. I swallow hard. Now's as good as any time. "But I can't save the world from a behind a desk somewhere."

Dad's smile is gone within a nanosecond. "Nonie…" His voice carries a warning: Don't start that topic again. Don't even think of going there.

Problem is, I have gone there already. I look up to him and scoot around on my bean bag, turning my back to the projection of the news. Deep breath. One more. He's gonna find out at one point anyway. "I took the academy's entrance exam last week."

Silence.

A muscle in his jaw twitches—but nothing. No outrage, no disappointment. Only silence.

"Did you hear me, Dad? I took the academy's—"

"I heard you just fine." It comes out as a growl. "Going behind my back. After we decided the academy wasn't for you."

I sit up straighter. We've had this discussion a million times over the years. "Wrong, Dad. *You* decided the academy wasn't for me. *I* decided it was." Which is why I took my chances and the entrance exam *this* year, when he didn't even think I was prepped for it, or there would've been a distinct possibility he'd lock me in my room to keep me from participating. He's kind of overprotective like that. Ridiculous, given the fact that he's working for the same organization he's trying to keep me from, but I guess that falls under parental schizophrenia, or whatever.

His lips press into a thin line. "Nonie, the academy—"

"Is going to give me exactly the education I want."

He huffs, then throws me a long and sarcastic look at me. "Really. If you got accepted, you *will* have to go through fight training, you know that, right?"

A shiver runs down my spine and turns into a stab in my left leg, a very real reminder of how *fighting* can end. "Yes, I know that I'll have to go through fight training." I can't say it makes me feel all warm and fuzzy inside, but I'll handle it. Let's call it desensitization therapy. "I'll be fine, Dad."

"*Fine.* That's what you say now. I don't want you in the academy, Nonie. If there's one favor you do me in life, please choose a different career. You can do whatever you want to, but don't enlist. It's not safe—"

Holy Sun and Stars! "Dad, I'm joining USEF because I want to be safe! Nobody can prep me better for all kinds of situations than them! The-day-we-don't-talk-about wouldn't have happened if I'd had even a bit of training—"

He slams his palm down onto the couch for the second time with two minutes. "Training isn't everything! There are situations in life you cannot train for, and I don't want you anywhere near them!"

I kick against the couch from where I'm sitting. "Well, tough luck, Dad! Because if I did even half as well on the exam as I think I did, I will be eligible for override recruitment under the gifted-and-talented-act, and I'll be going even if you don't want me to! Period!"

Dad's eyes pop wide. "You'd do that? Join against my wishes?" All anger is gone from his voice. He looks like a puppy kicked to the curb.

I deflate. "Dad…" What can I say? I know his aversion against me joining comes from a good place. I'm his only family, and he was this close to losing me once already. But enlisting, it's… it's not just a job for me. It's a calling, as stupid as that may sound. In the depth of my heart and soul I know it's something I must do. There's no other way for me.

So, I take the high road and try to be mature. "Dad, I'm sorry. I know this is hard for you, but it's my life. One way or another I'm going to join USEF, and… and I'd much rather have you in my corner, supporting me, than not." Can't help my voice break a bit with the last part. Not only am I his only family, he's my only family as well.

Silence.

Dad sighs and pinches the bridge of his nose. "You know, Shubert approached me today at work."

"Shubert?" The academy's dean?

"Yeah. Asked me how much I practiced with you for the exams. How much I prepped you."

I cringe. So much for keeping my secret. "Ouch." That's not how I wanted him to find out I skipped school and took the exam instead. Surprised my head is still on top of my shoulders and he hasn't said anything until I brought the topic up.

"*Ouch*, exactly." He looks down onto his hands in his lap. "When did we decide listening to your father's orders wasn't any longer on the agenda?"

My response comes faster than he expected. "When I decided it was my life and my responsibility. I'm overruling your authority in this case."

The last sentence catches him off-guard, as I knew it would. It worked once to make him see reason, maybe it'll work again.

"Overruling my authority…" Dad's mouth opens and closes once, before he draws a deep breath in. He huffs once and mumbles more to himself than at me, "don't like that phrase any better the second time around."

But: no yelling or getting mad at me. A win.

"Anyway, I guess the dean wanted to see how much I flexed my muscles to get you in, but when he saw my face…"

Oh, I can imagine. "He knew you didn't know I took the exams."

Because Dad would've either been pale as the wall from shock, or red as a lobster from anger. Either or, he wouldn't have been the proud tiger dad the dean might've expected.

Dad chuckles, but it sounds defeated. "One could say it like that, yes." He pauses, then leans to the side and reaches for his work briefcase. "He gave me something for you."

I cock my head. "He did?"

"Yes. But I need you to promise me something."

"Uhh, sure. I promise?"

"Nonie." I get a stern look.

Okay, okay. "Yes, Dad. What did you need me to promise?"

"That you will keep yourself safe. That you will not rush into anything headfirst. That you will listen to your inner voice. That you will—"

Sheesh. "Do I need to take notes?"

Dad smacks me over the head again, lightly. "Shut up. You can consider yourself lucky I'm not locking you in your room, but then… Apparently, fate does what she wants and sticks to it, no matter what I do to try to keep you out of her way." He sighs and produces a white envelope from the depth of his briefcase. Hope and anticipation spring to life. Whoa. I sit up straighter. Should he really—

Dad hesitates. "You know, when he gave this to me and I realized you'd gone behind my back to take the exam, I wanted to burn this."

I flinch. "Sorry I—"

"Nu-uh, let me. I wanted to burn this. Badly. But then I realized that you'd gone behind my back because I didn't give you a chance to be upfront with me. Had you asked me to take the exam, I would've said no, so I don't really have a right to be upset about you sneaking out. Don't get me wrong, I *am* upset, but…"

That little bit of hope grows roots and sprouts. "But…?"

"But I've come to see that you're right."

Whoopsie pie. "I am?"

"You are. What you said a minute ago, about having me in your corner? It's not only you making a choice, Nonie, it's me as well. And I can choose to stick to my old stubbornness, or I can choose to stick to my child, and frankly… I prefer the latter." He clears his throat, holding the letter up in an overly theatric way. "So here goes nothing. Nonie Thorburn, I am pleased to inform you that you have passed your entrance exam and psychological testing for admission to the USEF McGuire Academy."

My heart stumbles. Sun and Stars—should the letter truly be what I think it is? Dad cocks his head with a critical impression on his face. "Huh. Passed the psych test. I wonder, did they dig deep enough to find—"

I flinch from the memory. "*That* day? Believe me, they dug deep, found what they were looking for, and then rammed the shovel smack into that topic." Meaning, coming out of that testing alive and in one piece is proof how far I've come. Do I like talking about *that* day? No. Does it haunt me here and there? Oh, heck, yes. Does it interfere with my daily life? Nope, and I have that in writing from the academy, it appears.

Dad's gaze lingers for a full five seconds before he nods once. "Okay. Okay. To continue: It is my pleasure to inform you that you have been accepted with honors as the youngest student since the foundation of the academy system and to hereby officially welcome you to McGuire Academy in the Fall of 2291. We expect you to continue your current trajectory and look forward to you becoming a part of the USEF family."

No. Way.

The sound of my pulse swells in my ears. Did that just happen? Did Dad of all people just welcome me to the USEF academy? I must be dreaming, because, double whopper: One, Dad approving, well, kind of. Two, me, being accepted. It was a long shot applying at my age, but I had the grades, and—

"I did it," I whisper. "I'm really in."

Dad lowers the letter. "Yes, you are." A sad smile plays around his lips, but there's no anger. Only acceptance.

"You had that letter the whole night, and you still tried to talk me out of joining."

He shrugs. "Gotta give an old man time to adjust. Had to come to terms with a lot of things here." He opens his arms. "Come here."

I jump up and fly into his embrace, my arms squeezing around his neck so hard, he must have trouble breathing. "I'm in. And you're not mad." Un-be-lievable. Both of it.

I feel Dad nod in my hug. "No, surprisingly, I'm not mad. Only madly proud, because I know how hard that exam is. From now on, you'll have me in your corner, okay? And while I still prefer you go to vet school or something, I'm so very, very proud of you, Cadet Thorburn."

Cadet Thorburn. Moisture drops from my eyes. Can't be tears. Nope. Impossible. "Thank you, Dad." I sniffle, then pull away and reach for that letter. "Do you mind if I log in and see if I can register for classes already?"

"Now?" His faces scrunches up in confusion. "You still have—"

I protest. "But I don't want to miss AP placements, Dad!"

Dad lets his head hang in mock despair and waves a hand. "Yes. Go. Do your thing, Nonie."

"Thank you!" I smack a kiss onto his cheek before I jump up and dart past the open kitchen toward my room. I doubt anybody has signed up yet, or if they did, maybe they didn't have the credits to enroll for the classes I definitely want to take.

I hear my dad let go of one of his signature deep sighs behind me, and then, so quiet people with less sensitive hearing wouldn't have picked up on it he whispers, "And so it begins." Something in that whisper sounds so desperate, so defeated and resigned, it makes me stumble in my tracks.

A shiver runs down my spine.

I turn and look around the corner. "Dad? You okay?"

Dad drops his briefcase next to the couch and gives me a quizzical glance. "Considering all things, yes. Why?" He wears the exact same expression from before, the sad pride, if I had to describe it, but nothing hints at what I thought I heard.

"N-nothing. Never mind." I fake a smile and walk to my room, but the joy I felt a mere few minute ago has a hard time returning to its exuberant form.

And so it begins.

Another shudder runs down my spine, and this one won't go away even when I'm cuddled in my blankie with my PAD on my knees.

And so it begins.

Chapter Three

"Did anybody see you?" Admiral Grazer punches a command code into the door to the shuttle hangar to keep it locked. Wouldn't want anybody seeing a cadet in civilian clothing boarding a shuttle and taking it for a spin—especially if said cadet and shuttle ended up causing the war to flare up again.

Which they're not.

Because I'm going to nail this.

Bringing back the plants to cure humanity? Will do.

Not causing a war? Will do.

Absolutely no pressure. I wipe my sweaty palms across the outside of my thighs. It'll be all right. It'll be—

"Lieutenant? Hello? If anybody saw you." Grazer waves a hand through the air in front of my face, close to touching my self-sealing mask.

Oops, focus. "Y-yes, sir. Unfortunately, Admirals Conolly and Upinga were in the lobby." At three in the freakin' morning. Seriously. Of all people, I had to run into my mentors. The kings of inconvenient timing.

Grazer groans. "Those two. Of course. What did you say?"

"That I'm practicing for the finals."

"And they bought that?" He sounds surprised, and I can't fault him. He knows my grades. What the admiral doesn't know, is how badly I butchered yesterday's practice scenario with Conolly and Upinga. A blow to my ego, but a good excuse for today.

"Yes, sir, they did." At least I think they did.

Grazer rolls his eyes. "Sure hope so. Last thing I need is them sniffing around."

I cringe. There's not much love between those three, I know that. Hard to not notice it. Another potential reason why Grazer kept me at an arm's length. Besides Dad, I mean. After all, they have very different opinions and have clashed more than once. Or maybe it was just coincidence and me being sensitive, because well, here we are, Grazer choosing *the best*, as he said, for this mission.

I shake out my hands. No pressure. "The parameters still stand, sir?"

"Correct. Nothing has changed." Grazer holds out a PAD for me to place my palm onto it. "The shuttle's controls are transferred to your voice pattern and palm print. And voila, the *Odysseus*." He steps aside and gestures at the old, slightly rusty, grey shuttle behind him. "Don't let the exterior fool you. It might look old on the outside, but the inside is special. Admiral Mashaule personally oversaw the adjustments until one hour ago, and you should be proud to know it is stuffed front to tail with the best technology the USEF can come up with, all while keeping it seemingly civilian on first *and* second glance."

I glide one finger over the shuttle's hull. "Hey there, *Odysseus*." You and I, we're going on a mission. My stomach cramps, but I ignore it. "Thank you, sir. Please give my thanks to Admiral Mashaule as well— in secret of course." I wouldn't be here without him, that's for sure.

Grazer frowns behind his face mask. "I'm not sure thanks are in order." He lets his gaze roam over the *Odysseus*.

Ouch. And here I thought he'd get over Mashaule placing me in his division. Obviously, he's still holding a grudge.

For the longest, most awkward five seconds of my life, Grazer stays quiet, muscles in his jaw working. Then, he sighs once. "But you'll do fine, Lieutenant. Any more questions?"

"N-no, sir. I'm good." As good as it gets, at least.

His gaze softens. "Good luck, Lieutenant, and… it was an honor working with you."

His words slap me like a whip. Wait, what—honor to work with me? Says Admiral Grazer? And why does that sound more like a final good bye than a good-luck wish?

The admiral turns and strides toward the exit, and I barely get a response out. "Th-thank you, sir. The honor is—" The last part is cut off by the doors closing behind him. "All mine, I wanted to say." I sigh. That was weird.

And it doesn't matter, because now it's show time.

I board the shuttle, and within one minute I have her ready to go. Within another minute I'm out the space port and trailing along the course pre-programmed into the shuttle's systems, the one that keeps me off the radar.

Because from now on, I'm a rogue human.

Sounds just great. I draw in a deep breath, and cough. Ugh. Annoying mask. Taking it off, I suck in some sterilized air: much better. Relax, Nonie. You got this.

The *Odysseus* handles like any of the shuttles I've flown during my academy training. It may look its almost fifty years of age, but like the god it was named after, it has the potential to become a hero, if we pull this off.

I punch in the coordinates of the two jumps. Normal procedure would be to execute the first jump, then scan the coordinates of my arrival, then the second, but since we're in stealth mode, I won't linger at the first jump point. Can't, or the Quaneez' new stupid sensitive satellite system is going to announce my presence. So here we go, doing what nobody did before me as far as I know, and entering the coordinates for a second, a blind jump only a few seconds after the first. Nope, my fingers aren't shaking. I'm not nervous. Nu-uh. That's from… I don't know. From not eating enough.

My stomach's in knots, but yeah, that would probably also be because I didn't eat. Yup. Odd, how being here, about to break about a million rules, can feel so wrong, and yet so right at the same time.

Okay. I can do this. Humanity needs me. I won't get caught. I can do this.

I blow out that big breath in a harsh puff of air ending in a wheeze. If the admiral could see me now, all nervous like a complete newbie, I doubt he'd have chosen me for this. But no matter my racing pulse, he did choose correctly, because I'm ready. Get in, scan, locate plants, collect them, get out. All in under ten minutes to avoid *them* catching up with me. Ambitious, but doable. I hope.

I also hope the Quaneez are never gonna pick up on me in their space, or if they do, that they'll be late. That being said, better safe than sorry, so I take an extra twenty seconds to pre-program an off-course escape route. That wasn't in Grazer's briefing and I don't expect to need it, but I was trained by Upinga and Conolly. I learned my stuff, and it's a mere precaution.

Okay. Emergency-escape planned. Scanner prepped. Course laid in. Lieutenant—

I crank my neck.

Lieutenant ready.

"*Odysseus*, get ready for demat and warm up scanners. Let's rock this thing." I shake my hands and before I can chicken out, ram my finger down onto the console to engage the engines for the jump into enemy territory.

"*Executing.*" *Swooosh*—the shuttle transports me through space and comes to a standstill far off the beaten path and close to the borders of what we call our space.

Which means the next jump will bring me smack into *their* space. I suck in a big breath.

Enemy territory.

An act of war.

Odysseus doesn't give me any time to focus on the risks. "*Coordinates reached. USEF vessel USEF Guardian within hailing range.*"

Uhh, thank you, but no, thank you! Last thing I need is witnesses. "Disregard. Execute jump." Get me away from the *Guardian*. Who patrols this close to Quaneez space anyway? Way to go making the Quaneez nervous again.

"*Executing second jump.*"

Here goes nothing. The engines distort space around me, compress it into a neat, short bundle, and catapult me through lightyears of void to my destination. For one short, yet infinite moment, the stars stretch out, then zoom back to nothing more but bright shiny dots on the black canvas of vacuum.

And voilá—I've arrived smack on top of the H-class planet holding the only hope for humanity's survival.

"Bull's eye." Part one, accomplished. A silly little laugh bubbles up. I did it. I mean, the first part. Getting here. Now it's a matter of time. Of *timing. Speed. "Odysseus*, set countdown to ten minutes. Start." I need to be out of here before they realize I'm here and send over a Quaneez battle cruiser.

A beep comes from the *Odysseus'* console. *"Warning. Five million Quaneez life signs detected on the planet. Three Quaneez Battle Cruisers in orbit. We have not been scanned."*

I choke and cough. *"What?"* No. No, no, no—that can't be right! Five million Quaneez? Where are they coming from? Must be a mistake, this is an uninhabited H-class planet— *"Odysseus*, recheck coordinates!"

"We are located in a high orbit around H-155 in the Quaneez—"

"Cancel. Shields up and—" And what? What do I do? There are *five million Quaneez* down there—what the heck? Why didn't we know about that? What do I do? How do I get those plants off the planet and back home? They—

"Warning. Shuttle being scanned. All three Quaneez Battle Cruisers approaching."

Holy freakin—

"Odysseus, get those shields up *now!"* There are three, there might be more, we're not that good scanning for their silent propulsion drive. They tend to pop out of nowhere.

"Shields up and at one hundred percent. Three seconds until weapon's range."

Crap crap crap— "Evasive maneuvers, get me away from them!" I need to keep my distance. They won't fire if I'm close to the planet's atmosphere. If they miss... Quaneez weapons and planetary atmospheres don't go well together.

"Initializing evasive pattern delta four."

The *Odysseus* dives down so fast, internal gravity lags behind. My knees hit the console in front of me hard, pain spiking up my leg. "Ugh," I grunt, but no time to focus on any minor bruises. I've jumped into the deepest doo-doo ever: an inhabited planet *and* battle cruisers? Neither was in my briefing! What do I do? I rake one shaky hand through my hair. "Focus. Focus, Nonie."

"Battle Cruisers' weapons charging."

Oh, flickerbug—

I force a dry swallow down my throat. There is only one option. They know I'm here; the damage is done. I'm not going to shoot first. I'm the aggressor here. Either I get out ASAP, or… if I still want the plants, I only have one chance at this. One try.

I ball my hands into fist. *"Odysseus*, jump us to the opposite side of this planet, then initialize scan for long-range satellites and execute high-power level six scan. Do it now!" Get away from under their noses, scan the fastest I have ever scanned, demat the plants up… if I can do it in record speed, I might be able to get away from here with my life *and* the plants.

Might.

But at least it will buy me a few seconds. The Quaneez don't jump, like we do, and their drive is volatile this close to atmosphere-carrying planets. Meaning, it can ignite atmospheres. Not good, obvs. Error in design, I would say.

"Acknowledged." Within less than a second, space distorts and comes back to normal around us, only that the view of the planet below us has changed. The *Odysseus* displays a stylized outline of the planet, complete with a large core in its center, distribution of population on the surface, and all ships in orbit. *"Scanning. No Quaneez ships detected on this side of the planet. No long-range satellites detected."* Good, but—wait, what? Where is that super-sensitive satellite system Grazer warned me about? Never mind, I don't care. Makes the way out easier. Let's hope it'll take them a second to find me, because they assume I jumped home, not closer to them. I crack my knuckles. *"Odysseus*, prepare for demat and pre-programmed emergency escape while you scan."

"Acknowledged. Level-six scan of planet initialized. All three Battle Cruisers still in orbit on the opposite side of the planet, but moving in. Weapons' range in less than thirty seconds."

That's not what I would consider much time. Here goes nothing. Sweat runs down my neck. Eight more seconds for the scan, then enter coordinates, demat up a whole square meter of organic material, hoping I get what the scientists need, then jump out of here—

"Warning. Planet's core destabilizing. Warning. Planet's core destabilizing. Warning—" Alarms howl, hurting my ears.

"What—Core—?" My gaze flies to the readout on my console. The core—Its temperature is rising, and not only that: the core, which had been large already to begin with, is swelling up like an overinflated balloon. I don't think, I act. "*Odysseus,* cut scan!" What the hell—core destabilizing? How—

The moment I cut my scan, the core stops its expansion, but the temperature keeps on rising. *"Warning. Core explosion imminent. Core explosion imminent."*

No, no, no, no— That can't happen! It can't. Five million Quaneez—

"Core explosion in five seconds. Four—"

No, no, no, no—No choice. Dammit, I've got no choice! I clench my teeth so hard, I bite straight through part of my cheek. "Initialize emergency exit protocols! *Now!*" What kind of freakin' reaction did the scanner cause down there? Shouldn't be possible, shouldn't—

Like a maniac, I enter the commands to get me out of here, to get me to safety and away from this ticking bomb—

"Two—"

Oh, crap.

Now or never, correct coordinates or not. Only chance.

I slam my palm onto the button. "*Odysseus,* override safety protocols! *Jump!*" I yell.

Somewhere to the right of my view screen, a flash of lightning appears, a red beam shooting at the planet—and a millisecond later a wave of pure, blinding light bursts from H-155. The engines howl, space contracts around me, my skin burns—

Chapter Four

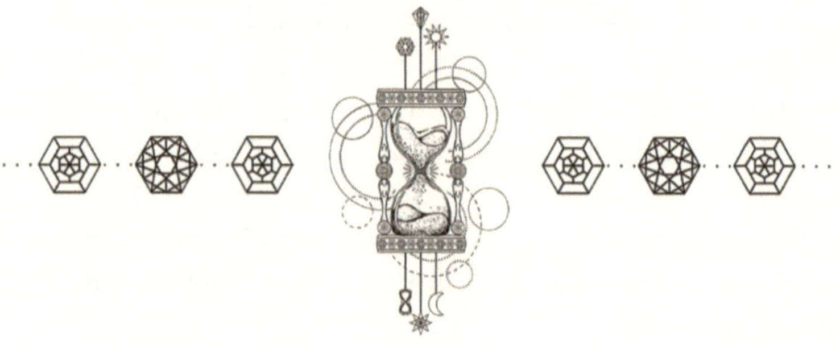

I still feel the weight of the brand-new lieutenant's pips on my collar. Okay, maybe not literally, those tiny things are almost weightless, but still.

Lieutenant Thorburn.

I like it.

What I don't like quite so much is the mission the admiral is sending me on. Its responsibility. *Hello, teenage girl—would you like to save the world?* Like, really?

In two days, all our fate will be resting on my shoulders, of all people. No pressure, none at all. So much can go wrong, so much… And then me and humanity are going to be in deep doo-doo. Especially humanity.

Seriously, giving this task to me, what did Grazer think? As good as it feels to be selected for a vital mission, there must be somebody better qualified than me. Jumping to the planet *in freakin' Quaneez-space*, scanning for and retrieving the plants, is a mission that would make most senior officers get wobbly knees, let alone a new graduate? Plus, I mean, I get the whole plausible deniability-thing, but seriously, what's so bad about the idea of having a senior officer fake-retire and let them pull this stunt? The Quaneez wouldn't care about—or understand—the difference, and the USEF could still use the rogue-human defense in case any other species complained *and* stand a better chance of getting their samples.

I wish Grazer had briefed me completely right there and then. Tomorrow is so far away, which means I'll probably have a stomach ulcer by the time I finally do get completely briefed and my questions answered.

I walk across campus past dozens of other students, none of them the wiser what happened to me. My whole life has changed in the last hour. Besides everybody wearing face masks, everything looks normal, which is weird, because everything is not normal. Not to me. Secret promotion, a more than important mission—but of course on the outside nothing's visible. Not my pips. Not the weight on my shoulders. Instead, it's pretending business was as usua—

"Cadet. How very convenient to meet you." A long shadow pops up next to mine—belonging to Admiral Upinga. My stomach twists into a figure eight. I need a private moment to freak out, not my mentor, one of the two people who know me best at the academy, observing and potentially interpreting my every facial twitch.

I clear my throat. "Admiral. Didn't expect you in this corner of the academy so late dyring the day." Most of the classes he teaches happen earlier.

"That would be because I was looking for you. I have something planned for you, Cadet."

What the what? "Uhh, something planned for me, sir? For today?" Nu-uh. I'm going to my room to panic. My afternoon is booked.

He nods. "For today indeed. See, I had this hunch you needed to be challenged more." Upinga folds his hands on his back and walks slightly bent forward, a habit of his. As a moderately tall female, I know where it's coming from.

I raise one skeptical eyebrow. *My* hunch would be to curl into a fetal position and pray to fate to be merciful. Or cry, at the very least. "Really?" Somebody passing us by greets the admiral. It's busy today. The last days and weeks before the year is over always fall into chaos thanks to people making up assignments and giving it a last desperate effort to bump up their grades. A group of three cadets walks past us, all of them a look of airy superiority on their faces. One sneers and the other makes a gagging noise once we're within ear shot.

Oh, hell to the no! "Hey!" I call after them. "What about showing some resp—"

Neither of them bothers stopping or turning around. The tallest of them, a guy a year under me, lifts his hand and pops out his middle finger toward me. "F off, *Maggot.*"

That does it. "You—"

"Cadet." Upinga lays a hand upon my forearm, effectively stopping my outburst before it had a chance to, well, burst out. "Ignore them."

Gah! Upinga and his calm! He would've had every right to call them out on their disrespectful behavior. Not greeting an admiral plus the way they behaved—that's at least a write-up, and only because Upinga is the forgiving type. Officially, it's insubordination, but either way, add the academy's anti-harassment policy to the tall guy's *Maggot*-slur, and the write-up turns into a permanent mark on his records. Maybe they feel they can hide behind those face masks, or else I wouldn't know why they'd be so stupid to risk a dishonorable discharge for insubordination.

I shake my head. "Sir, they—"

"They are young and blinded by what they're being told. We're not going to change their opinion if we stoop to their level."

I groan. "I wouldn't call adhering to academy protocol stooping to their level."

"But they will see it as an oversensitive reaction proving we're not on the same team."

"I see your point, but—"

"Then take a deep breath and ignore them. You've been doing it for years. Don't give in to them now."

Okay. *Okay.* I draw in a long, *long* breath through pursed lips and blow it out equally slow, then again. It makes me mad whenever my human colleagues behave like idiots. Not with me—I mean, yes, but whatever. Been there, done that, got used to it. Happens when you're known as the only kid ever to set foot on a Magellan spaceship and come out of it with a biosynthetic leg. Not that it was voluntarily or that I remember much, but still. So, no, I'm not mad for myself, but for Upinga, because it makes no sense. I can see them being afraid of the unknown, like of the Quaneez. Or of people and aliens we haven't encountered or understood yet, but of the Magellans? Of Admiral

Upinga? He is as human as an alien can get, and I really hope I'm not offending him with that.

Yes, Admiral Upinga is tall. Six-six, or something. But so are some humans. Yes, his hair is black and shimmers like an oil spill, but well, for example my hair is red-brown and I have a hint of that same stupid shimmer, and if Dad had more hair, he'd probably have it too. There you go, two humans for you with the same feature. And yes, Upinga's eyes are big and bigger than in humans, but to a girl who's been called "Kewpie-doll" all her life, a larger-than-normal-iris is nothing to get too worked up about.

So yeah, when looking at Admiral Upinga, it's clear he isn't from Earth, but it's also clear he's from the same mold. So are all other aliens we've come across so far, even the Quaneez, by the way, as far as we know. Maybe our general shape and form is a common masterplan around the universe. Maybe it's practical. And maybe that should tell us something, only we don't listen, or we don't want to hear it.

Or, like in the case with those three cadets, we're too stupid to add one and one.

Upinga motions for me to enter the Sim-building first. "To continue, I spoke to Admiral Conolly, and he agreed you should be challenged more."

I blink twice to get back on topic. After all these years, I'm still rattled by bullying, no matter the form. How Upinga, way more often the target than me, can switch to business as usual on a dime is a mystery to me. "Challenged more?" I sound like a parrot.

"Indeed. You're one lucky cadet with two mentors from two different specialties."

"I know that, but the way you're phrasing it, I'm wondering if I should run with all I've got." I was handed one special assignment today already, and it's sitting like lead in my stomach, heavy, eating away at me. Maybe one biggie per day is all I can take.

He stops in front of the doors to our tactical training suite. "Too late, Cadet. This day has been coming for longer than you know." He palms the doors open, letting me enter first. Great. With that one-liner, I can only imagine what special torture my two mentors have cooked up for me. *This day has been coming for longer than you know.* Translation:

your finals are nothing. *This* is the real deal.

Fantastic, really.

I enter the sim prep-room and snap out a quick salutation. "Admiral Conolly. Good morning."

Admiral Chase Conolly hits one more key on the computer console in front of him. "Top of the morning to you, too." His lips pull up in his typically half-mischievous Admiral Conolly-smile. "Take off your masks, guys. One, I've got the viral filters running since I got here, two, we want Nonie to breathe easy." He gets up and strides over to us with a spring in his step, rubbing his hands together, a move that emphasizes his considerable muscular frame. The admiral may be in his early sixties, but his body is fitter and better defined than many of my classmates'. Add blond, tousled hair, a broad chin and those bright blue eyes of his, and no wonder there's a Conolly-Fan Club in the USEF.

He shoots a questioning glance at his colleague. "You tell her, Zio?"

Admiral Upinga takes off his face mask and shrugs. "Barely. I doubt the cadet anticipates the extent of the exercise, although she has already considered running from it." Humor colors his voice, but still, I feel the need to protest.

"Hey! I was messing with you, you know that! I never back down from a challenge." And these two have *challenged* me more than any other instructors at the academy. I'm not even sure half of what they had me tackle was in the curriculum, but I won't complain. I feel ready for the world. Well, I felt ready for the world until Grazer turned me into Atlas with the weight of said world on my shoulders.

Still, the part about me breathing easy has me slightly worried. I take off my mask and place it on the console next to the door. Otherwise, it's easy to forget to put in on again. At least I'm lucky enough to be in a pod with my two mentors. They were the logical choice. I live alone in my dorm room, and I see Dad way less than these two. Sad, but true.

Admiral Conolly grabs a glass filled with an orange liquid and raises it at me. "Never have, and never will. We know." He takes a sip of what I assume is his usual Lubbeck's soda, but then picks up on his colleague's disapproving glance and sets it down quickly, wiping his mouth with the back of his hand.

Admiral Upinga sighs and pulls a chair from under another computer console. "Trip, stop drinking that stuff. Cadet, sometimes failure is not an option, which is why we're going through this."

I cock my head. "O-kay. That sounds trust inspiring."

Conolly lifts both palms in defense. "Don't get him wrong. All we're saying is we want you to be secure in what you do. Before you go out there, I mean."

Out there—like my mission.

I swallow dry. "Me, too. So, which scenario—?"

A sly grin pops up on both my mentors' faces.

Aww, come on! "Please no." I groan. With that intro, it's not hard to guess what's coming. My one weakness is combat. Always has been. And while I'm not great at it, I can hold my own.

"Please yes." Conolly falls into his chair and rolls over to the main console. "Anyway, Cadet, what we have for you is a combined exercise, a definite must before you graduate. Difficult to get approved, but finally, here we go." He adds a quick annoyed eye roll. For two admirals, my two mentors aren't big on authority and regulations. "We're going to merge two simulations together, like in real life. This could happen during any mission, and we want you to be ready. Therefore, you're getting the best of both worlds in one single exercise. Medical"—he uses a finger to indicate his colleague—"and tactical." He points the same finger at himself.

Fan-freakin'-tastic. That prospect only adds to my desire to curl up in a corner and rock myself to sleep. What have they cooked up for me? I tap the screen on the console to my right. "The— Oh, come on! Really? We've been through this a hundred times! Sirs," I tag on. Never been insubordinate, not going to start now. Thing is, I've been through both scenarios separately about twenty thousand times. Twenty million times. Twenty trillion-billion times. Upinga and Conolly are perfectionists, especially when it comes to these two exercises.

Cadet, you have ignored a chance to take out the automated weapons systems.

Cadet, you must know the way a Quaneez bunker is structured by heart.

Cadet, you must recognize their bio-signatures earlier and strike to kill. It's them or you.

Ugh. Any other instructors would've passed me with flying colors—they did with my classmates—but not Upinga and Conolly. I don't know how many times Conolly had me work on that ambush, or how often Upinga insisted I improve my medical care. *I don't care what risk it takes, this is your patient, and he is your responsibility until help is there. You don't discard that.* Hence, I stayed late and practiced more. And now they want me to combine it. "Merged specialties? Why?"

"Because you never know. You might be alone in the most important mission of your life." Conolly gives me a stern look, one that makes my throat go dry. Most important mission in my life? Uhh… are they hinting at what I think they're hinting at?

"Anything I should know, Admirals?" I squeak. Grazer said less than three people knew about this, and while I doubt either Conolly or Upinga are part of this crowd, it's a possibility.

Conolly tilts his head. "Besides that we want you to be prepared to complete missions on your own, without the back up of a team?"

My eyes pop wide. Now, wait a second! The academy is big on specializing early on. Cadets going into tactical get tactical exercises, medical get medical, engineering get engineering. Crossover is not in their curriculum. The only reason I got a broader education are these two admirals in front of me. Still, we've never combined any of those exercises, it's just not programmed into our curriculum. USEF soldiers work in teams, everybody according to their strength, so… My head swivels left to right, from one of them to the other and back. "Are you thinking what I'm thinking?"

"Most certainly not," Captain Upinga deadpans. "But enlighten us."

My heart skips a beat. "Are you… are you giving me this assignment, because you're thinking I might be accepted into Division Two?" While they've always supported me, I know they feel I'd be suited best in the Diplomatic Corps. Like them. Like my dad. But this exercise… It's perfect for a lone-wolf-soldier of the D-2.

Or for a poor fellow trying to save the world two days from now.

Admiral Conolly lays a hand on my shoulder. "Nonie, we *know* you're going to be accepted into Division Two. For the last years we've been getting you ready for what lies ahead, believe me. Do we wish you'd choose a career in diplomacy? Yes. Because you'd be perfect for it. But life works in mysterious ways, and while the dice have been cast, they haven't fallen yet. Meaning, we're still optimistic." He winks and claps my shoulder twice. "And speaking of. Let's put it this way: today's simulation is the most important test of your academy education. Of your career. Of your whole life." He gives me excited jazz hands, and I chuckle. Way to sell it.

"Okay, I got it. I will do my very best."

"That I do expect. Always." Conolly gives me a thumbs up and activates the console.

Alrighty then. I should consider that my trial by fire before the impending mission Grazer gave me. There's a reason why those two are my favorite instructors, but to be honest, it's not just that they're my mentors and challenging me like nobody else does. It's also not just the awe for their combined knowledge and experience I feel when I'm around them—there's something about both that makes me *want* to do well for them, no matter what they throw at me. If they were still out there, on a ship, I'd be the first in line to sign up and I can swear I'd follow their orders, no questions asked. Admiral Upinga is the best medical officer USEF has had in its existence. The research and treatment he brought to the Fleet is invaluable and should shut up all those *Humanity First*-idiots, but then again, they're idiots. And Admiral Conolly... rarely has somebody had better tactical insights than him. Add his knack for engineering, and there's the reason why we have the Conolly-theory on FTL-drives in the testing right now.

Their achievements, together with Captain Wildason's gave the academy the idea to reach out and recruit younger. Plus, Wildason, Conolly and Upinga are still considered the best commanding team ever in service, despite their youth when they started, and despite the fact they haven't served together in over three decades. Wildason's death changed the admirals' lives for sure, and sometimes, as childish as it is, I feel that he shouldn't have died. That it wasn't his time yet.

My gaze trails up to the framed picture hanging over the entrance to the simulation area, the only personal touch Conolly and Upinga brought to their control room. In the picture, all three of them are still young, not even twenty-five, I'd say, and yet they were veterans at that point already. Upinga and Conolly stand next to their captain on the *Pioneer*'s bridge, and all three look like they're ready to tackle whatever the universe throws at them. *The hotshot trio*, they were called, before too many people became racist and xenophobic and refused to call an off-worlder *hot*. I always liked that picture. It must be from their personal files, or else I'm sure it would be in the history books. They wouldn't pass on a shot like this. Not with the famous Captain Wildason radiating confidence and… I don't know, something warmer that makes me feel so sorry he's dead and I'll never get a chance to meet him.

I blush. Okay. Anyway. Maybe it's time to focus on what's important and deliver a good performance. I crack my knuckles, then check my brand-new super-awesome wrist-PAD's settings. Still amazing I have almost full scanning and interface capacities with this matchbox-sized tool. The exercise should go smoother with it. Speaking of: I reach for the medical belt and take it off the hook. Over the last years, Conolly and Upinga have pushed me through so many exercises, I can function through them on autopilot.

Huh.

I pause, a tight tickle running down my throat. "Admirals?"

"What's up, Cadet?" Admiral Conolly holds out the tactical kit for me.

Ugh, way to go to be sentimental, Nonie. I take the kit and busy myself attaching it to the belt. "I just… I don't know, I just wanted to say thank you for… for… you know, for training me." For not thinking of me as Tom Thorburn's daughter, like many of the other teachers. For not treating me like an abnormality. For helping me through the rough patches. For making me feel I had somebody rooting for me. For mentoring me.

They exchange a glance.

"It was our pleasure, Cadet. Training you always felt like… like it was supposed to happen." Upinga gives me a wistful look that makes Conolly chuckle.

"Aww, Uncle, don't get sentimental on us." He claps his colleague's shoulder, ignoring the annoyed expression that is Upinga's trademark reaction to the nickname.

"The point I was trying to make," Upinga says with an irritated glance at Conolly, "that I would like you to keep those warm thoughts of us in your mind when you go through your *favorite* scenario." He hands me an aerosol spray. "All we're working on is undoing what in our opinion is a flaw in your academic instructions. As a well-rounded officer you must be able to navigate a difficult situation and take care of your crewmen. You're not like them, Cadet. We expect more of you."

All protest I had in me dies with that one sentence. *We expect more of you.* They always have, and it's always meant a lot to me.

I take the spray, deflated. "Okay. I will try my very best to free the hostage and treat their wounds, while not getting killed by the Quaneez." Grr.

"And while not killing the patient, please," Captain Upinga says.

"And while not killing the patient." Obvs.

It's the last mission of my academy life, and the last prep I'll get for my upcoming mission.

I better nail it.

Chapter Five

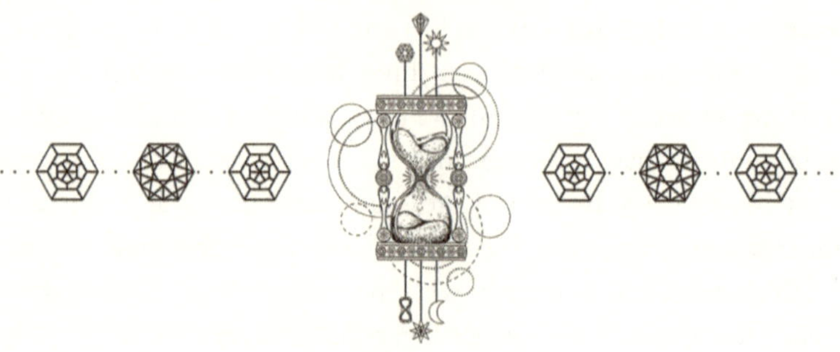

Somewhere, Day 0.

Waking up *hurts*.

Like, for real.

I groan and lift one hand to my forehead.

Ow.

Something's swollen. Bloody.

But I still have a forehead, that's a plus.

My next breath brings the sharp stench of electrical fire to my nose. "Damn it." I cough and gag, and damn it again, that hurts even more.

I force my heavy eyelids open. Blurry. So blurry. Smokey. Thick, grey fumes waft through the cabin. Crap. What happened? Wha—

Like a bucket of cold water dumped over my head, the last minutes come back to me. My scan—the core destruction.

Core destruction.

Five million Quaneez.

Those two sentences clear my foggy mind like nothing. How did I destroy the planet? How could my little shuttle possibly have come up with the power for such an unbelievable destruction? *How?*

We scan planets all the time—they're not supposed to blow up! They *can't* blow up just like that! And it can't, can't, *can't* have been me who did this, yet it seems it was: the graph the *Odysseus* displayed, was quite clear.

In the end, does it matter? Because that planet is gone. Destroyed. My presence killed five million living beings. *And* I destroyed the one hope humanity had to survive the flu-pandemic.

Nausea rises, pushing bile up my throat. What have I done?

"Warning. Internal fire. Extinguishers off-line. War—ning. Inteeernaaaal fiiiii—" Odysseus' voice distorts and cuts out.

Oh, heck.

I reach for the console and work myself up to standing. When did I fall? Breathing is hard. Must get that fire out. Must get—

My gaze drifts out the window in the front: trees with purple leaves. Bushes with yellow fruit. Some kind of insects with shimmering wings. What the—

"I crashed on a planet?" I *crashed?* Could I have been wrong and I didn't destroy H-155, but crashed there instead? But wouldn't then Quaneez be all over me at this point? No way they're overlooking a crashing spacecraft, shields up or not.

And it doesn't matter.

Every breath hurts and stings, and every second the temperature rises. I need to get out of here. "*Odysseus,* open hatch." I cough, and it comes with a wheeze.

Nothing.

Damn it, everything's fried.

I have to feel my way through the small shuttle toward the hatch, it's that smokey in here. Fire must be in the engines. Crap, crap, crap— how am I supposed to repair that? I need tools. Gotta take tools with me—

With a loud *boom,* something explodes in the engine compartment, rattling the *Odysseus.*

Never mind the tools.

I feel for the manual handle and crank it down. The hatch retracts the tiniest bit, but wide enough for me to squeeze through.

Another *boom,* and with this one the shuttle wobbles under my feet. Shoot.

I force myself sideways through the opening—

Wait.

Half stuck in the door, I reach for the weapons' belt attached to a magnetic holder on the wall and rip if off, then keep on squeezing myself until I spill out of the shuttle and into the wild. I stumble forward, barely catching myself before I fall.

The third *boom*—and when I look around, flames spill out of the engine compartment and lick over the *Odysseus'* hull.

Not good.

I suck in sweet air—breathable. Won't kill me. But within five minutes *I* have killed five million Quaneez and humanity's hope for survival. And I've stranded myself on a strange, foreign planet with no hope of leaving on my own.

No matter the breathable air. I might as well be dead.

Chapter Six

Three hours later, I'm exhausted, mentally and physically. It's gotten dark pretty fast, so hiking through this alien forest, making sure I'm not running into… *things*, alive or not, is more than draining. Add whatever injuries the crash caused, and that's not making it any easier. Can't really put much weight on my already weaker left leg, and my side hurts like crazy. Of course I did a quick scan with my wrist PAD, and although poor PADdy did get damaged during the crash, it tells me the same isn't true for me, at least not too much. A medical scanner would be better, but I'm fresh out of those.

A little voice inside my head whispers I have no reason to complain: I'm alive. A planet full of Quaneez isn't. According to the constellations, there's no way I'm on H-155. Wherever I am, the Quaneez planet is gone.

I should be happy. Didn't get the plants to cure the virus, but helped us eliminate part of a more chronic problem. After all, we're still at war, despite no shots having been fired in recent months. Killing five million of *them* in one single attack will get me the Iron Fist First Class. If I ever make it back, that is. So yeah, I should feel good. Five million enemies less to worry about.

But it doesn't feel good. Not at all.

Five million dead.

Because of me.

A sharp pang of nausea slices through me.

It's unbelievable this happened. Tha*t I* did this. The scale's too grand to grasp. Why didn't I know it was an inhabited planet? And had I known there was no super-sensitive satellite- and receptor-system to be found anywhere in the area of H-155, I would've scanned my destination point earlier as protocol demands and have known. I could've avoided all of this, I could've—

Could have.

Point is, I didn't, and it happened.

I have to live with it. Ouch, bad phrase, given the circumstances.

What are they going to do if I make it back? Pay me the kill-reward for five million dead enemies? Then I really should be happy. Problem is, as much as our training is focused on the war, I never expected to kill other than in self-defense. That's why I wanted to join D-2, to not be at the front lines, but to work from behind the scenes and help *save* lives.

Not take them.

But damn it, what happened? I scan, the core explodes—that's just not possible. Unheard of. And yet it happened. *I* made it happen, and then the resulting explosion must've thrown me quite far, or I was drifting longer than I thought for me to crash on a planet like this.

All I can do is try to survive and make it back home. PADdy tells me there's life here, and I'm not talking about insects. Large mammals, possibly human. And human life would mean I can get off this planet, and I can inform Grazer of the disaster I caused.

On the other hand—I'm pretty positive he won't see that part of my failed mission as a disaster. I minimized the enemy's force by a major number. The war—

Dang it. I freeze in mid-step. The war. What if my actions, my destruction of H-155, will cause a retaliatory attack on our colonies? They know I was there. If any of the ships in orbit survived or if they transmitted their data somewhere else and somebody else looks through their data later on, they will know I was there. And even if the Quaneez can't identify me, the *USEF Guardian* saw me before my second jump. USEF will know.

And then I'll be the one who killed five million Quaneez, couldn't bring home those lifesaving plants, and who indirectly caused the death of who knows how many humans by breaking the cease fire.

Holy cow.

I bend over, supporting my body's weight on my knees, as the true potential of the disaster I broke loose becomes clear to me.

The PAD on my wrist vibrates once. Turning my forearm slightly, I glance at its screen—

And pop right back up to standing, blinking a couple of times to make sure I read that right. Seventeen life signs, maybe a hundred meters straight ahead? At least one could be human, but could also be something out to eat me, can't tell with my damaged wrist PAD. And as much as I'd deserve to be eaten, I'd prefer it happened *after* I reported my failure.

Pewpewpew!

Shots!

Somebody yells out, and years of training and honing my reflexes pay off in this one moment. With one big jump, I dive behind a tree. Weapon's fire? What the—

Pewpewpew! Yellow beams slice through the darkness, hitting trees and bushes to my right about fifty meters farther up. *Pew! Pew!* More yellow beams. I release the snap on my weapon's holster without making a noise and draw the gun.

Yellow beams?

That's—that's Quaneez, their signature weapons, distorters! The Quaneez are breaking the ceasefire! I mean, after I destroyed a planet of theirs, so never mind, but… It's definitely them firing! Only Quaneez have this typical yellow beam, ours work on a different frequency, they're red. Thanks, PADdy, for breaking now of all times—I would've maybe liked to know a tad sooner those humanoids were Quaneez and I'm walking into the enemy's hands?

But then, who cares, the main message here is *Oh, crap!* Where *the heck* did I crash? Part of me still hopes this is an un-destroyed H-155, but even then, I'd be stranded without a working shuttle in the middle of enemy territory and without any means to bring those plants home.

But at least I wouldn't have killed a whole planet's population. I wouldn't mind *not* cashing in that kill-reward.

A yell comes from somewhere farther up front. "Hold your fire! I come in peace!" The words sound rushed, but they're plain, old, pretty English. A human! A human is down here with me!

Pewpewpew!

"I come in peace! I don't want you any harm!" the guy tries again, but it doesn't do him any good. Could've told him that. One, the Quaneez resist any attempts of communication. They just ignore us—until they fire that is. Two, they really don't like anybody intruding on their territory. We made that mistake when we first met them, and we're still paying for it.

More yellow fire slices through the darkness and into the area where the man must be, and finally—*finally*—he fires back. When the first beam shoots through the forest, I pump a fist. Red beams—he's not a civilian, he's USEF!

Zzzing! His red beams are woefully few compared to the onslaught of yellow, and he is not shooting to kill, he's shooting to distract and give himself cover.

I like the sentiment, but boy, does he need help.

My heart cramps painfully. And I guess the only help down here… is me. Before I can freak myself out too much, I sneak through the trees and bushes, keeping my eyes trained on the area I suspect him to be in. The Quaneez will do the same, so it's a question of timing who'll reach the guy first.

I really hope it's me. One, he clearly doesn't want to shoot the Quaneez, and I like humans who put ethics before a kill reward. Two, he's USEF, he must have a shuttle here or a ship in orbit. My means to escape.

His shots fall quicker now, rapid fire, and I take it back. Maybe he doesn't want to kill the Quaneez, but at this point, I doubt he knows how to do it, even if he wanted to. Man, he clearly didn't pay attention in his briefings. You don't shoot Quaneez with short-burst fire. I might suck at hand-to-hand combat, but I honed my long-distance skills. A few *pew-pews* won't kill—or even hurt—any Quaneez. To penetrate their whole-body armor fire must be focused for at least two seconds at the same spot, which is why they're so difficult to defeat in battle. And we've cranked the energy of our weapons up to what's technologically possible at the moment. Got us down from five to two seconds, and our stats improved, but it's still no easy feat.

My fingers hurt from holding them stiff around my weapon. I really… I really don't want shoot a Quaneez. Defend myself—yes. Kill? No.

I think I've done enough of that today.

The exhaustion I felt a mere minute ago is gone, kicked out of my system by a good, old-fashioned serving of adrenaline and fear. No matter how realistic simulations are, they never prep you a hundred percent for the real deal. Still, better than nothing. I send a quick mental thank you to Admirals Conolly and Upinga. Doubtful I'd be this calm-ish if it wasn't for them—actually, I know: given how weapons' fire always had the potential to trigger me, there's a distinct possibility I'd be hiding under the bushes right now.

The battle continues in front of me. The human can't be more than twenty meters in front of—

"Aargh!" He screams, and it ends in a yelp. Hit. Damn. Why the hell doesn't he deflect and demat up? What's wrong with him? Good for me he isn't out of here yet, but sheesh, I really messed up on a grand scale and blew up a planet, but he's clearly not able to follow simple SAR-rules.

Fifteen meters. Somewhere farther up front and to the left I pick up on reflections of the weapons' fire on what looks like a single Quaneez shuttle. Good. Matches the amount of fire. At least it's only one unit deployed down here, not more.

I pick up on heavy breathing. Grunting. Problem is, so will the Quaneez, and they will go for attack pattern delta and storm him. They're not known for their subtlety.

Ten meters. He hasn't fired in about twenty seconds. But they haven't stopped at all. Not good.

My heart hammers like crazy. I have one shot at this, and he better play nice. With one quick flick of my wrist, I turn my weapon over and press my thumb into the indentation we're told to ignore unless it's an emergency.

Yeah. I'm sure this counts.

The gun blinks red three times in quick succession. On the last blink I throw it in a high arch over where the guy must be hiding. It makes a noise when it travels through the greenery, and—*zing*—a faint, red force field pops up from where it landed, deflecting the yellow beams back to the attackers and protecting the guy and myself from the Quaneez entering until the shield runs out of juice. Here's to messing with their whole-body armor, so screw you, attack pattern delta. I've got sixty seconds, and I'll use them well!

Like a madwoman, I dash forward the last few meters. "Human incoming. Do *not* shoot!" Normally I wouldn't say it, the deflector shield gives it away, but with this guy… not the smartest of them all.

A grunted sound of approval is all I get, and then I'm there. "Summary," I bark at him under my breath. Too dark to see much, so I start patting him down according to SAR-protocol. He's covered in dirt—yuck. Stinks, too. Hope that's the mud and not him, although, who cares. Priorities.

"Who—" The guy sucks in a sharp breath. Wide, intelligent eyes set in a muddy face with high cheekbones and a prominent jaw stare at me through the near-complete dark. No face mask, but then, I'm fresh out of one myself. For one fleeting moment a feeling of familiarity tugs at my core, but I can't place it. "Summary *now*, soldier!" Tight schedule here.

It's obvious when he switches the gears from surprise to professionalism. "Unknown enemy. Too many, at least twenty. Got hit in—" He hisses harsh, when my hands feel over his sides.

"Your flank." Obviously. He's a tad tender there. Understatement probably, I know. "Breathing?"

"No problem."

"Good." That means it wasn't a full-on load he received, or else his lungs would already be spasming right now. "Do you have a ship in orbit?" Priorities.

"Y-yes." He nods, but it's a chopped movement. Paralysis is beginning. The movement lets his full, dark hair fall into his eyes, but his attempt of swiping it away fails. A hint of panic crosses over his face. "Can't move," he forces through clenched teeth.

Well, duh. I grab one of his arms by the sleeve and pull. As soon as he's half-standing, I wrap one arm around him and help him up. The movement makes his shirt ride up and me grab his bare flank instead of fabric. My palm connects with his skin—

A jolt of electricity shocks me. Like, for real. My breath hitches in my throat and I stumble, barely keeping us upright. I'm touching the guy with nothing more than my hand on his flank, yet I feel this touch through every part of my body like hit by a live wire, and I'm not being pathetic or girly here: This sensation is real. Physical.

And unimportant.

He gulps in air. "Holy—"

I shake my head once, fast. Focus. "Hail your ship. *Now.*" I wrap one arm around him and help him up. My hand burns and tingles where I touch him.

The guy puts way too much weight on me and his reply comes out slurred. "Can't reach 'em."

I grunt. "Huh?" The Quaneez are not known for their frequency blocking abilities. Their cruisers sometimes—oh, come on. "Did you counter the orbital interference?"

Silence.

"Seriously," I hiss at him. All looks and no brain, or what's wrong with him? I use my free hand to feel down his muscular body until I find the holster for his ground trip hablamate on his left. What a beginner. I flip the holster open, when twigs behind us break.

Frack! *Not* attack pattern delta!

Change of priorities. Leave it to the Quaneez to come up with new attack patterns during our cease fire. Not even the bad guys have decency these days. I ignore my conscience telling me I just eliminated a whole planet of theirs and thus have no right to talk about decency.

I rip the weapon out of the guy's hand, whirl around—

A yellow beam blasts through the darkness, missing us by less than half a meter. Shoot—someone breached the shield!

"Behind me!" I yell.

The guy doesn't move. *Can't* move anymore, probably. Pretty sure the paralyzing effects have set in. Dang it. I keep him up, but turn us sideways, so we're less of a target. I really don't want to fire on a living being, but my options are limited. My index finger hits the trigger—

Nothing.

What the hell?

Another yellow beam blasts by, this one closer.

"Crap." One lonely Quaneez soldier who thought out of the box, and I can't fire. "What the heck—"

I turn the gun over— Really? What possessed this dude to use a Mark Two? This thing is old, and—

PewPew!

And who cares it's old.

I release the safety and finally this thing does my bidding, I open fire and hold my beam at the area they attack from, as steady as I can without a guiding stabilizer. Finding and fighting a single Quaneez in the dark under stress and without a guiding system is not what I would choose if I could, but given this guy goes old-school on me, nothing I can do about it but defend ourselves and wing it.

And pray we won't get into any kind of contact fight.

Pew! PewPew!

Three more shots miss us, and now I have a location I can aim for and a Quaneez I couldn't disable—and he knows where to aim, thanks to me giving myself away, but the damage is done. No matter what, with only one guidance-system-free weapon, a dead-weight guy in my arms, and the force field about to expire, this is a battle I will lose, especially when it turns into close combat.

Fear wraps its tendrils around my throat and squeezes tight.

I won't lose.

I still have a responsibility to return home and report what I've done.

And—

With a little plopping sound, I'm sure I'm imagining my shield snuffs out.

Crap.

Priorities are shifting yet again. Gotta work with what I got, clock's a-ticking down. Desperation crushes over me, but it comes with an idea. I use my thumb to dial up fire frequency to max, turning my beam from red to bright orange. Adding disperse—

A wide, bright beam fans out from the weapon, so glaring I'd be blinded if I didn't close my eyes. The guy gasps and turns his head away, only too late. Sorry, man. Here's to hope the Quaneez won't like it either.

The second I let go of the trigger and holster the weapon, I scoot us over to the right and away from where the Quaneez saw us last. Hopefully, it will blind them or temporarily overload whatever guidance and scanning system they have integrated into their helmets' visors. I scoot faster. No direct shots at us, that's an improvement, but the guy is dead weight in my grip, and heavy. Muscle covered in slippery mud from head to toe is difficult to maneuver around.

I rip his hablamate off his belt, raise it—sheesh, ancient model as well—adjust for the interference and push the button. "Ground to vessel in orbit. Respo—" Static bursts from the speaker.

"-nally! Cou— ot -each—interfer-- -trong."

I really don't care. "Disregard! One crew member, injured, medical attention needed! Two for demat! I repeat—"

Steps, the noise of large bodies bursting through the bushes, movement on my left.

No!

I swivel and put the helpless guy out of the Quaneez' immediate line of fire. Give me that weapon—

The night lights up with a yellow beam and my right shoulder with a pain unlike anything I've ever felt. A strangulated grunt leaves my throat, drowned out by the same sound coming from the guy behind me.

Holy cow. Can't breathe. Penetrating shot, full blast, paralyzing. Must've gotten him too.

My knees buckle as pain overpowers me, dulling my senses into a repeating loop of panic. Must get out, must not get hit again. Must get out, must not get hit again. Must—

Something big barges toward us through the brushes, reeking of decay, and I wish I could raise my arm and fire, I wish I could—

A cool, prickling tingling engulfs my body, and before I can make out the exact numbers of Quaneez soldiers storming our location, the tingle blacks out my senses—

—and brings them back online less than a second later.

So bright.

Cool air.

Can't keep us up.

I collapse onto the hard, shiny floors, half buried under the guy, half on top of him. My body tingles where we connect.

"We got them, sir! Close call, but we got them!"

Wher—

Humans. There are humans around us.

The guy under me groans, and I force my eyes open. Blurry.

Somebody steps closer. Touches my pulse. The guy's neck. "Shit. What happened down there? Where's the rest of the ground team?"

That voice—

"Never mind, let me see. They both need treatment." Another hand feels my carotid, its touch barely registering. Dizzy. Blurry. Nauseous. I hear somebody hiss—

"Unexpected. What—"

The hand retreats, and a face appears in my line of vision. Large eyes. Hair that shimmers like an oil spill. Admiral Uping— "They're bad. To sick bay, both. Immediately."

I blink, and there's another face. Blonde, tousled hair. Bright blue eyes. Piercing blue eyes. *Admiral Conolly.*

Relief floods me. They came. My mentors. They got me out.

Drawing all the energy I have left, I suck in a deep breath and ignore the pain. Need air to talk. Report. Must give report while I'm still able to. "Too many down there. Ten. Or more. Mixed attack patterns. They fired first. He… got shot twice. Me, once. We—"

"Easy. Don't talk. It's okay." Admiral Upinga lays a cool hand on my forehead. He looks… different. Somehow. Huh.

Conolly steps closer. "Wait. I need more. Who attacked you down there? Did Kieran tell you anything before he got hit?"

Kieran? The guy?

Another breath that burns like fire and barely brings any air into my lungs. Paralysis is getting worse. "No. They fired first. I—" Crap. Pain, pain, pain. My eyes roll back as my body's demands for a temporary shutdown get louder.

The admirals exchange a glance. "Sickbay. *Now.*" Upinga waves over some Ensigns.

Conolly curses. "Zio, sickbay won't help me. I need details, if not from her, then from Kieran! If this is dangerous to the ship—"

"I'm not waking him up, Chase!" The sound of a discharging hypo needle warns me, then something cool presses against my neck, accompanied by the same sound. "I need the captain in sickbay, and once he is stable, then you can have all the time you want."

The captain?

With all the strength I have left, I turn my head to the right, to the unconscious guy I saved. Prettier in the light than the dark down there, as far as I can tell with all that mud on him. Black unruly hair, longer on top, shorter on the sides. Wide jaw bones, wide chin. Long lashes. *Four* damn pips on his collar—

Another hypo needle discharges into my neck. "That should do it. Now, sickbay."

I blink three times, fast. Can't think. So sleepy. Drowsy. Foggy.

Admiral Conolly stands up. "As you wish, Commander. But I need answers." He sighs. "Not my day today. So much for a peaceful ground mission. Attacks, shots… And to top it all off, who the freakin' hell is this girl?"

Then, everything turns black.

Chapter Seven

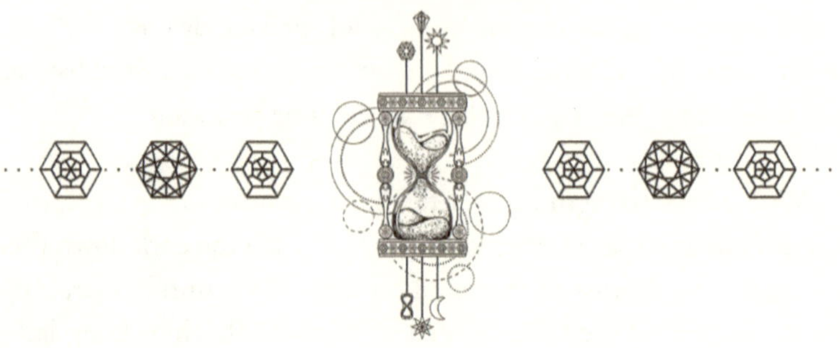

"No, Dad, I won't make it over for dinner tomorrow." Nerves bubble inside me. Tomorrow I'll be somewhere in Quaneez space, trying to retrieve the key element to fight the viral pandemic.

"Okay, fair enough, it's short notice. Saturday then." My dad taps something on the screen, probably his daily schedule.

Those nerves bubble up higher and bring up some nauseating flutters. "N-not good either." Saturday is debrief—I *hope*, because if it's not...

A messy, icky lump forms in my throat.

If it's not, what's left of me is floating in enemy space.

Can't very well tell my dad that though. It's bad enough he's calling, like, the minute he's back on Earth and while I'm in the middle of my very own mission prep. Time's a-tickin' down until my data disk auto destructs, and I better be prepped at that point. Can't very well tell my dad that either. I was hoping to be able to sneak out on my mission behind his back and without talking to him before. Might seem cruel, but this—seeing him and not telling him—is harder.

Alas, seems like my dad has a sixth sense when it comes to his daughter's secret undertakings. Tired as he looks, he called me first thing back on Earth. "Nonie, come on. We're on the same campus, but I see you less than any other student in the academy." The audio comes a tad time-delayed from the video thanks to the protocols securing every channel an admiral would call on, and it makes him sound even sadder.

My chest squeezes tight. Maybe I'm not made for D-2 after all, if keeping secrets from Dad is this hard. "Sorry, Dad. Dinner is so annoying with viral protocols in place." While it's nice to have options, it kills the mood to sit at a table with your dad, everybody in their own Virex-containment capsule. It's transparent, great, but I still feel quite uncomfortable in them.

Dad shrugs. "It is what it is. I'd rather have dinner with you locked in a tight capsule than not at all."

Of course he has to make it difficult for me. "Aww, Dad. That's sweet. Yes, me too. But right now, you're busy with your job and the upcoming elections, and I'm just busy with school. Last weeks, you know how it is." The lie comes easy though—that should count for something, right?

He rolls his eyes. "So I've noticed. I have cadets storming my office every five minutes asking for an extension of deadlines or to redo exams. From what I'm hearing though, you don't need to worry. Or is there something you're not telling me?" His sharp gaze penetrates me no matter the physical distance between us, and for a second, I swear he knows Grazer recruited me.

I shake my head and roll my eyes. "Besides the usual secrets kids keep from their parents? Nope. But give me some time, and then we'll have dinner, okay?" When I'm back. When I have a successful mission under my belt as ammo to tell him about my promotion and that I signed up with Division Two. I'll need it, because I doubt he's gonna be happy about my choice. Grazer's D-2 doesn't rank very highly in Dad's list of potential careers for me.

"All right, child of mine. But don't put it off for too long. I have a gift for you." He holds up a little box with a bow on top and wiggles it.

Granted, at seventeen, I'm not truly bribable with gifts anymore, but that doesn't mean I don't like getting them. A gift is exactly what I need to shake me out of the funk surrounding me for the last day. "From Mag-Two?"

"Fresh import from Mag-Two. Special order for you, Nonie." He winks, and I squee.

"Thanks, Dad! That's awesome! Can't wait to see what it is!" Because, corruptibility with gifts or not, Dad bringing something from the only planet in the USEF territory inhabited by non-humans is a rare treat. Especially because contact is limited to authorized personnel, which Dad as the Ambassador to the Magellans falls under. *Close contact with Alien Species is to be strictly prohibited to avoid contamination of the human race.*

Right.

Luckily for them, the Magellans like to stick to themselves. I feel like it's an extended middle finger at humanity: You don't want us? Fine, we don't want you either. Admiral Upinga is the only Magellan who left the tribe and joined the Fleet, and neither side, human nor Magellan, made it easy for him.

Over the years, lots of rumors came through the grapevine: exiled for his actions. Turned into a persona non grata. Forbidden to unite, the Magellan version of marriage. Upinga has never confirmed any of it, but neither has he denied it, and of course him staying without a partner only adds fuel to the rumors, never minding that he's also forbidden by law to have a relationship with a human female. In my opinion, all that only shows the extent of human paranoia, and I guess both, Admiral Upinga and Dad are carrying the brunt of those politics. I can't remember a single instance when Dad came back from Mag-2 and was well-rested. He usually looks a decade older and like he's in constant pain for about a week after he returns.

Doesn't change the fact I envy him like crazy. "Dad, I gotta say, I'm a *tad* envious you went to Mag-2. Again. How was it?"

Dad's tired face pulls into a smile and I don't need to hear the answer to know it. He's so easy to read, it's ridiculous. "Fantastic, Nonie. At one point I'll get permission to take you—or who knows, maybe I can give myself permission." He winks at me and I laugh.

"Ever the optimist that you're going to win the election and become USEF President, Dad?" Still can't wrap my head around the little fact that my old man might lead the USEF into hopefully better times. I wouldn't say it has made me any new friends recently, but oh well. Cry me a river.

"One can always hope common sense will win, and me with it. But all joking aside, one day I will take you to Mag-2, and either way and I promise you I'm not exaggerating when I say it will turn you in to a different person."

"More than they already have?" I chuckle and tap my left leg.

Dad flinches. "Well, yes. Differently so. They—"

"Never mind, Dad. Just pulling your leg, pun intended. You know me, I'm not mad at them for doing what they did. I just wish I remembered some of it. And, by the way, I believe you. But maybe take some of those *Humanity First* idiots there before me. They need a readjustment of their mental horizon more than I do."

That wipes what is left of his smile right off his face. "Point taken. How bad is it right now?"

"You mean politically? Nothing new, you've only been gone for four weeks, Dad. Today we had Chairman Roodt speaking for Humanity First on Campus—"

His look turns horrified. "What?" He leans forward so close to the camera I'm getting a good view of his forehead. "They allowed him to speak to *that* topic on Campus? Is Mashaule crazy? The academy is not political—"

I give him a sarcastic glance from under my lashes. "Really, Dad? Says the man who has given lecture after lecture on integration instead of separation and is running for USEF President?"

He flusters. "That's in my job description as the Ambassador—"

"I know, Dad, I'm just saying. It's lucky that you can reach so many of us when on campus. But you know many at the academy support Roodt's point of view. Have for a while." Which is why he spoke at least twice on campus before Mashaule was re-elected president almost three years ago. "But I also saw a group of students at the outskirts holding Vote-for-Thorburn-signs up. That's something, right?"

Dad perks up. "I like to hear that. Maybe there is hope after all. Mashaule is strong, politically. And with all that paranoia going on… It's hard to fight that." Especially if Roodt is spreading more paranoia. Mashaule's war and separation policy might look like the better alternative than my dad's integration and peace for all.

Well, my fingers are crossed. "If the Roodt-supporters don't scare everyone into voting for Mashaule, you should win this, Dad." Polls have been slowly turning sides, from Mashaule-heavy to a draw. Listening to Roodt and Humanity First, one could think we're being attacked from all sides—which we're not. Only the Quaneez have been hostile so far. In fact, I'd bet and say if we took the time to get to know each other, we might get along quite well. So far, we're keeping all encountered alien species at bay—even though they're friendly.

Dad sighs. "Humanity is going down the drain, sweetheart. I wish the Magellans were more outgoing and wanted to mingle with us, so that humans could see how amazing their culture is and how good-hearted their people are. Humans fear the unknown, and *I* fear the Magellan's self-imposed isolation is not helping them—or us—much." He frowns. "But since I mentioned humanity's decent into hell—you're wearing your… *thing*, right?" Dad gives me a stern look.

And here we go again. "Yes, Dad. I'm *wearing* my *thing*." I tap my left upper arm for him to get the hint. It's implanted. There's no way I could *not* wear it, unless I surgically removed it, and if I did, my dad would cross me out of his will. Or wrestle me down and re-implant the genetic masker I've been carrying around under my skin for a good eight years. *Honey, people can do all kinds of damage when they know your genes or where you're from*, he says, and while I used to think he was a tad over-protective, I have the scars on my neck and the limp in my leg to prove he wasn't and isn't. Genetic extortion is a thing, because genetic scanning and recognition is a thing, and we've seen where that can end. So I get it why he implanted the masker into my body. Nobody should be able to scan me and know my genetic—or isotope—make-up. All they'll get is a random DNA-sequence to lead them astray, because *if they knew you're wearing a masker, they'd cut it out.* And yes, before Dad became the liaison to Mag-2, he was in a couple of dicey situations, hence his dark streak.

Dad gives me thumbs up. "Just checking. Can't blame an old man for wanting to keep his daughter safe."

Safe. Like a fist to the face, his words sniff out the bit of peaceful ignorance I tried to erect around myself and bring back tomorrow's mission. "A-and I am. S-safe, I mean. Please don't worry." Famous last words and so wrong I couldn't even get them out without stuttering.

My dad's face pulls into what I call the puppy-look, the soft, loving, and warm expression only I get to see. I bet some of his students wouldn't recognize him all gooey for his only daughter. "I always worry, honey. That's in my job description as a father and nothing I could turn off at will. Especially not over the last eight years." *Hint-hint.*

I push my chin up high. I never have and never will let *that* define me, hard as it may be. "I know you worry. But *you* know I'm very well prepared to keep myself out of trouble." The words taste bitter in my mouth. Still, I hold his gaze, because Dad needs to understand I can make my own decisions. Like I did today. Tomorrow doesn't count as trouble. It counts as success, because I was chosen. Little me, not some tested war hero. Me, the broken one. The Maggot.

Dad cocks his head, the puppy-look turning part inquisitive father, part official admiral. "I'm not so sure about the keeping yourself out of trouble part, Nonie. Have you decided?"

Aww man, spot on finger into the wound. I keep my face blank. "Nope."

"Really? Because some high-ranking admiral I had the questionable pleasure of speaking to today dropped a hint."

Keeping the blank face, advanced level. "Admiral Grazer? I wouldn't know what kind of hint you could mean, or what has him in a good mood. Not privy to that, Dad."

"Interesting you're assuming it was Admiral Grazer, the head of the very division I don't want you near. No, it was actually Admiral Mashaule."

Oh. Odd. What kind of hint would he drop and why? "What did he say?"

"Not important." He narrows his eyes on me. "Just sayin', Nonie, to make myself really clear: I don't want you anywhere near Division Two. It's not a good place for you, believe me."

Terse silence stretches between us. Once, I think during my first week at the academy, I overheard Dad and Grazer fight. I probably remember it as way more scary than it was, but I was a newbie and easily impressed: *Silent infiltration, stripping rank, jail time, making yourself a target.* Big words were thrown around, every single one making it clear there was no love lost between them. "Dad—"

"This is not open to discussion. It's not safe."

My mouth opens and closes. I want to argue it's perfectly safe. I will be trained—I *am* already trained—and I'll be turned into one of the guys and gals who sweep in and save the day, the unsung heroes, the life savers. D-2 officers are trained to handle all kinds of sticky situations, and that's what I want to be able to do. Never again do I not want to be in control of a situation. I want all those tools, all those skills, and I'll be the safer for it—if I make it back home from my very first mission, that is. Something cramps in the depth of my stomach. I will. But yeah, today of all days it's hard not to see Dad's point.

"Nonie?" Dad leans closer to the camera. "I mean it. D-2 is not a good place for you. You know why—"

"Dad." We're not getting into this. Not now, hours before my first mission for, well, D-2. Hours before my actions will decide the fate of humanity. Hours before I may not—

Nope, really. Not going there.

Anyway. "I know your stance on D-2, Dad, but you also know I will make my way, whichever one I choose. I—"

"I know, Nonie, but—"

"*But* I really gotta go, Dad." Before I start crying that I may not see him again and that our last conversation was filled with my lies. Today's so not the day for an almost-fight-paternal-job-advisory talk, and just FYI, I have a self-destructing data disk waiting for me.

"Nonie, we're barely speaking for five minutes."

"Time I didn't even have in the first place, Dad." I soften my words by blowing him a kiss. Today is also not the day to end a talk with my only living relative in anger or with hard feelings. The lies are enough. The going behind his back.

He sighs, heavier than the last. "Okay then. You know I love you, right?"

Ouch. Right in the feels. "I've figured it out by now, Dad. Love you, too." Don't tear up, don't tear up...

The corners of his mouth move up in a warm smile. "Then stay safe and… may your First Sense always guide you back." He blows a kiss for me and then hangs up.

For a good twenty seconds, I stare at the area his image was projected to. My throat feels dry and raw. This was not the last time I saw my dad. I will be back, and I will have saved humanity.

Sheesh. I grimace. Sun and Stars, I should stop phrasing it like that.

But yeah.

Either I'll save them… or die trying.

Chapter Eight

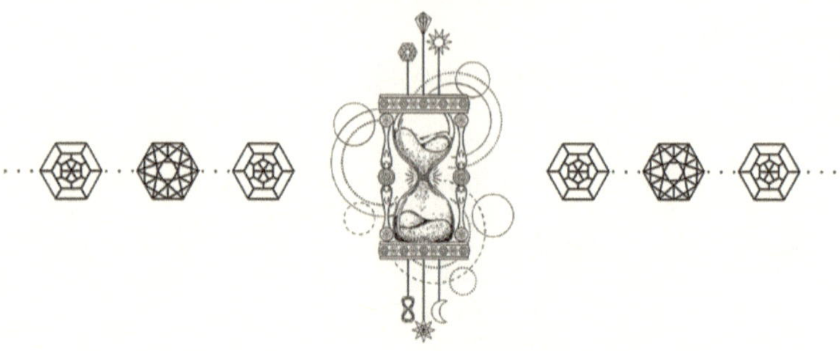

Somewhere, Day 0, Sometime

The first sense coming back to me is sound.

Beep. Beep. Beep. Beep.

Ow. Hurts my brain.

"… what are you telling me, Zio?"

Voices. Familiar. Faint.

Beep. Beep. Beep. Beep.

My chest heaves up with a big breath, and the beeping speeds up.

Sterile. Smells sterile here.

"I'm telling you that something is off." *Admiral Upinga.*

Somebody huffs—*Conolly!*—and like the volume was cranked up the voices become more clear. "Good description. The captain got attacked by someone on a presumably uninhabited planet. I'd say it qualifies as *something is off.*"

"That's not what I'm talking about, Chase."

"Enlighten me then."

One by one, my remaining senses come online, and with them awareness of my surroundings. My weight presses down into a soft surface. It stings when I take a big breath. Cool fluid drips into a vein in my right arm.

Sickbay. I must be in sickbay.

Headache. *Ow.* I lift a shaking hand to feel my face. The IV stings when I bend my elbow, and a small groan breaks free as I force my stiff muscles to obey my commands. Aftereffect of the Disruptor. First pain and paralysis, then only pain. *Only* in quotation marks.

Steps.

Somebody takes my hand and squeezes it. "Easy there. You've taken quite the load down there." That's Admiral Upinga. "Can you hear me?"

I nod and grunt. I can hear just fine, it's my eyelids that won't function properly. Thanks, dizziness.

"Wait, let me help you." The head of my bed moves up and brings me into a sitting position. "Better?"

I nod against the bout of vertigo, pinch my eyelids closed, and force them open. There. Conolly. Upinga. Feels like coming home. "Hi," I croak and squint against the bright light giving them a halo and making everything blurry.

Admiral Upinga checks the dressing on my shoulder. "Glad you're up. Was a bit worried about you." I think he smiles at me, but everything's hazy.

"I'm okay." *Ish.* "Would feel better if hadn't been for a full shuttle-load of *them* down there." One or two Quaneez I might've been able to handle alone. Three or four with the element of surprise and proper weapons. But one whole unit… that's tough.

"You saw their shuttle? Can you describe it?" Admiral Conolly steps closer to my bed and I go cross-eyed. Sheesh. Can't even focus my eyes.

"Nothing special. Old. Single unit."

"What do you mean?"

I know, I know. Conolly likes precision. "Ten soldiers." Two full units, and that Disruptor-blast to the shoulder would've been my least problem. Which reminds me: "Thank you for getting me. How'd you know where I was?"

Pause.

"You hailed us." Admiral Conolly steps closer to my bed, hands folded behind his back. I rub my eyes with the back of my hand, and finally both their features come more into focus.

"I know, but I mean all the way out here—" I look up to him and my next breath catches in my throat. What—

I rub my eyes once more, but to no avail. Yes, this is Admiral Conolly in front of me—blond, tousled hair, baby-blue eyes—but then he isn't. "What the hell?" I whisper.

Conolly looks… young. So young. *Too* young. Especially when he gives me the game face I've seen in action a million times, only then with more wrinkles etched into his skin. "We were exploring the planet, which brings up the question of how a lone civilian ended up on the same planet more than three quadrants away from Earth."

"I—" My mouth opens and closes like a fish out of water.

Conolly sighs. "What's your name?"

My jaw drops as the world around me begins to spin. "M-my name?"

"Yes. Your. Name." Every word is emphasized, one eye brow raised.

My name. I swallow dry. What the heck is—

"Chase, let her rest. Whatever they hit her with, I doubt it's easy to recover from." Upinga injects something into my left deltoid.

"A name isn't too hard. Or is it?" Game face cranks it up a notch.

"N—no. I'm Lieu— I'm Cad—" Stop. It doesn't feel right. I bite my lower lip and clear my throat. Play it safe. "I'm Nonie." My heart hammers like a drum, still bringing way too little oxygen to my starving brain. A nightmare. This must be a nightmare.

The admiral tilts his head. "Nonie…?"

Intuition kicks in. "Nonie Magnetta."

"Hello, Nonie Magnetta." Conolly's expression changes from business to more relaxed. "My name is Commander Chase Conolly, First Officer of the *Pioneer*, and this is Commander Zio Upinga, our Chief Medical Officer. Welcome aboard, and thank you for helping our captain."

My jaw drops. "C-commander? C-captain?" No. Wait. No. That can't be real. Must've heard—

Conolly sighs again and slows his speech, like talking to an imbecile. "Yes, *Commander* and *Captain*. I'm the First Officer. *Commander* Conolly. The man you helped on the planet—that's our *Captain*, Captain Kieran Wildason."

Captain. Kieran. Wildason.

I squeeze my eyes shut.

Open them.

Squeeze.

Open.

It doesn't change a damn thing.

Conolly still looks like early or mid-twenties, and Upinga… same for him. Young. Late twenties, maybe. *Twenties. Commander* Conolly. *Commander* Upinga. *Captain Kieran freakin' Wildason.* I don't under—

Like a lightning strike, the puzzle pieces fall into place.

Oh, by the Great Expanse, no.

No, please, no.

It's must be a nightmare, nothing else. Concussion. Maybe a hallucination dreamed up by a brain deprived of oxygen, because the alternative is impossible. Fiction. Against the laws of nature.

And yet it's the only valid explanation I can come up with, crazy as it sounds.

I stare at the two men I thought I knew like the back of my hand, who've become as close as family to me over the last four years. "Wh-what's the date today? Please?"

Conolly exchanges a worried look with Upinga. "May seventh."

My mouth is dry. "May seventh…?"

"May seventh, 2255."

2255.

Twenty-two years before—

Twenty-two years before I *will be* born.

And forty years in the past.

Chapter Nine

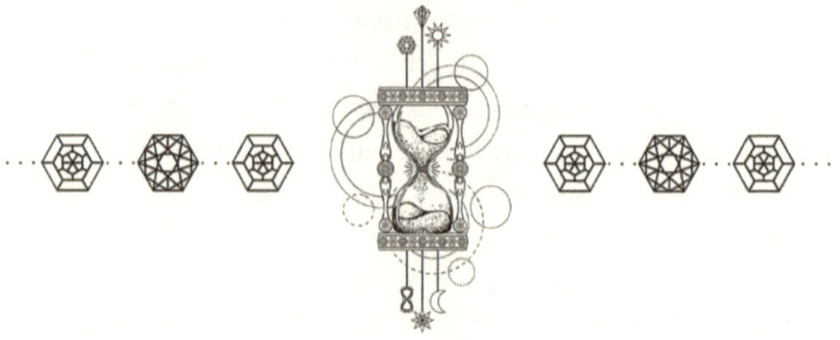

As soon as the bell rings, I leave Auditorium Three. No need to linger, it's not as if I wanted to chat, and even if I did, I assume nobody else would. Nothing I can do about that.

The hallway fills with students, most of them about to make a quick stop at their locker before heading over to Auditorium One, like me. Today's going to count as one of the most pivotal days in our Acade—

I stop dead in my tracks when my gaze falls onto my locker. "What the—"

With three quick steps, I weave through the crowd and swipe one finger over the words scribbled wide across my locker in all caps: MAG LOVER. The words won't smear. Sharpie. Great.

Who does that? My throat tightens and my eyes sting. Screw these idiots.

Somebody snickers behind me, and that sound, it brings my face to a burn. Snippets of whispered comments float by, none of them nice, and all of them like they were from the very beginning, singling me out and stamping me as an outsider.

Baby. Because I'm the only fourteen-year-old amongst eighteen-year olds, or even older students.

Traitor. Because Dad is the Ambassador to the Magellan people. Obviously, that *must* mean I work against humanity, for whatever reason.

Maggot. Because it's the leg that sets me apart from them, the leg that tells them the story I don't remember, the leg that makes me a *Maggot.* And gotta say, that one actually gets to me, each and every time. Although, what does it even mean? Maggot. Just because it shares the *Mag* from Magellan? Really? How uncreative—not that I want any idiots to come up with anything quote-unquote better, but still. Maybe it bugs me, pun intended, because it implies I'm one of the Magellans and at the same time makes it sound like that was wrong. News flash: it isn't! Yeah, maybe that's it—the fact that they use as an insult what shouldn't be one. All the old classics of messed-up academy behavior like *daddy's daughter, leech*, and *weirdo* high school has taught me to handle—especially *weirdo.* And to be honest, when I signed up for the academy, I knew competition was going to be fierce. What I didn't know was that all rules, decency, and good manners went out the window as well. Anything goes, as long as they can discredit somebody else and make themselves look better.

The snickers and whispers behind me haven't stopped, and judging from six months of academy life, I doubt they will. Or at least they won't until I show them what I'm made of.

MAG LOVER.

I open my locker, throw my books in there, and grab a Sharpie. Takes me less than five seconds to addend the slur. I step back to look at my work. Yeah. Much better. I cap the pen, pocket it, and limp away from my locker with my head held high, leaving the ink to dry on the cold metal:

MAG LOVER—AND PROUD OF IT.

Chapter Ten

Stuck on repeat, my mind plays through the same phrase over and over. *Twenty-two years before my birth.*

I'm in the past, *almost forty years* ago.

Can't make sense of it. How did I get here? How could I travel back in time? How could this happen? It's impossible. It can't happen. Time flows in one direction, and we can't reverse—

Conolly tries to check the pulse on my wrist. "You look horrible." Less experienced than Upinga, he feels around for and moves my wrist PAD aside to reach my artery. "But this is cool."

I rip my hand out from underneath his and turn PADdy away from him. "Th-thanks, and thanks. M-my dad gave it to me."

Upinga takes a medical scanner from the head of the bed and moves it over me. "I agree with the commander. You're quite pale. Do you feel okay?"

Do I feel I okay? No, not by a long shot! Still, I force a smile. "Y-yeah. Just… feel odd."

Upinga gives me a long, *long* glance that penetrates my lies and shoots right into the center of my disguise. "I could blame that on either your elevated heart rate and low blood pressure, or on whatever they shot you with down on the planet. It's going to leave a scar, by the way."

Conolly makes a slicing hand motion. "And I'll need to know which colony is using weapons like this and is going against their oath to USEF and Earth government, shooting at fellow humans. Whatever you can give me, please. Our scanners couldn't recognize anybody's life signs on that damn planet," he tags on, more as an afterthought to himself.

Which colony—?

I barely keep from facepalming myself. *Right.* It's 2255, the year we quote-unquote *discovered* the Quaneez. *This* Upinga and Conolly don't have much experience fighting the Quaneez. Yet. But—

Holy cow.

Like a punch to the gut, my stomach cramps.

Wait a second. They didn't recognize Quaneez life signs. That little tidbit of information together with what happened down there… Sweat breaks out on my forehead. If I'm right… I give a shy smile. Acting one-oh-one. "I'll do my best. What is that planet even called?"

Conolly huffs. "It doesn't have a name yet, which should make it clear you were way too far off the beaten path, girl. We catalogued and numerated the planet yesterday and it hails on the beautiful name T-12 from now on."

T-12.

No USEF-trained officer could hear the name of that planet without a shudder down their back: first contact with the Quaneez.

And I was there. Last night was *first contact* with the Quaneez, and I was the wild card on that planet. I'm very sure there is no mentioning of a Nonie Thorburn—or Nonie Magnetta—witnessing First Contact, so… Pressure and a bubble of fear grow in my chest, both expanding with every second my precarious situation becomes more and more clear to me. I'm in deep doo-doo. Seems to become a permanent condition.

Question is, did I already mess up? How badly? Did I alter anything—and if so, what? My brain scrambles to come up with history as it was supposed to happen. Obviously Wildason survived the night, but how did he get out of that dicey spot in, well, in the unaltered past? Cold sweat breaks out and runs down my back. Gotta be really careful from now on. I'm thinking, if I messed up already, it can't have been too bad, since the captain was supposed to survive, but what if I make it worse from now on? I could screw up the timeline and erase the future— my future.

Oh, Sun and Stars.

Nausea threatens to overwhelm me. My presence alone could change—or could have already changed—future events.

Everything's so fragile. At this point, nobody besides me here knows they were attacked by non-humans. They don't even know they've just encountered a new alien species. They're still thinking rogue humans, which is why the guy—sorry, *Captain Wildason*—didn't know a thing about defending against the attack.

Sun and Stars, I should've realized something was wrong. Thinking back, I felt off with a weird, uneasy feeling from the very moment I opened my eyes in the shuttle and, against expectations, wasn't pulverized. At the latest I should have added one and one when I saw a trained USEF officer struggling like this against the Quaneez. How I couldn't have known the second I held the mega-outdated weapon and hablamate, or the second Upinga and Conolly didn't recognize me, is beyond me. I should've made the connection.

But then, it's impossible.

Completely impossible.

And yet, here I am.

Conolly tilts his head. "So, how did you end up crashed on that planet? Give me the run-down, if you don't mind. And I would like as much information about that shuttle you saw as you can give me." He says it in an easy conversational tone, but I have known this man—or rather, I will know this man—for years. I know he's on high alert, and I can't hold it against him. Here's a girl on a planet so far off, it hasn't even been charted yet. I bet they scanned the planet before they dematted the team down, and I bet they didn't find me—because I wasn't there. Yet. Add said girl popping up off the beaten path rescuing the captain… yeah, I can't hold his suspicions against him.

I rub my forehead to stall. "Good question. It's all so blurry. Been there for a while. Two days, maybe?" Seems to be the safest excuse, because otherwise the *Pioneer* should have seen me crashing. Why they haven't I don't have a clue, by the way. And while I can come up with a BS-reason why they didn't find me on scanners, environmental disturbances, whatever, it's much harder to find an excuse why the *Pioneer*'s systems didn't see my shuttle crash landing. Two days is perfect, any more and it would be unbelievable I survived.

"Two days?" He exchanges a glance with Upinga, who scrolls through something on his PAD.

"Possible. All our scans brought back *interesting* readings."

Which would be the Quaneez life signs, not that I'm going to say that out loud.

"Okay, so you made it down there for two days. Fine. But really, I want to know how you ended up all the way here." Conolly makes an impatient hand gesture.

Focus, Nonie. "Honestly, I would like to know that, too." Truth, right there. I couldn't have jumped this far if I wanted to. No drive can cross a distance that huge, from H-155 to T-12. I grimace and rub that forehead some more. "I don't remember much. Systems' failure. Couldn't control her—smoke. Fire. Every alarm blaring. I—" I lower my voice. "I don't know." Again, truth right there.

Upinga closes the scanner and gives my uninjured shoulder a mild squeeze. "Not surprisingly so. You've been through a lot, meaning, you should rest some more. I anticipate that in a few hours you'll feel better. Come on." He looks at Conolly and nods toward the medical office.

Something passes between them, and to my complete and utter surprise, Conolly lets it go. "Of course, Doctor. Nonie, once you feel better, I'd like to know more about what happened, about you, and then we'll do our best to get you home as soon as possible. Until then, don't worry. You're safe onboard the *Pioneer*. Okay?" This time I get the full smile, dimples and all.

Relief washes over me. Saved by the bell, until I can think of more believable details. I nod so fast, the dizziness has a field day from it. "Yes, thank you, Ad—Commander." Thank you for not asking me those questions now, because I wouldn't know what to say.

"Of course." And with that, the two men retreat into Upinga's medical office at the far end of the sickbay.

Holy freakin' cow.

Unreal. This is unreal.

Never have I been more thankful to be left alone. To say I have to think is an understatement, because… yeah. *Because.*

Upinga said I needed to rest, but I could bet he's running a scan in the background to check for concussion after the show I just pulled.

Confused patient? Scan away. I know my Admira—

Nope. I don't. That's the point.

I know *Admiral* Upinga, I know *Admiral* Conolly. These two young officers in their early or mid-twenties? Never met them, literally. And that drives the point home like a sledge hammer to the face. I'm in the past, and my mere presence here might be altering it. Thanks to me, the world as I know it might not exist—or will never exist. Now, if that meant I didn't kill millions of Quaneez—

But it also means… everything. My presence here has the potential to wreak havoc on the timeline. Had I popped up in Somewhere, Idaho, no biggie. But here, on the famous *USEF Pioneer* at *this* time? There isn't a more vulnerable period in the decades before and after this—this is where the war started.

Not how I imagined I'd change the world when I woke up this morning.

The question becomes, what do I do? How do I get back? How do I behave here in the meantime? Have I already altered time, and everything I do from now on is negligible, doesn't matter anymore, the damage done? Or is my impact so far minimal, and the timeline will correct itself? That's the prevalent theory about time, right? If I remember that stupid class on Temporal Mechanics correctly, not every event creates a new timeline-slash-universe, but minor changes get smoothed out, I *think*. It's not like they taught the details of time travel at the academy.

The faint beep of a PAD being activated in the medical office comes to my ears, followed by a sigh from Admiral—*Commander*—Upinga. It's muffled, but I've always had good hearing. If I strain, I can even pick up their words behind closed doors: "What I wanted to say earlier, Chase. My research on her leads nowhere. No genetic match. Maybe some faint bonds to a family named Svenson in Chicago, but nothing that really tells me who she is."

Conolly speaks next. "Okay. So I assume she's one of the Starhopper Hippies. Not registered in our databank. She comes from money, you saw her fancy wrist device. Those rich people like their privacy, but the thing is, I don't like people who like their privacy too much. I also don't like her being out this far, all alone. Why? There's plenty of space closer and safer. Together with that attack on T-12... I don't know. Could be coincidence, but I have to assume it's not until proven otherwise."

"Point made."

"I see your frown. What is it, Zee?"

"Tough to say. Just have an odd feeling about her."

Pause.

"Dang you and your feelings." He sighs. "Odd as in bad, or not so bad?"

"In danger of repeating myself, tough to say. While she's obviously confused right now, she gave us a good sign out earlier after we dematted her up."

"I noticed. Suggests some kind of training. Ah, and we know one thing for sure."

"What would that be?"

"She has pretty hair like you." He chuckles, and Upinga huffs.

"Harr harr. Not what I'm talking about, Chase. All I'm saying is that I don't trust my scanner's readout."

"You always trust your scanner. You love your scanner." He definitely sounds even more concerned now.

"I love my scanner all right, but... the readouts are odd." Upinga says is with such conviction, I stop breathing.

"Odd." One word, so many implications. "Do I even know you? You give better descriptions than that, Zee."

"I'll give you details once I have them, Trip. For now you gotta live with me saying they're odd."

And that would be because of my masker. Oh Sun and Stars, thank you, Dad, for insisting I wear it. If I didn't, they would've found my family's genetic markers and made the connection to my grandparents or something. Or they would've noticed my isotopes don't date as anticipated. A shudder runs down my back.

Conolly sighs. "Do you think she is a security risk? Because from my point of view I'm not quite sure."

Pause.

I hold my breath, until Upinga replies after what feels like an eternity. "No. No, I don't think so."

Relief floods my system. Phew. Okay. Good. At least something is working my favor.

"Okay, then, Zee. I trust your intuition, as always, and I'll give her the benefit of the doubt, but… I'll start looking some more into her."

Ugh. Great.

One thing is clear: Until I figure out how to get back, I need to reduce my footprint here to invisible. As little interaction as possible. As little information as possible. Avoid anything that could alter the timeline.

My life and all of my world's future depends on it.

Chapter Eleven

Muffled voices wake me up. At one point exhaustion and worry must've won over and knocked me out.

"Let her sleep, Kieran. She took the brunt of the shot that you got into the shoulder and you were unconscious from a lower dose. She needs time to recover."

"I know, Zee. Just let me check on her, okay? If it wasn't for her, I'd be dead."

My eyes fly open. Deep voice, calm—holy cow, is that Captain Wildason?

Upinga makes a disapproving noise. "Only for a minute. No more."

"Promise."

The door to the medical office opens completely, and if I had any doubt about the validity of my time-travel theory, it'd be gone at this point.

This is Captain Kieran Wildason, one of only three recipients of the Iron Star, a Wunderkind at the academy, youngest captain in history, a legend. Like in the pictures and videos of him, he's tall, way taller than yesterday when he was doubled over from pain, and I gotta give myself props for picking up on the, uhh, *truly important* things in a life-or-death-situation, but I was right last night, no matter the mud he had on his face then: He's good-looking. More than that. Conolly—my *Admiral* Conolly—referred to him once as "pretty boy," and right he is.

Kieran Wildason is pretty. Masculine and pretty. His hair is so dark it seems to absorb all light around it, and like last night, wavy longer strands from the top fall into his face. The sides are kept short, which is probably why the style is still within USEF regulations, but even if it wasn't, I doubt anybody could look into those dark eyes and tell him to cut his hair. Not a female, at least. Add the high cheekbones and strong jaw, and I totally get it why my dad's generation is still fan-girling for this guy.

As it is, I can't help but stare as he palms the door closed, turns around and walks over to me with a self-assuredness worth my envy. His gaze falls right into mine and for the tiniest moment his eyes pop wide and his steps falter. Or it could have been my imagination, because I'm a tad distracted by that little *zing* shooting through my chest all the way down to my toes and the tingle it leaves in its wake.

Wildason stops next to my bed, and whoa, that sentence alone is close to inducing a stroke, because… Because it should be impossible. Because it's Kieran Wildason. Because he hasn't dropped his gaze from mine.

"Hi," he says with a small smile. Still looking straight into my eyes.

"Hi," I squeak back, my breath hitching in my throat mid-inhale and turning into a choked cough, the ugly kind with wheezing and gasping, because *ow*. Coughing hurts.

Wildason pats my back. "You okay?"

I fight for another choked breath and to control my embarrassment. "Yeah," I croak. "Thank you." The last part comes out better. Stronger.

His smile perks up. "You're… Nonie, right?"

"Yeah. Nonie. I am. I mean, I'm Nonie." *Sheesh…!* Some decorum please, Lieutenant.

The smile turns radiant as he chuckles softly. "I'm Kieran. Nice to meet you, Nonie." He says it slow and deliberate, like he really meant it. Oh, how I wish I could record those two sentences and play them back on repeat. Iron Star-recipient Captain Kieran Wildason says it's nice to meet me. To top it off, he's still looking at me with a hundred percent attention, completely focused, even when he is reaching for a chair and pulling it closer to my bed.

"So, that was you last night. Down on T-12." He sits and crosses his legs, completely relaxed and also completely unaware of the bout of panic shooting through me, because him mentioning First Contact gives me a good dose of straight-up reality. Yes, this is the famous Captain Kieran Wildason. No, it is not okay for me to be here and to be talking to him. So rein it in, Lieutenant, focus, and don't make it any worse than it already is.

I sit up straighter in bed. "Yeah, that was me. And nice to meet you, too." No matter the crappy circumstances and potential for even more disaster, it's still an honor.

Captain Wildason taps his shoulder where I can see parts of a white wound dressing peek out from under his collar. "Thank you for coming to my help yesterday. Things were looking pretty ugly there for a moment."

No kidding they did—actually, he has no idea how bad it could've gotten. "Anytime, Captain."

"Call me Kieran."

My heart skips a beat. "Kieran." His name rolls off my tongue. I'm calling the greatest captain ever by his first name.

Kieran leans into his chair, head tilted to the side, like he was trying to figure me out. "It was kind of unexpected to run into you on that planet." Unlike Conolly, he says it as a statement, not as fishing for information, and no kidding it was. Same here.

I smile and shrug, looking down at my blanket to buy myself another half second. Backstory coming up, right now. "I crashed two days ago. My poor shuttle didn't make it."

He flinches, then shakes his head. "Ow. Yeah, I heard. I'm sorry. We have what's left of it in Hangar Bay three. Had we—"

I shake my head to clear it. "Wait—my shuttle is here?" Not good. I mean, good because I need to get out of here, but not good because… because it's loaded with technology unknown to this time. What's not burned of it, that is.

"Engine's pretty damaged, from what I hear, so…" He lets the sentence trail off and I get it. That shuttle will be of no use for me any time soon, at least not without a major overhaul. A weird feeling of simultaneous relief and panic swamps me, so powerful it brings a wave of dizziness.

He sighs. "Anyway, had we known you were there, we'd have rerouted the *Pioneer* sooner, but we didn't pick up any distress signal at all."

Because I didn't send one. I rub my forehead. "Things went a tad too fast for me, and once I was down there… swoosh, fire, shuttle gone, and with it a lot of dreams and plans." It comes out more bitter than I planned, but truer words have not been spoken.

"I see. I'm surprised though to find a civilian this far into unexplored space. We should name T-12 after you."

I throw my hands up. "No. No. Please don't. No naming planets after me." First Contact on Nonie's Planet? Yeah, right.

The captain winks. "Kidding. USEF likes their boring names. But anyway, how'd you end up stranded? A sabbatical? But all alone? We're three quadrants away from Earth."

Heat rises up my neck. Here we go. Play it cool. He offered me a story on a silver platter, now I gotta go and run with it. "I know. I might've miscalculated my route a little bit." Commence more fake story and show.

"A bit?" Humor shines from his voice.

"Yeah. A bit much. Dad said to stay close to Earth, but you know…" I break eye contact and look down onto my folded hands.

"Dad's opinion didn't count?" The humor is getting stronger, and I realize my mistake. Mentioning a dad means there is family, which they will surely try to contact. To no avail.

"Dad… died. Shortly after he prepped me and set me up for the sabbatical." I cringe. Saying those words feels wrong, like I was jinxing my dad. "And I figured, he left me enough money, I'm done with school, I've got the shuttle, who cares if I explore? Nothing else to do, you know?" I remember Dad saying that when he was young, taking a sabbatical after high school was the in-thing to do. Some of the rich kids, they went the whole mile and took to space, and I get it. We had the technology, space was ours, we hadn't yet run into any enemies, and there was so much to explore. Granted, a few didn't make it back, and once the Quaneez came into play, nobody ventured out anymore, but for a while, it was freedom. For the rich, at least.

His face falls. "I'm sorry to hear about your dad. Is there anybody else we should inform we found you?"

"No." I shake my head. "I don't know my mother, and I don't have any other family." Truth again, right there. Look how well I'm playing this.

Wildason nods and leans forward, supporting his upper body with his elbows on his thighs. "So, you decided to throw conventions to hell and explore space. I like it." The smile is back, and it comes with a twinkle in his eyes that makes it way too easy to return that smile.

"Exactly. Why not?" I'm careful not to give too much background, motivation, or whatever. Too many details will make it harder for me to remember, and I don't want to keep on digging my own proverbial grave here. It's deep enough already.

Kieran laughs softly, and that sound, it shoots straight to my core. "I'm sure there are tons of why-nots, especially since one of them got you stranded on a planet far off explored space. If we hadn't been there—no, wait, let me correct that." He holds up one hand. "If *you* hadn't been there, *I'd* probably be dead. So never mind getting stranded on an unknown planet. Worked for me." He shrugs, and boy, if it didn't make him look so much more like a normal person instead of the famous legendary captain.

I smooth out the blanket covering me until not a single wrinkle is left. "I'd say we're even. I'd be stuck on that planet without you, and you… You know." Would *not* be dead. He made it out on his own in my official past, that much is clear.

The sliding doors at the far end opposite the medical office hiss apart, revealing Admiral—dang it, that takes some getting used to—Commander Conolly. With a few quick strides he's standing next to Kieran and me. "Captain. Good to see you up and running."

Kieran groans. "Running is pushing it too far. I'm sore as a mo—*Really* sore." His cheeks take on a pink hue.

"Maybe that's why the doc said to stay on bedrest another half day."

Kieran rolls his eyes. "Oh, come on, Chase. Not you, too. Zio has been breathing down my neck since I woke up—and probably while I was out of it, too. I'm not going to stay in bed and off duty any longer than necessary for him to run more tests. Besides…" He wiggles an eyebrow at me. "I needed to meet Nonie and thank her for bringing me back in one piece."

I give him thumbs up. "Like I said, anytime." Unless it interferes with the past, then count me out. Sigh.

Conolly nods at me. "And I thank her for that as well, although I would still like to see her in my office and hear her explanation of how she knew what to do to get you out of there, Captain." The look he throws at me I know only too well. It's the you-better-tell-me-or-else-look. He's not only my mentor—I mean, he *will* not only be my mentor—but he is—*will be*, gah!—teaching security at the academy. Looks like Upinga's concerns took hold in him.

Awesome, really.

I clear my throat. "Of course." Not that I could give any answer other than that.

Kieran looks up at Conolly. "That can't wait until she feels better?"

"Oh, of course. It's not like she was going anywhere." Conolly rocks back onto his heels, as I look from one to the other.

"I'm not?" Because, I need to get off this ship and away from anything and anyone whose actions could be altered because of my presence in this time. STAT.

Kieran grimaces. "I know, probably not what you wanted to hear, but we were in the middle of a mission and recent events made that even more *interesting*." No kidding. First contact with the Quaneez, and they don't even know that part yet. They might have a hunch, given the yellow weapon's fire and unknown technology, but it's not official yet. I don't need to know history, only protocol, to know the *Pioneer* is not going back home into explored space, but will be trying to find the unknown space ship from the planet in an attempt to establish communication with the presumed rogue colonists.

And while the team of the *Pioneer* is in for a surprise when they find said ship, this whole thing is very unfortunate for me, if it means I'm staying on board. Which is like sitting on a powder keg waiting for it to explode. I cringe. Bad comparison. I flash a quick smile. "N-no worries. I understand. I appreciate you taking me on board, but I don't want to become a nuisance either. Whenever you have a chance, just drop me off at the nearest populated planet. Doesn't have to be a Starbase, really." Because on a planet, I can melt into the population. On a Starbase?

Good luck with that.

Kieran rubs his thumb across his chin. "I don't think you could ever be a nuisance. I—" He looks down and clears his throat. When he looks up, his gaze crashes into mine and penetrates all the way into my soul. He tilts his head, assessing me. "You know, I wonder. Let me ask you something: Do you think they were human? The people down on that planet?"

Excuse me? I choke on my next breath. Do I think they were human? No. I *know* they weren't human. And even if I didn't know, I'd have suspected it.

The commander's head whips around. "Captain, this is not appropriate—"

Wildason lifts a hand. "Commander. Let me."

Conolly's mouth snaps shut, his lips pressing into a thin line.

Do I think they were human? What the heck am I supposed to say to that? When did the *Pioneer* find out those attackers were Quaneez? Now? When they encounter the ship the next time?

Only thing I can do is use common sense and do what feels right. I sit up straighter and go with my gut. "Your question alone implies you don't think so, and to be honest, I thought they weren't. Humanoid, yes. Humans, no."

"Why?" His gaze is glued to mine, evaluating every twitch of my facial muscles.

"Because their gestures were wrong. The way they moved." I'm not giving anything away here. And really, he wouldn't ask if he didn't already know, or at least suspect. It's kind of a non-brainer after what happened down there.

Kieran nods, a pensive expression on his face. "You're right," he finally says. "We don't think they were human either."

"Captain!" Conolly stares at him, mouth open, eyed wide. "Sir, this is classified—"

"Chase. Seriously. How classified can it be if she saw them and figured it out on her own? And I appreciate if someone can think straight under pressure and come to the right conclusions." He taps my blanket twice and gets up. "Anyway, duty calls. It was very nice to meet you, Nonie. I'll… see you around."

"Later," Conolly adds and tries to support Kieran by the arm, but nope.

"Nu-uh." He pulls his arm back. "Adult. Can walk on my own. Tell Zio to stop infusing your brain with nonsense."

Conolly rolls his eyes. "Yes, *sir*."

And with that, they leave sickbay, and me and my mountain of worries alone.

Chapter Twelve

The image of an older male in USEF uniform is projected into the air in the center of the auditorium.

"… was horrible. They were on top of us before we knew how many there even were. We were shot and blacked out from the pain—unimaginable pain—and when we woke up…" He shudders as his eyes take on a distant quality. "Can't remember much, like, details. But I thought I was in heaven. It was so quiet—so quiet I could hear nothing but my own breathing and that of my mates. Smelled like heaven. I thought I was done, it was over, and… I was kind of relieved." His features distort into a mask of horror. "I was wrong though. They came, like Lucifer from hell, and they reeked of sulfur and knew no mercy. Didn't listen, didn't speak, just tortured us without a word. The stuff they put into our bodies… like burning alive from the inside. Like burning alive. And I still hear them every time I close my eyes, every time I try to sleep. It never stops. It never stops, even in my dreams…" His voice trails out and the projection changes to a map of space, Earth in the middle, as always.

"In 2255, humanity had begun to push the boundaries of explored space," a male voice-over reports. "On May seventh, 2255 the *USEF Pioneer*, in the delta quadrant for a scientific mission, picked up on an unusual signature from an uncharted and at this point unknown H-Class planet. Captain Kieran Wildason and a team of two scientists transferred to the planet for investigation. Within hours and without provocation on their part they were attacked by an unknown humanoid species later called the Quaneez. While not officially recognized as the beginning of the Quaneez wars, many historians do consider this date its true beginning."

The map zooms out, a red zig-zaggy line moving from the H-class planet farther into space.

"The *Pioneer* subsequently searched for and found the unknown vessel. Hopes were high that despite the hostile first encounter peaceful communication could be established, and the decision was made to attempt communication to begin a peaceful relationship with a new intelligent neighboring species. Without provocation the Quaneez, true to their nature, opened fire on the *Pioneer*. Holding the values of the USEF to their highest standard, Captain Wildason did not return fire, but retreated."

The projection changes back to the *Pioneer* shooting through space. "For the next ten days the *Pioneer* resumed its search for the Quaneez, and eventually found the same ship on May 12th, 2255. The *Pioneer* observed the Quaneez ship pull into orbit around another Class H-planet after experiencing what looked like a malfunction. Several humanoids were dematted to the planet as their ship continued to emit smoke and leak electricity. The decision by the *Pioneer*'s commanding officers was made to send a single person to establish a non-threatening first contact and to offer help. Captain Wildason volunteered, was sent to the planet, Ursus 31, and was subsequently captured by the Quaneez."

The schematic of a Quaneez bunker pops up. They all look the same, but I know this is the very first one we encountered, because the drawing of the empty torture chair Wildason was in comes right after. Most of what we know about the Quaneez bunkers we know from this encounter, because whoever got that data did a good job collecting it and recalling details, like this chair. And… not many others survived to tell the tale, or if they did survive, they weren't… *intact* enough to give us more details. Kind of scary, forty years later, and also the reason why captains don't lead away missions anymore. Maybe the one commanding the ship should stay on board, responsibility and all.

The subtitles move on, a tad out of sync with the narrator. "During his three-hour-long captivity, Captain Wildason was exposed to Quaneez Mind Crucification and physical torture in an attempt to extract sensitive information about the *Pioneer* and humanity. Captain Wildason eventually was freed from captivity by a *Pioneer* crew member in a stroke of genius-idea—"

The image freezes with the subtitle *stroke of genius-idea* still on screen. "Enough for now, everybody." Professor Haggardy claps his hands. "This should be old news, cadets. You've all learned the basics of the Quaneez-wars in school. Now as first-year cadets it's time to give this a military spin and prepare you for what unfortunately will be the war of your generation as much as it is of ours." He waits for a moment until the last student has directed their attention from the bunker's freeze-frame to him and the topic at hand.

"The Quaneez wars started officially on May 15, 2255, with the Battle of Balthar. It has become the most destructive war humanity has ever been involved in. Until recently, there had been no cease fire, no weapon's rest, and there still hasn't been any successful contact or discussion with the Quaneez people. The death toll on our side ranks in the billions, on theirs it is unknown, but estimates go as high as twice our numbers."

Professor Haggardy's gaze scans over the cadets in the first few rows. We're all quiet. At a hundred percent attention. Pale. You don't talk about the toll the Quaneez wars took and joke around or give the topic anything less than a hundred percent. Many of us joined the USEF to defend our people, and many of us have lost either family members who were USEF officers who died in battle, or civilians killed on our colonies during Quaneez attacks. Meaning, this is serious.

"Cadets, this is the history you need to know like the back of your hand. Myers—name what's typical about Quaneez ships."

At my eight o'clock somebody jumps out of their seat and snaps to attention. "Silent Propulsion, as we call it. Very difficult to detect, therefore it is difficult to scan for the ships, or to estimate their numbers. That's one of the reasons why we haven't found their home world yet. Can't trace them, can't find them. And yet they can be on top of us within minutes."

Haggardy nods. "Correct." He chooses something on his pad and projects it into the middle of the round auditorium, replacing the still frame of the *stroke of genius*. "One should think a big space ship like this was easily detected on our sensors. Hint, it's not." He circles the aft of the triangular-shaped spaceship on his pad, the same area lighting up in red in the projection. "We've had luck tracing their exhaust, but with limited reliability. Disperses too fast. You'll learn more about that from Professor Yehodi in Tactics. He'll also give you some insight on theories in regards to potential locations for the Quaneez home world, or home worlds. Over the last two decades, we made finding their origin a priority, if for nothing else than to estimate their numbers." He frowns. "No people has unlimited soldiers, even though the Quaneez seem to have an abundance. We kill them, and it doesn't seem to make a difference. But I digress. Back to the silent propulsion drive. Meidan, why is silent propulsion a bad idea?"

Some guy to the left of me jumps out of his seat and snaps to attention. "Sir, because it reacts with planetary atmospheres. It's very volatile overall. Basically, it has a tendency to blow up or ignite an oxygen-rich atmosphere, and neither is obviously desirable."

"Maybe their engineers are working for us." Haggardy snickers. "But jokes aside, correct. Well done."

Meidan sits down again, looking way too full of himself, in my opinion, because ugh. What an arrogant answer. The moment we understand why they're not using that construction fault to zip over to Earth and blow us up, we'll be one step closer to ending the war. But what do I know?

"Moving on." Haggardy drops his gaze down to his pad, and two seconds later, the Quaneez ship is replaced with the image of a man in his early twenties, black, unruly hair, a strong chin, and eyes so dark they penetrate down to the bottom of my soul, no matter this being nothing more than a 3D-picture.

Captain Kieran Wildason.

Something about him gets me every time, something on a cellular level I can't explain. It gives my heart a little kick until it stumbles, it brings a tickle to my fingers, and I swear the day looks brighter when Wildason is a topic.

I frown. Grr. All that means is that I'm like ninety percent of my junior class: catering to the whims of the pathetic by idolizing a captain who's been dead for decades.

On the podium, Haggardy picks his next victim. "Scalzitti. Give me the one-oh-one on this man here."

Scalzitti jumps up. She scored with that task. "Sir, Captain Kieran Wildason was named the youngest captain in history after his heroic actions during the disaster of Alpha Rubrum. As we just saw, he was essentially the captain to make first contact with the Quaneez, and his team's groundwork in general and in regard to their shields and weapons is still much of what we rely on to this day. He received several medals of honor and distinction throughout his years of service and died in space at the hands of the Quaneez at age twenty-three."

"Correct, Cadet." Another image replaces the one of Captain Wildason, this one snuffing out the little tickle in my body: Commanders Conolly and Upinga, Wildason's first and chief medical officer, standing in their gala-uniforms next to an empty, black casket in their hangar bay. The symbolic space funeral. Behind them, the whole crew is lined up, and if I'm not mistaken, Commander Conolly is already wearing the captain's stripes at this point.

Scalzitti's voice drops lower. "His body was disintegrated at point of death, but to this day, his quarters on the *Pioneer* have been kept the way he left them. And, FYI, the *Pioneer* can be visited when she's around, since she's now an official museum."

Haggardy nods. "Well done. Such a pity, that is. I had the pleasure of hearing him give a speech once, when I was a young ensign, and I'm telling you that man had a gift. Such a pity." He shakes his head and swipes across his pad once, replacing the image up front with one of a Quaneez soldier. "Anyway, moving on. Monegain, list physical attributes we know about Quaneez."

Somebody scrambles up, and I don't need to look to know that person won't answer quite as self-assured as Myers and Scalzitti did. This is a difficult question, because as long as the wars have been going on, we know little about the Quaneez.

"Sir, we don't know much about the Quaneez." An audible hard swallow follows his statement, and I roll my eyes. Fake it until you make it, man. "B-but we do know they're humanoid with a physical strength surpassing our own. They—" He stops in mid-sentence when the double doors on the ground floor next to the podium open, admitting a handful people, all in gala uniforms.

We might only be first-years and new at that, but we know an admiral when we see one. Especially this one. Like one collective being, the whole class jumps up and to attention.

Professor Haggardy rolls his eyes at the interruption, but then turns to greet the visitors. "Admiral Grazer. Officers." He nods in greeting at the six people entering the auditorium.

Admiral Grazer is pretty much the head of the Academy, also the head of Division Two. He's the man to know around here, and rumor has it he is going to take a first-year mentee this year, and yes, I would love, love, *love* for it to be me. So much potential with him as a mentor, such a big stepping stone. Such an honor.

My heart pumps harder. Such an honor.

"Haggardy." Admiral Grazer shakes the professor's hand. "Sorry for the interruption. I'm giving the incoming faculty a tour of the academy—we have two alumni, but everybody else is from our sister academy in Europe." He steps aside, making room for the three male and three female officers, four captains and... two admirals.

A slight whispery hush goes through the auditorium, because, the two alumni? They're Admirals Upinga and Conolly, the former commanders-slash-later-captain of the famous *Pioneer* we've just been talking about! Whoa. Un-be-lievable. That is real-life history down there! My heart beats faster, excitement flooding my veins. I've never met either of them, and I have met quite a few important people over the years, thanks to Dad being an admiral with the USEF himself.

But: never did I meet Admirals Conolly and Upinga, two of the USEF's most famous Officers and leads of the OUTREACH division. They alone discovered what—how many more intelligent species? Three? So exciting.

And, judging by the palpable buzz and awe in the room, my classmates are on the same page. I'm pretty sure this visit today is going to be in everybody's report home during the next holo call, and yes, I'm going to tell Dad, no doubt about it. At this very moment I'm so proud to be at the academy. Meeting all these incredible people—it's amazing!

The professor nods like a wobble-head figurine. "Of course, Admiral. I can call a break—"

"Never mind, John. Carry on and we'll observe for a few minutes, then be on our merry way." Grazer claps the professor's shoulder and steps back in line with the others. Two of the visiting captains talk to each other in hushed tones, indicating something farther up in the auditorium with their chin. Admirals Conolly and Upinga on the other hand look over the attending first-years, scanning every face in the audience.

Intense.

Haggardy addresses the class. "At ease, students. Monegain, continue."

I could swear poor Monegain almost faints. He didn't get the best question to impress either the admiral or any of the new Faculty. Sucks to be him right now.

His voice breaks with the first word, but then he has himself under control. Somewhat. "What we know about the Quaneez. N-not much, is the short version. We don't even know the basics, whether their species is separated into females and males, or not. Current theory is they might be hermaphrodites?" The way he raises his voice at the end, it sounds like a question, which it shouldn't be. It's one of the current discussions, so just say it, man. We're completely underinformed, which is the reason why we call every Quaneez *he*, to make it easier. I really hope we're not offending the Quaneez with that—for all we know, they could be a female warrior race. On the other hand, given that we've killed billions of them at this point, I doubt mislabeling them was our worst offense.

Monegain pulls his shoulders back and juts his chin forward. Ah, gaining confidence, are we? "As we just saw with the officer in the video, nobody of the few who survived capture and torture by the Quaneez were normal. They were all… not quite *there*, mentally, so we don't have much intel. Like I said, we know they're humanoid, but stronger than us. They're very difficult to kill, and only a sustained beam to a single spot on their body will deliver enough energy to penetrate their armor and get the job done. Once they die, they disintegrate, which we think might be a function of the armor they're wearing, because they also disintegrate when we capture them. So far, we've neither seen a Quaneez without armor, nor had the chance to examine one, dead or alive. Because of that disintegration, I mean." One can practically hear the boulder rolling off his shoulders when he is done with his answer.

The professor gives him a short acknowledging nod, circling the armor in the image of the Quaneez soldier he displayed. "Thank you, Cadet. Now that we have visitors, let's crank it up. Anybody can recite facts from a book, but I want you all to start making connections. To think. To examine, to analyze, and to come up with your own opinion." He pauses for effect—or to taste the fear flowing through the audience with his last words. No matter the question, nobody wants to give an analysis or opinion in their second week of academy training. In front of everybody. *And* the admiral. *And* five other faculty members, two of them mentioned in every history book addressing spacefaring humanity.

As it is, Haggardy seems to have fun down there. He rubs his palms together with an impish smirk. "I would like you think about the next step in the Quaneez wars. Which tactic has not been used? How can we gain the upper hand? How can we win?" His gaze roams over the rows and rows of students until his face lights up. "Ah, let's ask our youngest. Thorburn. Go for it."

Me?

Oh. Crap.

All eyes are on me.

All. Eyes.

Including the admirals' and the captains'.

No pressure, none at all.

I give myself one half second to panic, then heed my own advice: fake it until you make it. I jump out of my seat, my left leg buckling the slightest bit when I snap to attention. "Of course, Professor. As a first-year cadet in my first week of training, I can't say I have figured out the secret to winning the Quaneez War, but I surely can make a suggestion."

"Go ahead, Cadet." Haggardy waves a hand through the air.

Okay. Okay. I can do this. It's an opinion, so it can't be wrong-wrong, right? Right? I clear my throat. Here goes nothing. "During the last decades of the Quaneez War, we have tried almost every tactic.

Withdrawal. Head-on attacks. Bombardments. Nothing has made a big impact on the frequency or severity of the Quaneez attacks. But there is one thing we haven't tried. Not hard enough, at least."

That little pause, where I catch my breath, that's where Admiral Grazer decides to step forward. "Is that so? And what would that be, Cadet?" Another hushed whisper flares up around me, adding to the pressure on my shoulders. An admiral addressing a cadet. Pigs are flying today.

I cock my head and look him straight in the eye. "Communication, sir."

His white, bushy brows shoot up. "Communication."

"Indeed, sir. We've been in this war for almost half a century, and while we know a lot about their tactics, we know next to nothing about them. Maybe we need psychology—or rather, understanding—to end this war. What does their culture value? What are they fighting for? How do they see life and death, or life after death? How—?"

Grazer's brows furrow. "Are you suggesting we sit them down with a therapist and *talk*?" The way he emphasizes the last word it's clear he's not happy with my suggestion, and I could swear the ground under my feet turns into quicksand.

"No, sir. I'm suggesting that, since our traditional military options didn't bear fruit, we focus on finding common ground. Establish peaceful cooperation via communication. Coexistence instead of warfare. Have—"

"Yeah, yeah, I get it. We talk. But what else can we do, Cadet? Wrack your brain and come up with something we can actually use. Forty years and we don't know their language, so I doubt we're going to crack it any time soon. What *else* can we do, Cadet?"

My stomach roils. "Well, sir, to be fair, we have not attempted to contact them besides the groundwork the *Pioneer* laid all those years ago. If we invested a small percentage of the war budget into establishing said communication, it could end the wa—"

"Cadet." This time the admiral's tone is harsh. *Sharp.* "I don't need a lecture by a first-year student, and neither do I need cloud cuckoo ideas that won't lead anywhere. The Quaneez have never answered a single hail of ours, and I doubt they're going to start now. I asked you a direct question to come up with more ideas, and all you do is give me *this*?" He spits out the last word. It's dead silence in the audience. Like, graveyard silence. Everybody's glad they're not in my shoes, and I feel them. I don't want to be in my shoes either.

"Sir, I—"

Grazer cuts me off with a slice of his hand. "You had your chance, Cadet. Disappointing. You're Admiral Thorburn's kid, aren't you?"

Aww, man. Part of me deflates. "Yes, sir."

He regards me with a long glance that cuts like ice. "I would have expected better of you. Our methods—"

"Are maybe not quite as successful as we'd like them to be. Ain't that right, Admiral?" Admiral Conolly steps forward, hands crossed behind his back, blue eyes boring into Grazer's.

A muscle in Grazer's jaw twitches. "Admiral, I don't think this is your area of expert—"

"I beg to differ. Don't forget we were there, Admiral Upinga and myself. We have more continuous hours logged fighting the Quaneez than anybody else, even after all these years, and even compared to you. And I can speak for the admiral and myself when I'm saying that I have to agree with the cadet. Communication is underutilized."

The lead in my stomach dissolves and turns into something feathery light taking flight. Maybe it's the sensation of being heard, of being understood. Getting backup from Admiral Chase Conolly… It doesn't get much better than that.

Grazer's jaw works overtime. "Underutilized. So is Darwinism."

"And decency."

The two men stare at each other unblinking. Something passes between them, something that speaks of years of issues, and while Conolly stays calm, with an open expression, Grazer's pulse is beating so hard in his neck, I can see it from up here. He pinches his lips together. "And this conversation is over. Carry on, professor." He turns on his heels and storms past Conolly and the waiting captains, which do their best to follow right in his footsteps.

But not Conolly.

Not Upinga.

Both stay back and look up at me, still standing, face probably beet red, but hey, still standing. Barely, but I'll take it. They look at me for a good ten seconds before Conolly nods. "Good thinking, Cadet. Keep it up." Then, they turn and leave, and I collapse into my seat.

What. The. Heck. Was. That.

Chapter Thirteen

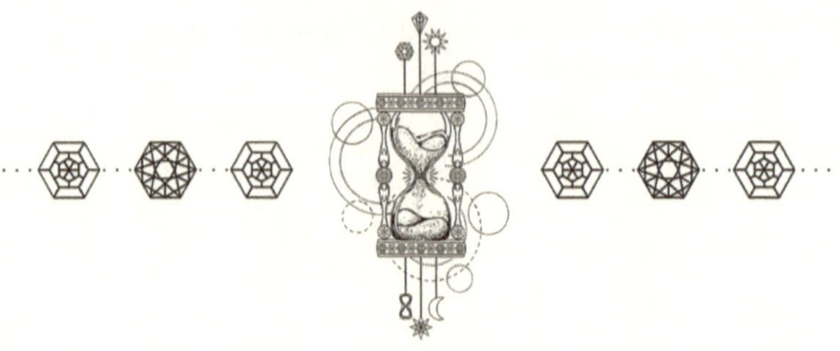

An ensign at least ten years older than me leads me to my quarters on deck nine. "Place your palm against the reader, please." He points at a spot on the right to the sliding doors.

It takes more than simple self-restraint to suppress a groan. Great. Palm print reader. Better than a retina-scan, but too bad that even in 2255 they didn't use keys anymore. I clench my teeth. "Of course." Yeah, let's get my palm print saved for eternity, splendid idea. I'm sure somewhere in 2291 this new timeline's future-Nonie registers at the Academy and is apprehended and questioned why her palm prints pop up on the *Pioneer* almost forty years ago

What a mess.

Instant sweat breaks out, but the reader still does its job. "*Profile saved. Welcome, Nonie Magnetta.*" Ugh.

The ensign points down the corridor. "This way to the lifts to the mess and gym, the direction we came from is the sickbay, and the forward-lift brings you to the bridge. You can use the comm system to ask for help, and the computer inside your quarters has been set for your use, minus restricted military information, of course."

"Of course." Wouldn't want me to find out whatever I surely got taught already during history classes or have stored on my little helper around my wrist, but I get it.

The ensign nods good-bye and leaves me alone.

Finally.

I enter my quarters and stop dead in my steps about a meter or so in.

Whoa.

A sensation of familiarity washes over me, like returning home after a long day. It hits me like a punch to the gut, adding insult to injury. Home. Right. No matter how often I've seen pictures of the *Pioneer* in every history book I ever read, no matter this is a USEF vessel looking much like its modern relatives with a tad more retro, this is not home. It's the opposite. This is the vast unknown, which is ironic, because officially this has all already happened. Only now I'm here as the unpredictable variable to change things up.

"Unpredictable variable. That's me," I whisper to myself as I cross the room toward the large window straight ahead, passing the couch and table on the left next to the door leading to the bathroom, the desk and chair-combo on the right, and the bed retreated into an alcove on the left in front of the window. A standard room, nothing special, outdated by over forty years, and yet it comforts my bleeding soul like a Band-Aid.

I'll take it.

No: I need it.

Can't really say things were going well over the last twelve hours.

I cross my arms behind my back and look out the window. Hello, space. Nice to see you, you're looking good today. So young.

I groan. Gallows humor, bad version.

My next breath comes in choppy, and that choked sound, the proof of how much I screwed up, brings tears to my eyes.

I don't know where to start. My whole life's shattered, but not only mine. That would be annoying, scary, and craptastic, but it's even worse: One stupid, *stupid* mistake has killed millions of Quaneez and keeps millions—billions—of people suffering, namely all those people waiting for me to return with the antidote. Waiting in vain, I should specify. Somewhere in that future they're first checking their watches, then checking their sensors, and finally see the planet blow up, and with it, humanity's hopes for a cure.

Do they even know I eliminated a large enemy population on that planet? Does it matter? To anyone, besides to me? And does it matter, now that we have a virus out to kill us, too?

I mean, they must know. We have sensors sensitive enough to find freakin' plants, they better know—

Holy—

I suck in a wheezy breath that brings absolutely no oxygen to my brain.

Dizzy.

Reaching one hand forward, I lean against the window. Holy Sun and Stars, they know—no, *he* knows. I swallow hard.

All of a sudden, everything makes way more sense than before:

Grazer sending me on this mission. Grazer, who really doesn't like me. Who was annoyed that Mashaule got me into his Division.

The dizziness worsens. I don't like where this is going.

You know what, Lieutenant? You're getting maybe a tad too conspiratorial. Sure, Admiral Grazer disliked me so much, he came up with this ridiculous mission, hoping I'd get killed by the Quaneez. I can't be the first student he isn't a fan of, and I doubt he has a habit of ridding himself of them.

Ri-di-cu-lous.

But still, the bad taste stays. Too many little things were off in this mission, and they all… they all have to do with Grazer.

One, Grazer didn't tell me the planet was inhabited. It very much was. Which is something he should have known. He knows about freakin' plants on that thing, then he knows it's inhabited and circled by freakin' Quaneez battleships.

Two, Grazer told me to be on the watch for their long-range satellite system—the system I didn't detect a trace of—presumably to keep me from scanning ahead and discovering said Quaneez population. Why else tell me to jump in blind? No scans, meaning, I couldn't have detected I was jumping straight into an enemy fleet.

Three, just to re-emphasize, Grazer really doesn't like me. He didn't want me in his division at all, had it not been for Mashaule.

Why, oh, why does it make sense?

This doesn't look good. I really don't like where this is going. It can't be. I must be adding one and one and arriving at three, not two. I must be wrong, I must. Admiral Grazer wouldn't set me up to fail. To *not* bring those plants—

Why would he do that?

I lean forward and support myself with my hands on my thighs. Breathe, Nonie. Breathe. Grazer didn't set me up to get killed. Absurd. Just because he isn't my biggest fan, doesn't mean he would want to kill me—

Heck.

Maybe it wasn't a plan hatched with the sole purpose of getting rid of little Nonie Thorburn, but what if he didn't *mind* getting me killed in the process? If he used me as an expendable chess piece, as an end to his means? But then, what means? Destroy the Quaneez planet and potentially restart the war? Nobody would benefit from that. Plus, he explicitly warned me to *not* start a war, so—

Yeah. Right now, it's not my biggest problem. Some weird twist of fate kept me from being blown up, which I appreciate, but it also got me stuck forty years in the past, which I don't.

I straighten up and tug on my shirt, as if it was a uniform top. Pull yourself together. Neither self-pity nor wallowing in misery has ever helped anybody. I'm a lieutenant of the USEF, I can deal with this.

And even if I couldn't, I must.

I crank my neck and shake out my hands. Okay. Mental note, if I ever make it back: have a nice heart-to-heart with Grazer. But since that's a good four decades in the future, I have to focus on more pressing issues, namely, plans for survival. I need those, because I know Conolly, no matter the rank. He's not done with me. The only reason he held off questioning is because of the captain, and once my puppy protection has worn off and he gets me alone, I better have my answers neat and ready to his satisfaction.

All right. Okay. Planning. I press both palms into my eyes and blow out a puff of air. Focus.

One, I need to keep a low profile. Altering the past is a big no-no. I'll have to see if I can delete my palm print from the record, or alter it, or something. Whatever waves my appearance here caused, I need to smooth them over to minimize my impact and keep my own timeline intact. Two, if anyhow possible, I need to return to my time. I can't stay here, a foreign body in the past and a constant danger to my very own future. So duh, yeah, I need to find out how to return to my time, if that's possible at all. Maybe, given the fact that I somehow ended in the past, there is a way back somehow.

Which leads me to the third part of my plan, gathering knowledge. I need to look into what brought me here, so I can hopefully use the same mechanism to bring me back to my time. Here's to hope it doesn't involve blowing up a planet, because that would for one suck, and for another be impossible. I don't know how I blew up the first one to begin with.

Also, I need to brush up on the details of what happened in May 2255. Knowledge is power, and that power is key to avoid any pitfalls and worsen my and my future's situation. Thanks to my little wrist PAD, the latter part of my plan shouldn't be a problem. It holds a myriad of files on our history, plus USEF archives of past missions. I should find what I need in there. Yes, it's broken, but come on, not all data can be lost.

Fourth, I need to check on my shuttle. If anything is salvageable, I need it. If anything even hints at future technology, it needs to be hidden from anybody in this timeline or destroyed.

Wonderful.

Yay me.

I let myself fall into the couch with a view of the window and lift my left wrist. "PADdy, activate." The home screen pops up in front of my face, displayed at the perfect reading distance for my vision. It wobbles and warps for a second, but then stabilizes, ready for input. So not completely *kaputt*. Good. Imagine Conolly had activated it accidentally in sick bay. No better way than advanced technology screaming in his face to announce I'm from the future.

Anyway. "Show me the *Pioneer*'s records, 2255, May seventh and ongoing." I keep my voice down to a whisper. The *Pioneer* doesn't have any surveillance in their guest quarters—as far as I know, at least—but it doesn't feel right to talk any louder.

A split second later, a menu with about a hundred items scrolls over my screen. Oy. Okay. That will take some time to sort—

The boatswain whistle sounds through the speaker system.

"Attention *Pioneer* Crew. This is Captain Wildason. Prepare for jump. Repeat, all hands, all stations, prepare for jump." His voice is deep and steady, no trace of the pain or injuries his encounter with the Quaneez caused.

Captain Wildason is tough.

Captain Wildason—*Kieran.* Still can't believe I've met Kieran Wildason. I've talked to him. And more: I've felt him all over when I checked for injuries. A small grin spreads over my face. Had I known it was him, I'd probably enjoyed that encounter more down there. All muscle, all trained and well-defined, from what I could tell. And in sickbay, he was as nice as Admirals Conolly and Upinga always said. No, not nice—normal, in a good way. Cool-normal. Attractive-normal. The way he looked at me—

Stop right there, Nonie.

Stop right there.

I scoot higher into the couch. Focus, and priorities.

Kieran Wildason shouldn't be either.

Keeping the timeline intact on the other hand, should.

With a deep sigh I open the first file.

Here's to luck.

Chapter Fourteen

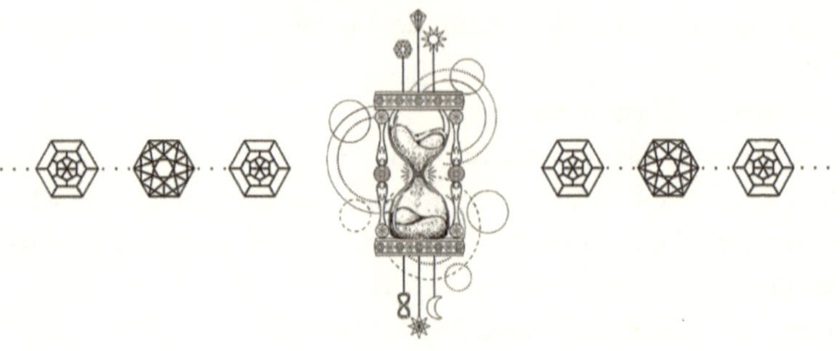

"**...m**ake sure Earth belongs to humans! It's in our nature to expand, it's not in our nature to be conquered or to bow to anybody! Humanity First!" Bits and pieces of the rally held at the center stage sound across campus, making me feel more on edge than I already am. No wonder with all the venom they're allowed to spew. It'd poison anybody. Not even the good number of Vote-for-Thorburn-signs held up by people protesting the xenophobic messages can undo the feeling of hopelessness that comes with any of these speeches. Pity those self-sealing masks don't come with a mute button.

I scurry on faster. Can't stand that stuff.

At the next security checkpoint, the officer holds up a hand, the epitome of seriousness and professionalism. "Credentials, please."

I roll my eyes. "This is the third time within five minutes I'm being stopped on my own campus. While wearing a cadet's uniform and doing nothing out of the ordinary, unless you consider walking to be against regulations." The first time they stopped me I got it, the second time I was annoyed, and the third is a tad too much.

The lieutenant shrugs in a way that's supposed to make me feel better, but doesn't. "Orders are orders, Cadet. You're Admiral Thorburn's daughter, aren't you?"

And here we go again. "Yes, I am. And why would that make a

difference?"

"It doesn't, Cadet. Of course not. May I see what is in your pockets?"

My jaw all but hits the floor. "In my pockets?"

The security officer rolls his eyes, then gives me the fakest smile behind his face mask. And yes, I can tell. "Did I not speak clearly enough? In. Your. Pockets."

Some other cadet next to me passes the checkpoint with a short nod of the second security officer. Huh. Okay, once more to clarify. "You want me to empty out my pockets. Like everybody else." I give a pointed glance to yet another cadet passing the station next to us without as much as an ID-check, let alone without showing the contents of his pockets.

The officer is unfazed. "Exactly. Just FYI, with Chairman Roodt giving a speech, you won't have an easy time anywhere on campus tonight. Security is on high alert." I'm not quite sure whether he emphasized the *you* or not, and in the end, it doesn't matter if he meant me personally or all of us cadets. Thank you, Travis Roodt and your annoying politics.

I turn my pockets inside out. "Sufficient?" Because apparently, I'm a danger to the chairman, being the daughter of a man who openly defends the complete opposite political opinion and is running for USEF presidency.

"Yes. Carry on." He motions for me to continue.

"Thank you so much," I say, but my sarcasm is lost on him. He's darting over to the next victim—student, I mean. That guy doesn't look any happier than I did. That's a good sign, I'd say. I'd be more worried if students didn't mind the security checks—and some of us don't, because they're so behind what Roodt has to say, they'd go through way bigger inconveniences to hear their idol speak.

From my point of view, Admiral Mashaule shouldn't have allowed him to speak here, or better, anywhere, at all, but it's not my choice to make. If I was allowed to vote, I'd have a choice, but that's another precious few months until I turn eighteen, and it'll be after the next elections. Sorry, Dad. But I would totally vote for you otherwise.

Just can't wait until it's over, one way or another, because apparently profiling is a thing. The main annoyance of those security stops is the fact that I'm being singled out at every one of them.

Luckily for me, I don't get stopped again until I reach the administrative building and then Grazer's office. I crank my neck. Here we go.

I knock on the door and look straight into the facial recognition screen. My heart hammers like crazy, which is weird, because absolutely nothing hangs on this meeting. I got the mission assigned already, I know it's going to be dangerous and difficult, and this briefing isn't going to change a thing about that. Still, my body disagrees and insists on adding a bout of nausea and end-of-the-world sensation to the mix.

Guess that's what hearing all that Travis Roodt-crap does to me.

The doors slide apart, granting me entrance to the admiral's front office. Lieutenant Campos, his secretary, greets me with a little wave. "Hello, Nonie. Back so early? I'm not sure I can squeeze you in, he's pretty busy."

Well, yeah, busy with me. "I have an appointment for today." Five minutes early, but better too early than too late.

The secretary frowns. "No, you're not on the schedule."

Huh? "Uhh, I think I should be?" I must be on the schedule, unless I understood Grazer wrong, but I don't think so.

She looks up at me. "Is it still about career choices for after graduation?"

In a matter of speaking… "Yeah." Kind of.

The lieutenant types into her interface. "Let me see if he has a few minutes."

Few minutes? I don't need a few minutes, I need a few freakin' *hours* for this! A *few minutes* for a life-or-death mission's briefing…? Gosh, that nausea is getting worse. Maybe I should listen to Dad and stay on Earth after graduation. If this is anything like the jitters I'll have before any mission…

A pinging sound announces an incoming message on Lieutenant Campos' interface. "Ah, lucky you. Go in there, Nonie. He's got ten minutes for you." She points at the door, already focused again on whatever she was doing before I interrupted her.

Wow. Ten whole minutes. How are we even supposed to be

touching the very basics? Mission briefings for our student tests take longer than that, and they're way less complicated, to say the least!

Nonetheless, I force a smile. Maybe that's the difference between a cadet and a lieutenant. "Thank you, Lieutenant Campos."

The doors to the admiral's office slide apart for me, revealing Grazer's more than spacious office with a view of the main campus out of the large, floor-to-ceiling windows on the left. Like the very first time when I came in here, the view still mesmerizes me. The admiral sits behind his desk, reading glasses on his nose, a PAD in his hand.

"Nonie. Come on in, Cadet." Admiral Grazer motions for me to step into his office. The moment the sliding doors hiss shut behind me, he drops the facade and gives me a smile. "Lieutenant. Appreciate the punctuality."

Punctuality when I wasn't even on the schedule? But never mind, probably part of secrecy. "Of course, sir." Could've been here earlier, if I hadn't been held up by those annoying security stops. On the other hand, they made me be on time-ish. Otherwise, I would've looked way overeager. Or over-panicky, because let's be honest, since the admiral informed me of my upcoming mission last night, I've been… slightly pre-occupied with not freaking out too much.

It's a great honor, but an even greater responsibility.

But I can do it. If a man like Grazer believes in me, I can do it.

I *will* do it.

The admiral taps on something on his PAD and, with a quick pull-and-flick motion of his wrist, throws a graphic into the air between us.

"Earth." He points at the blue planet I'd always recognize, no matter how many others with water on them we discover. "And the Quaneez' space." No need to circle that, but he does. The displayed image glows bright between us, the red of enemy space piercing my eyes and not improving my lingering headache at all. "As you can see, the distance is quite far, which is why it took long-range sensors a while to pick up on those plants. We have a satellite here and here," *point-point,* "close to their border. Usually, we scan for ship-movements, but with the current situation, Admiral Mashaule had to dedicate them to look for anything that could help us. We're desperate."

I cross my hands behind my back. "I understand, sir." Very well, actually.

Grazer rubs his eyes and sighs. Dark, saggy circles under his eyes are proof of how critical the situation is. Even the lines in his face seem deeper today, like he was running on empty. Or, maybe it's the face mask emphasizing that feature. Either way, he looks like he needed a vacation. "I know, Lieutenant. You're the sharpest available knife in our drawer right now." A tired smile accompanies his words, but nonetheless satisfaction blows up my ego until I stand ramrod straight. Sharpest knife in the drawer. I waited four years for him to finally realize he should've picked me as a mentee. Not that I regret my mentors—never—but I kind of want him to regret his mentee.

Because I would've been a perfect fit for him, and he didn't pick up on it.

Anyway.

Here we are, and with Grazer finally seeing the light and switching to Team Nonie, I better keep it up, or else my fame will be very short lived. Literally.

Grazer carries on. "And those skills of yours are the reason I need you to do this, Lieutenant. I would like to save us all from both, the virus and an all-out war with the Quaneez. I don't trust that cease fire. I really don't. I don't understand it, and therefore I can't trust it. How could I if it's a cease fire we don't understand?" He groans. "Sometimes I don't get Conolly and the St—"

String Bean, I know. Before he can complete the sentence and slur, I interrupt him. "Communication has been challenging with the Quaneez, sir."

"You don't say, Lieutenant."

My cheeks turn rosy. "What I was about to say is that at least Admirals Conolly and Upinga found a way to stop them from attacking us." However coincidentally that might've been—it never happened before, no matter what we tried. To the Quaneez, it doesn't matter what we do, they fire. We've lost so many colonies to them. Unprovoked. Not even all human, but also alien settlements. Like they enjoyed destroying what we terraformed bit by bit.

Grazer harrumphs. "As I said, I don't trust them or the cease fire, especially because passivity is not a way of warfare I can subscribe to.

Alas, there are louder voices in the USEF right now supporting this, your father being one of them, so my hands are tied." His lips press into a thin line, and my cheeks are on fire.

"I apologize, Admi—"

"Never mind, Lieutenant. Back to matters at hand. Your mission. You will need to be quick, because Mashaule's intel has it they set up a new network of receptors through their space. They will notice you jumping into their territory." He takes a paper and turns it for me to see: a classic display of the Quaneez space, embellished with red diamond symbols—excuse me, hypersensitive receptors. Grazer gives me a questioning look. "You know what that means."

I do, and it changes things, as in turning it from barely doable to basically impossible. It takes quite a lot of willpower to keep standing straight, but I manage it. Barely. Wobbly knees do not a lieutenant make. "Yes, sir. I assume I have less than ten minutes until Quaneez' ships arrive, since this planet is off their inhabited zone, but within patrol parameters." Fifteen minutes, if I'm lucky. Like, really lucky. How the heck am I going to pull that off in less than—

"Correct. It also means you cannot scan H-155 before you jump there. It will alert the Quaneez."

I flinch. This gets better and better. Meaning, not. "Ouch. *That* sensitive? Frustrating. Those receptors are going to be a tactical game changer." And not only for my mission, but for every future jump close to them. Protocol demands we scan the area we intend to jump to, but if that's like waving a flag and screaming *hello, here we are, incoming!* then obviously it's not a good idea.

Grazer drops his gaze to the desk. "Agreed. But let's not worry about later. For your mission it shouldn't be a problem. You have the coordinates, and you'll jump blind. I don't like to give you that order, but Admiral Mashaule's data is quite convincing."

Jump blind… A million warning signs light up inside my brain. All my instincts, all my teaching is against it, but… this is me, playing with the big kids now. I swallow. "Understood, Admiral."

He nods. "Good. Now that that's clear, the next point to remember is that while speed when collecting the plants is of the essence, the most important is the speed of your scan."

Huh? "My scan?" Why would that be a factor?

The admiral sighs. "I trust you kept your skills up and still can perform a Level-6-scan?"

Puh-lease. "Of course, sir."

"In less than ten seconds?"

My brows furrow. "In under ten seconds?"

Grazer rolls his eyes. "That was my question, Lieutenant. You will need a Level-6-Scan to find the plants, and it will need to be under ten seconds to avoid detection by their new satellite grid." He hammers a finger onto the paper he showed me a minute ago. "So?"

Crap. That's quite the receptor network, so okay, valid point, but not important, in the grand scheme of things. I shake my head. "Sir, I don't think you need to worry about the scan alerting the Quaneez. If they have a network of receptors, they'll see my arrival, and if nothing else, they'll read my engine's signatures. Me scanning the planet for the plants is a negligible spike on their radar, no matter how long it takes."

"Don't you think I know that, Lieutenant? But if Admiral Mashaule wanted somebody on this mission who increases the risk of failure by being slow, he would have chosen somebody else. Meaning, we have the *absolute pleasure* of working together because of your skills. So, can you do it?"

Doesn't he get it? That scan is the least of my worries. What about fragility of the plants, storage methods, data I could send before I even take off, in case something, uhh, *happens*. I step forward. "I will do my very best to localize the plants in as short a time as possible and reduce my time on the planet to the bare minimum, sir, but in order to do that, I need more information on the mission. Like, where are the next Quaneez outposts. The location of the highest concentration of plants. Quantity to harvest. How to store—"

Grazer waves a hand, annoyance flashing in his eyes. "And we will get to that, Lieutenant. Can you pull off the scan, yes or no?" His jaw tightens as he glares at me, and I snap to attention.

"Yes, sir. Record at 8.5 seconds. Sir." Fastest A&T—assessment and target—during battle drill. Bought me a ten-point advantage over the runner-up.

The admiral releases a harsh breath. "Good. That is the most vital part of your mission, a fast Level-6-scan as soon as you arrive, Admiral Mashaule was very clear on that. Without it, the rest is doomed. Do you understand, *Lieutenant?*"

All right, all right, I got it. "Yes, sir. Understood, sir." I keep my eyes straight ahead. If Grazer wants a fast Level-6-scan for whatever reason, he gets a fast Level-6-Scan, no questions asked.

He gives me a crooked smile. "Wonderful. That scan will help you tremendously. Without it, you won't find the plants to demat up. I assume you understood my instructions."

"Of course, sir." Still don't get it, but whatever. He's the boss.

"Wonderful." Grazer stands up and hands me a data disc. "Fine print is on here. The disc will delete its contents in two hours from now, so I suggest you go study. Dismissed."

Dismissed? Already? That was it, for a mission this magnitude? A *data disk?* "Yes, sir, but—"

The admiral drags the glasses down his nose and gives me an annoyed look over their frame. "Yes, Cadet? What else is there?"

I cringe at the use of my official title. "Sir, if you don't mind, I have a few more questions for clarification." Understatement. I have a million. Shouldn't we talk it through, so that I'm not only clear about the parameters, but crystal clear?

"You do?"

Loads. Do I demat down to collect the plants? Do I demat them up right after my scan, without collecting them? Let's start more broadly. "Yes, sir. For example, if I may ask, what class planet is it?" I hope it has an oxygen-bearing atmosphere, but there are some that grow life without O2. That would obviously slow me down if I needed to demat to the surface, and I would need more equipment and tools, which Grazer needs to assign to me. I can't just waltz into Materials and demand a space suit etc.

Grazer raises an eyebrow. "Do you have a problem with reading a data disk, *Cadet?*"

I look straight ahead. "No, sir. But I figured with this mission—"

He holds up a hand, and my mouth snaps shut. "Maybe that's why we usually don't send younglings on life-saving missions, but Admiral Mashaule seemed to think you'd do fine with *this.*" He points at the data disk, takes off his glasses and rubs a hand over his eyes. "To make you feel better, it's a regular, uninhabited, good old Class-H planet. There you go, not that I expect you to set foot on it." The admiral pauses, then shakes his head with a small frown playing around his lips. "If you stick to your mission parameters, I'm not expecting any surprises. *Dismissed.*" He waves a hand at me. Guess this meeting is over.

"Thank you, sir." I salute, turn sharper than a ten-year-veteran, and march out of his office and his building. The moment the doors close behind me, I blow out a big puff of air.

He's not expecting any surprises. Good for him, because all I can think of is what could go wrong. I really hope this disc contains all the answers to my questions, because if not... I could be responsible for millions of deaths from the flu, or millions of deaths if I cause the war to flare up.

Neither nor is an attractive prospect.

Chapter Fifteen

Today is my second full day on board the *Pioneer*. It's the second day I don't leave my quarters, the second day I try to figure out how I got here and how to get back, and the second day I do my very best to get over the nightmare that tortured me during sleep, and inconspicuously access their systems to erase myself from their ship's memory.

And, surprise, it's not going well. Besides the part where I don't leave my quarters, I haven't made any progress at all, unless it counts to keep my footprint in this time to a minimum. Then, yay me.

So, so frustrating.

Thanks to a wee bit of talent for programming and coding I'm usually good at this stuff, especially on a single-layer unscrambled security database like on the pre-Quaneez-hyperprecaution *Pioneer*, but…

But.

Can't erase myself without triggering alarms. Not from down here. From the bridge or main engineering, maybe. But from my little quarters I don't stand a chance, which means I'll have to work on a different strategy. Feels great to waste two days on that revelation.

And speaking of waste: It's also great to have about one million scientific articles on my oh-so-wonderful and more-broken-than-not dear PADdy, but not so cool that none of them speak about time travel.

I know, big surprise once again, but still disappointing. The only thing I found worth looking into is the mentioning of an article about a gravity-assisted slingshot maneuver that holds the potential to destabilize space-time fabric and cause quote-unquote *irregularities in the time-space-continuum.*

First problem is, I haven't even seen the article itself, because it's a Magellan work and not featured in my database or the *Pioneer*'s, and yes, I checked. Second problem is, *irregularities* don't mean time travel. Third, if they did, it wouldn't mean to time-travel in the right direction, let alone to the correct date.

Meaning, this doesn't really help me at all.

My chest heaves with a silent sigh as my gaze drifts out of the window. I've noticed the *Pioneer* set course away from the planet where I, uhh, *rescued* Kieran. According to the log on my PAD, they're ordered to find the foreign-slash-Quaneez ship for species confirmation and to establish first contact. Ah, the good old days before Humanity First's paranoia seeped through the USEF. If it wasn't for the *Pioneer*'s work, we wouldn't be in contact with half as many intelligent species, and I define *contact* in a loose way, thanks to said paranoia. Alas, for the current scenario, I wish there had been more of it, because I'm fairly certain that at this point Captain Wildason and Co have picked up on the ionic signature of the Quaneez ship, which has dropped off after a few parsecs. As per my information, we're—they're—searching for that ship to find out more before we hail them to initiate an official first contact.

Problem is, none of them know that ship has sailed the moment they attacked us down on the planet. Pun intended. The Quaneez are very much aware we're looking for them. They're playing their game with us, and to say I want to run out of my quarters and warn the crew is an understatement.

If I could warn them, if I could modify their approach, I could stop them from running into their trap and maybe stop the Quaneez wars from happening. I could prevent the damage to both sides, could prevent misery and heartbreak, torture and kidnapping, destruction and death. I could.

But I can't.

Because doing so would inevitably change the timeline, and I'm not about to play god and change what has already happened. Who am I to say one way is better than another? As much as it hurts me to think this way, I cannot alter the past, even if I think it's for the better. What about the people who will never be born because of my changes? What if me keeping us from the Quaneez wars backfires? One disaster avoided, but another Pandora's box opened? I can't even begin to fathom what kind of problems me intervening would cause.

Still, it is so unbelievably frustrating.

I move my hand through the image PADdy beams into the air for me and close my fist, turning the display off. "I need something," I whisper and let myself fall backwards onto the couch. "Anything." A tiny morsel of information, anything to latch on for more research. I don't care how long it takes, but I need something to keep me hoping, to keep the despair at bay that's been looming over my head ever since I got here. Because no matter what I'm telling myself, I know I haven't digested or progressed what I did—what I did in my time.

Five million.

Five million gone. Because of me. How could I cause this? The image of the graph on the *Odysseus*, my scan triggering something inside that core and inflating it, was featured quite prominently in my latest nightmare, by the way. How is that even remotely possible—the core explosion, not the nightmare?

I ball my hands into fists. I will figure it out. And at one point I will own up—

A melodic beep chimes from the door.

Huh? Is that… my doorbell?

I swing my legs off my couch and sit up. Who'd come to visit me?

The bell rings again, and alas, only one way to find out, so I get up and walk toward the door. "*Pioneer*, open doors."

Nothing.

"Ope—ugh." I blush before I place my palm on the reader next to the door. Yeah. Voice control for visitors was not integrated into Starships at that—*this*—time.

The doors slide apart—and my eyes pop wide. "Captain." Captain Kieran Wildason is standing in front of my door. Those two days of recovery have done him well. Gone are the dark circles under his eyes, gone is the hunched posture. This is Captain Wildason how he is displayed in the history books.

"It's Kieran. Hey, Nonie." He raises a hand, then scratches his neck. "How ya doing?"

"Uhh, fine." *Pause.* "And… and you?"

A smile dances across his face. "Better. Turns out the doc has more than torture medicine in his cabinet. Some of the stuff actually works." The scratching turns into massaging his neck. "Can I… Can I come in?"

I all but jump aside. Sheesh, where are my manners? "Of course, come on in."

The Captain—Kieran—walks into my quarters, and I swear the light shines brighter, the air smells fresher, and the cabin shrinks to tiny proportions just from his presence. Maybe I should have Upinga check my head.

I point to the couch. "Have a seat. Anything to drink?" Because I've become fabulous in blending future soda mixers from what I have in my dispenser here. Happens when one tries to stay out of view, but needs something to soothe her wounded soul.

"That would be nice, thank you." He sits down in the very spot I sat a mere minute ago, leaned forward, arms resting on his knees.

I mentally high-five myself for keeping the quarters clean and my soda stash stocked. Thank you, academy, for prepping me for this one moment in my life: Captain Wildason in my quarters. A tiny voice pops up saying that the academy prepared me to save lives and bring those plants home, not to host a famous captain, but I ignore it. Not the time for it.

"So, what brings you in? I'm far off from the bridge." I unscrew the bottle that holds my special concoction and pour both of us a glass.

"Actually, I wanted to come by earlier, but I've been busy. Turns out finding that ship—and those aliens—is a tad more difficult than we anticipated."

Then don't. Don't find them. Don't get dragged into a war. Don't. I fake a smile. "You're going to find them eventually. I heard the *Pioneer* is home to the best."

That compliment earns me a true smile, dimples and all, making my tummy flop. "Why, thank you. Our reputation precedes us."

I place a hand over my heart in mock reverence. "And it will follow you for decades to come." So, so true. Maybe I should use this technique to avoid lying. Or, maybe not. Maybe I just shouldn't talk as much.

"Anyway." I take both glasses, hand him one, and nod my chin toward the window. "We changed course. You're searching in an uncharted star system." Uncharted for this time period at least.

His eyes light up. "So, you're not just a Starhopper. You know your constellations."

Of course I do. And I refuse to see that as a problem for the timeline. "That, and there's a nebula we're flying through currently. That kind of gave it away. But, yeah, Dad thought it'd be best if I knew what I was doing." It's neither a lie nor giving anything away.

"Your father prepped you well."

"That he did."

We both take a sip of our soda. Kieran's eyebrows shoot up. "This is good. I didn't know we carried that on board."

"You don't." I give him a conspirator grin. "I mixed it." Knew he'd like it. Admiral Conolly drinks the official version of it all the time, back in good ol' 2295.

He raises his glass. "Not bad. You're multi-talented, Nonie. Which makes me hope you might have more for me—information wise."

I'm sure I do, but my lips are sealed. "Such as?"

"From the encounter on the planet. I need whatever I can get about the aliens who attacked us. Anything. Commander Conolly said when you woke up you said something about *if you had a proper weapon*, but I saw you use my weapon, and you did shoot—and not badly at all," he adds with a small, crooked smile. "So I was just wondering what your experience down there was. I really can use every detail."

My mouth opens and closes. "I… don't really have much, you know. It all went all so fast."

"And yet you acted like a pro." It's meant as a compliment, but it stings like an insult. A pro. I wish. Clearly I've shown to not be a professional, or I wouldn't be in this predicament here.

"Well, I did what instinct told me to do."

Kieran cocks his head. "I think I saw you hold fire onto a single spot on the person's armor. That was instinct?"

Oy. Crap. Counterattack: "What would you have done if a single blast didn't do it?" I throw up my arms. "I really didn't want to die down there." Would've deserved it, but still didn't want to.

"Neither did I, but clearly I wasn't on top of my game. Couldn't even reach the *Pioneer*." He pauses. "How did you know there was orbital interference?"

I put on a look of confusion so fast, I should get some kind of acting award for that. "I didn't know there was orbital interference."

Kieran gives me a look like, *really?* "You asked me if I had *countered the orbital interference.* If I remember correctly, you were quite annoyed at me for not coming up with that myself."

"Nu-uh." Insert strong head-shake here. "I'm pretty sure I said *potential* orbital interference—"

"You—"

I lift both palms up. "Hey, just problem solving. You can't reach your ship, what could be the reason? Like I said, I really didn't want to die down there. I'd call it great teamwork and yay, we made it out. Right?" I swipe a strand of hair out my face that didn't need swiping.

Kieran's lips quirk at the corners. "Right. Hats off for quick thinking then. Makes me wonder—was your father USEF?"

I almost spew out my sip of soda. "What?" I mean, great we're off the other topic, but this one burns just as hot. My dad—

An eye-opening epiphany strikes: Dad is *here.* In this time. *Of course* Dad is here. Young, about the same age as the famous Captain Wildason sitting in front of me, only Dad should be an ensign or lieutenant maybe, I'll have to do the math, but he's here. Weird just got weirder.

Kieran flinches. "I'm… I'm sorry, I know it must be hard for you to talk about your dad. I just thought with the level of professionalism you showed down there—" His cheeks take on a slight pink hue as one hand creeps up to his neck again, rubbing it. "I… I just figured you'd have some kind of training. Maybe by him."

Some kind my butt, a whole academy-education! But not that I could tell him that. I fix a quick smile onto my face. "Sorry, I didn't mean for it to come out like that. It's just… Dad used to say I was perfect for USEF, and it was always a dream of mine to join. And you're right.

He made sure to train me as well as he could. You know, better chances to ace the entrance exam." Good enough to explain my very much USEF-heavy behavior down on the planet. What kind of ordinary civilian handles herself like that?

The captain drops the hand from his neck and wraps it around the glass once more. "Ah, that explains it. And he did well, because you have potential, Nonie. Keeping your head straight in a situation like down there, thinking on your feet under stress, recognizing star systems as we fly by... I have lieutenants who can't do what you pulled off." He pauses, before a smile tugs on his lips. "If you ever need a recommendation for your application for the academy, I know a certain captain who owes his life to you, so..." He winks, and that wink brings something to a dance right behind my navel, then coils lower.

Before I know it, I've returned his wink. "I'll keep that in mind. Expect to find the papers in your inbox sometime soon." For the shortest moment I really—*really*—consider handing in generic USEF-application forms to him. Why? Because heck, getting a recommendation from Kieran Wildason is just... just... just *whoa*. No words.

His smile widens. "Cool. And you'll be one step ahead of your fellow cadets, no matter your age." He tilts his head. "How old are you anyway?"

"Almost eighteen." With a maturity level of a twelve-year-old, or else I wouldn't give my age like a preschooler.

Kieran chuckles. "So, time to get your applications ready. Eighteen and above, most recruits are around nineteen, besides me, maybe. I joined at seventeen. The academy made an exception because I did a good job with the exam and because my father was a high-ranking admiral."

I know, I want to say, followed by, *that's kind of what it was like for me.*

But of course I don't.

Instead, I hold up the soda bottle with a face splitting grin worthy of a product commercial. "Some more?" Awkward is my middle name.

Kieran holds up a finger and downs his glass, then holds it out for me. "Thank you."

"Sure." I pour the soda—

Click.

The lights turn off without a warning—

Click.

Back on.

What the—

"Ugh!" Kieran scrambles back from the soda assaulting his thighs.

Crap. "Sorry, I didn't see—"

He waves a dismissive hand, then taps the coin-sized hablamate on his left shoulder. "Wildason to bridge. Care to elaborate?"

Conolly's voice comes through the speaker integrated into the hablamate. "Temporary glitch, sir. Something happened to the power transfer from engineering. We're looking into it, but it's under control. Shouldn't happen again."

All color leaves my face. *Not* a temporary glitch. I'm very sure this was *them* hacking our systems. As of now, when the lights went out, the Quaneez have accessed parts of the *Pioneer's* computer system and downloaded as much as they could without detection, something we never managed in return.

I don't think they ever got to shield data or our weapon's technology, but they got something, giving generations of engineers enough reason to double- and triple secure our databases. I wonder where they're sitting in this darn nebula, hidden, stalking us stalking them.

Brr.

Reliving history is scary.

Kieran rolls his eyes. "Sure hope so. Thank you, Commander. Wildason out." He taps the hablamate again, and the little light indicating an open channel turns off. "That was—" His brows scrunch up. "Are you okay? You're kind of pale—"

I jump into action. "Yes. Sorry. Totally got you. I mean, the soda did—" I clutch the bottle to my chest with one hand while frantically wiping his thigh with the other, as if I could do anything against the liquid already seeped into the fabric "Really, didn't see. Sorry—"

He catches my wrist in the middle of another futile wiping motion. "Nonie." His voice is calm, deep, and shoots right into my soul.

I freeze. His fingers wrap around my wrist with ease, and while his hold is firm, it's not uncomfortable.

Quite the opposite.

Warmth steals through me and curls my toes.

"Y-yes?" I swallow hard.

"Don't worry about that soda." How he can be so calm, I don't know—well, I do. Obviously, I'm the only one with hormones going crazy. "You hear me?" Humor colors his voice, and yet he still keeps his fingers wrapped around my wrist. I look up, and as my eyes lock with his, I suck in a sharp breath. Crazy as it sounds, I don't just *see* him. I *feel* him, all the way in my core. Static passes from his skin to mine.

"Y-yeah." I work on another swallow. Sheesh. Pathetic, Thorburn.

"Okay." Slowly he releases his hold on my wrist, dragging one coincidental finger across the back of my hand as he withdraws his. No matter it's an accidental touch it burns where his skin touches mine. *Burns.*

For a moment neither of us says a thing, and while it still holds a touch of awkwardness I can thank myself for, it's surprisingly comfortable.

Kieran keeps his eyes on mine, and if it wasn't ridiculous, I could swear his cheeks take on a slight blush. "So, Nonie, why I originally came by, since I wanted to ask anyway… I was wondering… I mean, if you'd like, of course. Only then."

I cock my head. "Huh?"

Kieran's mouth opens, then closes. He lets his head fall forward in mock despair and groans. "Wow. Okay, I totally messed that up. Amazing." He shakes his head and laughs to himself, and when he looks back up, his eyes hold a little twinkle. Together with the red in his cheeks… it makes him a whole lot adorable. "I was trying to ask you if you'd like to have dinner with me. And Commanders Conolly and Upinga, I mean." The red deepens, but he keeps looking at me.

And I don't know how to react.

At all.

My gut screams yes, my brains counters with a hard no, and like Kieran's before, my mouth opens and closes like a fish out of water.

The captain flinches. "Oy. Tough decision, eh?" In that one

sentence he sounds so Scottish, it breaks the tension. I burst out laughing.

"No. No. Not at all. I just didn't expect it." I chuckle some more. Decision? Made. "But the answer is yes. Yes, I'd love to." My gut high-fives itself and my brain finds a corner to hide in and cry. Me? I'm okay with it, because it feels right to get out of this room and have dinner with the Hotshot Trio.

Wow.

It feels right. Well, yeah, usually I can trust my intuition pretty well, but I should consider said intuition being a few decades off right now. Meaning, whenever I have a quiet moment, I need to digest me having dinner with the Hotshot Trio further. All aspects of it.

Kieran flashes a wild sort of grin that seriously shoots down into my very core. "Awesome, Nonie. Then it's set. Eighteen-hundred hours, my quarters." He puts his soda down. "And if you don't mind, bring a bottle of this, please."

"Yes, sir." I give him a mock salute. "Consider it don—"

A shrill, deafening siren screams through the speakers. *"Red Alert. Captain to the bridge. Red Alert. Captain to the bridge. Red—"*

Kieran jumps up and slaps the hablamate on shoulder for the second time within three minutes. "Wildason to bridge. What's happening?"

Chase's voice comes through the integrated speaker. *"We found a ship, Captain. They could be connected to the attackers of T-12."*

Kieran tugs his uniform shirt straight. "On my way. Do not engage, do not hail until I'm on the bridge."

"Understood."

"Wildason out." He grabs me by the sleeve. "Come on."

"Come on—"

"Chase said you've seen their shuttle. If they're the same people, I'm expecting similar designs and features in their mother ship." He jogs toward the door, dragging me with him. "You're coming to the bridge with me."

Chapter Sixteen

'm darting through the *Pioneer*'s hallways following in Kieran's footsteps.

Quite surreal, yet here I am.

My quarters are not on the direct way to the bridge, but also not that far off, but during this short sprint at least twenty crew members have to jump out of our way—that would be twenty crew members who now have seen my ugly mug running after the captain. Great. Just great.

As on every USEF ship, the doors to the bridge open automatically when they sense the captain approaching.

"Captain on the bri—"

"Report!" Kieran comes to a stop next to Conolly in the command chair in the center, and me… I skid to a halt just behind the doors.

Holy cow.

The *Pioneer*'s bridge.

Hello, history. Nice to meet you.

Like in the picture hanging in Admirals Conolly and Upinga's office, the command chair is in the middle, facing the floor-to-ceiling and left-to-right window up front. Several working stations are strategically distributed throughout the bridge: Helm and Ops in the front, science and communication a tad behind the captain's chair to the left and right, engineering and backup systems lining the wall to both sides from where I came in. Everything's kept in white and off-white, the *Pioneer*'s color schemes, contrasting nicely with the black consoles. As always during alert situations, the lights are dimmed and nobody pays me any attention. I think the communications officer saw me, but he's focused again on his readouts, like everybody else.

My heart hammers to the rhythm of the sirens. Maybe I can stay out of this one and keep exposure to a minimum. But then, I'm also on the bridge… Hope flares up. If I could use PADdy to access one of their stations—

Commander Conolly all but jumps out of the command chair. "Long-range sensors picked up on a ship about fifteen minutes ago. We altered course to investigate—"

"Was that when the power outage happened?" Kieran has a seat in the chair and types something in the pad integrated into a holder on his right.

"Yes and no. The timing holds, but we didn't pick up on anything that could point to *them* being the reason for it." Funny how he says *them* like millions after him will in the next decades.

Kieran nods. "*Pioneer*—silence alarms." He makes a slicing hand motion and the ship responds, muting the annoying screeching sound. "Better," he sighs. "Do we have scans or a visual?"

"Visual, sir. Hayes?"

"On screen, Captain." The science officer—Hayes, apparently— brings the scan of the vessel up on the front windows. If I remember correctly, the *Pioneer* was one of the first ships to not have screens acting as pseudo-windows, but actual thick, thermoglass windows with integrated display capacities, a standard of my time.

"Thank you." Kieran leans forward. "Magnify."

Pop—the image of the vessel jumps to ten-fold magnification of a triangular, aggressive looking ship with unfamiliar markings. Everybody on the bridge sucks in a sharp breath—besides me.

Kieran und Conolly exchange a glance. This should be the point where they're sure their opponent is definitely not human, as expected. The markings on the hull, the shape of the vessel, the green glow of their silent propulsion drive… clearly not human-made. Definitely Quaneez.

Definitely Quaneez—but… why aren't they attacking? Shouldn't they be? And yes, *should* is too strong a word in this case, I know—but nothing's happening. Typical Quaneez behavior is to shoot first. Here they are, sitting in space, facing us, waiting. *Not* attacking.

Sweat breaks out and runs down my neck. Was that me? Did I alter something? Did I knock out the one Quaneez who was supposed to start this war when I fought back on T-12?

Interesting how hope and horror can live so close together in a person's heart.

Kieran turns half-way in his chair. "Nonie, what do you think? Recognize it?"

Everybody on the bridge turns and looks at me. There goes staying out of this one. Granted, most give me an interested-yet-disinterested look, and they're not the ones I'm worried about. The ones who look at me with interest—they're the ones giving me the jeebies, because they actually engage enough mental faculties to potentially remember me: Helm. Ops. Science. Communication.

Commander Conolly throws a quizzical glance at his captain, but Kieran ignores it. "Would you say it looks like the shuttle on the planet?"

No way around it now, and at this point they kind of know it without my confirmation. "Yes, sir." The *sir* comes without second thought, and the moment it's out a small smile pulls on the corners of Kieran's mouth.

"There you go, Commander. Nice job finding them, Thaler."

The helm officer nods. "Anytime, sir."

The captain turns half-way to his first officer. "I feel like I've seen a ship like this before. Reminds you of something, Chase?" He nods his chin at the view screen.

Conolly focuses on his read-outs. "I was thinking the same, but can't confirm. We don't have enough data from Alpha Rubrum. Zio?"

The tall Magellan shakes his head. "Magellan data is insufficient, or at least what I have access to. It's possible, but that's all I can say."

"Gotcha." Kieran nods.

Ops chimes in. "Sir, the readings don't match anything we have in our database. Some of the features I can find are similar to what the colony on Zephyr Two came up with, but unless they've totally revamped their design..." And came up with a new form of drive...

Kieran exchanges a meaningful glance with his two senior officers, then claps his hands. "Thank you, Lieutenant. And listen up, people. I think at this point, it's fair to say this is a first-contact type situation. I'm not counting the one on T-12, I feel we got started on the wrong foot on that one. Suggestions?"

Thaler speaks up. "But with that in mind, sir, shouldn't we leave them in peace? I'd say that encounter was a good taste of what might happen if we engage again."

Hats off to Thaler. I hope she remembers years from now she called it as it was.

Somebody else speaks up, to the right of Thaler: Ops. "But Command wants us to establish contact with them, so it doesn't really matter—"

Kieran holds up a finger. "But it does matter how we do it. Barge in, like we did on T-12 and annoy them, or knock on their door and wait for somebody to answer. Wouldn't you say so, Manazari?" Kieran looks at the guy at Ops.

"Yes, sir. Question becomes, what is a light knock at the door for them?"

"Suggestions, team?" Conolly looks around the bridge, eyes skipping over me as I'm trying my best to look neutral, while my insides are screaming to back out of this. Reverse course, forget we ever ran into them, and save billions of lives on both sides… and including the millions that were my fault.

I bite down on my tongue so hard it bleeds.

Can't change it. Am not allowed to change it. All I can do is use this situation to my advantage and access their systems from here to erase myself. Feels a tad opportunistic to abuse Kieran's trust like this, but it's a necessity. I throw a glance to the console on my right. Not yet. Too much going on.

"Low-range hails, sir?" That's communications coming up with the idea. "I would recommend against scanning them, as they have not scanned us yet—" Wrong. *Not scanned us*, as far as they know, at least. "—and might perceive a scan as a hostile act or invasion of their privacy. I also wouldn't want to blast full-power hails over, just because they have been known to blow a fuse on our older ships, and I don't want to risk doing that to them. Again, a gentle knock, not kicking down the door, to stick with your metaphor, sir."

Kieran nods. "Agreed, Chocho."

At this point my breathing is a wheeze. I'm not sure whether I should hope for Chocho to be right and what I know about history to be wrong, or for the Quaneez to do what my history tells me they did: attack. At least the latter would mean the timeline was intact. Great consolidation when it also means the beginning of a war that will kill billions.

Kieran motions at Chocho. "Make it so. Low-range hail, simple message, *we come in peace*, in all known languages, including using the ones from the Magellan databases and binary."

"Yes, sir." On my right Chocho gets to work. "Sent." He confirms it with a nod.

Nerves bubble inside of me. I can't help the internal countdown starting in my brain. How much longer until the Quaneez decide they really don't like us? Ten seconds? Less?

"Thank you, Lieutenant. Now the ball's in their cor—"

The Ops console alarms. "Sir!" Manazari's hands fly over the display. "They're powering their weapons!"

I close my eyes. There we go. History, on repeat for me to see. And it doesn't make me feel better one single bit.

Kieran jumps into action. "Red alert! Shields up. Resend message! Now!"

"No response, sir!"

"Shields are up. Distance to ship 50 km!"

"Ship's moving into attack position! Their shields are up and—"

"And what?"

"And they're weird, for a lack of a better term. I don't think we could penetrate even at full power—"

"Sir, I'm measuring an unknown energy in their weapons—I can't say what kind of damage those will cause!" Hayes does his best to sound professional, but anybody can hear the fear in his voice. For a moment, everybody stares at him—and I inch closer to his station, as if I wanted to have a look at his data.

Conolly darts over to science, positioning himself between me and the station, spoiling my attempts to sneak into their system. Dang it.

"Show me the readouts!"

"Chocho, any response?" Kieran.

"Nothing, sir. Resending on all frequencies—" Chocho.

"Enemy firing!" Manazari.

"Brace for impa—"

Boom! The ship trembles and rocks with the impact of Quaneez disruptors. Somebody yelps out on my right, but the grav stabilizers keep us all from falling. At least three different alarms start blaring, adding to the cacophony of noise.

"Report!"

"Shields holding, down to ninety percent! Unknown weapon. It's still eating through our shields. Down to eighty-five percent. Eighty!"

"Charging again!" Manazari's hands fly over his display.

Chase looks up from the science console. "Captain! Return fire?"

For one tiny, yet endless second silence hovers.

Kieran balls his fists, then slams one onto the armrest. "Negative. We're not starting a war today. Ops, keep the shields up, and Hayes, figure out how we can stop that stuff gnawing through our shields. Thaler, reverse! Back us out of here, *now!*"

Conolly is next to Kieran in two quick steps, his voice lowered as he talks to the captain. Here's to good hearing. "You don't want to retaliate? What if they perceive this as a sign of weakness and come after us?"

"Then it's an active act of aggression and we deal with it. But this…" He points at the screen. "This should not be a reason for two people to start shooting at each other. For all we know—"

"Incoming!"

I press myself against the wall a moment too late. The next impact jostles the ship like somebody kicked a can across the floor. The grav stabilizers kick in with an unfortunate delay making me lose balance as I get thrown into the console to my right, then to the floor. Ow, but— yes! I slide my thumb over the PAD to activate it, reach for the rim of the station to pull myself up, and hope PADdy can get the job done.

"Shields holding, but down to fifty-two percent! Grav stabilizers offline!"

Ah, not delayed, out. First systems' failure I appreciate.

"Charging again—"

"Helm!" Kieran is up, body wound tight as he stares at the screen. "Get us out of here, maximum jump, any destination. Now!"

"Aye, sir!" Thaler needs a max of three key combinations and space distorts in front of the bridge's window as the engines compress it and catapult us lightyears away from here.

Three seconds later, space looks different. A nebula. Two suns. No Quaneez cruiser.

PADdy, the most awesome PAD ever, vibrates at the exact moment when I pull up to standing. Done.

Nobody says anything, but I can feel the relief in the air, mine as palpable as theirs, although it comes with a serving of betrayal for abusing the situation and installing my virus.

Kieran blows out a puff of air. "All right, people. Let's gather our bearings, do damage control, and fix what needs fixing. Reports to me within the next five minutes. Commander, from now on your priority is finding a way through those shields. Notify Commander Upinga, I want something to counteract whatever they use to shoot us with—and that will be a standing order until we know how to hold our own against them. I'll be in my ready room informing USEF." He pulls his uniform shirt straight and walks to the door on the left. "I'd say that was too close a call."

"Agreed, sir." Conolly takes over the command chair.

Nobody pays me any special attention in the back, and I appreciate it. If they did, they might see the disgust in my eyes, and while I could always say it was from the attack, it's not.

It's from knowing how history is going to play out from now, and that I did nothing to stop it, but everything to make sure I wasn't affected by it.

Chapter Seventeen

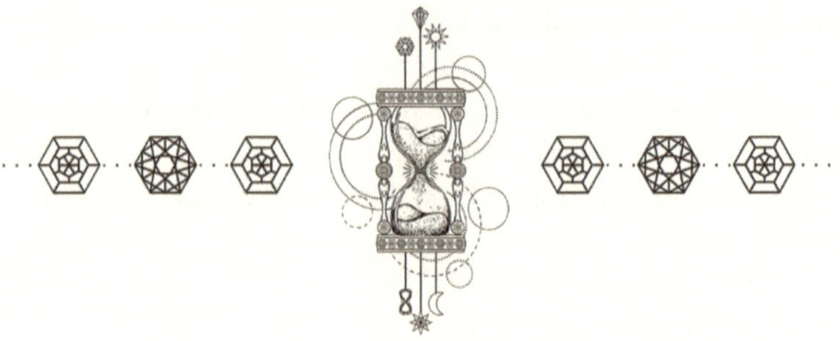

McGuire Academy, Auditorium One, Year 1, Match Day

uditorium One has never been fuller, at least not since I started at the academy. Every row of the student section is filled, and even on the opposite side, the faculty side, only a select few seats remain untaken. Three hundred people fit in here, and we're all lined up and focused on the dean below, the lion in this modern take of a roman arena.

No wonder: It's Match Day.

Finally.

To say I'd been looking forward to this day since I stepped onto academy grounds six months ago is an understatement. I've been working toward it, grooming myself to be the best version of a cadet I can be, doing my very best to impress the faculty.

Given the fact that I'm currently ranked first in my year, I'd say it's been going well, and yet I'm nervous. So much hangs on Match Day. Some call it Dooms Day for that exact reason. Shows what an emphasis the academy places on good mentoring. For us students, our career may depend on it. Getting the right mentor is like winning the lottery, and not getting a mentor… Not good. If a cadet can't score one of the few mentors, they're not top-notch material. Obviously, it's not an official mark on anybody's record if they don't succeed in getting themselves a mentor, but unofficially, it's damage that can't be undone.

For the last six months, the USEF academy's faculty had time to observe us. To test us. To look at all our test results, review videos of our performances, and talk to us. All to make up their mind whom they want to take under their wings for the remainder of their academy life.

During that same time, us students spoke to older semesters to get their point of view on the potential mentors we fancied, interviewed with the faculty members we sought out, and came up with our two-person ranking list, just like the faculty did.

And today is Match Day.

Excitement is in the air, although we're all trying to play it cool. And failing, most of us at least. At least half of us are going to walk out without a mentor, or with not their first choice. Which is still better than group mentoring, to be clear, but still. Let's not kid ourselves, the ability to attract a mentor and match with them will make any cadet an asset. No pressure, right?

Eventually, the dean clears his throat, and like somebody pulled the plug on the noise, it drops to absolute zero. A few of the faculty grin when they see us all but snap to attention, but come on. You all were here once. You know how it is.

I spy my dad higher up on the faculty side, chatting quietly with one of his colleagues. It's kind of weird to be on the receiving end of mentorship after seeing him mentor a new student every few years. Cue dinners at our place and late-night help, when the finals came close. Some of his former students have become family to us, and we're still in contact with all of them. Dad has made good choices whom to pick, and I really, really hope I inherited his sixth sense for that, because I definitely got ambitious with my rank list. But then, I have a good CV under my belt, plus six months of ranking first in class. I should be ambitious, right?

My first choice is Sebastian Grazer—Admiral Sebastian Grazer. As the head of Division Two, he would make a fantastic mentor, especially given the fact that I have made it clear I want to go into D-2 later on. My skills are what he's looking for, so I'm optimistic this is going to be a home run.

Choice two, in case the home run isn't going to happen: Captain Naomi Rangel of the *USEF Adventurer*. She is my kind of gal. Smart, tough, one of the best captains the Fleet has to offer. Working with her and being her mentee would mean the world.

Down below, Dean Shubert lifts both hands in greeting. "Welcome, students, welcome, faculty. Every year it pleases me to see a full auditorium of young, motivated cadets waiting for a mentor to guide them through the next years of academy life. Let me tell you, mentoring is the very heart of our academy. Mentoring, dedication, and skills. No surprise the USEF's McGuire Academy is the leader in education worldwide."

Applause breaks out, accompanied by a few *hear, hear* calls and even more pointing up the ranks to the big boss himself, current USEF president Admiral Jaxon Mashaule, a Los Angelino, luckily for us. No other branch gets visits from him as often as we do. He has kept our head above the water as the president for the last ten years, and even before that he served as an advisor to the president at that time. Fair to say that no other admiral knows war with the Quaneez as well as he does. Some actually say it's all he knows, but then… it's all we need right now, sad as it is.

Dean Shubert picks up on that. "And of course, a very warm welcome to Admiral Mashaule." He makes an effort to pronounce his name exactly the way the Admiral likes it: Muss-WHOLE. French pronunciation, as the admiral likes to emphasize. Higher-ranked officers have lost their positions for calling him Mash-all, or worse, placing the emphasis wrong, MASS-hole. Nothing good ever came for those poor souls from that unfortunate pronunciation.

The dean, clearly happy to have that obstacle passed safely, carries on. "We are always honored by his presence and grateful he could join us today for another day of making history." A mischievous glint lights up in his eyes. "Now, I could stand here for hours and praise our wonderful institution, or I could speed it up and give you all what you want. And because I'm feeling the excitement in the room, let's get this party started. Students, when I call your name, please stand up. Faculty, the same goes for you. If your name hasn't been called, you will be grouped into the combined class mentoring. Remember, we only have a limited number of mentors for a whole year of students, so competition was tough." He reaches for a PAD and activates it. "Aberforth, Sigourney."

Somewhere behind me somebody gets up, and at least two hundred heads turn in that direction. Sigourney's pale face flushes pink. Sucks to be the first in the alphabet—or maybe not, because she was called. She has a mentor.

The dean checks his list. "Captain Jeremy Jones."

An older man with dark skin and a warm, open smile gets up and waves at Sigourney, who's doing her best not to faint. "Ohmigod, Ohmigod, Ohmigod," she whisper-squeaks under her breath, totally audible for half the crowd, and for sure for the dean, who is visibly working to suppress a smile.

"Congratulations, Cadet. Well matched. Next. Archer, Desmond."

Archer, Desmond, matches to Lieutenant Commander Belfast and can't believe his luck. Neither can the next, and the next, and the next. With every passing matched student my anxiety grows. Unbelievable how long it can take to get to T. We pass the As, Bs, and Cs. The Ds, Es, and Fs. Someone, please speed this up, I'm about to get a coronary, and I'm not the only one. Everybody is on edge and emotions are running high, with anxiety still the dominant one.

Gs, Hs, Is.

The students who get their first choice beam across their whole faces. The ones who are not quite so lucky to get their first choice are still elated. Especially compared to the ones who get skipped. When we get to the end of L, the guy next to me whispers quietly, like a prayer. "Lohman, Lohman, Lohman, Loh—"

"Mesropian, Julian. Please rise."

The guy lets go of a sound so full of disappointment and sorrow, it breaks my heart. No single mentor for him. Group mentoring it is. I turn to look at him. "I'm sorry." There's not much else to say, really.

He takes a slow and deliberate deep breath. "Thank you." He keeps his eyes straight ahead, and I get it. Stay professional, don't let them see how it affects—

"—matched to Admiral Sebastian Grazer. Congratulations, Cadet. Very well done." The dean claps, and half the audience falls into the applause.

Wait, what— I heard that wrong.

But no.

Admiral Grazer stands up and waves at *Mesropian, Julian*, whom I could swear I've never seen in class in my life.

No. No, no, no. That didn't just happen. Admiral Grazer didn't match with some nobody—no offense, *Mesropian, Julian*—and not me. Can't be. I'm perfect for D-2! All I ever wanted is to go into D-2!

Admiral Mashaule gives an approving nod of congratulations to Admiral Grazer that chases all doubt from my mind. It's real. I didn't match with him.

Panic wraps around my throat and squeezes. The next breath comes in with a wheeze, and so does the one after. I worked my butt off for the last years to first get into the Academy, then to get into Division Two, and while not getting Grazer as a Mentor doesn't mean I won't, it's a set-back.

A harsh one.

Maybe I should've told him the truth during the interview—

A pang of something sharp lights up inside my chest. No. That's private.

I suck in a breath and shake out my hands. Get a grip, Thorburn. Life's not a party, so cut your losses and move on. This is done and over, and Grazer assigned to somebody else. I can't change it.

But I can—and will—deal with it.

The dean has already moved on, and all I can do is keep up a mask of professionalism, as if my best shot hadn't just gone up in smoke.

Mrzadeh, Shaideh.

Napa, Victor.

N'gumba, Chukwuka.

Nieman, Jessica.

To say my heart hammers like crazy would be an understatement. It doesn't really beat, it flutters, barely pumping any blood. Sweat breaks out and runs down my neck. Did I do something wrong in my application? Was it not clear I'm the best this year, in all categories? Is it something that I did? Where did I ruin my chances to match with Admiral Grazer?

Oazu, Chioma.

Okawa, Grace.

Ortega, Antonio.

Palomino—

"Matched to Captain Rangel, *USS Adventurer.* Congratulations, Cadet."

The ground opens to swallow me whole. I see Captain Rangel wave over to Palomino, whoever that is, but it doesn't register. Something in my brain keeps me from truly understanding what just happened.

My two picks.

My two picks are gone.

I won't get a mentor.

I won't—

Schlagman, Joseph.

Szubota, Kaiden.

Tahmasian, Janice.

Trumeba, Abioye.

That's when I stop breathing. When my name is skipped and it becomes painstakingly clear that there is no mistake, no error in the match, no mix-up that could explain my two picks being assigned to somebody else. None of that. I wasn't matched, because I wasn't good enough to be chosen as a mentee, period. The smallest sound of disappointment leaves my throat, a mix between a sigh and a pitiful moan that can't have been loud at all. Still, somebody snickers behind me, then whispers to their neighbor. More snickering.

My neck burns, and so do my cheeks. I sit up straighter and hide all my emotions, all my disappointment, all my regrets behind a mask of professionalism. I feel the guy next to me, Lohman, scoot a tad away from me, and I can't blame him, because the snickering gets louder. *Schadenfreude*, at its best. I bet they feel better now that *she* hasn't matched, the one who leads the ranks, Thorburn's daughter. The Maggot. Bet it confirms all the rumors I'm only first because of my name. That something is wrong with me.

On the other side of the auditorium, Dad types frantically into his PAD, jaw tight and eyes narrowed.

He must be disappointed in me. How embarrassing for him—his daughter, not matched, rejected by the faculty, his colleagues.

As if he felt me looking at him, he lifts his gaze, and his features soften when our eyes connect. No, I was wrong. He's not disappointed in me. He's sorry for me, and I don't know if that is any better.

Not really.

The smallest sad smile plays around his lips when he mouths something to me. *You're okay.*

I am? Doesn't feel like it. Around me, the match continues, but I'm not really present. My mind has checked out, keeping my body still and my face an unreadable mask. All for show, because I've been reduced to nothing but a shell. Never have I felt more inadequate, stupid, juvenile, and rejected. What did I think? Picking two of the most sought-after mentors the Academy has to offer? Why didn't I play it safe, and add one dud—at least then I would have the dud, but a mentor to myself. Now all I have is group-mentoring.

"—matched to Admiral Thorburn. Congratulations, Cadet. Well done." Somewhere to my right a classmate of mine waves at my dad. Another match made in heaven. I'm sure he did better than I did, but at this point that's not really difficult.

Because. I. Did. Not. Match.

Is this the first time ever the student with the highest score didn't match? Possibly. Actually, I could bet so, and I bet the others know it too, or else I wouldn't get those glances. Those whispers around me. I can feel the venom, spitefulness, and malice in each and every word trying to penetrate my shields and pierce my soul, but I won't let them.

The dean puts down the PAD and takes a long, satisfied look through the auditorium. "What a wonderful session. Congratulations to everybody who matched, what a great achievement. To those who didn't, I wish we had more available Faculty—"

"You would if you'd read your messages."

Every head turns toward the auditorium's entrance on the right and the two men walking in. First, only their outline is visible against the harsh light shining from the double-doors they entered through, but with every step closer onto the floor of the auditorium more and more details emerge, and with them more and more of the students break out in hushed gasps and whispers.

Dean Shubert pulls his uniform straight. "Gentlemen. A very untimely interruption—"

"A necessary interruption, Dean. I wondered why we weren't

invited." Admiral Chase Conolly—*the* Admiral Chase Conolly, formerly of *the USEF Pioneer*—crosses his arms in front of his chest. "Really, you're a hard man to get a hold of. Secretary doesn't know where you are, never time for a meeting. And we've tried, haven't we, Admiral?" He turns to the tall man next to him—and no way if I'm the only one starstruck, it's Admiral Zio Upinga, also of the *USEF Pioneer*. Two of the most famous officers the USEF has to offer, two thirds of the hotshot trio and the heads of the OUTREACH Division—both here, with us first-years. Actually, for the second time with us first-years if I count the stupid, embarrassing history-class encounter from a few months ago I swore to myself to never mention again.

Upinga nods. "We have. But for whatever reason, there must have been a mix-up. We were told the ceremony was tomorrow. We barely made it back to Earth in time." Admiral Upinga regards Shubert with a piercing look of disdain. "A more-timely manner of communication would be advantageous, Dean Shubert."

Admiral Grazer gets up, a harsh sound of rustling against the background of awed silence. "Admirals, this is hardly the time or place. You can meet the dean—"

"Apologies, Admiral, but apparently we can't." Conolly adds a slight bow to his interruption. "Combining active duty with academy teaching seems to be adorned with one heck of red tape."

Conolly throws a poignant glance up to Admiral Mashaule, whose lips press into a thin line. "For good reason, Gentlemen. And maybe you should consider sending in your applications on time if you would like to be considered."

"Huh." Conolly rubs his chin, and I swear a hundred girls around all ovulate simultaneously. "On time. Interesting. Say, Dean, did you receive our applications on time, or are you saying that the receipt sent out from your account is false?"

The whispers around me get louder. Somebody behind me murmurs to their neighbor, "They really want to mentor? *Both?* Does that mean I still have a chance?" A surge of lightning shoots through my veins. Does that mean *I* still have—

Yeah. Better not get my hopes up. Didn't work out so well a few minutes ago.

The dean flushes bright red under their scrutinizing gaze. "Oh. Uhh. N-no, that should be correct. But I didn't see— Maybe a mix-up. It must be a mix-up. I—I apologize." He throws a glance up into the faculty side of the audience. "B-but no matter what, Admirals, the Match is done."

Conolly smiles, dimples and all, and when the girls in front of me swoon like crazy, I wonder how they can't see the steel behind his eyes. This isn't only about not getting a Mentee. This runs deeper.

"No worries, Dean. I'll tell you what we'll do. No matter the paperwork, you can hardly dispute Admiral Upinga's and my qualification for mentoring. Or can you?"

"N-no, Admiral, of course not. It's just that—"

Admiral Grazer is on his feet, on the defense. "For heaven's sake, Admirals! You are holding up the whole class—"

"For a worthy cause. The Academy never has enough mentors, or am I mistaken? Admiral Mashaule?" His pronunciation sounds more like *MASShole*, but I could be mistaken. Admiral Conolly lifts his gaze to the upper gallery, and so does everybody else.

For the shortest moment I think I see something close to annoyance flash across the admiral's face, but then it's gone. He stands up and lifts his hands. "Gentlemen, please. I have to say your behavior is very irregular, Admirals. I would highly recommend you stick to protocol as you transition from active field duty into academy life."

"Of course, sir." Admiral Conolly nods sharp, but keeps his eyes trained on the head of the USEF.

One-Mississippi.

Two-Mississippi.

Three-

Mashaule's chest heaves up and down with a sigh swallowed by the distance. "That being said, you are correct. We never have enough mentors. Which is why I would suggest, Dean Shubert, to let the gentlemen proceed." And with that he sits down again, waving a hand as if to say *on you go*.

Admiral Upinga bows his head, and Conolly salutes. "Thank you, sir. Then let's make this fast and easy on everybody." He takes the dean's PAD from the table, scans over the list Shubert used to announce the matches, then hands it to his colleague, pointing at something. "Admiral Upinga and I have chosen our mentee." I swear, everybody who didn't match in the last thirty minutes sits up straighter, and even some of the ones who did match do. Admirals Conolly and Upinga are going to mentor one of us—it doesn't get much better than that. Like jump-started, my heart jolts back to life, thumping hard in my chest. There's no way I *cannot* hope…

Admiral Upinga gives the PAD back to Conolly and nods. "Sometimes I wonder how near-sighed some of the faculty are." He says it with a smile, but there's bite behind his words. "Honored faculty. Whatever your reasoning, the conclusion you came to was wrong. But even better for us. Would you like to do the honors, Admiral?"

Conolly rubs his hands together. "My pleasure." He turns and addresses the crowd of very excited cadets in front of him. "The student we will be mentoring has an impeccable record, refreshing new views, and enormous potential to change the world." His gaze travels through the audience and falls right on me. "Please rise, Nonie Thorburn."

Chapter Eighteen

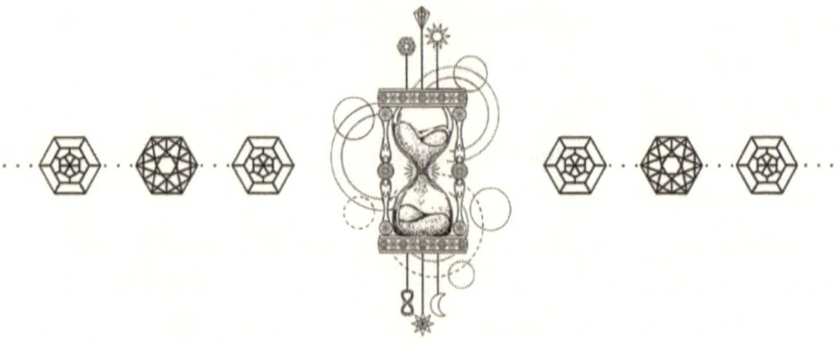

'm five minutes late, but on purpose. Being early to an invitation is mean, since the host might not be ready, and being on time is way too eager, so all that was left was being late.

Fashionably late.

I stop in front of Captain Wildason's quarters. For a moment I had hoped he'd cancel dinner after the stand-off with the Quaneez, but nope.

Last chance to turn around. Blame my cancellation on a stomach bug, something—anything—to stay in my quarters instead of walking seeing eye into this minefield.

My stomach cramps with the thought of going back. Maybe it's hunger, maybe a gut feeling, maybe nothing at all, but okay, it's all the answer I need. I'll go with my gut then. It's—surprisingly—oftentimes right.

I dry my hand on my thigh and press it against the reader on the right. In Kieran's quarters, the doorbell must be ringing, and I imagine him getting up and walking to—

The door slides apart, revealing the young Commander Conolly, greeting me with a smile and a tip to his forehead, like an abbreviated salute. "Nonie." He steps aside. "Come on in."

"Th-thank you, Commander." Ugh, stupid stutter. I've got to get used to Conolly being young, I mean, he isn't going to age in front of my eyes, and I can't stare at him every time I see him. That being said, how could I not? He's dressed in off-duty standard leisure attire and it fits him like a glove. That man is all muscle and will still be all muscle when I officially get to know him in a few decades. I know that much.

What I didn't know was that the fifties tailored their uniforms much more than they do now. In my time, I mean. To say they emphasized the important parts would be an understatement. Conolly looks hot in his uniform, as weird as it makes me feel to even think that, or to acknowledge that well… he's hot. Blond, tousled hair, eyes bluer than the sky, a wide chin and prominent, high cheek bones—yup, he's ticking all the boxes for most women. Still does in my time. Dad told me once the number of fan clubs for the "Hot-Shot-Trio" haven't gone down over the last decades, and I get it. Especially seeing them young.

Oh yeah, I get it.

"Nonie. Glad you came." Kieran's voice comes from the right, the kitchen area—and there he is, in the same leisure uniform as Conolly, an apron around his front, spatula in one hand and holding on to a pan handle on the stove with the other.

Forgotten is Conolly and his tight uniform. He has nothing on Kieran—on Kieran in the kitchen. His dark hair falls into his face when he looks down into the pan and the food he is preparing. Every move is purposeful and smooth, like he had done it a million times, and with every one of those moves I can observe the muscles playing under his uniform shirt. And when he turns back, throwing another glance at me over his shoulder—

Holy cow. It's really warm in here.

"Ah, you brought the contraband," he says with a smile.

All I can manage is a wide-eyed nod. Sheesh. Pull yourself together, Thorburn. "Of course I did. Fresh brew, so to speak. Thanks for having me." I hold up the bottle and put it down on the dining table. Maybe being thrown into the past has muddled with my brain. Seriously.

Conolly grabs some plates from the cabinet and begins to set the table. The whole scene has something so domestic and normal, I can't align it with what history said about these two tough guys. "What can I help with?"

"Nothing," Kieran says. "Almost done, and Chase got it covered.

Right, Trip?"

Conolly rolls his eyes. "Yes, and stop the nickname."

"What?" Kieran lays a hand over his heart and gives his colleague an innocent look, wide eyes and everything. "Commander Chase Conolly, triple C—Trip. The crew loves it. All I'm doing is showing you the same love."

"Sure, you do." Conolly comes back for silverware. "Better pour all your love into your cooking, or else I can book us a suite in sick bay. Zio is going to be thrilled."

"As if you ever did not like my cooking."

"There's always a first time." When the commander turns away to set the table, Kieran makes a quick face at him and sticks his tongue out, shoulders quaking with a suppressed chuckle.

I lean against the island separating his dining- and kitchen area from the living room. "I didn't know you cooked." I realize my mistake the same time as Kieran regards me with an odd glance.

"How would you? Plus, I don't advertise it. I like to keep my chef on board, thank you very much. This is only for the odd evening." He turns off the stove.

"Don't let him fool you, Nonie. He cooks all the time," Conolly calls over from setting the table.

"Shut up, Chase." Kieran threatens to throw a potholder over at him, and I laugh.

"No worries, your secret is safe with me. I like to cook too, happens without a mom and a busy dad." I think I was eight when I started making my own dinner because Dad was held up at work one too many times.

His mouth curls up into a soft, regretful smile. "Same here."

Right, I forgot. Half-orphan. Like me. Hey, I'm sure though he knows more about his mom than I do. Oh well. Details.

Conolly aligns napkins with the plates for everybody. "You recovered after that interesting afternoon?" The way he emphasizes the word makes clear he is talking about the Quaneez attack.

I shake out one hand and give my voice a little jitter. After all, Nonie-the-civilian should be appropriately frightened by said encounter. "Barely. That was quite scary. I hope we're far, far away from that ship at this point."

Before answering, the commander looks over to Kieran. Of course he doesn't trust me completely. I'm the unpredictable and unpredicted variable—seemingly innocent enough, yet out of left-field. Only when Kieran nods, he answers me. "We are. For now at least. Orders are to return to the location of the encounter and find that ship. And then…"

And then. I cover my short wince with an eye roll. "Does that mean I better fix my shuttle and head back to safety?"

Conolly flinches. "Well, about that. I had a look at your shuttle. It doesn't look good, as I thought."

I cringe. Dang it—what if he finds evidence of future technology? "Oh. Uhh, how bad is it?"

"Right now, the *Odysseus* is a smoking heap of metal in our hangar bay. With lots of time, even more replacements, and if you're willing to eat the cost, it might fly again, but right now, I'd call it totaled. And I haven't even gotten that deep into its guts."

My shoulders slump forward. "Right." Funny how his words open a mixed bag of feelings. No shuttle means less flexibility. I can't hide, I can't run, I'm stuck. But no shuttle also means no evidence of when I'm from. "Thanks for checking it out."

The commander looks up. "Sure."

Behind me, the doors hiss apart. "Good evening." Commander Upinga enters the captain's quarters, holding a container with a lid.

"Zio, you bring dessert?" Kieran turns the stove off and wipes his palms on his apron.

"I did, but not what you requested. Since I'm responsible for your health, I refuse to worsen it by adding chocolate to your diet."

Kieran groans. "Aww, man! You can't do that to me, Zee! What about those antioxidant effects—"

"Not enough to make up for the calories and sugar." He puts the dish down on the kitchen island, and Kieran lets his head hang.

"Dark chocolate?"

"Nope."

"Oh well. At least you're here." Kieran frowns at the clock.

"Some of us had to do this thing called work, Captain." Upinga manages to lace that sentence with an extra-serving of sarcasm, and the other two chuckle.

Conolly pours my special mix into everybody's glass. "Told you he'd complain about late shift, Kieran."

"Merely stating a fact." Upinga nods a hello to me. "Feeling well, Nonie?"

"Yes, thank you, Commander. Much better." I take a seat where Kieran points to, across from him at the dining table. Upinga takes the chair at the head of the table to my right, Conolly to my left.

"Glad to hear that. That was quite the injury to your shoulder. The captain is still dealing with the aftermath."

Kieran throws him an annoyed glance. "No, I'm not. I'm perfectly fine."

That reply earns him the most tongue-in-cheek expression from Upinga. "As you say, Captain. Then I'm sure those headaches and body aches are mere side effects of getting old."

This time Kieran does throw the potholder. "Somebody tell me this is enough to grant you a night in detention for subordination."

Conolly shrugs. "Meh. Maybe for disrespecting a superior officer. But you know Zee, he'd love a night in the brig in peace and quiet, so I doubt he'd mind."

Upinga cocks an eyebrow. "I'm kind of invincible like that."

Kieran groans with fake despair. "I'm so lucky to have the two of you as friends. Nonie, please don't listen to anything they say today. Clearly, they're out to torture me."

A small smile tugs at my lips. It's like coming home to a certain degree. Conolly and Upinga still do that teasing to each other. "I'd never. For the record, that was a nasty hit down on the planet." We're lucky we survived. Quaneez weapons suck. Badly so. I rub one finger over the spot where I have a new sunburst-like scar, courtesy of that shot to the shoulder. "And FYI, I also still feel the aftereffects. You're not alone, Kieran." For a moment I think I did something wrong, because like they choreographed it, both Conolly and Upinga cock an eyebrow and look at their captain.

Kieran ignores the pointed glances from his officers. "Thanks, Nonie. At least somebody here has empathy. And they're exaggerating. We've been in dicier situations before." He serves Upinga his meaty stew, then reaches for my plate.

Conolly cocks an eye brow. "Not really."

Kieran frowns. "This is where you normally agree with your captain, first officer."

"Agreeing with you is not in my job description. In fact, the opposite is listed there. And if I think about it…" Conolly holds one finger up. "Well, only one comes to mind, if you're honest."

Kieran pauses in mid-motion, head tilted to the side. "Nu-uh, that was different."

Conolly gives him the eye. "Really, Captain?"

"Really, Commander."

"I would argue that in either situation you barely escaped with your life—"

"For completely different reasons, Trip."

"Be that as it may, you can't blame Zio for being worried about you."

Kieran gives Upinga his plate, filled to the brim. "I'm not. But this wasn't Alpha Rubrum."

That jostles a memory. "Alpha Rubrum?" Why have I heard that before?

Commander Conolly nods. "The Magellan outpost until about a year and a half ago."

Right, that's why I remember: The first Magellan outpost decades ago, if only for a few years, and the *Eclipse* rescuing the Magellans from there. Dad was a young ensign assigned to the *Eclipse*, and part of said rescue mission. Aww. "Until it was destroyed, right?" A meteorite shower. After that, the Magellan's moved closer into quote-unquote our territory and settled on the planet we now call Mag-2. Obviously, that was before Humanity First got more of a footing in our society.

"Correct. And during that destruction Kieran almost got himself blasted into nothingness."

"He *what*?" I sit up straighter. Yes, Alpha Rubrum is the reason Kieran was promoted to captain, I knew that much, but maybe I'm a bit fuzzy on the details, because— "Blasted into nothingness? How? Why?"

"Because the good captain prioritizes differently than *others*." As Conolly takes a bite of his stew, Kieran gives him an odd look.

"Come on. Get over it. Bas has paid—"

"Well, *somebody* had to, although in my opinion punishment was not quite fair. Not enough, also not fair. Mashey always had Bas do all the dirty work to distract from all his shortcomings."

Kieran repeats himself with forced calm. "As I said, Bas has paid for it. I could bet he's more sorry about it than we could ever imagine, and honestly, to a certain degree I understand him. You protect the ones you love."

"So did you, only you protected everybody with us."

Kieran makes a face. "I never said I loved you guys. Most days I can barely stand to see you, but since we're trapped together on this floating heap of metal… No offense, *Pioneer*." He pats the table. "But as we have established through countless hours of debriefing, the option I chose was the only viable one."

I feel like I'm a tad behind the times, pun intended. "Okay, if I may ask, what happened?" All I heard from Dad was that it was one of the most important missions of his life—life-changing, in fact, since it got him into the diplomatic services.

The commander loads another bite of stew onto his fork while he regards me with his head tilted to the side and an odd expression on his face—an expression I've seen countless times. If I know my Admiral Conolly, he's going somewhere with that. "Okay, why not. See, Nonie, all three of us were young officers assigned to the *USEF Eclipse*—"

"*You* are *still* young," Upinga interrupts him. "I on the other hand have been and always will be more mature than both of you together."

"Oh, shut up, Zee." Conolly balls his napkin and throws it at his colleague. "Those few years you have on us—"

Upinga evades the incoming projectile, keeping his expression completely neutral, with a touch of fake innocence. "Obviously those few years make a big difference." He points at the napkin now lying on the floor.

"Whatever," Conolly grumbles. "As I was about to say, we were on the *Eclipse*. Our ship was assigned to render humanitarian aid to Alpha Rubrum, since the planet wasn't quite as stable as we and the Magellans had thought, and quakes and seismic shifts had pulled a number on the Magellan Colony. Command decided sending the only USEF vessel with a Magellan on board was a good idea, but our captain at that time disagreed."

Kieran frowns. "I don't know, Chase. You can't say that. Mashey has his shortcomings, but you're accusing a USEF captain of not following orders and, pretty much, racism."

"Oh, please. Let the official logs say one thing. We all know it went down differently. A captain who sends his complete crew off-board to quote-unquote facilitate help and then leaves orbit?"

"He says he didn't. Remember? There was nothing in the logs. *Malfunction in the sensors* causing the *Eclipse* to not pick up on the attacking ship."

Attacking—

"Sure." Conolly's voice drips with sarcasm. "Only interesting that Zio found those odd particle traces on all key systems he would need to alter the log."

"Commander." A muscle in Kieran's jaw pops. "Careful."

"Yes, sir. But you know my opinion."

"That I do."

Okay. Okay. I don't remember any of this. Why-oh-why don't I? Alpha Rubrum, Magellan Colony, humanitarian disaster, Meteorite shower, Kieran promoted for coming up with an idea and saving everybody. The other stuff? Never heard about it. I work on a dry swallow. "S-so, what happened, Commander?"

Conolly cocks another eyebrow, tilts his head and pauses. "Call me Chase. You're on a first name basis with the captain already. I'm Chase. Zio." He nods at Upinga.

My cheeks are turning into a supernova in no time. I've known these guys for years, and they're *Admiral* Conolly and *Admiral* Upinga. Maybe I can go down to addressing them as commanders instead of admirals, because, let's face it, rank changes in the USEF, and we're used to adjusting. But first-name basis? With all three? Technically, they're not that much older than me—in this time at least—but they outrank me in either time and old habits die hard. But boohoo, too bad, so sad— am I really complaining about them asking me to call them by their first names? Not my biggest problem. I fix a smile on my face. "Chase and Zio, got it."

Conoll—Chase gives me a thumbs up. "Wonderful. And to answer your question, what happened was that the colony got attacked and that neither the first officer nor the captain were there to help us."

"What?" I all but drop my fork. That is *so* not something I remember, neither part of it. Meteorite shower! *Meteorite shower!*

"You heard correctly." Chase takes a sip of his soda and gives the drink an appreciative nod. "Weapons' fire raining down on us, first officer MIA from his post, and the *Eclipse* not in orbit."

Unheard of. Seriously, that didn't happen. "You're kidding me." It should've been in the books! Dad should've said something! He would've mentioned it—that's a biggie!

"Oh, no. I wish I was. Our first officer was busy getting it on with a Magellan female—"

"Phrasing, Commander," Zio cuts in. "We form a union once. For life. I'd much rather prefer you call it bonding, because it is a connection on both, a mental and physical-chemical level. It alters physiology. Permanently. And believe me, that female he was *getting it on with*, has not gotten involved with anybody else after Bas because of that. She never will, and neither will he."

"Sorry, Zee." Chase raises his glass. "You're right. I get annoyed by the Alpha Rubrum incident, you know that."

"Hadn't noticed," Kieran mumbles under his breath.

I have a hard time picking my jaw off the floor. This is not what's in the books. Not at all, and I don't even know where to start. "Wait— am I getting that right? A human senior officer and a Magellan female— I mean, isn't that—shouldn't that be—"

"Forbidden? For whatever reason it is. Not that I think it should be." Kieran shrugs.

"Whoa." I fall back into my chair. "And even if we disregard that it's still, what—immediate dismissal from the service, dishonorable of course, for leaving his post—"

Upinga gives me an odd glance. "You know your academy regulations one-oh-one."

Uhh… I blush. "I want to join at one point. And friends of mine go there already." I drop my gaze to the napkin on my lap.

Conolly points his spoon at Kieran. "See? Even a civilian gets what the higher ups ignored."

Kieran sighs. "I get it, Chase. I wish it had come differently, and to a certain degree, I don't blame Bas. When it comes to the captain… maybe there was a reason for him to keep some information from Command, or to take the *Eclipse* out of orbit."

"You're saying that because you're a captain now and because *you* wouldn't just leave your team hanging." Chase pauses for another sip of soda. "Gosh, this is good. What is that?" He regards the glass and turns it in his hand before he sets it down again.

Quick as lightning, Kieran darts forward and snatches the bottle off the table. "Don't you dare. It's mine. Nonie made it because I asked her to bring it. Right, Nonie?" He presses the bottle to his chest in mock desperation.

I stretch my hands out from one to the other, like a referee. "No fighting, gentlemen. There's enough for everybody. I can always make more."

"And you'll have to. This is fantastic." Chase drains the last drop from his glass. "But to finally get this story done, the colony was under attack, everybody panicked, no leaders in sight… so Kieran took over."

I whistle through my teeth. "You saved them." It's a statement, not a question. That part I know he did. Although at this point it's clear some of my information was… *flawed*, for whatever reason.

Kieran wipes his mouth with the napkin. "I did what everybody else would've done—"

"Only that nobody else thought of it," Upinga says.

"Nor would everybody else have confronted the enemy in a shuttle with non-functional weapons." Chase puts down his spoon.

"I didn't know that," Kieran protests.

"And you were lucky the attacker retreated."

"I've never said I wasn't. But come on, don't blame that on me storming into a situation gung-ho, because I didn't. We were under attack. We can't call for help, because first thing they do is destroy the Magellan's communication array."

"Didn't even want to talk to us. Big f-u smack into our faces." Chase growls.

Kieran tilts his head. "It was an attack, Chase. Those rarely are polite. Anyway, rigging one shuttle's shields to tap into the colony's power grid and extending the shields was the only way to protect everybody. And we needed to defend ourselves, and we couldn't do that from the ground. That's why I took that one remaining shuttle up—"

"Only to realize the weapons and all secondary systems were off line."

Kieran harrumphs. "Not a pleasant surprise after lift-off, believe me."

I straighten out my napkin with shaking fingers. Why does this sound so much different than what I know? Has history already been altered? Was it something I did? Saving those people, I remember that part of history. It's what got him promoted to captain: thinking on his feet in a dire situation, saving the lives of the Magellans and all *Eclipse* crew members—only I thought his shield saved them from a meteorite shower.

I tear little pieces off the napkin. "So… who attacked you?" Besides the Quaneez, we have no enemies. And the Quaneez were not yet in the picture.

"I don't know." Kieran lifts and drops his shoulders. "Once I was up there and realized I took the one shuttle that was being overhauled… I hung there in space, kind of at an angle to their ship." He tilts his head and upper body to a forty-five-degree bend. "All I saw through my window was part of a ship, no more. Tried to hail, but communications were down, like most other secondary systems. Of course I thought that was it for me, but they didn't shoot. Ten seconds later, *zoom*, they were gone."

"Whoa," I whisper.

"Whoa indeed." Chase serves himself some more stew. "We still don't have much to go by, and just because Command wasn't happy with how it went down, I wouldn't be surprised if this becomes need-to-know at one point. Wait till the captain makes admiral, then it's a potential mark he's going to eradicate from the records while holding this over Bas' head until the end of time."

"Chase—"

"Anyway," Conolly interrupts, "long story short, Kieran was trying to make a point we had been in dicier situations before, mine was, only one came to mind."

Kieran reaches over and pulls Chase's plate out from under his spoon. "Wrong. Mine was that you're getting yourself in dicier situations, and now you've got to pay for it. Hope you're full, because I ain't feeding you anymore tonight. You're making me look bad."

"Ey!" Chase protests and reaches for his plate.

"Nu-uh." Kieran holds it up and out of his friend's reach, a certain glare in his eyes that softens with every second, until it turns into an almost child-like joy. "Say you're sorry. Say it. Say it!"

"All right, all right, whatever! Sorry," Chase grumbles. "Now give me my food, you—"

"Yes?" Kieran holds the plate higher, a wide grin on his face.

"Nothing."

"Thought so." He hands the plate back to Chase and chuckles to himself.

In that one moment something shifts in my perception of him, like a curtain was drawn and the lights switched on, or rather, as if I'd put on glasses, bringing my vision to a sudden sharp and clear 20/20.

I've got to say, the history books didn't do him justice. They didn't capture his spirit, his verve, his… I don't know, his aliveness, for the lack of a better word, and duh, of course they didn't. But still. He's so much more a person than they made him out in the books, and maybe that's the point. Since I first saw Kieran, my brain has been trying to align him with the historical captain-figure he is bound to become. Of course I was starstruck, in awe, and full of respect. What I failed to do was to see Captain Wildason as Kieran, the person—as a twenty-one year-old regular guy, who happens to be really, really good at everything USEF, but who's also just a regular guy, like there are tons at the academy right now. Well, in the future, I mean. Okay, or now as well. Or— Gah! Doesn't matter. Point is, he's so much more a person rather than a historic figure, and I'm beginning to see him as that: Kieran. Not Captain Wildason. Kieran.

I clear my throat. "So that's what got you promoted to captain."

"I guess so." Kieran says it like it was no big deal.

"With Mashey recommending him for the promotion he probably groomed Bas for," Chase adds on.

"He will get there eventually. He knows his stuff. He's good people. You know that."

Chase holds both hands up. "I do. I do. I bet you in twenty years, he's going to outrank us all, once this is water under the bridge."

Kieran lays a hand across his heart. "And if he is, then we'll all sleep better knowing a man with his heart in the right spot is in command. Now shut up with those old stories and tell me how much you like the food, or else it's the mess hall for both of you the next few weeks."

"Yes, sir," they both say in unison, and Kieran shoots them a fake stern glance that turns into a barely hidden smile when he's sure they're focused on the food.

For about half a minute we all dig into the stew, which is really good, I must say. Hearty and well-seasoned. Eventually, Chase wipes his mouth with his napkin.

"Nonie, I was wondering… Since we're talking about attacks and you more or less just had your own… When you were stuck on the planet, how did you manage to stay undetected by those people?" He says it with an innocent undertone that is anything but—rather the opposite, and it turns this conversation into a slippery slope. And here I was, wondering why he told me that story. Now I now: soften me up. Make me feel like part of the team. Get me to trust him and tell the truth. I know my *Admiral* Conolly, and *Commander* Conolly is not far off from his future self. Of course, he was going to ask. Wouldn't expect him to truly trust me otherwise.

I'm not the only one picking up on the pitfall behind his question. "Trip." Kieran drops his spoon, his voice carrying a warning.

"No, really, I'm wondering. You were there for two days from what you told us. You survived what a trained USEF officer nearly didn't. I'm only curious about your strategies."

Kieran shoots me an apologetic glance. "Never mind him, Nonie. He's just paranoid."

I shake my head. A normal question to ask, to which I need to find a normal answer. Normal-ish, at least, without disrupting the timeline. "It's oka—"

"Paranoid? I wouldn't call operating within my job description paranoid, Captain." Chase's face pulls into a scowl. "I'm merely asking a question that pertains to the security of the ship and of our crew. Anything we can find out about those people helps, and Nonie has been on the planet longer, and, if I may add, more successfully than you, Captain. And after today…"

Kieran sighs, then waves a hand. "If you don't mind, Nonie. Tell him what you can, or else he'll be thinking you cooperated with them. I wouldn't put it past him." He glares at Chase, who only shrugs.

"Safety first."

Better than Humanity First. I wipe my mouth and drop my napkin to my lap. Time to play the game. "What would you like to know? How I survived the crash? Easy answer—no clue. Blacked out, woke up, there I was, shuttle smoldering. Made it out just in time, and now my poor baby is a charred piece of rubble. What else—how I survived on the planet? Also easy. Search for water. Check. Observe wildlife, preferably mammals, finding food. Check. Eat the same, hoping our bio systems are compatible. Check. What else?"

His fingers drum a soft rhythm onto the table. "Fair enough. How about those people down there?"

Now it gets tricky. "Here's my two cents on that. Yes, I did crash, and yes, I did not have any means to leave the planet, but that doesn't mean I'd automatically assume everybody I met was friendly. I saw signs of them after about a day on the planet. And while I really wanted to run there and get help… I dunno. Those guys were weird. I mean, whole-body armor? Really? Plus, I saw them shoot some kind of weird weapon at wildlife. They sort of freaked me out and I stayed away. Figured evaluating my options was better than running into something head over heels and regretting it after." I drop my voice and my gaze, and add an exaggerated hard swallow.

Chase's drumming stops. "Did you see them without the armor?"

"No." Nobody ever has.

He raises a dubious eyebrow. "How did you know to use a shield against their weapons?"

Because that's the first line of defense against the Quaneez the *Pioneer* discovered, and it's taught to every cadet in every USEF-Academy on Earth.

I meet his gaze head-on. The time to underplay this is over. "You're not truly asking this, are you? What else was I supposed to do? I had one weapon, and neither my nor Kieran's return fire did anything to them!

Anything! My dad once said, sometimes you gotta go big or go home, and since going home equaled being killed—freakin' killed!—down there, I hope you can understand why I went all out and tried what I could to make it out of there alive!" I fall back into my chair and cross my arms in front of my chest. I'm a tad dizzy, not from my performance, but from the fact that I know I'm teetering on the edge of what I'm allowed to do—to say—in this timeline.

Silence.

Then Kieran lays down his silverware and asks the one-million-dollar question. "What would you do in my place? With those people? You saw what happened today."

My entire body tenses. Not the question to ask me, really. On my right Zio stops chewing, the hand holding the fork inching down until it rests against his plate. His eyes are wide, their black even deeper than normal, like sometimes when his older counterpart is spacing out.

My throat feels insanely tight, the last bite of stew going down like chalk. "I—I don't think my opinion matters for this."

"Why wouldn't it? You've seen as much of them as I have, or maybe more. You've shown great judgement so far. You used your gut instinct well down on T-12. What does it say now?"

To run.

No, not true. That's what my brain says, to run and not look back, to get off this ship and hide until I'm sure I can't alter the timeline. My gut apparently hasn't caught up with reality. It insists everything will be fine. So I force a smile and go with what I know is safe. "I think the USEF has a good approach. I mean, at this point those people fired first—twice. I guess making sure they won't kill humanity is in order." It takes more than self-control to not cringe with those words.

Kieran cocks his head, figuring something out inside his head. "You're trying to be PC."

My mouth opens, then snaps shut. *Busted.* Heat invades my cheeks, and I guess it's enough of an answer, at least Kieran grins.

"I'll take that as a yes. Good to know we're on the same page here."

I groan internally. Just great. At this point I can only hope this didn't give Kieran the push to go against USEF orders, or it will be bye-bye history.

Chapter Nineteen

It's two in the morning and I really, really want to punch something. Or, if I can't have that, at least throw something. Hard.

Alas, it would be very impolite to destroy my assigned quarters, so I resolve to the only acceptable solution: I bury my face into the thickest pillow the couch has to offer and scream into it. Like, scream-scream.

Sun and Stars, this is so frustrating.

I shove the pillow off my face and give it a good jab with my left before I let it drop to the carpeted floor. How many hours have I been at it? Fourteen? Fif—no, wait, seventeen long, annoying, frustrating and vexing hours that haven't brought me one bit closer to anything.

I still don't know why or how I ended up forty years in the past. And I still don't know how to get my sorry butt back home to my present—because time-travel is impossible, tells me all the research I can come up with. Or, maybe I'm not looking at the right data, 'cause obviously I'm here, but still.

So, so frustrating.

Maybe I should focus on the small victories, since they're all I have to show for seventeen freakin' hours of work. Thanks to yesterday's visit to the bridge and my PAD's set-up, the *Pioneer*'s computer will do a facial recognition scan on all staff every twenty seconds. Whenever it finds my face—insert awkward selfie right there—it is instructed to blur out my features reaching back to when I came into frame. I'm kind of proud of myself for this feat of sneaky programming, although to be honest, it only takes care of part of the problem: I'm still scanned in Upinga's medical records. I'm also sure I'm mentioned in Kieran's and Chase's reports, because that's what captains and first officers do, they report when something happens, and me quote-unquote rescuing Kieran from an unknown enemy qualifies at that.

Alas, that's a problem to be tackled another time. Right now, there is absolutely nothing I can do about it, since any intervention beyond what I pulled off in those seventeen hours exceeds the programming power of both, myself and my little PADdy. Meaning, I need to crank it up, and pronto. We're still searching for the Quaneez cruiser, and once we hit the Balthar star system I need to be off board, or I will become a witness to the outbreak of the Quaneez wars and forever memorized in countless databanks. Good luck deleting all of that.

But: praise where praise is due. I drop a kiss on my PAD's sleek silver exterior. "I'm so glad I've got you, PADdy," I whisper at it. I don't even care whispering at one's electronics is probably the first sign I'm losing it. Blame it on sleep deprivation. But either way, I'd be lost without my wrist PAD. All those *extra-features* I got installed are worth their weight in gold. They would be worth their weight in platinum if PADdy hadn't been damaged during my crash, but even damaged and running on half capacity it's invaluable.

Problem is, no matter how awesome and helpful good ol' PADdy-O is, I'm stuck. I need more scientific data, which is my biggest problem, because there's absolutely nothing in the *Pioneer*'s systems. That I can find, at least. Why did that freakin' H-155 blow up? All I did was execute a high-powered scan, and it's not like that held the energy to blow up anything. So what did I do wrong? How did I mess up everybody's future?

I rub the back of my hand across my eyes. Fact is, I'm stuck. I need help, and I can't get it anywhere on board. I—

My door bell chimes.

Uhh..?

It's, like, two in the morning.

Still, I roll myself off the couch and sort my leaden extremities enough to at least resemble a human being when I drag myself across the room and to the door. I place my palm against the reader and the doors slide apart.

"Evening, Nonie."

I blink twice. Three times. "Kieran?" It's, like, two in the morning. Wait, I said that already.

He lifts and drops a shoulder, a shy smile playing around his lips. "Computer said you were still up, so…"

A pleasant rush invades me and I step aside. "Come on in."

"Thanks." As he walks past me, I get a whiff of his cologne. Something spicy with a hint of butterscotch that tightens the muscles low in my stomach. Pretty yummy and pretty amazing he still smells so good this late at night, especially because he looks like I feel. His hair is tousled and dark rings adorn the area under his eyes. The amount of stubble also speaks for a longer-than-normal shift, and so does the yawn he stifles when he falls onto my couch.

I take a seat at the other end of it, draw my legs in and turn toward him. "Long shift?"

He nods. "That, and haven't been sleeping well."

Boy, do I know the feeling. The past doesn't make for good R&R.

Kieran rubs his eyes. "So yeah, that doesn't help. Plus, we're still searching for that vessel."

I know. "How's that going?" And I know that, too.

"Depressing, actually. I spoke with Command and the orders are clear, but…" He yawns again.

"But you don't agree with them." I don't have to ask this as a question, the answer is in his very body language.

"No, I don't. How'd you know?" His voice holds a bitter tone to it. "This is out of my hands, frustrating as it may be. We're following protocol and orders, and we'll see if it leads to success eventually." And success could mean *making new friends* or *assessing the potential enemy* after they killed USEF officers on T-12 and attacked the *Pioneer*.

I dig my fingernails into my palms. Not bursting out with what I know is a level of restraint I should be proud of, because all I want is to tell him. *Don't follow them. Abort. Take the consequences of ignoring an order over causing a decades-long war.* But I don't. Instead, I take a deep breath and say the first thing coming to mind. "It'll all play out the way it's supposed to."

Kieran chuckles. "You sound like Zio."

My head whips up to meet his gaze. "Like Zio?"

"Yeah. He's full of this philosophical stuff."

Don't I know it. And I should focus more on keeping a low profile, dang it.

Kieran rubs both palms over his thighs. "Anyway. My team has been busy and productive, but we're still not getting any usable results about those attackers. I'm collecting all the data we have on their ship, propulsion, build, etc., to bring to the Magellans. I'd like to know if they've encountered them before. So, we're having a rendezvous with the M-3. I need a second opinion."

"The M-3?" I sit up straighter. The M-3 is the Magellan flagship for exploration, no matter the decade I'm in. Every M-1 ever built serves as the political flagship for their government, every M-2 is always the battle flagship, and every M-3 is always the one for exploration—a true and dedicated science vessel.

Kieran's smile widens. "You've heard of the M-3?"

That one is easy. No danger to the time line. "Puh-lease." I wave a dismissive hand. "It's only the most famous science vessel in the world. Of course I've heard of it." Heard of it—and been there, not that I remembered anything.

"Wonderful. Well, then I assume you'll be pleased if I tell you you're going to join us tomorrow."

I blink. "Join you for what?"

"For our visit on the M-3."

"Me?" I squeak. Oh, heck no! Not a good idea, *so* not a good idea! That's the opposite of flying under the radar, that's announcing my presence with a bang! Not many humans of my time can claim to have set foot on their ships or their planet. My dad has-slash-will. Maybe a handful of others. That's about it. I don't count, because I was—will be—unconscious for most of it.

"Yeah, you." He leans back into the couch. "Zio suggested you should come."

Wait, what? "Zio wanted me to come?"

"He did. Said you were way more lucid than I was after I got hit, and he wants all the information given to the Taro. Per him, she has the strongest First Sense of all Magellans, and I *might not be of much use as an eye witness.*" He adds air quotes. "I need Taro Magona's point of view on those aliens. And the Magellan's data of the Alpha Rubrum incident. You know, the one Chase told you about yesterday?"

"I remember." How could I not? "But… you think they're connected?" That would be news to me, but I'm not claiming I'm a history buff, buzzword *meteorite shower.*

Kieran shrugs. "Can't rule it out. We have absolutely no data from the *Eclipse* because of that *systems failure,* or whatever, and while the Magellan colony had been conducting high-intensity long-range scans looking for more surviving Magellans, I don't have access to that data. Heck, I don't even know what they picked up on, if they picked up on anything. But that ship we're searching for… it rings a bell. And I want to make sure I'm not missing anything."

"Sounds reasonable." Could it be possible that attack… I mean, that the Quaneez did that? If so, why isn't that in our records as the first contact? I don't like that one single bit. It gives me stomach pain.

"Yeah, right?" He rakes a hand through his hair. "Chase is working on a way to keep our shields functioning and to break theirs, but they're proving to be quite the tough nut to crack. And I feel sorry for Zio already with the amount of studies he's doing on the crewmen killed on the planet to find out how to antagonize the yellow-beam weapons." A shadow falls over his face. "At least I'm hoping their deaths will be *good for something,* you know?" He uses more air quotation marks for the last part of the sentence. Little does he know that in fact both of his senior officers will come up with trailblazing work in regards to the Quaneez. Without them, we'd have taken much longer to penetrate their shields. Conolly is one mean engineering nerd, considering he graduated in Command, and Upinga… there's a reason he's hailed a medical hero in my time.

Me, though… I'm as unnecessary during that visit like a boil on the butt. For many reasons. I swipe a strand of hair out of my face. "Honestly, I don't think I have anything to contribute. I've given you all the information I have already, and knowing how selective the Magellans are when it comes to visitors… I really don't want to be causing any inconvenience." Or changes in the timeline.

Kieran chuckles. "Well, consider yourself the first civilian to meet with the Magellans then. Will look good on your resume, future cadet."

Those two last words shoot into my heart like a dagger. Future cadet. That's exactly and quite literally what I am, if history holds its shape. *If.* The smile on my face dies and withers away.

Kieran's brows furrow. "What's wrong?"

"N-nothing." I fake another smile, hoping it will resemble a real one. "Just—" Come on, find an excuse! "Just feel like I'm already inconveniencing you, and now I get special treatment and to go to the M-3. I should stay here. And Magellans like their privacy. What if I mess up with them? I'm not trained—"

He leans forward and taps my knee closest to him with a finger, and that tiny bit of contact, it shoots right into my heart. "You're not going to mess up. I believe in you, Nonie."

Said heart stops and takes a second or two to stumble back to activity. I still completely. "You... do?" That wasn't just a sentence thrown out—it sounded like he meant it.

He nods. "I do. One, you saved my life. Two, I'm getting... well, let's call it good vibes, for a lack of a better term. And three, I said it before, you've shown more skills than many of my officers, and..." Kieran shrugs and drops his gaze to the floor, a slight pinkish hue flaring up on his cheeks. "I don't know. It makes me trust you, I guess."

Aww, come on—right in the feels, even though I'm not quite sure if I should feel good for gaining his trust or bad for my ultimate deception. I cringe. "Thank you. That's very nice of you to say, but I'm a tad uncomfortable with visiting the M-3. Really. Like an intruder, who shouldn't be there." Hello, truth.

Kieran sighs. "Look, I get it. It's a big step. But a Magellan himself suggested it, and I trust Zio, which means, so should you."

Well, I do, but in this case, Upinga doesn't have all the data, or else he'd lock me in my room and never let me come out to avoid contamination of this time. "I don't know. I'd rather stay—"

Kieran deflates. "Okay. Like I said, I get it." He cocks his head, something mischievous lighting up in his eyes. "Then I'll have you hail USEF Command for a personal report—"

Oh, dang it. That's even worse! "Never mind, I'm coming with you," I blurt out. Anything is better than getting my mug recorded by the USEF decades before my birth.

He gives me a thumbs-up. "Good choice picking the lesser of two evils. I would do the same thing. Avoid the administration whenever you can." He finishes with his signature grin, the one with dimples and all, the one that shoots straight down to my core.

I groan. No kidding. "Yeah. Nothing worse than a start into academy life when they know you already as the girl who crashed her shuttle." Plausible excuse, served on a silver platter.

"I'll make sure then to phrase it differently when I send my report."

My heart skips a beat. He hasn't sent it yet? "You—"

Kieran's gaze snaps right into mine. "Thanks for agreeing to come tomorrow. I'm hoping your information will help the Magellans identify the species. At this point I need all the help I can get to find out what I can if we want to keep the peace." He rakes his hand through his hair again. Boy, that hairdo is getting a workout. Work-through. Whatever. "I'm getting more and more pressure from Command to ignore establishing a relationship with these people, and to let the weapons speak instead, but…"

"But? But you don't want to start a war."

"No. I don't want to start a war. I've lost two officers to those people already. I don't intend to lose more. I say they don't want to meet with us, we let them be and hope they reconsider at one point when they're ready."

"I like your plan better." Not that it ever will come true, but still.

"Thank you." He sighs and presses the balls of his palms into his eyes. "It's frustrating sometimes, but that's the nature of the beast with a military hierarchy. And I've got to give it to them. Usually, the admirals have a good overview and often know more than we do. They see the bigger picture with the intel they get from all the sides, not like us. Not as limited. This situation on the other hand…" Kieran drops his hands and shakes his head. "Hopefully, the couple of centuries the Magellans are ahead of us will yield something useable for us, even though they're far from their original home at this point—or maybe because they are far from their home. Because if not—and if I have to follow orders to the T—I'm worried we're going down a path we shouldn't. All my instincts tell me to stay away, to give those aliens the space they want, but…"

"An order is an order." I get it. I've lived it.

A sad smile plays around his lips. "Exactly. Only, I really don't want to go down in history as the guy who started a war."

"Yeah," I whisper. "That'd suck." And while history is going to judge Kieran Wildason a hero, I don't think that's truly his concern. It's the war. The loss of life. The fact that it could've been avoided.

And that we're heading full-speed toward it.

Chapter Twenty

"Good afternoon, Admiral." I stand ramrod straight at attention, and I'm pretty sure I'm doing a moderately good job for a newbie-first-year cadet. Eyes straight ahead. Posture rigid. Shoulders back. Good thing he can't see inside of me, or else he'd know my heart was missing every other beat: nerves.

"At ease, Cadet." Admiral Grazer doesn't look up from his PAD when I obey his order, relax my stance and fold my hands behind my back.

And wait.

And wait.

Aaand wait.

I'll wait as long as it takes for the admiral to give me a minute of his time, because I'm here to make him realize how much potential choosing me as a mentee could have. I'm not about to screw that up with impatience.

So, I wait.

While the admiral is reading over something on his PAD, I let my gaze drift around the room. This must be the nicest office of them all. I've been to a few, obviously to Dad's, but none of them are as big or have as good a view as Admiral Grazer's. The view is stunning from this high up in the Admin Tower. The whole campus is on display below us, all the way to the beach and ocean training grounds. And the interior isn't too shabby either: dark mahogany furniture, comfy cushy chairs, shelves filled with books over books. I wonder if Grazer chose the dark wood because it contrasts with his white hair and makes him stand out even more. How old is he? Mid-sixties?

The admiral chuckles over something he's reading, then—finally—drops the PAD and looks up at me. "Cadet." His brows narrow as recognition flares in his eyes. "Cadet Thorburn, correct?"

"Yes, sir." Here's to hope he doesn't remember me because of that stupid question Haggardy gave me when he dropped by class at the beginning of the year. Nope. He probably recognizes me because he knows my dad, and Dad has tons of pictures of me on his desk.

The admiral raises an eyebrow. "To what do I owe the pleasure?"

Deep breath. This is it. I step forward and hand him a data chip, then snap right back to attention. "I would like to formally apply for your mentorship, Admiral."

The eyebrow climbs higher. "Would you now?"

"Yes, sir."

I can't be quite sure, since I'm keeping my eyes trained on a spot somewhere above his head—Basic Training one-oh-one—but I think I see the hint of a smile playing around his lips. He tosses the data chip in the air and catches it. "At ease, Cadet. Your stance is giving me a muscle spasm just from looking at you." He lays the chip down onto his desk, aligning it with the PAD in the middle. "Tell me why you think I should pick you."

Excitement surges through me. I've practiced this, and not just once, but about a million times. "Yes, sir. As you know, I'm the youngest applicant ever admitted to the academy. I've been studying more than hard to make that goal happen, which shows I do have a good work ethic, and I know that's important to you." Because he dismissed a student from mentoring before, when he couldn't keep his grades up. "I plan to continue the way I started my academy training—in the top one percent of our year, and with that I do not only mean our academy, but of all USEF Academies worldwide."

Grazer's eyes widen. "Really? Aren't you reaching a bit too high, Cadet?"

I pull my shoulders back. It makes me look more official and older, and I need all the advantages I can get, besides being tall. "No, sir. So far, I'm ranked number one for our academy, and number two world-wide." And I intend to leave the current world-wide number one to follow in my dust within the next week or two, once exam scores come in.

"Impressive, Cadet. But good grades will go down well with any mentor. Why pick me? Or rather, why should I pick you?"

Because since that day five years ago all I want is to be like *her*. Be prepared for all kinds of situations. Be ready for what life throws at me, good or bad. Of course I don't say that. I go for the official version, the one that doesn't give away what only Dad and I know. "You're the head of Division Two, Admiral. My ultimate goal is to join D-2 and two become a strong member you can rely on. I know it's a long and rocky road, but I'm prepared for it and willing to go the extra mile, no matter the cost." It's what kept me going after the abduction, what made me study and train like a madwoman.

Grazer purses his lips, looks down on the PAD, and taps something on it. "Your record says you're taking an expedited course load?"

"That is correct, sir." Who needs six years for the Academy anyway, right?

"At your age?" I get a raised eyebrow with that.

"Also correct, sir."

"I see." He continues to read on the PAD, then frowns. "You passed advanced self-defense before admission to the academy, and yet that's the only grade…" He looks up at me. "Combat not your thing, Cadet?"

I keep looking straight ahead, face blank. This question doesn't bother me. It doesn't. It was to be expected, after all, it's my only not-perfect grade. "I'm still in the top ten percent." And it took me a lot of sweat and tears to get there, especially the latter.

A smirk appears on the admiral's face. "Still, seems like a let-down looking at everything else… And you know that Division Two focuses heavily on combat training, don't you?"

"Yes, sir. Like I said, top ten percent, trajectory steep." I chew the inside of my cheek. I can crank it up. I can. My mind is stronger than those memories.

"Huh." Grazer raises an unconvinced eyebrow. "We will see." He taps the PAD's display. "It says here you speak three human languages—and some Magellan. Huh. I'm curious, why bother, Cadet? All of them speak Standard English."

Why bother? Isn't that the wrong approach? "Sir, I figured knowing a people's language was a good way to understand their culture, since culture is formed by language and vice versa. For example, the Inuit—"

"Yeah, yeah, I got it, Cadet. Thank you." Grazer waves a hand and continues reading, his head cocked to the side. "You won the Lichtenstein-Award for critical thinking two years in a row. Only two years, huh? What happened this year? Topic didn't suit you?"

Not in the least. "As a two-time consecutive winner, the rules prohibited me from participation. Sir." Or else I would've rocked it. I hope.

Finally, *finally* the ice breaks and the admiral chuckles. "You're quite something, Cadet. I didn't think your father's genes would produce somebody so determined." Something in his eyes changes as they bore deeper into mine. "And speaking of. What is your stance on your father's integration policy?"

What is it with him and asking those kinds of loaded questions to first-years? This is leading down a slippery slope, no matter what I say. Still, I snap back to attention. Anything regarding family ties to another admiral needs to be treated with the utmost professionalism. Nobody should be able to say I'm using his rank as a stepping stone. "Sir, Admiral Thorburn's integration policy is well thought-through and deserves more recognition with the broad public. As you know, the Magellans have proven to be a true friend of the human people. They have helped us tremendously in many aspects—"

"And yet they have never even offered their help with the Quaneez."

"They have given us technology and medical advancement we're using every day fighting the Qua—"

"Not what I'm talking about, Cadet. Manpower, that's what I'm talking about. If we're such good friends, how do you explain that?"

I barely keep from flinching. "Sir, we do not have a contract with them, meaning, the Magellans are not obligated to help with manpower, and, given the fact their whole culture revolves around peace and conservation of life, they're unlikely to ever send troops—"

"But what if they got attacked? Would you, if you were in command, send troops to help them?" His light eyes stay on me, evaluating my reaction.

And the answer is an easy one. "Yes, sir. Even if they wouldn't pay us back if the situation were reversed, I would defend them."

"Why?" I can't tell whether he is pleased with my answer or not.

"Because friendship is not about equal pay. It's about helping with what the respective party's strength is. Ours is strategic thinking, exploring, and, well, warfare. Theirs is medicine, technology. Friendship is a cooperation. We scratch their back, they scratch ours. Only we're using different tools."

For the length of at least three hurried, stumbled heartbeats, the admiral stays silent. Did I go too far? Go too much pro-Mag? Is he—

"Strong words, Cadet." The admiral switches off the PAD. "Thank you for your time. Dismissed."

I salute, turn on my heels and walk out of his office.

Dismissed.

Question is only, dismissed from this meeting, or from the list of potential candidates?

Chapter Twenty-One

"Everybody ready?" Kieran throws a glance at Chase standing on his right and Zio on left, then at me right behind the tall Magellan. "Weapons stayed here? You've got the data?"

Chase nods with the first question, Zio with the second. "I added Commander Conolly's results to mine. We don't have much yet, but there's progress."

"Wonderful. Nonie, ready for the second demat in your life?"

I give him a thumbs-up from behind Zio. "Ready whenever you are." For the umpteenth demat in my life. Normal to a USEF cadet of my generation and time, but obviously not for Nonie, Starhopper extraordinaire of this timeline. Now, if he asked if I was ready to visit the M-3, the answer would have been... complicated. From a preparation point of view, I've been ready to visit the Magellans for years—heck, I've been eager to do so. From a safety point of view? I should keep my sorry butt on the *Pioneer*.

Kieran signals to Allison Lopez manning the console straight ahead of us. Guess it's one of those days where the Chief of Engineering is taking over the demat. "Go for it."

Lopez nods and types into the console. A warm, tingling sensation engulfs first my chest, then spreads to the periphery. Arms, legs, head. For a second my vision blurs—

—and then focuses again, only that I'm not looking at the *Pioneer*'s white demat-room, but at a congregation of five Magellans in a much bigger room with intricate decorations covering the light blue walls.

The female Magellan in the middle of the five steps forward, raising one hand in greeting. "Captain Wildason. Welcome to the M-3. May your First Sense always guide you safely." Her voice is somewhat raspy and rough. She is one of the tallest Magellans I've ever seen, maybe even taller than Zio, and about his age, I would guess. Her jet-black hair shimmers like an oil-spill, which I've got to say goes well with the dark-blue uniform she's wearing.

"Taro Magona, may your First Sense always guide you safely. Thank you for flying to rendezvous with us." Kieran motions at us around him. "This is my first officer, Commander Chase Conolly, and I'm sure you've met or heard of my chief medical officer, Commander Zio Upinga."

Magona nods a short greeting at Chase, but when she looks at Zio, her face turns into an impassive mask. "Zio Upinga. It has been a while."

Zio lowers his head. "Indeed, it has."

"We wondered if you even remembered your people."

"My memory has not been affected by working with humans, Taro. And if you're referring to the fact I did not visit Mag-Two recently, I would like to remind you that I was not in any way encouraged to visit after my decision to join USEF."

Ouch. There it is, the rift I knew about but never saw. Back in 2295, Admiral Upinga's relationship with his people is more relaxed, but a few decades earlier, it wasn't. The Magellans have quite strict guidelines when it comes to working with us, and Zio was the first—and only one—to break out.

Before Taro Magona can reply, Zio carries on. "And to avoid diving into a lengthy discussion of internal politics, I would like to introduce a guest we brought." He steps aside to reveal me. "Nonie Magnetta. I think you will find what she has to say most fascinating."

I swear, the eyes of all five Magellans pop wide when they fall on me. Like, comically so. If they had never seen a human, or, if they didn't expect me coming. Magellans are not known to be open to visitors. At least those five get themselves under control in less than a second.

The Taro bows slightly. "Nonie Magnetta. It is nice to meet you."

I return the bow. Comes in handy to hide my annoyance at their reaction. "And may your First Sense always guide you safely, Taro Magona." I could've even delivered that in Magellan, because Nonie Thorburn is only half-bad at it. But then, Nonie Magnetta wouldn't know any Magellan, so I stick to—very polite—English. They might not be big fans of visitors, but this one is a well-behaved visitor. I know my Magellan, and my Magellan one-oh-one.

The Taro ignores my response and addresses Kieran again. "Captain, let's talk." She turns around and walks through the room toward a large table and chairs at the other end closer to the large, ceiling-high windows. Part of me is disappointed we're not going to be led through their ship. Maybe I would've recognized something. Maybe it would've triggered a memory of things yet to happen. Even if not, I was truly looking forward to seeing more of it, but then at least I'm here. For the second time. Not many humans can say that.

I take the rear of the group, only followed by the last Magellan who manned the demat controls. He touches my shoulder. "Your leg."

I stop and whirl around, bringing his hand to drop off my shoulder. "W-what?"

He looks down at my left leg. "The readings were off when I dematted you over. What is it?"

My jaw drops. "Uhh, I had an accident once—"

"Ah." He nods. "Bioengineered. Good work." And with that, he speeds up and walks past me, taking a seat at the right of the table next to Taro Magona and his colleagues, leaving four chairs on the opposite side for us humans.

Holy Sun and Stars—I didn't even think about the Magellans picking up on my leg! The differences are so subtle, nobody in USEF would know if me getting it hadn't been such a big story.

Unease makes me sit straight as I slide up into the chair next to Kieran. Oh. Big. Obviously, these were not made for humans. They're a tad too high, even for somebody tall as me, but then I'm nowhere near Magellan proportions. If I stretch, my tippy toes can reach the floor, but otherwise my feet dangle like somebody sat a kindergartner on an adult chair.

The Taro folds her hands in front of her. "What can we help you with, Captain?"

Kieran reaches for the PAD Zio brought. "I would like to get your input. We ran into a hostile situation on T-12 three days ago. Two of my crew members were killed and I only made it out because of Nonie, who'd been stranded on that planet." He taps something on the PAD, which is why he's missing the raised eye brow of the other Magellan sitting next to the Taro when he mentions me.

Uhh, excuse me, guys? Yes, girls can do that. Rescue people. I cross my arms in front of my chest. Never thought the Magellans were chauvinistic, but here we go.

Taro Magona tilts her head. "In that system? That's unexpected. I don't think we have tracked any ship movements in that area for a while."

"Well, neither had we, but still they were there. I don't have much, but this is the data we have on their ship." Kieran pinches something on his PAD and makes a flicking motion with his wrist, transferring the data into the M-3's computer system.

Magona activates the screen in the table in front of her. "Interesting. That drive is unlike any I have seen in use before."

Zio lowers his chin. "We were hoping to compare it to the readings the Magellans collected during the Alpha Rubrum incident."

The Taro leans forward, hands on the table. "You're thinking they could be the same." She pauses, looking at the data again. "It's a possibility. The design does look familiar. Of course, you're very welcome to the data we collected, but keep in mind that we were running long-range scans, trying to penetrate deep into the Magellan Cloud until our arrays were destroyed during the first salvo of attacks. We were not focused at all on close-range, so data is limited. But,"—she leans back, leaving her hands flat on the table—"it might still prove helpful."

"Appreciate it, Taro."

"Of course, Captain. Without you, what is left of our people would be gone. We're forever indebted to you." She bows her head, and Kieran blushes.

"Taro—"

Magona holds up a hand. "We are. And while we get the data for you," she nods at one of his officers, "I'm interested in hearing some more about the attack, if you don't mind."

The other Magellan starts working on a keypad appearing in the surface of the table in front of him. Kieran motions his hand at him. "Thank you for that, and of course, any details you need, Taro."

"Thank you. As we're staying in this part of the galaxy, I'm hoping we won't encounter a new enemy, but I would rather be prepared. What did you note about the beings themselves?"

"Down on the planet?" Kieran scratches behind his ear. "Not much, I was running and hiding from an enemy I couldn't see, and when they did come into view, they shot me with whatever and I was not quite lucid anymore. Whole-body armor. Helmets. I didn't see any electronic devices they could've used to scan for my signature, but then that could've integrated in their helmets."

The Taro cocks her head. "Interesting. Did you do anything specific that might've caught their attention?"

He shrugs. "I don't know. Nothing comes to mind. And they stayed on my tracks until Nonie saved me."

Taro Magona directs her attention at me. "Could you describe the attackers, Nonie?"

Of course I can, but this is where my game starts. I purse my lips and nod. "Of course, although I don't have much to add to the captain's description. Tall. Humanoid. Their faces were hidden behind mask-like helmets, and they wore, like the captain said, whole-body armor or uniforms."

"Did you by any chance get a closer look at their uniforms? Any details you remember?"

I fake-deflate. "Ugh. It was so dark… Like, mostly red, and they had this symbol here…" I tap my right shoulder.

"A symbol?"

"Yeah, it looked like…" I shake my head and sigh, like I was frustrated with myself. "Maybe if I drew it? Would you mind?" I tap the table in front of me as a means of asking for access to their systems. And once the screen is activated, PADdy should be able—

Taro Magona raises an eyebrow. "No need to go through that trouble. A description will suffice."

"Is your First Sense misleading you these days, Taro?" Zio stares at the other Magellan, unblinking, keeping those dark eyes of his trained on the female Taro.

And it works.

Magona's eyes roll back for a second, like she was annoyed by Zio, but then she gives a slight shake of her head. "You're right. A picture says more than a hundred words, I've heard humans say. Please, go ahead, Nonie Magnetta."

"Thank you," I say. A screen and keyboard spring to life in the table's surface in front of me, like for the other Magellan. Okay, here we go. I pretend to scratch myself next to PADdy while brushing my thumb over the activation spot. My heart cramps once. If this goes wrong, I might find myself in the brig of either ship, and then bye-bye going home.

Bye-bye to making up for what I did.

My throat constricts. Easy, Thorburn. At least fake being calm and trust in your sneaky programming. If all goes well, my little PAD will find a way into the Magellan's systems, get me what I need and install the same blur-my-features-mode as on the *Pioneer*. I kinda feel bad about that, but hey, I'd like the timeline to stay intact, as crappy as parts of it may be. I just hope this trick doesn't get old and works twice. Pretty-please, fate? I feel like you owe me one.

The others watch in silence while I draw. My hands are steady, which I'd consider a major win, because on the inside I'm as jittery as they come. Come on, PADdy, come on! How hard can it be to initiate that stupid intrusion and extract the data? This is 2295 tech, it should easily beat forty-year-old Magellan programming! Or, maybe I should also consider no alarms blaring a major win, no matter how much or little I'm getting out of this. And if I can pull this stunt a second time, first on the *Pioneer*'s bridge and now here, I should give myself a major pat on the back.

After about a minute and a half I can't draw it out any longer. Pun intended. Either I got the data at this point, or I didn't.

I hit enter and clear my throat. "This is what it looked like. Roughly."

The Taro checks out my graphic. "Interesting. I cannot say I recognize it though. What did they attack you with when you were stranded on the planet?" She lifts his gaze at me.

Truth? "Actually, they didn't really notice me until I ran into Kieran."

Magona exchanges a glance with one of her officers. "But once they did, what kind of weapon did they attack with?"

I nod. "Yellow beams." My thumb and index finger form a fake gun that I fire.

"Yellow beams, no visible technology, and whole-body armor." The Taro closes her eyes for a second. When she opens them again, she looks straight at Zio. Something passes between them, something I can't interpret, but eventually the Taro gives a small nod and breaks eye contact. "I can neither say we've ever encountered this race before, nor that I would want to. I would attribute the described behavior to a warrior race with an extremely high level of aggression."

Well yeah. You can say that.

"But also, Captain Wildason, I'm afraid I have bad news."

"Bring it on." Kieran leans forward, supports his upper body with his forearms resting on the table.

"It's possible that the attackers you encountered are the same as on Alpha Rubrum. You're welcome to look through the data we've collected to come up with your own opinion, but knowing said data by heart, I can tell you already that no clear identification can be made. However, no matter that, the descriptions you have given me make it likely this is a race we have heard of before."

"And why is that bad news?"

"Because, while their existence was said to be hearsay, if it is not, you have encountered a very hostile people, Captain."

Kieran flinches. "I can tell. Why hearsay?"

The Taro folds her hands in front of him. "Because it is said that no species who encountered them survived for longer than a few decades."

Kieran blows out a harsh puff of air, and so do I. A few decades? I mean, considering that humanity isn't doing too badly, but... what does it mean for our future? That we're ultimately doomed, no matter what? Nausea rises, bringing bile with it.

"Taro, are you sure—"

"Unfortunately yes, Captain. We had our suspicions after Alpha Rubrum, but not enough data. With what you gave us now, I'm fairly certain you have encountered whom lore calls the Quaneez."

Quaneez! She knows they're the—

"Quaneez." The apple in Kieran's throat moves up and down.

Magona nods. "Correct. Quaneez is the Magellan word describing…" She looks at Zio for help.

"Silent assailant," Zio translates.

"That would fit," Kieran whispers.

Silent assailants. Definitely fitting—I never knew their name meant something. I never thought about how we knew their name if we never talked to them either.

Chase raises a hand. "Taro, if you don't mind me asking, what does rumor say about their tracking or technology? Oftentimes there's some truth to the lore, and obviously as the first officer and chief of security, my main concern is safety. The way the captain described it, he and our officers were more or less hunted down on that planet. Now, I assume there must have been some kind of technology—some kind of scanner or device—to help them. I'm looking for anything as wild as a guess as to how it works so we can protect against it. Any information could improve our chances to develop a counter and camouflage our signatures."

Taro Magona sighs. "Unfortunately, I don't have anything useful for you. Legend says they come to destroy, and those legends are centuries old."

Meaning, the Quaneez way of life has been working out well for them so far.

Chase frowns. "Worth a try. Thank y—"

"Could they be tracking by scent?" Kieran drums a light rhythm onto the table top.

"By scent?" The Taro shakes her head. "It would be highly unusual for a spacefaring race to rely on biological over technological senses, especially because it would be useless in space."

The drumming continues. "I know, but doesn't it make sense? Duarte and Lingo were shot within the first few minutes after we ran into them. I used mud, more as a visual camouflage, and after I covered myself in it, they definitely took longer to find me. If they used technological scanners to find me, the mud shouldn't have been a problem."

"You're thinking because your natural scent was masked." Taro Magona circles her nose with a finger.

"Yes, but then—" Kieran's gaze darts between me and the Taro. "But then Nonie would've been found earlier. She wasn't covered in mud, and yet she survived for two days on the planet. So never mind. Stupid theory."

I blush. Big lie right there, not that it mattered. Forty years later and we still don't know how the Quaneez do it. Those helmets of theirs must be pure tech magic, no matter what we try to disturb their readings.

Kieran turns to me on his left. "What did you do to keep hidden?" He asks it without any malice, without any accusation in his voice, and yet I feel like I've just been called out in the biggest lie of my life.

Heat rises to my cheeks, cranking up my blush to a burn. "I—" I don't know. We've never been good at evading the Quaneez. We tried shields, we tried scrambling our bio-signals, and nothing works. We land on one of their outposts, they know we're there. Cost us hundreds of thousands of people until we decided to minimize stealth attacks and hand-to-hand combat and rather focus on large-scale assaults. "I don't know. Maybe they were busy with you?" Which still doesn't explain the two days I supposedly spent down there without being attacked, and judging by Chase's look, he's thinking the same. Dang his intuitions.

Upinga and Magona exchange another one of those glances. Seriously, Magellans have these communicating-without-words-looks perfected. Hands down. Then Zio turns to Kieran. "It would make sense, Captain. Our team was the bigger threat." Competitive me feels a tad offended, because if we're honest, I was the bigger threat: at least I knew how to shoot them. Alas, not the point.

Kieran gives me a smile so honest and warm, it brings the guilt inside my stomach to a boil. "Well, I'm glad we kept them busy then."

Taro Magona rises. "If I can give you one good piece of advice, Captain. Stay away from the Quaneez. Nothing good will come from another attempt at contact with them. Only death."

Chapter Twenty-Two

USEF Pioneer, Day 4 on board, somewhen in the evening

'm done sitting in my quarters. Like, done-done. It's all I ever do. All I *can* ever do.

I've exhausted the materials I brought from the M-3, and what has it brought me? About as many questions as I had before. What I thought had the potential to give me a leg up feels more like it knocked me down a peg, at least optimism-wise.

Theoretically, according to one very smart Magellan scientist, time travel should be possible. He proposes time is not linear, but nonlinear, meaning, it doesn't just flow in one direction. So far, so good. I can subscribe to that theory, because here I am, in the past, upstream from where I was before—so yes, I've definitely gone backward when old-school theories say we can only go forward. That being said, it's not quite unexpected nobody knows how to throw an ordinary organic being like myself out of its natural downstream flow and make them go back in time.

Everything sounds so impossible.

I push off the couch and stretch. There's another research paper linked that sounds promising, but from what I can gather it blew up together with Mag-1 when their sun went supernova.

To make a very long afternoon and evening short, I have nothing to show for it.

A big sigh escapes me. So frustrating. Alas, here's the thing: no matter what the physics—and the possibilities or chances—are, I most likely need a ship for whatever I want to do, be that attempting time-travel or just get off the *Pioneer*.

I glance at the clock: 22:30 hours. Nightshift. "Perfect," I whisper. At this time, it should be nice and quiet on board, ideal to check on the *Odysseus*, otherwise known as the *smoking heap of metal* left after my crash-landing. Here's to hope something is salvageable, despite Chase's assurance to the contrary. Even if it's a long-term project, I'll need to get the shuttle fixed for whatever the future holds for me. Pun intended.

And, to be honest, it feels good to come up with some kind of activity to hopefully end my predicament. This inactivity, the whole being at this time's and fate's mercy, is not my thing.

Long-term project, here I come. I brush a finger over PADdy. "Schematics *Pioneer*. Hangar Bay Three from this location." The PAD springs to life, projecting the fastest route into the air in front of me. Okay, easy-peasy, not far. "Deactivate. And thank you, PADdy. I'd be lost without you." I cringe. Second time I'm talking to my PAD, as if it wasn't bad enough I named it. Get a grip, Thorburn!

Anyway.

The doors part and release me into the hallway. As expected, it's completely empty. Forty percent of the crew, i.e., shift one, should be in bed, the twenty percent of shift two either in the mess hall or unwinding somewhere, and the last forty percent, i.e., shifts three and four either busy at work or not out for work yet.

This time is kind of the sweet spot on any ship: when the majority of the day is over, most of the crew are tucked away while the active shifts maintain function, nothing more. Limits traffic in the *Pioneer*'s corridors. It's so quiet, only my uneven walk and the louder tap of my left foot hitting the ground harder than the right is disrupting the silence. Kind of my trademark, at this point.

Still, I stay alert to, I don't know, bend down and tie my shoe to hide my face or whatever. I'm not that stupid. I can erase myself from the computer, but not from 400 memories. And here's to hope again those forty years will make Upinga and Conolly forget what I looked like until they meet me again at the academy. There are many Nonies, so that alone shouldn't spark recognition. Right? I'm hoping that together with a good serving of disbelief they'll only say *Oh, we once knew a Nonie, she looked kind of similar to you*, and not *Say, why did we meet you forty years ago.*

The *Pioneer* at night has something calming and soothing to it. The hallways shine in bright white, the walls with their slight concave design look fantastic, and everything still smells new. Did I mention I like this little ship? Even in my time she's still flying, only she's a museum, traveling from colony to colony for school classes to visit. I never got to see her though. During elementary school, our teacher tried several times and couldn't get us in. Too busy. It's obviously a popular field trip.

The next corner brings me to the aft lifts and a few meters farther down to Hangar Bay Three.

I place my palm onto the reader until it turns green and the doors open to a large, high room with crates on either side and what's left of the *Odysseus* directly in center.

And that's not pretty.

I stop dead. "Aww, man." Chase was right. If she is ever going to fly, she'll need more than just TLC. *Full makeover* is more like it.

Like in a trance, I move forward, gaze roaming over my only hope to either get home or at least away from here. The shuttle's formerly fake-old exterior has some real street cred now. Its white-and-silver hull is charred all over, like somebody took a ginormous brush of soot and went crazy with it. The rear is worse, right where the engine compartment is. Was. I don't know. I can't even tell if the engine is still in—

"Hey, Nonie."

I twitch and jerk—

"Over here." A hand waves from the rear of my shuttle—at the ground level. What the…?

A squeaky noise and grunt later, Chase, on a board on wheels, rolls out from under the shuttle. "Coming to check on your baby?" He sits up and wipes his hands on a cloth.

I blink twice. "Uhh—yeah. Yeah. I needed to see how bad it was."

"Pretty bad." He points a thumb over his shoulder at the engine. "Most of your secondary systems are fried. So is air and propulsion. I haven't gotten all the way in, so there's hope parts of the sub-jump drive are salvageable, but I can't guarantee it."

A spike of something shoots through me, although I'm not sure whether that's from the fact that something might be useable or that he has not gotten into the depth of my engine, i.e., found out its secret.

I come closer and drag one finger over the *Odysseus'* hull. Feels rough, thanks to the burn marks. "Thanks for checking her, Chase, but I think she's a lost cause." Ow. It hurts to say those words, no matter I hope they're not true.

"No worries. Engineering is my hobby. If it wasn't for Kieran, I'd probably have gone into that instead of Command, so with that as a disclaimer, I wouldn't necessarily say she's a lost cause." He gets up and throws the cloth onto the floor. "The hull is intact, for example. Just doesn't look pretty. From what I can tell after a preliminary scan is that helm control is repairable, and the engine…" He shrugs. "Not as bad as I first thought, but we'll have to see."

No, *we* don't. "Never mind, Chase. I don't want this to take up more of your time, really."

"You know, this is my way of relaxing. I needed a break from analyzing that shield data anyway. Whatever stuff they're using, it's giving me a headache."

Oh. The Quaneez' shields. Right, he's the one who figured out how to penetrate them and demat within their parameter. And speaking of Quaneez: "Glad I could provide a distraction then, but really. Whenever we're back in USEF space, just throw me and the *Odysseus* out at the nearest colony, and I'll figure it out." I shrug, like it's no big deal.

His eyes narrow. "Seriously? You think that's gonna happen? Then you haven't met Kieran. I can promise you he's not going to drop you off somewhere, but deliver you either home himself or get you onto another USEF-vessel to do the job."

I cringe. Both means more exposure, and more potential changes to the timeline. "No, really, I don't want to inconvenience—"

"Nonie." He tilts his head and raises his brows. "Really. After what the Taro told us about those Quaneez-people and knowing how easily they destroyed Alpha Rubrum, assuming it was really them… Space isn't quite as safe anymore for star hopping."

No kidding, although I think it took another year or two until everybody got that message. "You're probably right, but I still can't accept that. It's too much of an inconvenience. If you don't mind, talk to him, Chase. You all have done so much for me, I can't—"

"Yeah, you still will have to, probably." He winks at me. "I don't think that part is negotiable."

I drop my hand from the *Odysseus'* hull and wipe it on my pants. Choose your battles. And strategies. "Okay. Okay. Thank you. Not necessary after already saving my butt, but thank you. But please, then you do me a favor: Stop wasting your time on this." I gesture at the shuttle. *Stop wasting your time, stop digging around, stop risking the timeline and go back to discovering that shield modulator.*

Confusion crosses his face. "You don't want me to repair her?"

"Nope." I shake my head so fast I get dizzy.

"Why not? I really might be able to fix the engine. Or I'll have Allyson help me."

And exactly that's my problem. If he finds out about me—and once he or Allyson dig deeper into the engine, there's no doubt they will— the timeline is altered and there's no guarantee it's going to restore or not change my future. Then I'll have wrecked not only humanity's rescue, but also humanity's future. How many billion lives am I going to have affected then? Including the Quaneez on H-155? Fair to say countless, because billions is going to be too small a number.

Panic rises and constricts my throat. "Don't fix it. Please. I could never repay it. Don't fix it." It comes out more pitiful than I intended to.

Chase's brow pull into a frown. "But, Nonie, if I—"

Gosh—just don't, Chase! "My dad gave the *Odysseus* to me before he died," I blurt out with the only excuse coming to mind that might— might—stop him. "He said he trusted me to do well out there, even on my own. It was supposed to be my journey of maturation. So... if I want it to fly again, it's something I need to do by myself. To prove that his trust in my abilities wasn't misplaced. Or at least not too much." My voice withers down and breaks at the end, because, really, I can't take yet another thing going wrong.

Chase sighs and walks over to me. "Okay. I get it. I honestly do."

He takes me by the shoulders and directs me to the opened shuttle door, then pushes me down to have a seat on the ledge. "Look around. It's not too bad in here. Why don't we do the following: You check her out yourself, and if you need my help while you're here, I'll be happy to. Okay?"

I force out a smile. "Okay." That at least buys me some time.

For a moment, neither of us says anything, then Chase scoots up onto the shuttle's step to sit next to me. "Hey, Nonie? Don't get me wrong, I'm only asking because I'm curious. When I scanned the *Odysseus,* I noticed traces of Setayashi radiation, and…" He makes a shrugging gesture. "That's pretty rare. We still don't know much about it."

Setayashi radiation? "I don't know anything about it," I croak. Never heard about it, but whatever it is, I don't want it. All it does is scream out loud something isn't right here. *Great.* Maybe it announces time travel. I close my eyes. From one close-call to the next, each and every one scraping another layer off my excuses and fake stories.

"See, our knowledge is limited on that, but I checked, and there's absolutely nothing in the parsecs around T-12 that could give off this kind of radiation. So… I was wondering what else might've happened with you. *To* you." He gently rocks his shoulder into mine, but the good-natured approach to this topic doesn't help the panic curling around my stomach, tightening to a hard coil.

He knows.

He knows my story is a lie. From here it's only one small step and I'm exposed. I suck in a harsh breath. "I—"

I only have one chance: lie more, while partially coming clean. The tight coil of panic turns into pain, bringing a hefty dose of nausea with it. "I'm sorry," I whisper, and I actually mean it. I *am* sorry. For everything. For lying. For deceiving him and the others. For maybe screwing up their future, as well as mine.

"For what?" He keeps his voice low, calm—but oh yeah, he knows my story's fake. He's had his eye on me since I came on board, and just because we're friendly at this point doesn't mean he wasn't attentive and thorough.

I suck in a choppy breath. "I didn't crash two days prior. I don't know when, but not that long before I found Kieran. Hours, not more." My throat constricts from the pressure around it. I hope I'm making the right decision here. "I was far off, somewhere in uncharted space. I scanned a planet, and there was this flash of light—and next thing I know I'm crashed on T-12—only I didn't know where I was until you told me." One embarrassing silent tear escapes me, and while I wish I could blame it on good acting, it's rather the proof of how much this is getting to me.

Chase twists his upper body to get a better look at me. "Why didn't you say so in the first place?" He rubs one palm over my shoulder blade. "We could've investigated when we were still closer."

"Investigated what?" a third voice chimes in.

Both our heads whip up and to the right.

Chase clutches his heart. "Zio. You scared the living daylights out of me."

"Apologies, Chase. I was not aware neither the sound of the door nor of my steps were enough to announce my arrival."

Conolly rolls his eyes. "We were talking. But anyway, love it that I'm not the only one taking a break from the captain's orders."

I flinch with his words. Job well done, Nonie.

Zio shrugs. "I can only spend so much time with dead bodies doing autopsies."

Chase grimaces. "Ugh, no kidding. Then brainstorm with me here. Turns out Nonie's story is a bit different from what we thought." Chase inclines his head toward me.

"Is it?" Zio cocks an eyebrow, regarding me with the same mix of attention and evaluation he will use on me forty years later.

I blush. Appreciate Chase's phrasing, but still. I give the Magellan my best game face. "Yes. I was afraid I did something wrong." I drop my gaze to the floor. Truth, right there. "I mean, I scan that planet, there's this flash, and next thing I'm crashed where you found me, lightyears away from where I was before." I look up at Zio, swallowing hard. "What did I do?" What I really mean is, what the heck got me to this location and to this date? Any insights, any theory, I'll take it.

Zio pulls over a chair and sits down. "Chase?"

"Definite pick-up on Setayashi radiation. Oddly enough, some

Tau-particles as well. Nothing else abnormal. Fire started in the engine compartment, I assume due to overheating the emergency brakes when crashing through the atmosphere. Haven't gotten into the data yet, but doubt there's much left."

"Setayashi radiation?" His brows form a V. "Interesting."

"It is?" I squeak.

"Indeed. It only occurs naturally a split second before a planetary core rupture."

I don't need to fake the pained facial expression, it's there on its own, no problem. "A planetary core rupture?" Triggered by me. Sounds impossible, because I shouldn't have that kind of power, no shuttle does—heck, no spaceship does—but yet I saw it happen. Core temperature rising, core size doubling—*flash*—gone.

"Correct. But as you can imagine, it is very hard to destabilize a planetary core. The Tau-particles are even more unexpected and unexplained. They're not a naturally occurring particle." His gaze bores into mine. "Unless it was a terraformed planet."

My stomach drops. I get the implication. Terraformed, equaling inhabited, equaling he's wondering if I blew up a whole people. Here we are, about to find out they're talking to a mass-murderer.

Self-preservation kicks in, at its finest. I shake my head. "No. No humans on that planet." That's as honest as I can be. I really don't think it was terraformed, we should've known that. Or maybe it was, and our data was old, so the USEF missed that planet's transformation. It's not like Grazer would've included that in my briefing, given that he left out oh, only the most important part about it, like five million Quaneez living there, or battle cruisers in its orbit.

Eventually I will have to come clean to Upinga and Conolly about how I messed up when—*if*—I ever make it back, but for now, I just can't. Plus, if I admit to this being a populated planet, guess what's going to happen? Correct, they're going to send ships to that area, and then: *Hello, Quaneez. Nice to meet you. Oh, and wait, the planet isn't destroyed? Oops...!*

Yeah. No. Can't have that happen either.

Zio raises a slow eyebrow at me. "All right." He pauses and thinks for a second. "What kind of scan did you use?"

"Uhh… my dad taught me one that's called Level Six?" My voice sounds fake to my own ears.

"Level Six? For us at the USEF that would mean a high-powered, focused beam—"

"My dad loved everything USEF, so I think that might be it."

"Do you remember any details of the planet? Composition, atmosphere, its name?"

I rub my eyes and let my head hang. "Unnamed, too far off the beaten path, way deep in undiscovered space. I don't remember the sector. Maybe I can find it when I look at a map, but…" I shrug. "I'm not good with that without my computer. And no, I had no time to check the readings. Scan, alarm, flash, crash. That's it."

Zio rubs his chin. "Something's missing. I can't think of any mechanism that could be responsible for transporting you any distance through space, no matter if a level six scan or an explosion are part of it. I wish we had more data. It's fair to say that if that planet exploded, you wouldn't be here, but pulverized."

"Right," I squeak. How I wish he were right.

"I don't like not understanding the physics behind it, but at least we can assume for now that it was an unlucky combination of events that threw you off course, meaning, I don't expect any of this to happen again."

My jaw drops and the next breath comes in wheezy. That's what I was worried about—my journey here beating the one in a million odds. A once-in-a-lifetime thing.

Bile pushes up my throat as realization hits me like a fist to the gut. I'm stuck here for reals. Even if I could replicate exactly what I did and blow up another planet, I wouldn't know where or when I'd end up. I couldn't direct it. A total crapshoot.

And worse, let's not overlook the biggie here: I'd have to potentially destroy another planet to replicate the events. And that's not going to happen ever again. I hug my elbows.

Never again.

Chase shows Zio his PAD. "Found this here, too. I'm sure this triggers a memory, eh?" He tilts it so that a schematic of my shuttle is visible, red dots marking several junctions in my secondary systems.

"Huh." Upinga raises an eyebrow. "How could it not? These particles I only saw once before, but—" He pauses, staring straight ahead.

"But what?" Chase elbows him into the side.

Zio blinks twice. "Can I use the scanner for a second?"

"Sure." Chase hands it over and watches Zio enter the commands for his scan and move the tool's invisible beam over the shuttle's core. "Whatcha got?"

"Not much. The only systems showing those particles are diagnostics."

"Not data recording like with us."

"No." Zio hands the scanner back to Chase, who gives it to me. "Here. You keep it. Everything I have on the *Odysseus* is on here, so in case you do want to start fixing it, you can."

I take it and lie it next to me. "Thank you." Hallelujah! One problem less to worry about. Nothing worse than Chase looking through the *Odysseus'* readouts in a quiet moment and finding what I don't want him to find.

Zio's gaze follows the scanner. "By the way, I noticed your shuttle's scanners are quite interesting."

Uhh, yeah, like, forty years more advanced. "My dad liked to tinker with stuff."

The Magellan nods appreciatively. "He should've become an engineer. The modifications he made to those scanners…" He points at a few junctions in the schematics. "Interesting, indeed." Blue dots appear on top of some of the red ones. Zio's brows furrow. "There was a theory in a Magellan article once—"

Oh, hell to the no—knowing my Admiral Upinga it could very well be the time-traveling-theory one I've been looking at. He is one walking encyclopedia, that man, i.e., this is way too close to home. I stick out my tongue at him. "Are you always quoting articles?" Weak distraction, but all I have.

Chase laughs out loud next to me. "He does. Wait till he finds a topic dear to his heart. There will be no stopping him."

Zio folds his arms in front of his chest. "Excuse me, how come it's okay for you to have engineering as your hobby, and I'm not allowed to follow up on science?"

"Puh-lease, Zio." Chase makes an exaggerated wave with his hand. "Because you're a Magellan. We wouldn't want you near our technology."

"Unless it's medical."

"Exactly. Because while we do trust you to put us back together, we're still not quite sure anybody else but a human should be in a position of power."

Forgotten are my means of getting here as they exchange a glance speaking of years of frustration. *Humanity First* hasn't even been founded, and yet...

I shove my hands under my thighs. "It's that bad already?"

"Already?" Chase rolls his eyes. "It's never been good, Nonie."

I cringe. Sheesh, close call: *already*. I clear my throat. "I meant, I would've thought USEF—"

"Whatever you're thinking, nope." Chase scoots off the wing and brushes the soot from his uniform pants. "USEF is as bad as the general population. Point in case, Zio would science the heck out of everything and everybody. That's what he was born to do. Seriously. But the USEF..." He sucks in his lip and weighs his head to the left and right. "How do I say it? The USEF likes to parade their one Magellan as a sign of inclusivity to the public, but when the doors are closed..." He lightly jabs Upinga in the shoulder. "Then they make sure this one here is restricted to medical sciences. Less potential for espionage."

Zio rolls his eyes. "As if we needed that. We were spacefaring when humanity was still burning witches."

"I know that," Chase says. "But to your detriment, one of the characteristics of humanity is fear of the unknown. And to them, that's you, as open as they pretend to be." He huffs. "One can only hope humanity will grow and evolve, or else I'm really worried about our future."

Chapter Twenty-Three

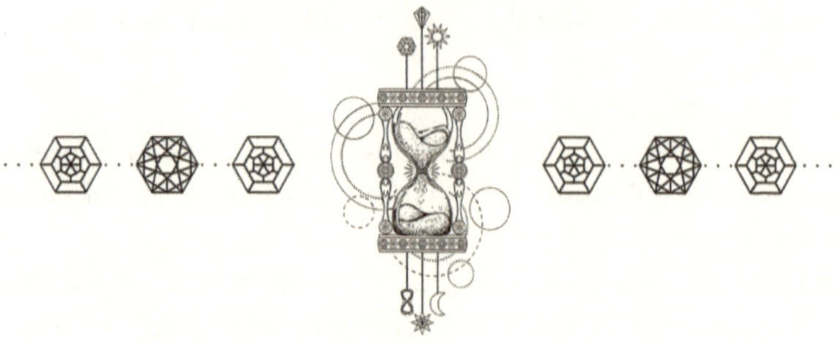

It's one of those days where homework and assignments make up most of my day and they just won't stop coming. Only good thing is I'm sitting in one of Admiral Upinga's ginormous office chairs, which is way more comfy than the academy's regular chairs making it easy to sit criss-cross-applesauce. Admiral Conolly is going over some technical manuals and safety reports, while Admiral Upinga swipes across his PAD and sends me another file. "Make sure you go over this one before the finals. I would like a written summary by tomorrow morning."

Here's to maturity, because I don't groan, I don't roll my eyes, and I don't let my head hang down. Another assignment. Ugh. I mean, I'm going to graduate in less than a month, how much more do they want to pile on? But there's a reason I'm still leading the scoreboard, and that would be my two mentors and hard work. I accept the file on my PAD on my lap with three forceful taps. Sometimes it's slow to respond. "Will do." There goes sleep for tonight.

Admiral Conolly gives me a sideways glance. "You need a new PAD, Cadet." He points at my good old fourth-generation PAD. Not the newest of the new, with a big scratch from an unfortunate collision a few years ago and a tad slow here and there, but I love it. Yeah, it's bulky, but fine. It had my back all through academy and never once ran out of juice or hung itself up. I give it a loving pat on the frame.

"Naah, I'm fine. It works." Reliably so. Granted, sometimes it needs some gentle convincing, but we're a good team.

"Huh." Conolly doesn't sound convinced. "Maybe we shouldn't have assigned you so many tasks over the years."

"Then I might not have become valedictorian, sir." I might also have fewer dark circles under my eyes, but oh well.

"Agreed. And hey, we know you like to be prepared for everything and anything. Just helping you along, the way only your two all-knowing annoying mentors can." He raises his Lubbeck's soda in salute and takes a sip.

Admiral Upinga's eyes narrow. "That's your second bottle today, Trip."

Conolly flinches. "Come on, Zee. There's not much sugar—"

"Too much."

"I'll work it off later in the gym."

"You better," Upinga growls under his breath. Admiral Conolly's soda intake has been an issue ever since I met them. I like Lubbeck's too, quite a bit, actually, but I'm nowhere this addicted.

"Hey! I always do! This wouldn't be here if I didn't!" Conolly flexes his biceps.

Upinga points to Conolly's stomach. "That would also be flatter—"

"Unfair! Not a single gram of fat—"

And here they go again, like an old couple. I lift both my hands in a calming manner. "Really, gentlemen. The two of you negotiated a historic cease fire, and yet you can't keep peace amongst yourselves." I add a theatric sigh. *Men.*

The admirals' mouths snap shut as they exchange a glance of the kind that makes me feel like I'm missing something. "What?"

"Nothing, Cadet."

"Really." I find I'm having a hard time believing that.

Conolly cocks his head. "Uncle Zio?"

Upinga's jaw twitches once while he stares straight ahead, eyes as dark as the night. "It might be beneficial for Nonie to know."

"To know what?" We were just talking about Lubbeck's, for crying out loud!

Admiral Conolly leans forward and supports his weight with his arms on his legs. "Okay then. Since you mentioned the cease fire…"

My heart skips a beat. "Yes?"

"There's not much Zio and I did to facilitate that."

Huh? "But you negotiated the treaty."

Conolly flinches. "Strong words. Way too strong for what really happened. They're only calling it a treaty so it sounds like we—slash the USEF—actively worked on that."

I cock my head. "You didn't?"

"Hell yeah, we did. For years. It just didn't happen by any means of intervention we attempted. The only thing we did differently this time was going in blind and holding our fire—and that was accidental, I might add."

My jaw drops to the floor. "We *accidentally* held fire?" Since the wars started forty years ago, we have not been known to hold our fire, let alone by accident.

Conolly sighs heavily. "Zio and I had taken a shuttle into the Quaneez' territory. We came prepared to be shot at and destroyed, but we also came with everything we could imagine might help to communicate with the Quaneez and make them see reason. Unfortunately for us, we encountered a meteorite shower. The shuttle got damaged pretty badly. Sensors were offline, communications too, weapons. Everything besides basic life support."

"Uh-oh." A shudder runs down my spine. They're both sitting right in front of me, so obviously they made it, but still. Sounds less than ideal.

"Uh-oh indeed," Conolly continues and reaches for the soda bottle on the table. "We hung in space, blind, deaf, mute, unable to defend ourselves—"

Upinga takes the bottles of Lubbeck's away from his colleague's prying fingers. "And we didn't even know the Quaneez had arrived until we looked out the window."

"Holy cow," I breathe. In our experience that's usually the last thing people see before *boom*.

Conolly frowns, most likely more because of the soda being taken from him than the actual story. "The battleship came close. Stopped. That's the point where, believe me, Zio and I were counting our last seconds. Not the way we wanted to go. But… nothing happened. After a few minutes they left. No shots fired. No nothing."

"Whoa." I seem to have lost my ability for longer, more coherent sentences, but this is… *whoa*, for all intents and purposes.

Upinga takes his PAD and a box of paperclips and holds them in the air. "Since then, Command has issued the order for all ships encountering the Quaneez to mimic what we did, and since we don't really know what exactly caused them to not fire, they all tilt their ships forty-five degrees aligned to the nearest sun, shut down their secondary systems and hold still." He rotates the paperclip box accordingly.

Admiral Conolly sneaks a hand under the table and retrieves the Lubbeck's. "We're taking it as a sign they don't want to fire, and believe me, until we find a way to communicate better—heck, at all—we'll take it." He pours himself some more soda while Upinga is turned around to return the paperclips to their original resting place.

I shake my head twice. "That's quite the story. Quite scary." Because, what if it's a minute tiny detail we don't know about that convinced the Quaneez not to fire? Like, moon in the second house?

"Agreed. But, since that's not a problem we're going to solve today, back to you, Cadet." Conolly takes another sip and sticks out his tongue at the other admiral when he isn't looking. "Your PAD. What about one of the eighth gen? The wrist PAD? So much more convenient. Especially since they now come with holo-control, meaning, you can get actual work done. No need to lug around such a big piece of technology. Small is better." His thumb and index finger form a circle the size of a wrist PAD. "They come with fully integrated scanning options, a large data base, and they look cool."

I shrug. "Love to, but Dad said just because I'm an only child doesn't mean I need to be a spoiled only child." I think his exact words were something along the lines of it won't do me any good if he kept spoiling me. I beg to differ, though. I think it's him trying to correct the over-protective and therefore spoiling behavior he fell into after he got me back, half-broken and with a limp.

"Sounds like your father. How's he doing? Haven't seen him in a while."

Neither have I. I shrug. "He's busy. And when he's home…"

Conolly grimaces. "He's grumpy?"

I give him a thumbs up. "How'd you know?"

The admirals exchange a look, one of the type that makes me feel like I'm missing something. "Especially coming back from Mag-Two, I'd expect him to be quite drained. It's... taxing for him, to say the least." Conolly shoots a questioning glance to Upinga, who gives him a confirming nod. "Also, your father always has been and still is... *nervous* about your career choice."

Nervous? Nope. More like mad at me for it. If I'd say he'd been *trying to convince me* to go into a different direction it would be too soft a phrasing. "Well, I don't think his dad—my grandpa—was happy with Dad joining the USEF. He still did it. Best example I can have to stick to what I want to do."

"Meaning," he says, "you still want to do this? Division Two?"

"Yes, sir." Division Two is right up my alley. It suits my strengths; it suits my personality. Mostly, at least.

Conolly sighs and looks once more up to Admiral Upinga. His colleague closes his eyes for a short moment, then gives an almost imperceptible shake of his head, which in return prompts Conolly to focus on me again. "You might get into situations that feel less than ideal for you." *Hint-hint.*

I pull my shoulders straight and lift my chin. I'm not defined by this one event. "Then I will adjust and overcome whatever problem there is."

"To clarify, I did mean hand-to-hand combat." To Conolly's credit, he says it completely neutral, which is the only reason why I don't feel antagonized. Plus, even to somebody out of the loop, my weakness would be obvious.

I sigh. "I'm doing my best. It's getting easier." Meaning, less sweaty palms, less jitters, and less blanking out when fighting. I'm calling that progress. "Nobody has ever said anything." My grades in self-defense are great at this point, no wonder. Combine OCD with a touch of PTSD, and out comes a moderately possessed student aspiring perfectionism. And since nobody can look inside me, they also don't know I barely keep it together most of those classes.

"Of course, nobody ever said anything, Cadet. You have walls up the size of a medieval barricade. All I'm saying—all we are saying—is that you don't need to choose a service that doesn't suit you completely to prove something."

"I'm not—"

He holds up a hand. "And keep in mind who is heading D-2."

Yeah. *That's* the downside, not my faulty mental programming. I deflate. "You think he's not going to accept me." Because he didn't choose me as a mentee all those years ago, and while I think we're on neutral ground, apparently Admiral Conolly begs to differ.

He cocks an eyebrow. "No, I don't think that. He'd be stupid to not accept you. But I do think he doesn't fit your personality. Your ethics." A slight tick of his jaw accompanies the last sentence.

Admiral Upinga pulls up something on his PAD and, with a flick of his wrist, projects it into the air between us. "Exploration. Discovering new civilizations. First contact. You have a special talent to know what's right, and how to take the correct approach. We need somebody like you to overcome humanity's narrow-mindedness. You're a natural at negotiations, at finding compromises. That's what you're good in, Nonie."

A special talent. Warmth spreads from my core into every cell of my body when I understand what he's saying. "You want me to follow in your footsteps."

Conolly lifts an approving thumb up. "And you should listen to Uncle Zio, Cadet." He chuckles, clearly amused with himself, and ignores Upinga's annoyed expression.

"Chase, shush. Nonie, both of us think you'd be perfect for the diplomatic corps, for OUTREACH." The way Upinga says it, with complete dedication and belief, I gotta say, I'm *this* close to tearing up.

"Really?"

"Really. Alas, we know you're most likely ending up in Division Two, knowing your scores and preferences. But keep in mind those other talents of yours. You're going to make your way, no matter what you choose. You will graduate to become a fantastic officer, and we couldn't be more proud of you."

Okay, now it's really an effort to keep those tears at bay. "Thank you. I—"

"Nu-uh." Conolly opens a drawer. "Don't go all sappy on us. Yet, at least. While we're on the topic, here's a little something, an early graduation gift, since we're both going to be away over that special day." He lays a little rectangular box onto the console in front of me. "You may go sappy now."

Whoa. "A gift?" I look from one to the other. "You're giving me a gift?"

"So it would seem," Admiral Upinga deadpans, his dark eyes as deep as space itself. "It is customary and appropriate to give our best student something she could use to her advantage."

My brain gets hung up on two parts of his sentence. Part one: "Your best student—I'm your only student." Their one and only mentee.

Admiral Conolly grins. "Still makes you our best one."

I roll my eyes. "Okay, I'll take it. So, can I open it? And check whatever is in there that I can *use to my advantage*?" Which would be part two of what my brain got stuck on.

"Of course." Conolly gives it another push over to me.

Within three seconds I have the box open. I mean, who gets gifts from their mentors? Nobody I know, that's for sure. Not even Dad does that. It does feel special. Who would have known that one fateful day during my history class so many years ago would lead to this? Admiral Conolly once said the day I spoke about establishing communication with the Quaneez he saw something in me he was missing in most others: compassion. Empathy. That's why they chose me. And dare I say it has changed me for the better?

The inside of the box is stuffed with tissue paper—and underneath shines the newest of the new PAD wrist computers. My eyes pop wide. No way! "That's why you've been dissing my PAD!" This thing must've cost a small fortune! It's small and sleek, and I bet it projects a screen bigger than any of the old models. "That's... I'm speechless. You shouldn't have—"

Conolly chuckles. "Yeah, we should hav—"

"It's way too expensive!"

"It's fine, Thorburn. We won't go hungry. And I meant it when I said you needed something newer than that fourth gen. You deserve it. Cheers to that." He lifts his Lubbeck's in a toast. "And we're sure you'll make good use of it. It's the 100-centrabyte version. I took the liberty of uploading everything I thought was important for you onto it. Plus," he lowers his voice, "this one was developed specifically for the USEF. It has a nice additional bundle of *features*."

I bite my lower lip. "Thank you. I don't know what to say. Now you turned me into a spoiled only-mentee. Thank you."

Conolly winks once more. "You're very welcome. I gave it my personal spin, because I know you like to be prepared. If you ever feel the need and sudden urge to read up on a ship's manual and security schematics, it's all on there. Especially the schematics. Made sure of that." He keeps a straight face, humor shining from his eyes.

I laugh out once. He got me there, I love to be prepared. Having the rug pulled out from under my feet once makes for a pretty much compulsory need to plan for all possible options. Except boring schematics, maybe. "Yeah, right. I'll look right into those." *Not—* because I can't imagine any scenario in my life I will voluntarily look at the sleep-inducing schematic of any vessel out of my own free will.

"I bet you will," Conolly replies.

"Of course she will," Upinga agrees.

For a moment they keep the serious façade, but only for a moment. Then both of them burst out laughing and I join in.

I love those guys, really do.

Chapter Twenty-Four

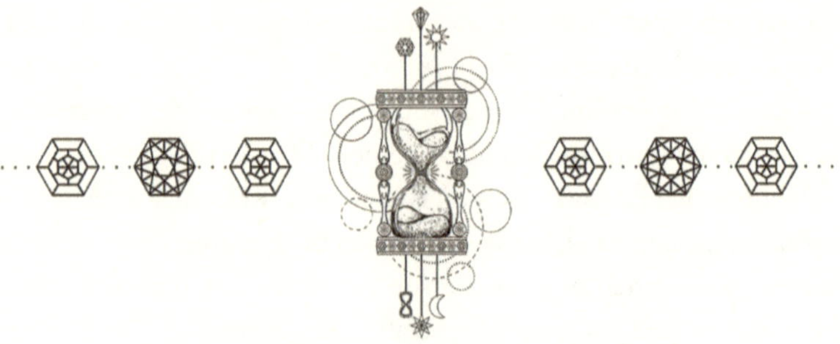

feel like an intruder.

I mean, I *am* one—this isn't my time. I shouldn't be here. Surprisingly, that's not what I mean. It's this sneaking around the *Pioneer*'s hallways during nightshift for the second time within an hour that makes me feel like I'm doing something wrong, even though I'm doing nothing more than going back to my quarters.

Zio offered to walk me back, but I figured being seen with one of the senior officers would make me more memorable to the rest of the crew, meaning, might as well have saved myself all the hours I spent hidden away in my room. And since that's the only successful thing I'm doing in this timeline, hiding away, I should stay an expert at it. I let go of an annoyed sigh.

Since that conversation with Zio and Chase, I can't get rid of this tiny, nagging sensation in the back of my mind telling me something about my-slash-the-*Odysseus'* scan was off—I know, big surprise, right, since it made a whole planet explode. But I wish I knew—

Oh, idiot me—I can check! I toss the scanner Chase gave me in the air and catch it. Appreciate him giving this to me on so many levels. One, it means I can start working on repairs in my own time without anybody's involvement. Two, I don't need to worry about him discovering what he shouldn't discover. And three, he might've done the hard work for me and analyzed my scanners.

I fast-scroll through the data until—

My index finger freezes over the controls.

Interesting modifications, Zio had said. I thought he said it was because of the forty-year advance they have on scanners of this time— but that's not it. The read I'm getting on my scanners doesn't look normal. At all.

"Holy Sun and Stars." Anger crashes over me. That read-out is *so* not normal. The proof of what I suspected stares me right in the face.

What the heck did Grazer do to my scanners? And no matter what, they still shouldn't be able to blow up a planet! A battleship of the newest generation can't do it with all its firepower, so the thought of one little shuttle destroying a whole planet with nothing but a scan is beyond ridiculous. Yes, the drive on Quaneez ships can ignite oxygen-rich atmospheres, but that's still a massive energy requirement and it only blows up the atmosphere. *Only* in quotation marks, by the way. Causing a planetary *core* explosion with nothing but a mere scan sounds about as likely to happen as staring at a corn kernel and expecting it to pop.

But still, it doesn't change that I saw it happen, that I saw what my scan did. The moment I cut it, the core stopped expanding, but the damage was done, the temperature kept rising, and then *boom*. And I have the proof right here, on Chase's scanner.

How much does Grazer hate me to come up with two ways to get me killed? Either by the Quaneez, or by a planetary core explosion, risking humanity losing access to those potentially life-saving plants—

If they truly exist.

Maybe they were never real, and it was nothing but Grazer finding a way to kill two birds with one stone: use me—get rid of me—to extinguish those Quaneez. What a bad judge of character I am. Never would've thought he wanted war. Never would have thought he'd be able to pull off such a cunning, disgusting maneuver that—

Footsteps are coming toward me from around the corner. Ugh. I straighten up, drop my gaze to the floor and lift a hand to my eyes as if I was swiping some non-existent hair out of my face.

Don't look at me. Don't look at me. Don't look—

The footsteps stop.

Aww, come on just keep on goi—

"Nonie?"

I drop my hands at the sound of *his* voice. Of course. Couldn't have been just anybody, had to be *him*. Oh, well. At least it's not another new person who can now claim to have seen time-traveling Nonie. I wave with the hand that did the longest hair-sweep ever. "Kieran. Hey."

He gestures down the hallway. "What'cha doing up here? Couldn't sleep?"

"I could ask you the same thing," I squeak. Why is fate trying to make my job even harder than necessary by throwing Kieran into the equation at every turn?

A tired smile tugs on his lips. "And then I'd tell you that you're right. Sleep is hard to find these days. I…" He shrugs. "It's not important. And don't worry, I'm not judging. I find myself walking around *Pioneer* quite often. It helps me think."

Oh, well. I guess answering his question for once isn't risky. "Well, I wish it would help me think. Was checking on my shuttle. Needed to see how bad it was."

Kieran grimaces. "Pretty bad. I walked over there after dinner with Chase. He wanted to look at it some more."

I point my thumb over my shoulder. "Yeah, ran into him there. Doesn't look good." Especially the scanner readouts, apparently.

His face falls with pity. "No, it doesn't. Not really. But Chase can—"

Holding up my hands I shake my head. "He's busy. Everybody's busy. I'm already abusing your hospitality by staying much longer than I should." No kidding, right? "I don't want him to spend even more time on my ship. I've more or less said goodbye to it, unless I can fix it myself." I add a sad sniffle for conviction.

Kieran tilts his head. "Huh." He pauses, sucks in his lower lip for a moment, then lets go of it. "You look like you could use a pick-me-upper."

"It's so not my day today." And that would be courtesy of finding the proof that Admiral Grazer was *never* on Team Nonie. The smile I give Kieran is more fake than anything else.

He pats my shoulder. "I feel you. So yeah, pick-me-upper it is, captain's version."

"Which means?"

"You'll see. Come on." With a small nod toward the direction he was going in he walks past me. Now, I could *not* walk with him. I could find an excuse, turn around, find the nearest lift and go back to my quarters. It would probably be the smartest move.

On the other hand… the damage is limited, if there is any: I'm not "contaminating" this timeline any more, because he knows me already. And really, a pick-me-upper sounds fantastic.

"Coming," I say and fall in step with him. An easy decision that feels right. I like you, gut feeling.

Kieran leads me down the A-hallway to his quarters close to the front lifts. He palms it open then steps aside for me to enter. "Welcome back."

I enter the room, the lights springing to life the moment the sensors register a warm body. "Thank you." Kieran's quarters, for the second time. It should feel more monumental, because I'm in Captain Kieran Wildason's quarters, but it rather feels… normal. Right, somehow. Maybe because somewhen over the last few days I stopped seeing Kieran as the famous captain he was—is—but as a normal guy, who happens to be the captain of this ship.

The *normal guy* crosses the room toward the living area and pulls his uniform shirt over his head, leaving him in a short-sleeved USEF-issued undershirt. With one quick motion, he tosses the blue uniform top behind the couch. "Don't judge me, I'll clean it up. But this is the best part of the day." He stretches, and there goes *normal*. Each lean muscle is noticeable under this thin shirt, popping up like they wanted to impress me—and they do. My mouth is dry all of a sudden, and my stomach does this hollowing-thing again, sending ripples down into my toes. All I want to do is drink in the sight of him, that strong frame, the dark, tousled hair, the boyish charm that can be so young, and yet so old at the same time. Amazing how he affects me. Scary, but amazing.

Kieran turns toward me when I don't move. "Have a seat." He points at the couch, and I unfreeze. Way to go, Nonie.

"Yeah. S-sure." I shake my head once to clear it. Okay, hormones, we gotta keep it under control, okay?

Kieran grabs two bottles of water from the fridge. "I would love to offer you more of that concoction you brewed the other day, but Chase took it all. I'm afraid you might have to mix more, or else he's going go into withdrawal." He throws one bottle over that I catch.

"No problem. Happy to help your first officer with his addiction." I cringe with the last sentence. Boy, even *Admiral* Conolly still drinks Lubbeck's every day. There's definitely a pattern emerging. Good to know he had developed that little addiction even in my time and without my help. See? Not hurting the timeline.

Kieran falls into the couch on the other side of me. "Ugh." He rakes a hand through his hair. "Long day."

I nod. "If you're coming off your shift only now, no kidding. Any progress with the Quaneez ship?" It feels fair to ask, even if I know the answer.

"Nothing. They must know we're looking for them, and I bet they're evading us. Once in a while, we pick up on a trace of something that could be exhaust, but they sure are difficult to track. I doubt they flew through this nebula, but here we are, trying to find and follow somebody who wants neither nor." He points a thumb over his shoulder at the window, where clouds of blue, purple, and red pass by the window, illuminated by some distant star.

I take a sip of my water. "Still frustrated about that?"

"Beyond belief." He sighs. "Every instinct screams to let them be, that we don't know if we're possibly aggravating them. I wouldn't like somebody stalking and following me, why would they?"

"True." I wish I had the freedom to tell him to listen to his instincts, because he's right. "But your orders still stand, I presume."

"That they do, and they're unlikely to change. There's only so much weight the youngest captain of the fleet can throw into the ring." It sounds bitter, and I'm not surprised. As long as I can remember, Dad has complained about the higher-ups, and to a certain degree it's normal, I guess. It becomes a problem though when the desk jockeys lose touch with reality and don't trust their officers' instincts. Like in this case.

A small smile tugs on the corners of my mouth. Obviously, I can't tell him, but history is going to judge him to have been right, and not Fleet Admiral Jones. Actually, the countdown to a new lead for the

USEF has been initiated. Bye-bye, fleet admiral, so long. "So, what's the plan then?"

"Same old. Find, follow, observe, use every opportunity to make contact, but so far, not even the first task has worked. Obviously," he adds and grimaces with a sip of his water. "Which is why I think this day calls for something else than water. Or rather, something more. I.e., my special nightcap." A mischievous glint lights up in his eyes. "Can you keep a secret, Nonie?"

Can I? "Well, yes. Shouldn't be a problem." Especially in the grand theme of things. I'm all about secrets these days. And, at this point assuming that my theory about Grazer is true, I'm not the only one. Sigh.

"Good to hear." He winks, gets up and sneaks over to the desk. "I told you my dad is an admiral with USEF, right?"

"You did." Admiral Niall Wildason, recipient of the 2246 USEF Expeditionary Medal for his services, and current—at this time—head of the Deep Space Explorative Services. My dad took classes with him when he was still a green cadet at the academy. If I remember correctly, Admiral Wildason died about ten years ago, which would be a good twenty-five years after—

Pressure squeezes my heart tight to the point of pain.

Which would be a good twenty-five years after his son.

Misery washes over me. When people say they don't want to know what the future holds, they're right. I wish I didn't know Kieran's fate. I wish I didn't know when and how he was going to die, but mostly I wish I could tell him and warn him. No, correction: I wish he didn't have to die. It doesn't feel right. Every time I think about his death, it hurts, in a nauseating, dizzying way. So, so unfair.

Kieran carries on at the desk, unaware of my inner freak-out. "So, my dad is not the warm or cuddly type, and neither is he the trusting type. I once heard his first officer say that the day my dad called him by his first name was like he was knighted."

The little chuckle he gives chases away the clouds of misery hanging over me. "Really?" I regard him skeptically. Kieran is so different, I wouldn't have guessed that about his father.

"Really. It only took Dad five years." He rolls his eyes. "Anyway.

Because of his trust issues, he made sure he was always one step ahead of whatever he perceived as necessary. Which means, he liked to keep secrets. And speaking of—this here is top secret. Got it?" He lays a finger across his pursed lips.

"Sure." I wave a lazy hand. At this point, Top Secret is my middle name.

"See? Good things happen to those I trust." Kieran winks at me, wiggles his finger in a dramatic gesture, then brushes his thumb along the edge of his desk. *Click*—a little thin drawer pops open, and I laugh out once.

"No way. A secret drawer?" Integrated into the desk's wooden surface board. Old school, but classy.

Kieran grins. "A secret drawer. Low tech. My dad had one installed on board his ship, the *Exploration*. When I got my own command, he had the same one installed here, as a gift for me. Only, I feel I'm misusing it. I'm sure Dad had important files in there, data discs of whatever was truly important. Alas, in lieu of any such intel, I only keep one thing in here, away from the prying eyes of my chief medical officer…" The jazz hands are back, only this time he reaches into the drawer and retrieves—

"Chocolate?" A thick, large bar of dark chocolate, wrapped in golden-red paper, promising a great depth of flavor.

Kieran rolls his eyes in a mocking way. "I know, I'm such a rebel. Don't tell me you expected booze."

"Booze? Never. I'd be worried if you had some." Starship captain plus alcohol equals problem. Case in point, the USEF *Determination*. Maybe in a couple of millennia, we'll get their intel of what it feels like to be stuck in the event horizon of a black hole.

"Me, too. And FYI, Zio is very strict about sugar on board. Increased inflammatory reaction, dependence, blahblah, don't ask him, he's going to give you an hour-long lecture."

Which I have heard several times already, thank you very much. I keep my face straight. "You don't say."

"Oh, yes. Which is why as the captain, I've taken the step to secure at least some supply of chocolate. And I'm keeping it safe. Hence, the drawer and my secret stash of up to twenty regular-sized bars of chocolate." He falls into the couch again, tears the wrapper open, and breaks off a piece for himself, then hands the rest to me. "Help yourself."

"Thank you." I pop a piece of chocolate into my mouth. Yummy stuff—but the yummiest about it is watching Kieran. It's like a religious experience, really. He closes his eyes and bites off another piece of chocolate, savoring it in his mouth. A little moan leaves his throat, and sue me if it didn't bring something to a coil inside of me. He slides lower into the couch, the epitome of relaxation.

Something warm pools deep inside my body. Huh. Look at that. In this very moment, despite the overall crappiness of the situation, I'm actually… happy. Thank you, Kieran. Thank you, chocolate.

"This," he whispers, "is what I need when the day was rough." One eye pops open. "I hope you're not judging."

"Me?" I swallow. "Are you crazy? You just gained a whole bunch of coolness points with that secret drawer of yours. And the fact that you had chocolate in there… seriously, Kieran. Bonus points." I reach for the bar and tear it out of his hands. "Now share some more, you egoist."

He laughs and lets go of the bounty. "Go for it." He watches me from under his lashes as I pop another piece in my mouth. "Do I still get coolness points when I tell you I have my dad send survival packages with chocolate from Earth, whenever he has time?"

Aww. "He does that?"

"Yeah. He knows Zio—respects him like crazy—but he knows what a stickler he can be."

"I think it's sweet, in more sense than one."

Kieran laughs with my words. "True, but despite his trust issues—or maybe because of them—it's proof my dad and I have always been close."

I look down at my shirt and smooth out a wrinkle with my palm. "Is that because you grew up without your mom?" His eyes pop open, and I hurry to add my explanation. "When you made dinner, it sounded like… it sounded like you were raised by your dad."

"Like you were." His voice is softer than I thought it would be, and it catches me by surprise.

"Yeah, like me." It's not that I ever missed-missed a mother. Well, yes, somehow I did, but then… it was and is normal for me to only have

Dad. It's hard to miss something—or someone—you don't know.

Kieran takes back the chocolate and breaks off another piece for himself. "What happened to your mom? If you don't mind me asking, that is."

"Not at all." There are absolutely no emotions connected to talking about my mother. Again, what you don't know… "Her name was Kelia. She died a day after I was born. Apparently, something went wrong during birth, so…" I smooth out my shirt some more. How we're sending people through space, but still lose women in childbirth is unfathomable to me, but it is what it is. Dad only told me after I bugged and bugged him, when I was twelve or so. He didn't want me to feel guilty. Thing is, I don't. I feel sad that this happened to her, but I don't feel guilty. I wish I met her, I wish I knew more about her, but it's nothing I can change, so whatever.

Although—

Sun and Stars, I *still* haven't truly digested the implications of where, or rather, *when* I am. At this point in time, my dad is still young, and my mom still alive. Maybe they're already together. A little spike of something close to hope shoots through me. If I stay stuck here—*if*, not when—I might just sneak a peek at her. Maybe. In disguise. Or whatever.

Kieran sits up and leans forward. "I'm sorry."

"Thank you, but I'm okay. My dad did more than his best to make up for her." Cue spoiling his only daughter and blending it with academy-style discipline. Talk about mixed messages.

He picks at his cuticles. "My mom died on board the *Journey* when I was seven."

I cringe. Remembering from history lessons versus hearing it from him is different. Much different. "Ouch. Malfunction in the drive, if I remember correctly?" The *Journey*-disaster is the reason why engineering limited jumps to a certain distance. The drive gets too volatile on longer jumps.

"Yeah. I was supposed to be on board with her, but Dad wanted to show me off to his colleagues at a conference, so he took me with him." Sorrow radiates from his body and rolls over to me in palpable waves.

I mirror his position and lean forward. "You miss her."

"Every single day." The way he says it breaks my heart open.

I reach out and lay my hand on his forearm. "My dad used to say, Mom was watching from some plane of the universe we just haven't discovered yet. And he sounded pretty convinced, so…" I wink at him to lighten the mood, and Kieran's eyes light up.

"I like your dad. Sounds like a man I'd like to meet." He realizes his mistake the second the words leave his mouth. "Sorry, I forgot, I—"

"Never mind, Kieran." I wave a hand through the air. He actually has met my dad before and will meet him again, for all I know. I don't want him to feel bad for something he doesn't need to feel bad for.

A flash of lightning shoots through the room. Kieran's head whips over to the window. "Whoa, I guess Zio was right."

"With what?"

His face lights up. "See for yourself. Come on!" He jumps off the couch and crosses the distance to the window in three large strides. "Seriously, come on!"

"All right, coming." I'm off the couch and next to him in five seconds. "What's the emergency?"

He chuckles. "No emergency, but a pretty cool natural phenomenon. Rare, according to Zio, like, once in a lifetime." He points at the clouds of blue, red, and purple nebula passing in front of his knee-to-ceiling window. "Apparently, this gaseous cloud is electrically charged and our presence shifts its charge and releases the energy in flashes."

The Upinga-Effect of Energy-Generation! No way—I mean, I learned about it. Of course I did. But I didn't know *this* must've been when Admiral Upinga came up with the theory behind it.

"Wow," I whisper.

"Yeah, wow," he whispers back. "Computer, lights."

With a little *plop,* I'm sure I'm imagining the lights turn off, leaving us in the dark, the only light the faint colors of the nebula illuminated by the star in the distance.

I've been to space since I was little. I've seen a lot, and I've come to take its vastness and beauty as normal. But this… is different.

The moment the lights are gone, the universe opens up in front of me. The darkness behind me engulfs me, making me feel part of what's going on outside the window, as if the lights had been a barrier. With it gone, the darkness of space claims this room and us standing to watch. The colors of the nebula shine so much brighter than before: how they dance, waft, change, how gaseous tendrils sneak out and wrap themselves around each other to melt into a new color I can't even begin to describe.

Out of nowhere, like a rip in the fabric of space, lightning shoots through a cloud of purple and pink, zig-zagging down a path to our left.

Kieran and I both suck in a breath at the same time.

Another flash of lightning zaps by, this one so close its path burns in my dilated pupils, and it starts a natural phenomenon I've heard about, but never seen. All around us, the gas in the nebula lights up, like a myriad of glowworms had sprung to life. The colors shift from one end of the spectrum to the next, gaining intensity and dying down slowly until the effects of the lightning bolt are gone.

"Holy cow," I whisper. "I always knew space was beautiful, but that…"

Out of the corner of my eye I see him turn toward me. "Stunning," Kieran whispers hoarsely. I swear I hear him swallow after.

Another streak of pure white crackles through the nebula, the short illumination and our reflection in the window confirming what I thought. Kieran isn't looking out the window, but at me.

Heat rises in my cheeks. He—

Lightning jags across the nebula, this one so close it almost hits us. I twitch and turn toward him. "Whoa! Did you see—"

Mistake. Big mistake.

My gaze collides with his, the connection ensnaring me with such intensity, it all but holds me captive. With every breath, the air in the room grows heavier, with every second our eyes stay connected something behind my navel coils and tightens. As if the Upinga-Effect had transferred to organic objects the air between us feels charged. Heated.

Neither of us reacts to the next bolt of lightning. Or the next, or the colors dancing in front of our window. The next flash of light is enough to see the pulse jump in his throat as fast as mine.

Kieran inches closer.

Closer.

Closer, until we're standing toe to toe, barely any space between us.

The whole front of my body tingles from his proximity.

He bites down on his lower lip, and the look he gives me does amazing things to my stomach. Nothing in this world could stop the warmth building in my chest—but it *needs* to stop. This is dangerous territory I'm treading on—

The back of his hand brushes against mine, his soft touch shooting like lightning not just through space, but also through my body. "Nonie," he whispers—and slips his fingers through mine.

My heart pounds so hard, my chest hurts. Kieran glides his thumb over the back of my hand, and I swear something unlocks inside of me. Out of nowhere I feel this need, this yearning, this want for him so intense it causes my lungs to seize up and my heart to skip a beat.

My entire hand—no, entire arm—tingles and buzzes from his touch, its wave moving up my arm, my shoulder, my chest, until my heart tingles and buzzes just the same.

His touch sears through my skin, branding me and setting me on fire. The next brush of his thumb draws a small gasp from my throat, one I had no chance to hold in. Kieran's pupils dilate with that sound. He raises his other hand to my face—slow, so slow, I would have ample time to move away.

But I don't.

I watch his hand come closer to my face, heart jack-hammering away at an unhealthy pace, pumping way too little blood. What am I doing? I need to stop this.

I need to.

I—

The speakers in his quarters spring to life. "Captain to the Bridge. Code Purple. Captain to the Bridge. Code Purple."

Kieran's hand freezes in midair. For one tiny second, he closes his eyes, then lets go a deep sigh. "I'm sorry. I have to—"

"Never mind. Go." I'm dizzy. Seriously. Dizzy. Out of breath.

Kieran squeezes my hand once and gives me an apologetic smile. "Wait for me?" He doesn't stick around for a reply, but turns around and jogs to the door, leaving me alone in his quarters.

Again, for emphasis: *leaving me alone in his quarters.*

At this point, probably the most dangerous place for me to be.

Chapter Twenty-Five

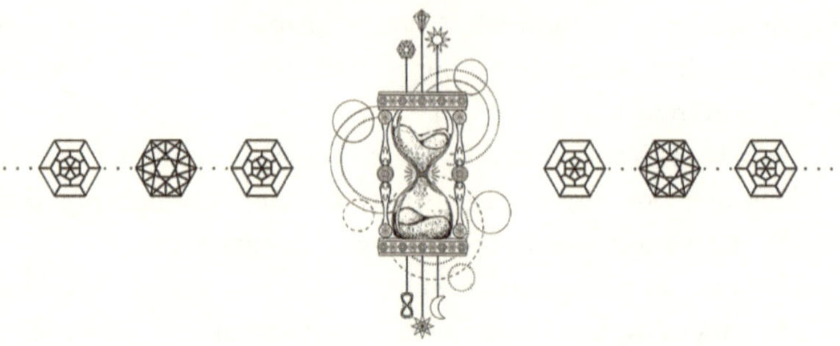

I throw my bag onto the couch in Conolly's and Upinga's office. Adrenaline buzzes through my veins, begging me to let it run free and punch something. *Anything.* My skin pricks with anger and annoyance. What is wrong with people these days? Seriously, what—

"Well, good morning, Cadet. What has your knickers in a bunch?" Admiral Conolly looks up from behind his desk, leveling me with an even gaze.

I let myself fall into the soft, cushy fabric next to my poor, abused school bag. "Nothing." Crossing my arms in front of my chest, I stare at the coffee table as if it personally had offended me.

Hint: the table is innocent. It's everybody else who's just a raging ass—

"Really." Conolly's response is as dry as they come.

"Really." If he looked closely, he might see little puffs of steam rising from my ears. Alas, I don't think he's looking *that* closely. Conolly pushes his chair back and walks over to the coffee table, holding his PAD in one hand and his soda in the other.

He takes a seat in the chair opposite from me. "Then why does your usual sunny disposition equal more a cloudy rainy day?" His voice turns teasing. "Don't tell me you're having boy trouble."

That breaks the tension and I chuckle. "Nope. No worries. None of these idiots would be worth my time." Meaning, they won't come near me with a ten-foot pole: admiral's daughter. *Thorburn's* daughter.

Conolly nods. "Ah. One of those days."

"Yeah, one of those." I can add today to the long list of idiotic stuff that has happened to me at the Academy.

"Care to elaborate?" Conolly lays his PAD face down onto his lap.

Sigh. Might as well. Conolly and Upinga have heard all my complaints. More than my dad. With him I try to hold back. I don't want him to see how some of this stuff affects me, mainly because… "They pulled the admiral's daughter crap again."

His face distorts into a frown. Both of them know my ongoing issues regarding that topic. "Ouch. But in which direction?" Because there are two: the "you as the admiral's daughter get everything blown up your butt, so we hate you," and the "your father, Thorburn, has crazy political opinions. We don't like him, so we don't like you either" categories.

I let go of a big puff of air. No way around it, might as well tell him. "Actually, a mix. Professor Nadjarian gave us an assignment. An essay about war tactics. Pick a year, then come up with comparisons, success rates, suggestions. I picked 2257."

Conolly cocks one bushy eyebrow. "I see."

Of course he would get it right away. That's the year the *Pioneer* was withdrawn from the front lines of the Quaneez War and reassigned to explorative duties, while the *Groundbreaker* took over leading the war efforts.

He takes a sip of his soda. "So what did you come up with that Professor Nadjarian didn't like?"

I look him straight in the eye. "My conclusion was that under Captain Wildason and the *Pioneer*, the emphasis was on avoiding battle and trying to find peace with the Quaneez. Once the *Groundbreaker* and Admiral-then-Captain Grazer took over, it turned into a whole new ballgame. More attacks, higher numbers of soldiers recruited. More Quaneez ships were destroyed, so it was deemed a success—"

His warm eyes stay on me. "But you don't think so." Not a question. A statement. He knows me well.

"No. I don't think so. I think that for the last decades we've been missing out on something important. All we do is fight, with minimal effort to stop the war other than by wiping out the Quaneez. I don't like it, I think it's short of view, and that's what I said." And that's what got me the suggestion to *maybe read up more on history* and *understand the value of our battle maneuvers, and not just trust on my father's position for me to pass my tests.*

Conolly chuckles. "That's so typical you, Nonie. Couldn't hold back, could you?"

A smile tugs at my lips. "Nope. It needed to be said."

"And while I agree with you, you know that Professor Nadjarian is a big fan of Admiral Grazer's. I doubt she would accept an essay openly criticizing the head of Division Two."

I shake my head. "Well, you know I'm a big fan of Grazer's too, and I'm not criticizing him at all. He was put in charge, and he had to try a different approach to win the battle. None of our friendlies really fared any better either."

"Besides the Magellans."

I roll my eyes. "Yes, besides the Magellans." For whatever reason the Quaneez don't hesitate to attack our worlds and ships, or most of the friendlies' worlds and ships, besides Magellans. Proves how little we understand about the Quaneez' reasoning. "But my point was, Grazer's tactic worked from a certain point of view. We died less, they died more. But why did we change it up? Why reassign the *Pioneer* to explorative missions, when we hadn't exhausted all options? From what I can read, you guys were praised like crazy for leading the war." Seriously, I don't get it. Can't be that the *Pioneer* was too old or not top of the line anymore, and therefore a risk during battle.

Conolly lays a hand over his heart. "Thank you very much. And you're right. The admiralty was happy with our work. Everybody was, public included. We connected with several new friendlies and for the most part kept the Quaneez at bay. "

I throw up my hands. "See? So why did they reassign you? They kept their best horse in the stable, their best chance to eventually get peace. They all say we did so well those last decades, but honestly, since the *Pioneer* was removed from war duty—" Conolly holds up a hand, and I stop mid-sentence. "What?"

For the longest second, he regards me in silence until he nods once to himself. "You think you can keep a piece of information to yourself that's beyond your clearance level?"

My eyes widen. Beyond my clearance—I lower my chin in a sharp nod. "Yes, sir."

He holds my gaze. "Good." The short pause following stretches anticipation close to torture. "We requested reassignment."

My jaw drops. "What?" I didn't see that one coming. Requesting reassignment—and getting it granted—from battle is… unheard of. "Why would you do that?"

"You can figure it out yourself. You actually gave the answer already. Look at warfare when the *Pioneer* was in charge versus when the *Groundbreaker* took over."

My brows furrow. "Okay. When the *Groundbreaker* took over, we fought five battles in the first two years with a total of over five billion casualties on both sides." An unimaginable number.

"And before, under the *Pioneer*?"

"Under the *Pioneer*, a greater emphasis was made to avoid casualties of any race, human or Quaneez. The *Pioneer* defended, but did not attack."

"Unless ordered to do so by Command." He points over his shoulder, indicating the admiral's building next door.

And—*click*—the pieces fall into place. "You weren't okay with that." It fits them. Conolly and Upinga have never been the ones to put fighting over finding solutions. Hence, they eventually went into the diplomatic corps.

He nods. "Exactly. We—especially Kieran—were not okay with it. Not at all." Conolly's mentioning of famous Captain Kieran Wildason brings a shiver to run down my spine. It's so awesome they knew him and worked with him. And not just that, from the stories I'm hearing they were friends. Good friends.

Conolly shrugs. "The signs were there, for years. The admiralty wanted this gone—wanted the Quaneez wars over. The faster way from their point of view was by dominating the Quaneez, meaning either our complete victory or them surrendering. And to get there, they needed battles to be won and the enemy's population to be decimated." His lips press into a thin line. "Our captain wouldn't have it. Yes, in the beginning, we responded to their threats and defended ourselves, and from what we know at this point, that might have saved humanity from a swift and detrimental war to our disadvantage."

"You mean the Battle of Balthar." The beginning of the war with the Quaneez. That battle was make it or break it—and the *Pioneer* made it. Had they not, all experts agree the war would've gone in a completely different direction.

"Correct. We had to defend ourselves." Admiral Conolly takes a sip from his Lubbeck's soda. I swear, he drinks a gallon of that every day. "But over time it became clear to us that something else other than pure aggression must be driving the Quaneez to fight us. Only by then our political direction had changed, focusing on victory and dominance instead of negotiations and peaceful efforts, so we requested reassignment to OUTREACH."

And that's where both admirals are still active, in the USEF's most underfunded branch tasked to discover new species and civilizations. Used to be the biggest department, but thanks to the *First Party* and *Humanity First,* they're down to the two admirals and a handful of officers.

My brows furrow. I don't get it. I mean, I get the reassignment-part, but it feels odd. Wrong. That story makes sense, yet it doesn't—and I know I'm not making any sense with that either. What I also don't get is why I haven't heard about it, or why this is beyond my clearance level. "So why was it not made public? Why isn't any of this in the books?" One should think Captain Wildason's refusal to dance to the tunes of the higher-ups would make news. Big news.

Conolly puts his glass down. "Nonie, you know who writes history, right?"

Well, duh. Have heard that one before. "The winner."

"Or the one in power, which equals the USEF. If the most famous captain and crew announced they thought the war tactics were the wrong approach, what do you think would've happened?"

"The USEF would've lost the support of the general public."

"And then funding, and then somebody wouldn't have gotten re-elected, et cetera, et cetera. Exactly. So it was in their best interest to grant reassignment and keep us quiet." He pinches the bridge of his nose with two fingers. "Oh yeah. Those were the good old days."

Oh, holy moly, I can read between the lines. "They bought your silence by granting you reassignment." I don't need to phrase it as a question, because the answer is obvious in Admiral Conolly's frustrated expression.

"They did, because it suited them. But it suited us as well. Kieran chose a good point in time to transfer the *Pioneer* out of the battle zone and into exploration. The *Groundbreaker* was brand new, their newly promoted captain eager for battle and to prove himself. And Grazer never liked to share the spotlight. The USEF didn't need us to fight the Quaneez—they needed us to explore, bring hope to humanity, to help, to rescue, and to be the breath of fresh air and the good news that wasn't coming from the front lines. So we struck a deal. We wanted to focus on finding allies, on finding a way to peace that did not include the annihilation of one or the other race. And in the beginning it went well, but…"

"But?"

"But then Kieran died, and all plans went to hell."

Heavy silence hovers, the kind that hurts even after decades. And while I never knew Captain Wildason, I feel their pain. Maybe not as if it were my own, but I remember that picture from the history class, the one with the empty coffin and the whole crew of the *Pioneer* paying their respects. I remember how white and pale Conolly and Upinga looked. How I thought from the very first time when I saw this image in school and I never thought I'd meet the two officers in person that they didn't look like they lost their captain. They looked like they lost a friend. Kudos to my intuition, because I've never heard anybody talk about a fellow officer like Conolly and Upinga talk about Wildason, like he was a part of them—a part they still miss every day, a part that shouldn't have died. And I agree. It feels wrong for the captain to be gone, like, from the bottom of my heart I feel like he should be here. He could've contributed so much more to USEF and humanity. He could've changed the world.

After a while and a few more sips of Lubbeck's for the admiral I clear my throat. "How… how was he? During those days?" I've heard many a story about Kieran Wildason, so many, I feel like I was there, like I knew him myself. But still, no matter how much the admirals tell me about their former superior officer, I can never get enough of him. Maybe it's fan-girlish or whatever, but I suck up all the information I can get on him, all the stories. Everything.

A wistful smile tugs on the corners of Conolly's lips. "How he was? On fire, Nonie. On fire." He sets the soda down. "Best man I've ever worked with. Best friend I've ever had, together with Admiral Upinga. A man of principle. Against what history may say, he wasn't a typical Mr. Popular. I mean, he was, everybody loved him, but he took no pleasure in it." His eyes take on a distant quality. "Kieran had great leadership skills. A captain who didn't just see black and white, but all the shades in-between. At least with everything USEF. As a private guy you were either in his circle of trust, or out. In fact, there were only three people I can think of besides his father he trusted completely. Let's just say there were a couple of things in his past that made it hard for him to trust anybody, so we got it—and we were lucky enough to call ourselves his friends."

I pull my brows down. "What happened?" *A couple of things in his past…* way to go being ominous.

Conolly gives me a wistful smile. "Not my story to tell."

I barely suppress an eye roll. Who then is going to—

The admiral hands me a glass of Lubbeck's. "Kieran always strived to make the world a better place. Always. And you know, over the recent months, I've come to think he was a bit like you, you know?" He chuckles. "His father was an admiral with USEF, just like yours. No mom—sorry—also just like you. Mostly though, neither of you could sit by quietly when things were not right. And Kieran knew things weren't right. If he were here right now, he'd be the first to call for more peaceful negotiations. Unfortunately, the USEF has lost their footing a little in that regard during the last decades. But yeah, you remind me of him."

My cheeks feel really warm all of a sudden. Happens when you're being compared to the famous Captain Wildason. Even if we had nothing else in common besides an admiral as father, I would feel honored. "Th-thank you, but that's just flattery. You all, including of course Captain Wildason, you all made history. And let me repeat that for emphasis: You. *Made.* History." High-achieving as I am, I'm not delusional or a maniac.

Conolly levels me with an even gaze. "How can you know you won't? And guess what? The funny thing about history is, you don't know you're making it. Oftentimes it's not special while you're at it. Working with Kieran was… normal, in a certain way. It was always us three. That was the default since the academy."

"You three. The Hot-Shot-Trio."

The admiral chuckles with my mentioning of their nickname. "Ah, that name. Been a while."

"Sounds to me like you're missing the attention, sir. They still have those fan clubs, you know?" I wink at him and Conolly laughs.

"Thank you, Cadet, but no, thank you. The publicity helped, but honestly, besides feeling flattered about the attention, we weren't the biggest fans of those clubs. Kieran hated them the most."

"Why?"

A pensive look crosses his face. "Because he had his issues with the public's perception of him. On the one hand, they worshipped him as the youngest captain of the fleet. His heroic deeds. As the protector of humanity. On the other hand, they said his dad—an admiral—paved the way. His results were coincidental. Luck. Now add a fan club that focuses on his looks and women trying to hook up with him…" He shakes his head. "He never trusted any female who came on to him. What sounds like any man's dream was never ours. Never his."

Huh. "I've got to say, until now I thought having a fan club was really cool, but the way you say it it sounds rather sad."

"I think for Kieran it was. To be honest, I ran with it. I was young, in my twenties. But the pretty boy—"

"Pretty boy?"

He shoots me a glance from underneath his lashes. "Don't tell me you don't find him attractive, Cadet. I wouldn't believe you."

I blush. "Well, I mean… yes. But I'm trying really hard to not have that interfere with my judgment, sir." Especially after what he just told me.

"Thank you, Cadet, and rest assured you're not alone with that. I remember hundreds of women lined up in front of the USEF headquarters after we returned from the Dartagnan Mission. Bras were thrown, if I remember correctly."

I grimace. "Seriously?"

"Seriously. Kieran though…" He looks at me with this odd assessing-slash-melancholic glance. "There were no flings. No temptation. Kieran was the most dedicated and faithful person I've ever known. Until he died. So…" He shrugs. "Hot-Shot-Trio or not, fan girls or not, it didn't matter to Kieran."

A different voice comes in from behind me, together with the swooshing sound of the door. "Hot-Shot-Trio? Are you back to reminiscing about the famous, unbeatable, oh-so-awesome Hot-Shot-Trio?" Admiral Upinga sets a mug with steaming hot liquid down on the table and takes a seat next to his colleague, his tone conveying nothing of the disapproving look he gives his friend's Lubbeck's soda. "Those were the good old days. Kind of the only time I've been idolized that much, not that I could've taken advantage of it." He says it completely neutral, but to me, his words sting. Magellans mate for life. So did my dad apparently, because he hasn't dated once since my mom died, as far as I know. But sad joke aside, Magellans do *bond* for life, as they call it. Unfortunately for Admiral Upinga, neither are the Magellans quite inviting him to visit Mag-2, nor are the humans making it any easier: *Human-Magellan mating*, as they so beautifully phrase it, is forbidden by law. No exceptions, not even for somebody as decorated and prestigious as Admiral Upinga.

Conolly's lips press into a thin line. "Gave Nonie a bit of a run-down of that. Got to it after talking about the Battle of Balthar and about Kieran."

A shadow falls over Upinga's face. "Oh." He holds his mug up and blows onto the liquid. The steam smells of something flowery. Must be one of his Magellan teas. "About Kieran as in…?"

"As in why we resigned from the front lines."

Upinga chokes on his tea. "Security clearance, *Admiral?*" He coughs and shakes his head at his colleague.

Conolly shrugs. "She would've found out eventually, Zee. And you know Nonie can handle the information. Can't you?"

I sit up straighter. "Of course, sir." I think I could handle intel beyond my clearance level when I was six. Little bits and pieces of information float around, and if Dad hadn't made it clear how I was supposed to handle those, I might've spilled stuff I wasn't even supposed to know about—not that I understood any of it, but still.

Admiral Conolly clears his throat. "We also talked about Kieran as in him hating the fan clubs." He drums an annoying rhythm onto his thigh as Admiral Upinga takes a careful sip from his tea, the wraps his hands around the cup.

"I see." He arches a brow at his colleague.

Conolly lifts both hands. "Don't look at at me like that, Uncle Zee. That's your area of expertise."

Upinga wraps both hands around the cup, a muscle in his jaw twitching once with the nickname. "Indeed." He regards me with what I call his x-ray vision. Maybe it's because of his larger eyes, or because they're so black they seem bottomless, or it is the proverbial burn in them, but whenever he gives me this intense stare, I feel like he's taking me apart one atom at a time.

Upinga blinks once. "The fan clubs. I think Kieran's unhappiness there resulted from them reminding him of something he couldn't get for himself. As an active USEF captain, it's basically impossible to have a relationship—"

"Unless it's an impossible relationship," Conolly quips, raising his Lubbeck's in salute.

Upinga rolls his eyes. "Yes, *that*, Admiral. Let's talk about making the impossible possible."

Conolly grins. "Well, if anybody could make the impossible possible, it's Nonie, no matter the topic."

My head swivels from one to the other. "Wait, what are we talking about now?" I feel like I missed half of what's being said—because it isn't being said.

Admiral Upinga sighs. "Never mind. As my people tend to say, time will teach you." A shadow falls over his eyes as he repeats, "Time will teach you."

Chapter Twenty-Six

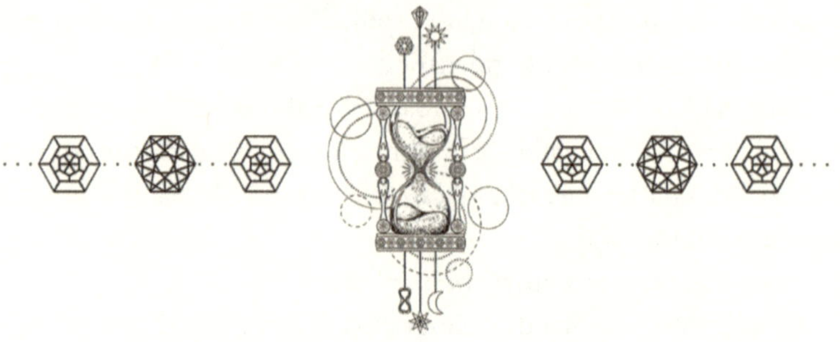

Of course I don't stay in Kieran's quarters and wait for him. As soon as my mental faculties come online again and win the battle against my hormones I'm out the door and all but running down the corridor toward the safety of my quarters. No sound has ever been more soothing than the doors closing behind me and the silence of my little space.

Holy. Freaking. Cow.

My heart hammers so fast it skips nearly every other beat—and it's not from running. What was I thinking? What did I do? Could anybody please smack some sense into me? If the bridge hadn't called him, I doubt I would've stopped what was about to happen, and I know what that was.

I let myself fall against the door and slide down until I sit on my butt.

Yeah. I know what that was.

And while I wish I could say me wanting for him to take that step was a momentary lapse in sanity, I also know it wasn't. I wasn't brain amputated in there. It's not like I could forget where and when I am and what repercussions my actions could hold, but—

Exactly: *but*. But I chose to ignore that because being with Kieran feels right. Good. No, scratch that: *great*. I groan, draw in my legs, and let my head drop to my knees. Let's face it, I'm in deep. A sarcastic chuckle tears from my throat. Strong observation, Thorburn, really. So astute.

But nonetheless correct on more than one level.

Kieran is my Achilles heel in this time. Without much exaggeration, I'm developing a constant craving for his presence, and it's getting worse every day, eating away at my defenses. Every time I'm near him, I feel this magnetic attraction, like he was pulling me in and there was no way to resist. All I want to do is give in and see where it takes me—where it takes us—but that's just plain stupid. There is no *us*. There is nowhere it could take us.

It's a dead end.

I cringe. Bad phrasing, because it could literally be a dead end, and then I not only ruined humanity's chances for curing the virus and survival, but I might've even altered the timeline and done worse damage. Sounds familiar.

I cannot underestimate the danger Kieran poses to me, and the danger I pose to the timeline.

And still, during that one minute in front of the nebula… All I wanted was for him to make a move. And if he had, I wouldn't have stopped him. Without being too melodramatic or thinking too highly of myself, that make-out session would have changed the course of the universe.

One kiss and it would've killed mine.

And I can't let that happen.

Fact is, this is a crossroads. For all I know, I'm stuck in this time forever. Yes, I got here somehow, but that doesn't mean there's a return ticket. I still don't have a clue what brought me here or how to replicate it, which means I have to assume I'm going to stay in this time until I die. Then, of course, I have a responsibility to not disturb what's about to happen. This is what's been giving me a headache ever since I arrived: I can't alter the past—my past—without affecting the future. Whatever I do here ripples forward and changes the course of what is supposed to happen. And granted, my impact might be minimal and not make any difference at all, but what if it isn't? What if my presence here, if any actions here alter the timeline as I know it? I can't risk that. I'm not willing to play God—or Russian roulette—with fate.

I lift my head off my knees and tap the screen on my wrist PAD. "Search: Kieran Wildason. Girlfriend."

PADdy thinks for half a second, then projects its answer into the air in front of me: *No entries found.*

Re-phrasing. "Kieran Wildason. Relationships."

No entries found.

"Kieran Wildason. Affair." That word sounds dirty and makes me feel a bit stalker-ish, like I was invading his privacy.

No entries found.

I blow out a puff of air. What was I hoping to find? An entry about me? How was that supposed to be there, genius? Or maybe something else, like the proof he had a girlfriend or that he had none? What is either or going to tell me or help me with? I know he was never interested in any of the female fans as the *Pioneer*'s captain. The admirals told me at one point, when Captain Wildason was a topic, as so often. So why do I bother, besides to torture myself?

Another groan leaves my throat, this one carrying an extra serving of self-made misery. Whatever his lack of girlfriends means, I have given myself the answer. I can't risk getting involved with Kieran. He is too much of an important figure in history. What if I screw him up? No matter what kind of relationship we'd have, it would change him. What if he makes a different decision because of me? Because I'm on board, or because we broke up, or because of who knows what? A relationship will change him, and it might change the timeline.

Conclusion, not that it's a news flash: I can't get involved with him—no more than I already have, which… might be too much already.

Pain knots itself around my heart and squeezes tight.

Hands off the captain, Lieutenant.

It's my only chance to keep the timeline intact.

Chapter Twenty-Seven

For the last day I've been proactive, and boy, does it feel good. Or, okay, let's put it this way… it feels better than sitting in my quarters and hiding from Kieran like a coward. No, wait, rephrasing again. It feels better than waiting for fate to decide how to toy with me next, because in a matter of speaking, I've still been hiding from Kieran, only under the *Odysseus*, or in her engine compartment. Nothing helps to distract from unwanted thoughts like something else to focus on, preferably something that could improve my overall situation.

So look at me, what a responsible and mature person I am, staying away from Kieran *and* trying to save the timeline Grazer risked by pulling this stunt on me.

I glance down at PADdy. It's late, twenty-three hours and change, and everybody should be in bed or on shift. According to my PAD's log and the calm traveling of the *Pioneer,* we're still searching for the Quaneez without anything new to report, which translates into Kieran hopefully sleeping in his quarters at this time.

Meaning, break time is over. Time to get back to work.

I sneak out into the empty hallway, half expecting to see Kieran standing in front of my doors, because… I was mostly at the *Odysseus* and not in that much, and my door bell rang twice in the last twenty-two hours, and that's only when I was in. Not that I'd been counting the time since the impossible almost happened.

It rang twice and I didn't answer it either time.

Coward.

Nope, mature time traveller.

Anyway.

Priorities: The *Odysseus* is coming along fairly okay-ish, considering I'm no mechanic and have only been at it for a few hours. Admiral Conolly stored tons of data on PADdy when they gifted it to me, and while there isn't much that stayed intact on it in regard to time travel, there's more than enough in regard to ship manuals. Maybe, if I'm really lucky for a change, she'll at least fly after a few more hours of work. I don't expect wonders, just the basics. Please.

I'm so deep in thought I notice the footsteps coming around the corner too late to hide, so I stop at the window on my right looking into the gym, waiting for the person to pass. Luckily for me, somebody's sparring, so standing here in the middle of the night and looking into the gym doesn't seem too odd. And the two men dressed head to toe in full sparring gear are good enough to warrant some attention: Kicks are flying, punches being exchanged and dodged, everything happening at a dazzling speed.

The steps come closer, closer—and stop right behind me. Of course they do. Ugh. Somebody chuckles. "Man, are they at it again?"

I ignore him. Just move on, dude. Nothing to see here—

One of the guys fighting unleashes a spinning heel kick that hits its target dead center.

The guy behind me whistles. "Nice."

As much as his presence annoys me, agreed. Those two are good—at a pretty high level. One of them is dressed in a black shirt, the other in a blue, both wearing protective head gear, shin guards, and all the other necessary shebang one needs when fighting with somebody who knows what they're doing. And they do, especially the guy in black. Looks like even four decades ago, the academy taught them their golden nugget of wisdom: in your mind you've got to know without a doubt you're going to win, or else you won't. And Black Shirt's body language looks exactly like that: Determined. Un-shakable. Like he's got this. His attacks are too fast to be blocked by the other guy, let alone countered.

Whenever he lands another punch, he follows up with two or three more strikes, until Blue Shirt is too distracted by an uppercut to his spleen and drops his defense. That's when Black Shirt moves in and throws him over his hip.

Blue Shirt lands with a splat and a groan I can hear through the window.

"Nice, Captain!" The guy behind me pumps a fist.

My hands fly up to cover the little gasp. Captain? Kieran?

He must've picked up on my movement, because he glides around until he can see us, and the second he does, his face lights up behind the headgear with the most joyful expression. I'd be lying if I said it didn't bring my cheeks to warm. Which means, I better get going—

Kieran points at the door. *Come on in*, he mouthes and waves at me.

The guy behind me chuckles. "Looks like captain would like to see you. Nonie, right?" He pats my shoulder, and now I turn.

"Y-yes—Hayes?" From the bridge, science station?

"Yup. Go on in. Captain's orders." He directs me toward the doors.

I dig my heels in. "No, I need to—"

"To do what the captain says. From experience, I can tell you that if you don't, your next sparring session won't be pleasant." His palm hits the reader next to the door. "There you go, kiddo. Have fun in there." He chuckles again, and with a push, he shoves me over the threshold into the gym.

I stumble in, scrambling to gather my bearings, heart erratically pounding, especially when I take a breath and catch his scent—Kieran's scent—hanging in the air. The same familiar ache pools in my soul and ties it into Gordian knots.

Blue Shirt—clearly Chase—groans some more. "Really? Witnesses to my humiliation?" He fumbles for the headgear's velcro.

I point at the door. "Yeah, I should probably leave," I croak. "Sorry to interrupt." I spin on my heels—

"Stay, Nonie." It comes out part order, part request, and my legs lock on their own accord. Screw you, USEF training.

Kieran takes off his headgear and uses his shoulder to wipe some sweat off his forehead. "And come on, Chase. It's in the captain's job description to be the best on board." He winks at me, and I drop my gaze as fast as I can. Not getting myself into deep waters here.

Chase curls into a ball on his side. "Not in self-defense. That's my job description."

Kieran grins, and that grin… Maybe I should get my head checked. Or my stomach. Or my sanity, for heaven's sake!

"Pet peeve, you know that."

Chase pushes himself up to sitting and massages the area of his spleen. "Pet peeve my butt." He works himself to a standing position, favoring his left side. "Ow. You need a new hobby." He bro-shoves Kieran in the shoulder and staggers off the mat. "I'm done for tonight, thank you very much."

Kieran's face falls. "What? We just started!"

Chase cuts an eye at him. "Feels like I just got finished."

"But we got the gym for another hour!"

"It's not as if we had to pay for it. And if you're so eager, show Nonie some self-defense moves. Always comes in handy." He points his thumb over his shoulder at me while limping to the door, favoring his left side with every step.

"Me?" I squeak. Nope. Nope. Not a good idea. I take two steps backward. "Maybe—"

"Maybe you should stay where you are, Nonie." Chase gives me a stern look that melts into something the slightest bit mischievous as he turns to the door, mumbling to himself under his breath.

As the doors close behind him, silence hovers, and for the first time with Kieran it's a bit awkward.

Kieran scratches his head, then drops his hand. "He doesn't like to lose."

I swallow hard. "I can tell." It's a trait Admiral Conolly still possesses forty years later. It's one of the reasons we get along so well. He wants me to be best at whatever I do, and I thrive with that competitive spirit. With most topics. Usually.

Not today though.

Silence resumes, and it's heavy. Last night hangs in the air, unresolved, but a dead end from where I'm coming from.

Kieran clears his throat. "So… you wanna give it a go?" He works a hand through his hair.

"What now?"

"A little self-defense practice?"

I cringe. "No, thank you." I'll pass. For many reasons.

"Why?" He comes closer, palms open and out toward me. "Afraid you're going to hurt me?"

"N-no." With every step he comes closer, I take one back.

"Afraid I'm going to hurt you?"

I shake my head. I can hold my own, I know that. I started Krav Maga when I was nine. Learning how to defend myself was the only thing that brought at least some kind of security back into my life. Lots of bruises came with training at that level, so being hurt is not what I'm worried about. None of the physical bruises can hold a candle to the bruises left on my soul.

"Okay. Then let's do this."

My back hits the wall, and Kieran stops about half an arm's length away from me. Heat radiates off his body, and I swear mine comes close to spontaneous combustion as his gaze travels over me. My heart thuds against my chest with a strength surely bruising me on the inside, and I don't think I'm breathing.

At all.

Kieran holds out a hand. "Join me? On the mat? Please?"

That careful, almost begging last word, more whispered than spoken loud, it tugs on a heart string and reflex takes over. I reach out and put my hand in his. "Okay." The second my skin touches his, a warm sensation spreads through me. This is right. It feels right. Which, again, means I need my sanity checked.

Kieran's smile travels up to his eyes and lights them up. "Awesome! I can show you some simple moves—"

"It's fine. I know how to spar," I blurt out.

Interest sparks in his eyes. "Really?"

"Really." Add the academy training to the Krav Maga, and I know how to handle an opponent, no matter their size. Granted, after seeing Kieran fight, I don't expect winning, but I expect not losing too badly.

I don't dwell on that though long enough to admit to myself I may know how to handle an opponent, but still don't know how to handle myself during a fight.

Kieran leads me to the mat. His thumb does a swiping motion across the back of my hand that shoots spikes of electricity all the way down to my toes. "Your dad, I assume?"

Easiest explanation. "Yeah."

Kieran lets go of my hand and curls his finger at me. "Then get your butt onto this matt, Nonie Magnetta, and show me how it's done." The way he looks at me… There's more behind his words. Something that turned yesterday awkward. Something that's been there since I met him, something that I don't want to acknowledge, because I can't.

Still, I nod and crack my knuckles. "Challenge accepted. Don't complain later I didn't warn you." Look at me. I'm the freakin' queen of fake it until you make it.

He laughs softly. "I'll keep that in mind."

A tickle of panic rises inside my chest. What if I can't handle it? What if—

No.

I will handle it. Like at the academy. Walls up, and off we go. I slip out of my shoes and sweater and begin with some warm-up jumping jacks. I'm not going into this cold. Kieran grabs another pair of MMA-gloves from a box in the other corner and holds them up. "Comfortable with these?"

As comfortable as I can be. "Sure."

Kieran jogs back and hands me the gloves. "Karate? Taekwondo? Muay Thai?"

"A little bit of everything." I slip into the gloves and get into a fighting stance. "Ready." On the outside, I'm calm, on the inside… as well. Deep breath, Thorburn. You've got this. This is routine.

Jitters run down my spine, but for a change I'd blame them on Kieran. Let's be honest here. Sparring is a battle I had to fight, literally, with every class I took since I was nine. I do spar, I do fight, but it's never with pleasure. It can't be. But then, a tiny voice whispers in my ear, this is not about the fighting. It's about Kieran.

Heat invades my cheeks and I raise my gloved fists to cover the blush. It's *not* about Kieran. Will not be about Kieran. Ever.

We touch gloves, and it's *on*. Kieran begins to move, testing my reactions. I keep the distance between us. Am not running into an attack in the first few seconds. Gotta get my footing and avoid going down into ground fight at all costs. Yes, I saw him fight, but I haven't felt him fight yet. Big difference. He throws a jab at me I block without a problem. A test balloon.

Jab.

Another one. Blocked.

Jab.

Blocked.

Cross.

Harder. Good punch, but good defense on my part, too.

Jab-cross!

Ah, now we're talking.

The more my defense holds, the faster Kieran's punches are coming, and the less he's pulling them. Guess he's figuring out I won't go belly-up right away. Time to counter.

With his next move forward, I sidestep his attack and counter with a round house kick to his mid-section. He blocks it just in time, but I do see that gleam light up in his eyes. Oh, yeah. We're so on.

As if my kick had broken the restraint, Kieran cranks it up.

But so do I. It's an automated response born from years of training and the compulsive need to never lose again.

Within a few seconds, this is a full-on sparring session, no different from the one he had with Chase.

And for the first time ever... I'm kind of having fun with it. Every move is like a well-coordinated dance. Attack, evade, counterattack, move, test, attack. Within less than a minute, both of us are breathing heavier, and it's no surprise. I'm on the balls of my feet, giving my best to be fast and unpredictable. Same with Kieran. He feints a combination punch but goes for a kick I block so hard, I know I'm going to have a picture-worthy bruise on my shin when this is over.

But so is he.

I catch his kick to my midsection with an *oomph*-sound. Dang it. His legs are too long for me. Keeping him at a distance has me at a disadvantage, and I don't like that. Well, then I'll have to turn that around.

With the next attack, I don't move back, but forward. My uppercut hits him right in the solar plexus. The same *oomph*-sound breaks from his throat as he doubles over the slightest bit—

It's all I need.

I wrap one arm around his body and grab his sleeve with other. A quick turn of my hips, a quick squat and buck, and Kieran is flying over me and landing on the mat with a smack rivaling Chase's from a few minutes ago.

Yes!

Admiral Conolly's words from my first year at the academy come to mind. "Being smaller than your opponent doesn't matter. Using it to your advantage does." Words of wisdom I soaked up and made my own.

For a split second, I hesitate. Should I go to the ground—

Yes.

I keep holding on to his arm and drop to the ground. Armbar next—

Problem is, Kieran also trained at the academy. And with Conolly, young Conolly. He knows what's coming, and before I can get a good grip, he rolls over and yanks his arms free. In the last second, I close my guard around his waist, trapping him between my legs.

But it traps me as well—on my back.

A raspy sound breaks from my throat.

Doesn't matter. Doesn't matter. I'm good from here. I can handle it.

My next breath comes in even wheezier.

Ignore it, Nonie. Could be worse.

But also could be better.

I aim at his face and punch—

Kieran's eyes widen as he deflects my attack. Lightning quick, he drops down, bringing his upper body to squish into mine.

Too close.

My sharp breath inhales his scent—vanilla and something manly I've come to identify as Kieran—but doesn't bring any oxygen.

Must get out of here.

Too tight.

Can't breathe. Too tight.

Must get out—

He passes my guard and comes into a mounted position on my stomach. His hands find my shoulders, glide down my arms—

Must. Get. Out. I buck my hips and wrap my arms around his back. Avoid punches. Get out.

Get. *Out!*

The body on top of me tenses against my movement.

Hands find my wrists and pull them down.

No.

No, no, no, don't hold me—

Weight is shifted. Pinning my hands to the ground.

Fingers tighten around my wrists. Dig into my skin.

Ground is so cold. Bites into my skin.

Hungry. Afraid. Going to die here. Die—

Fingers relax. "Nonie? Come on. Fight me."

Fight—

Fight.

I'm not giving up.

I'm not helpless. Never again.

A deep, menacing growl breaks from my throat.

Not. Helpless.

With one lightning fast, chopped movement, I buck my hips. Yank my arms down my body.

The man didn't expect it.

My counter throws him up and over my shoulder, when I turn the buck into a roll.

"Holy—" Something flashes in his eyes, some kind of awareness mixed with a hint of… fear?

It doesn't register to me. My mind has taken me to a different place, a place long blown up and gone, but still so ever-present when I close my eyes. So dark, so cold, so full of fear. *Of death.*

I finish the roll and come up on top, the man under me. Before he has a chance to recover, I ram my knee into the inside of his thigh. I'm not being taken into his guard. Never again.

"Ng-uh," he grunts, body curling up in an automatic movement when I stretch him too far.

Never again.

I climb out of his guard, keeping my weight on the man who took me, who wants me dead. This is my one chance for payback. For freedom.

I grab his collar with my left hand and ram my right fist down into his face. Damn him, he deflects my punch.

"Whoa! Nonie, sto—"

Harder. Must punch harder.

"Shit! Nonie—"

Harder! I let go of his shirt and unleash a flurry of punches at the guy who's in my nightmares, who's—

"Nonie! Nonie! Nonie! Damn it, I—" He covers, he deflects, but he doesn't punch back. It's my chance. My only chance. I can—

Barely dodging my last punch, he jackknifes up, wraps both arms around me and lets himself fall back, pulling me down pinned to his chest in an improvised bear hug.

No! "Let go!" A scream tears from my throat, carrying all the pain, all the worry, all the suffering I had to endure at the hands of this man.

"Easy, Nonie. Easy—"

"Let. Go!" I grunt into his ear, I twist my body, stretch my legs trying to roll off of him, but he has me tight and my arms trapped. "Let go!" Images dance in front of my inner eye, images I don't want to see, I don't need to see to feel the panic rising, suffocating me one memory at a time. And it turns me into a crazy banshee. The arms around me hold me like a bench vise. He keeps himself so close to me, I can't even head-butt him. But I want to. I *need* to. Like a switch flipped, all conscious thought is turned off and panic mode initiated. I buck, twist, turn, and try everything in my power to get out of his hold, because if I don't, I'm going to be dead, I'm going—

"Shh..!" His lips brush over my ear with his soft sound. "Shhh… It's okay. It's okay. You're safe. It's all right. You're safe—"

I'm not safe. I—

The arms hold tighter, but one hand sneaks up to the back of my head, into my hair. "I've got you. You're safe. I've got you, Nonie."

Such a soft voice. Not harsh, not dangerous.

Such a soft touch on my head.

Such a soft brush of his lips across my ear. "It's okay. I got you,

Nonie."

I blink.

What—

Like a fog parted and the sun came through, the panic retreats one painful tendril at a time.

Sun and Stars, what was that? A strangulated sob breaks from my throat, one I couldn't suppress even if I wanted to. My heart hasn't caught up with my mind yet and hammers away at an unhealthy dizzying speed, but the rest of me is exhausted. I was *there*. In my mind, I was *there*.

Only this time, *she* didn't come and save me.

Chapter Twenty-Eight

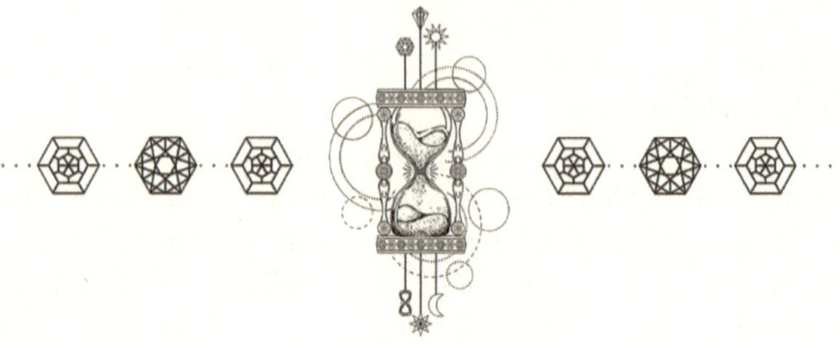

I 've always been good at multitasking, but I've got to say, the last months at the academy have improved that greatly. Perfected it, actually. At this point I can walk, look at my PAD, read and understand what's on it while walking to whichever destination I need to go, *and* keep an eye out for superior officers to salute.

Mad skills? I got them.

I doubt I'd survive the academy without them.

Last week, the USEF made a news announcement we had discovered another planet suitable for colonization. Nothing too fancy, a regular class C planet, but with both, a longer orbit around its sun and a slower rotation around its axis. Once it's terraformed, imagine having a year of five hundred days, and a day of thirty-six hours. Heaven. I might actually get more than five hours of sleep every night then.

I pass a group of third-year students on their way to flight school. No need to look at them to feel their eyes on me, and no need to peel my ears to hear their comments.

…so unfair she took two mentors… nothing special about her… because of her dad, I'm sure…

Ah. I can see word has spread already. Two days later, and I'm the talk of the academy. Again. Fantastic.

One of the students does a hard, sudden swerve into me as we pass, ramming his shoulder into mine. My PAD goes flying to the ground, skitting over the gravel, display down.

"Oops," he says, then snickers as he gets high-fived by his friends.

For one moment, one teeny-tiny moment, I consider ramming my fist into his face. Then common sense and reality kick in and I don't. That's not me. Hasn't been me for a while. So I do what people told me to do since I was nine: I ignore him. Yes, hitting him would make me feel better, but the fallout after isn't worth it. Not difficult to see where this would go: him and his friends would swear he accidentally bumped into me and I retaliated with an uppercut to his chin. I'd get detention, a permanent mark in my file, and my dad another worry on the list of worries he already carries. Imagine explaining that to him. I hate fight class, but pick fights on campus.

No, thank you.

I pick up my PAD with a sigh and wipe its display clean. Oh, great. A stupid scratch right across the display. Fantastic. The group of third-years moves on, once in a while one of them throwing a glance back to see how I react. Yeah, you showed me. Idiots.

I wonder if they had had the guts to pull this off any closer to my dad's office, but then I know the answer: nope.

And it doesn't matter.

I enter the admirals' building my dad's office is in. As annoying as it can be to be known as Thorburn's daughter, at least I can see my dad when he is actually in and not somewhere for a conference, a meeting, or off-planet.

I take the glass elevator on the outside of the building to the thirty-third floor. Many of my professors have their offices here, so I keep my PAD in my bag for now. Don't want to seem too dorky or impolite.

As I walk down the hallway to Dad's office, I hope he's feeling okay. He just came back from Mag-2, and boy, they must work him hard over there. I don't remember him ever returning from one of those trips and not looking about a decade older and like he just got his wisdom teeth removed—without anaesthesia. Usually—

The door to my dad's office opens just before I was ready to knock, and out steps—

"Admiral Conolly." I snap to attention, then see the second, much taller figure exiting behind him. "Admiral Upinga. Sirs." What are they doing in Dad's office? Dad never mentioned working with them, besides serving on the same ship when he was a junior ensign, I think. But nothing beyond that—and I know, because I would totally have been into it if he had.

Admiral Conolly's eyebrows fly up to his hairline. "Cadet Thorburn. Uhh, hi. How'ya doing?" He moves out of the door into the hallway.

"Fine, sir. Yourself?"

"Fine." I get a quick smile, but it comes with a flash of *something* in his eyes I know all too well: pity. I've seen it in my dad's eyes, my counselor's eyes, my principal's eyes. Everybody who *knew* looked at me like that, and I've hated it every single time.

Admiral Upinga walks past me. "Cadet." Him I can't read, or at least he doesn't give away that he knows the one defining story of my life. Maybe Dad didn't—

My head whips around to my dad sitting behind his desk. One look and it's clear he did: guilt. He looks guilty under all that fatigue and malaise courtesy of his latest stressful trip to Mag-2. Does it mean I feel sorry for him? Right now, no. Not in the least.

I pull on all the professionalism I have. "Have a great day, Admirals."

There's that pitiful smile again, partially overplayed by what I think is Admiral Conolly's general upbeat nature. "We will. See you next week for mentoring."

"Yes, sir." I wait until both have turned away from me and are walking down the hallway. Then I step into my dad's office and close the door. Oh, he knows he's in trouble. I get that sheepish look from under his lashes.

"Nonie—"

"You told them!" I point one accusing finger in the general direction of the hallway. "I can't believe it, Dad, you told them!"

Dad flinches. "It's not what you think—"

"No? It isn't? Then tell me why Admiral Conolly looked at me the way he did! Something has changed, and right after you talked to my two new mentors? You told them!" Unbelievable! I thought we were over this, done with it. At school, yes, I understand. But here? Years after? He knows I want this story to be gone!

Dad raises both hands. "Calm down, Nonie. Sit."

"I don't want to sit!"

"Sit, *Cadet*." He points at the chair. Not a suggestion. An order.

My lips press into a thin line. "Yes, *sir*." Grr.

Dad leans forward onto his desk, hands folded in front of him. "Take a deep breath, Nonie. It's okay. It's all okay. You hear me? They are your mentors. They… need to know certain things about you."

Certain things. "May I speak freely, sir?" He wants to play that game, I can play it too.

He shoots me an annoyed glance. "Yes, child of mine, you may speak freely."

Thank you. I throw my hands up. "They did not need to know *certain things* about me, Dad! It's in the past—"

Dad harrumphs once. "That it is all right, but it won't stay there, Nonie. It won't stay in the past, I can guarantee that to you. Don't you get it? Things can happen—"

"Things won't happen, Dad! I'm not the helpless little girl I was—"

"I know that! But if you can improve your skills, so can they! And I'd rather have the two people you should trust the most on this campus besides me knowing everything—and I mean *everything*—about you and keeping you safe rather than risk anything happening to you ever again! Do I make myself clear?" Fire shoots from his eyes, and I deflate.

"Yes, Dad." I know he wants what's best for me, but sometimes I wish he'd dial it down a notch. When Dad goes into full Nonie-protection mode, nothing is impossib—

Crap.

I cock my head, blood pressure back up to one-eighty from the one possibility that would be worse than telling them my story. Way worse. "Please tell me you didn't ask Admirals Conolly and Upinga to become my mentors. Please tell me you didn't." It would be so, so typical. I can see him pulling strings. He knows how much mentoring means to me—to any cadet—and he knows his last name's affect on my career. I wouldn't put it beneath him to ask somebody—

"Nonie." He gives me *that* look, the one I get whenever I say something I should know better. "Really. I am protective of you, which is, by the way, in my job description, but I am not messing with your academy life. I told you when you applied, you're on your own here, and it is for your benefit if I stay away from you as much as possible." His face distorts with those last words. He hates the latter part, but as we have seen on that one fateful day so many years ago, a strong political stance comes with a lot of enemies.

I blow out a puff of air. "Oh. Okay. Right. Sorry, Dad."

He nods, a small smile tugging at the corners of his mouth. "And I'm sorry I blindsided you by talking to the admirals. You have to understand though, I needed to check in with them, I…" He searches for words, mouth opening and closing, before he sighs. "I had to. It was time."

"It's okay, Dad. I'm sorry I overreacted. I get it. I may not like it, but I get it." I stick my tongue out at him. "As long as I know I got my mentors on my own, and not because my dad pitied them into choosing me—"

The smile turns wistful. "No worries. That was all you, Nonie. Everything you did. They wanted you to be their mentee. Nobody else. It was all you."

Chapter Twenty-Nine

All tension leaves my body, and I collapse on top of Kieran.

Kieran.

Not *the man*.

How could I mistake him for—

Yeah. PTSD. Triggered, at its finest. So much for the academy's assessment and clearance.

The next breath comes out chopped, and it hurts.

"It's okay, Nonie." Kieran keeps his hold on me, and only slowly does he loosen the pressure around my arms. He never lets go of my head, the mesmerizing play of his fingers bringing goosebumps to my skin. He never stops murmuring sweet nothings into my ear.

And now that I'm back to normal, it sets me on fire.

Every brush of his lips against my ear shoots down to my core, igniting it like a supernova, every gentle, massaging touch of his fingers in my hair brings a strange kind of heat to build up deep inside my body, and every second we're flush on top of each other sends sparks down to my toes.

I feel the same tug in my belly, the same yearning, the same longing as before, all morphing into a sensation I can't name—or better, I still don't want to name. It comes with too many complications to be acknowledged, but still it's there, lighting me up from the inside.

It takes me a good half minute, but eventually, I notice Kieran's touch has changed from protective and soothing to… something else. Something warmer, softer, and a whole lot hotter.

What was a strong grip on my head has turned into a play of his fingers with my hair. The arm wrapped around my back has slid down to lie on my waist, his fingers skimming over the area in circles. And best of all, it's not just my heart racing. I swear, I feel every beat of his like a drum through his chest as it reverberates into my body until I can't tell which beat is his and which is mine. His chest rises and falls out of rhythm, each and every warm breath stirring my hair.

I close my eyes as a series of shivers dances over my skin. This is unreal, what I'm feeling. What I think Kieran might be feeling. It's completely unreal.

And it can't happen.

No matter how badly I want to push my body harder into his, no matter how right it feels—it is wrong.

This is neither the time, nor the man for me to fall for.

Kieran curls his hand around my neck, and my heart pounds so hard my chest hurts.

I need to stop this, before I can't anymore.

With an effort close to moving a mountain, I push myself up and roll off him to the side. His fingers grace over my flank when I move, and those shivers from before turn into chills dancing down my spine. For a moment I lie on my back, panting. I might be physically separated from him, but I'm still drawn to him. I feel him lying next to me, just like I feel him turn his head and look at me.

Not meeting his gaze is harder than it should be.

I close my eyes and bite on my lower lip. Sit up, Nonie. Now.

Obeying my own command, I crunch up to sitting. What the heck was that? My melt down, and then… yeah. *That.* I rub a palm over my eyes. Intense. Everything.

Rustling next to me tells me Kieran is sitting up as well. I'm still not looking. If I did, I don't know what he would see in my eyes. Actually, I do know, and it's nothing I can afford to have him see. Regret lodges in my throat, thick and heavy and hard to swallow down.

Kieran scoots around until he's in front of me, legs criss-cross applesauce, just like me. He taps a finger onto my knee. "You okay?"

Okay for real? No. Okay for now? "Yeah," I say, and nothing more. Not trusting my voice yet.

His finger lingers for a second, then drops off, leaving my stomach hollow. "Want to tell me what that was about?"

Oh, hell to the no! I'm not pouring out my heart about him—

"When we fought," he clarifies, as if he had read my mind.

Oh. *That.*

I swallow hard. Problem is, *that*'s not any easier to explain.

He waits, but when I don't reply, he gives my shoulder a slight shove. "Talk, Nonie. That's an order." He peers down at me with soft eyes and a little wink. "Because something is going on, and it's not going to get better if you don't talk about it."

Well, I'd rather talk about *that* than about what happened as I was lying on top of him. Choose your battles, right? I suck in a deep breath and look up at him sitting across from me, face neutral, eyes holding a warmth that, to be honest, was always there since I met him.

And here we go, the defining story of my life. "I was abducted when I was a kid."

His eyes pop wide. "Whoa. Okay. Didn't expect that."

I huff. "Neither did I. Or my dad. I was nine years old and grabbed on the way back from school. They held me hostage for a couple of days, somewhere hidden, obviously. Two people. They hit me. Badly. Especially after I tried to escape." I tap my left leg. "Shattered knee from when they beat me with an iron stake."

Kieran's jaw drops. "What the—" He swallows visibly. "Is that why you limp on that side?"

A little sting shoots through my chest. Having my inadequacies pointed out is never fun, and even less so when it's Kieran. "Yes and no. It's probably just me subconsciously treating that side differently. It's not the leg. It's fixed up pretty nicely, though." Thanks to the Magellans. They were close, they offered to help, and here I am, as good as new with a biosynthetic knee joint. A human doctor would have amputated above the knee with the amount of damage, I was told. I rub the knee some more. "And I consider myself lucky my kidnappers didn't shatter my skull, like one of them suggested. They were like good cop and bad cop. Bad cop kept saying how they needed to kill me, good cop was holding him back."

A shadow falls over Kieran's face. "But he didn't let you go."

"That he didn't. Quite the opposite." My voice drops to a whisper. "Bad cop was gone, and good cop was alone with me. He cut off the rope they used to bind me, threw me on the floor and himself on top of me. He held my hands above my head, just like you did—"

Kieran groans and buries his face in his hands. "I'm sorry. I'm so, so sorry, Nonie. I didn't know, I—"

"No." I reach out and, for a change, it's me who touches his knee. "It's okay. I'm over it, most of the time, but sometimes I get triggered." Not always in the same position. Not always in the same way. But always by something from those few days, sometimes as little as a whiff of something, and *boom*, I'm back there, helpless, scared.

He looks up from his hands, eyes holding a pain that reflects my own. "It's not okay. Not remotely. Did he… did he—"

"Rape me?"

He nods.

"No. I got lucky. I was freed just in time." A small smile pulls on my lips. It's fair to say that one moment defined the rest of my life. So far, at least.

Kieran blows out a puff of air. "Thanks to the Sun and Stars. USEF?"

"Yeah. A single soldier, clad in black, the patch for Division Two on her shoulder. I'll never forget what she did for me." How she broke in, all bad-ass in her black uniform, rainbow-swirl patch on her arm, how she disposed of Good Cop, who wasn't a good cop at all. How she checked me, hugged me, and told me all would be well. "You gotta understand, I didn't know what to do. I had no means of helping myself after my leg got destroyed, and I was scared shitless and in more pain than I'd been in my entire life. Then comes this soldier, and she is everything I'm not. Tough, strong, and totally the boss. I think I've been idolizing her ever since."

I remember her carrying me out of my prison, walking uneven under my weight, and, because I was too afraid to be alone, her holding me on her lap as she was piloting the shuttle to rendezvous with the

Magellans. I was lost to fear and panic, so I only have blurs of memories left, but funnily enough, the one thing that stuck to my mind for whatever reason was the ring she wore. I remember her holding me, and depending on how the light hit it, a multitude of colors shimmering on that simple band on her left hand, a little like her division-patch.

Kieran tilts his head. "So that's why you're trained so well."

"Yes." Not a lie. That's when I decided to join the USEF, even though Dad wasn't quite happy about it. He looked more than pale after the same USEF officer, my savior, gave him a report a day or two later, but from there on, he damn well made sure I knew what I was doing. I think he was still hoping he could avoid me joining the USEF, but my mind was set. "My dad helped to train me. I made it my goal to never ever be in a situation like that, where I didn't know what to do or how to help myself." And, until a few days ago, it worked out fine.

He nods. "It explains your level of training."

"It does." Because even though he doesn't know I'm USEF, I got to where I am because of that incident. I am who I am because of it.

"Who were the guys kidnapping you?"

I huff. "Good question. We don't know. They must've had helpers, because they escaped."

Kieran's eyebrows dip down deep. "From a USEF facility?"

"Correct." One day they were there, next morning they were gone. No video evidence, nothing. As if they just vanished into thin air. To say Dad threw a fit would be the understatement of the decade—no matter which decade. He watched and re-watched that surveillance video a million times, meaning, even though he tried to do that when I wasn't around, I did catch a glimpse here and there. And to be honest, it didn't re-traumatize me as he feared. I liked seeing those two men all beaten up, with swollen faces. Made me feel that at least a bit of justice was served.

"Do you… I mean, would you like me to look into it some more? When we're back in USEF space? I'm sure I can dig deeper and see what evidence was there. Maybe, with today's methods, we can find clues they overlooked all those years ago."

Oh, heck, no! That's the last thing I need. I should've modified my story, but blame it on a temporary loss of sanity. Why I didn't think about that? "Thank you, Kieran, but it's fine. I'd rather not be reminded of it. I'm done with that chapter, and believe me, stuff like this," I point to the ground we fought on a few minutes ago, "doesn't normally happen. It was just—"

A flush steals across his cheeks. "I know. I…" He pauses, then drags in a long, deliberate breath. "I was shot when I was ten. And in certain situations—"

My jaw drops. "Wait, what? *Shot?*" He got *shot?* When he was ten? Why don't I know that? Shouldn't I have heard of something of that magnitude, given who my mentors are?

He nods. "Yeah, shot. I had tremendous luck. By all accounts I shouldn't have made it, but…"

"What happened?" I stare at him, eyes wide.

"Good question." He sucks in a harsh breath through purses lips. "My… my caretaker—babysitter, if you will, although I hated that expression at that age. She'd been with our family for years. Closest person I had to a mother. One day… I don't know. One day she acts all secret and takes me out into the fields, where the raspberry farm is. Pulls a gun on me—boom. Point blank." His voice is low and husky. "I drop right there, and I promise you I knew I was going to die. Even at ten, you know."

"Yeah. You do," I whisper hoarsely. That's how I felt—at the end of the road. Until I saw *her*, at least.

Kieran chews on his lower lip. "I lay there, face smushed into raspberries, feeling the blood running out of my chest. There's gun fire, screams, yells—next thing I know a medic is injecting me with something, telling me all is going to be well. Don't know how they got to me this fast, but she saved my life."

"Holy crap." I blink hard.

"Yeah, right?"

"Your *sitter?*" How messed up is that?

"Yup. The whole thing became top secret because Dad thought rather than her having lost it somebody could've turned her against us or blackmailed her, but we never found out any details."

"How come?"

His eyes meet mine. "Because she killed herself on the spot."

I flinch. "Ouch. I think your PTSD outweighs mine."

Kieran chuckles. "And I don't think you can grade PTSD. But my point with this whole story was, I get it. Certain scents remind me of what happened. I don't do well with blood at all. I hate raspberries. So I get why you reacted the way you did."

I point a finger at him. "Okay then, here goes nothing, but still I'm doing the math. I freak out during fights, and you don't trust easily." Of course. It makes sense. After a betrayal of this magnitude…

He regards me from under his lashes, a slight color tinging his cheeks. "Figured that one out already, huh?"

I blush. Well, yes. With a little help from the admirals. I draw an invisible pattern onto the mat. "Wasn't too hard. You're different when you're with Chase and Zio."

Kieran nods appreciatively. "Good pick up. And you know what's funny?"

"Enlighten me."

"I said it before and I meant it. I trust you too, Nonie."

The words come out with brutal and disarming honesty, and they hit me right into my center, waking all those butterflies to flutter up and soar—*boom*, straight into the wall of impossibility. I clear my throat. "You've said that before. Why? Why would you?" I am the biggest fake, and yet I seems to have wormed myself into Kieran's trust.

The blush on his cheeks deepens, and I'd be damned if it didn't revive those stunned butterflies. "Do you really need to ask?"

"Well—"

He fumbles for the hem of his shirt, and then, in one fluid movement, it's gone. A deja vu of last night hits me, only that this time he doesn't wear an undershirt. My brain whirls as it takes in Kieran in all his beauty. The strong chest. Defined pecs. Eight-pack abs. The fine trail of hair under his belly button.

And the two sunburst scars, one on his right upper chest, one dead center.

Kieran keeps his gaze glued to mine as he reaches for my hand. "Easy, Nonie." He takes my hand between his and lifts it up.

It doesn't take more than this little touch to switch my senses to hyperawareness. The world around me is filtered out, leaving Kieran in more than 20/20 clarity. Maybe I'm imagining it, but I could swear I hear his heart hammer away in his chest, as fast as mine.

He places my palm above the scar on his upper chest, the one that mirrors my own. "This is why I trust you. I was nobody to you. You had my gun. My hablamate. You had all means to leave that planet. You could have let them shoot me. And yet you protected me. With your life."

My face heats up. "Of course I did." Without second thought. And I would do it again.

A lazy smile travels up to his eyes. "Then don't ask me why I trust you."

He holds my hand in place, warmed between his chest and his palm. The apple in his throat moves up and down… and his thumb swipes across the back of my hand.

Once.

Twice.

Again—and every little brush of his skin over mine shoots sparks across my body to sizzle in my core, kicking my hormones into overdrive. My heart does this fluttery thing and my stomach twists into a figure eight, but in a good way. I'm glad I'm sitting, because my knees are wobbly. Like, seriously weak. The intensity in his eyes, the hunger… it leaves me dizzy. Breathless.

Must get up.

Well, should get up.

Or, *maybe* I should get up—

Another brush of his thumb across my skin roots me to the mat, and like out of reflex I skim my index finger across the scar underneath it, the skin hard, yet velvety, and instantly addictive.

Kieran's entire body jerks as if he'd been shocked.

Seeing his reaction to the smallest touch—I was wrong. It's not addictive. That's an understatement. It's addicting, empowering, and mind-blowing.

And I want more.

I draw all my fingers in, nails scraping across his chest, savoring every inch of the movement.

His breath hitches, and that sound… sends rippling tingles down my body.

Kieran's gaze drops to my mouth. We're both breathing faster than normal, heavier, maybe because we both know what's coming next, no way around it. Our bodies are as close as they can get without touching any more than we already are. His chin tips down. Mine stretches up. We're both leaning in, and—

As if we're drawn in by magnets, our lips crash together, leaving no room for denial, no room to find an excuse. We both want this. We both need this. He moves his lips fervently over mine, teeth nipping at them, every little bite exquisite and oh-so-good. This kiss—this kiss is more than I could've ever imagined, unleashing such a powerful raw sensation, I won't ever be the same.

Kieran's fingers tangle into my hair as he draws me closer, my fingernails dig into his chest, and little tremors course through me. A breathy sound leaves his throat, mingling with my ragged breath. Taking advantage of my parted lips he slips his tongue into my mouth—

Oh, Sun and Stars. His tongue playing with mine, his hand on my face, his body so close I can feel the heat radiating off him… Nothing else exists besides Kieran and me. I'm out of control, tumbling head over heals into the vast unknown, the un-precedented, the impossible. And it feels… mind-blowing. Right. Meant to be—

A sharp spike of reality shoots right into my brain, the part that hasn't surrendered to my hormones yet.

Meant to be?

What the heck am I doing?

I've officially gone certifiable. Obviously.

I can't be kissing Kieran.

And yet I am.

Crap.

I freeze, like paralyzed by the weight of the world on my shoulders. I messed up. Again.

I messed up.

Messed up.

Messed—

"Hey." His breath is warm as he presses his lips against my cheek. "Too fast?"

Too fast? Hell, no. I want nothing more than throw myself at him and continue where we left off, and then some.

But that's not an option.

My next breath comes in with a wheeze. "I'm sorry." I untangle myself from him and scoot back. "I'm sorry, Kieran."

His brows narrow. "Sorry?"

I nod like a bobble-head figure. "S-so sorry." I scramble to my feet. Must get out of here. Off this ship. Away. Away, away, away.

"Nonie, wait." He jumps up to standing and reaches for me. "If I went too fast—"

"No." I yank my arm away from him before he can get a hold of me. I'm apparently as stupid as they come, but not that stupid. One more touch, one more skin-on-skin contact, and I can't guarantee I'm not going to cave.

And if I did, so would my timeline. If it hasn't already.

Hurt reflects in his eyes. "I'm sorry if I went too far. I—"

I lift both palms. "No. It's not you. It's me. I—" I can't believe I'm giving him the lamest excuse in the world. *It's not you, it's me.* Gah!

Keeping my palms up, I back toward the door. "I made a mistake. I'm sorry. I—"

The hurt in his eyes cranks it up a notch, and mine fill with tears. I'm such a disgusting idiot. "So sorry." It's a whisper, nothing more, and the last thing I'll ever say to him.

I turn on my heels and run.

Chapter Thirty

It's been twelve hours and forty-three minutes on the dot since Kieran and I kissed.

Not that I was counting.

It's also been twelve hours and forty-three minutes on the dot that I have neither slept nor thought of anything else other than the way he looked at me. How it felt when his lips brushed over mine. How those raw, beautiful sensations took over my soul one fiber at a time.

I groan and drape an arm over my eyes. No matter how long I lay on my bed staring at the ceiling, it's neither going to undo what I did, nor make anything better. Especially not the memory of the hurt in his eyes when I said I made a mistake.

Damn it.

I *did* make a mistake, but it wasn't kissing him. Well, yes, but not the way it sounded. Kissing Kieran was right. Boy, was it ever. But kissing him in this timeline, screwing up the future, was not. I'm sorry I hurt him, but it was best to cut it out before we were in too deep. This way he'll get over me and—

I jackknife up to sitting.

Holy cap.

What if—

No.

Can't be, for two reasons.

But what if—

What if Kieran Wildason never had a girlfriend because I screwed him up?

No. I shake my head. Ridiculous. Ridiculous for two reasons, as I said: One, way to go thinking highly of your kissing abilities, Nonie, but I doubt this one kiss—any one kiss—would have the potential to keep somebody from dating afterwards. No way it was either *that* good or *that* bad that he swears off kissing after me. Right?

Two, if—*if*—indeed kissing me made him hold off relationships after, it would mean my presence here was a time paradox, a temporal loop where I was here before, doing exactly what I'm doing now, kissing Kieran, *screwing him up* for him to never date, and for that information to make it through the grapevine of time to me back in my time at the academy, courtesy of Admirals Conolly and Upinga.

Yeah.

One would think if that was the case, the admirals would've warned me. I roll my eyes. The idea that both of them kept something like this secret for all those years is beyond absurd—and maybe I shouldn't waste any brain power on that, but on solving my many problems.

Problem One: Kieran.

Problem Two: Returning to my time.

Problem Three: Curing-slash-saving humanity without killing a planet full of Quaneez.

Enter Problem Four, the newest of the bunch and the only one I haven't really digested yet: dealing with Grazer. Which kind of circles back to Problem Two—can't deal with him if we're separated by forty years. Would love to rub it in though that I survived his sinister attack. Would also love to see the look on his face when he hears I traveled back in time, because let's be honest, I doubt he planned for that to happen.

So with all four problems it's easy to see the common thread. I need to get off this ship and my butt in gear. Yes, I've been trying to find out what I can, but I'm stuck. I've gotten all from the USEF and Magellan databases I can, and it's time I try something else to get away from here.

And if I can't, then I need to hide—better—and let this time ride out its natural course—

Oh, crap.

For a split second my muscles cramp up, halting my breathing, and maybe even halting my heart. What if—

What if that's the only way to make up for what I did? What if… what if I will never make it back to my time by any other means than natural progression? The thought is both, horrible and hope-inspiring, because… because even if I have to age for the next forty years, I will get to the date that saw me destroy humanity's only hope for survival.

And once I do, I could get those plants before I blow up the planet and before I get thrown into the past.

Maybe that's my destiny. Sitting out my life in the past, then bringing those plants to Earth in forty years. And maybe, just maybe, having forty more years available to me will help figuring out communication with the Quaneez, and then I can get them to evacuate before Nonie the Destroyer comes barging in.

I ball my hands into fists. One way or another, I will fix this as much as I can. Either young Nonie will, or old Nonie will finish what her younger self couldn't. Tears sting in my eyes. Not how I wanted this to play out. None of it, but…

I swing my legs off my bed. Toughen up, Thorburn. Toughen up, stop acting hormonal, and get it done.

"*Pioneer,* locate Commander Conolly." Time to take Chase by his word.

"Commander Conolly is in the captain's ready room."

Aww, crap. That means Kieran is there as well. I tug on my shirt to straighten it. Well, maybe even better.

With strong strides I cross the room and exit left into the hallway, for once not caring much about being seen, maybe because I have bigger fish to fry.

It doesn't take me long to make it to Kieran's ready room. Deep breath. Okay. I stand up straight and press my palm against the reader. Inside the room *Pioneer* will be announcing me—

The doors slide apart, granting me access.

Here goes nothing.

I step inside, nodding a greeting at Kieran behind his desk and Chase, sitting in the chair in front of it. "Kieran. Chase." The second door leading to the bridge is closed and the window behind Kieran darkened to minimize the motion effect of the stars.

"Nonie." His tone is not ungentle, but also not very welcoming. "What can I do for you?" Same goes for the look I get. Guarded, I would call it, and I can't blame him after the way I left him.

I stand straighter, hands folded behind my back. It's not affecting me. It's not. "I would like to ask Chase if his offer to help me fix the *Odysseus* still stands, and once it is fixed… I would like to request to leave *Pioneer* and make my way back to Earth."

Silence.

Chase turns around farther in his seat. "Where's that coming from? We're out in the middle of nowhere—"

I keep my eyes fixed to a spot above Kieran's head somewhere. Unfortunately it doesn't keep me from seeing the short flicker of hurt crossing his face, and it translates to a heavy pressure in my chest. "I think it's been long enough I took you up on your hospitality."

Chase shakes his head. "Seriously? I mean, yeah, I can help you and I can have Allyson look into it as well, but—

"Thank you, taking up one person's time is enough. I might need some more materials or tools, but I think I can fix most of it myself." And keep the *Pioneer* crew from discovering even more about me.

Chase gives me an annoyed glance, ignoring me and continuing where I interrupted him. "*But* think about it. Timing is bad. We're as far out as humanity has ever been, if anything happened—"

"Then I'll deal with it."

I do catch the short roll of his eyes. "Really. Worked out well the first time if we hadn't come by. Why are you so desperate to leave—"

"If Nonie wants her shuttle repaired, we will help her. Whether she leaves the *Pioneer* in this area of space or not remains to be seen, but if she wants to leave, she can leave." Every single one of Kieran's words rumbles through me, rattling the defenses I erected around my heart.

"Thank you, sir." *Sir.* Dang it, it just slipped out.

Chase frowns. "What's going on with you two here?" He looks from me to Kieran and back.

"Nothing," Kieran and I say in unison.

"Right. Obviously."

Kieran clears his throat. "It was a matter of time, Chase. Nonie—"

Sirens howl. *"Red Alert. Captain to the bridge. Red Alert. Captain to—"*

Both, Kieran and Chase jump up. Kieran has crossed the room before Chase has maneuvered himself out of the tight spot from between the desk and his chair. The doors to the bridge hiss open.

"Report!" Kieran bellows.

"Sir, we found them!"

"On screen!"

Chase jogs onto the bridge. "Chocho—any hails?"

"Negative, sir. They—"

The doors close behind them, leaving me alone in Kieran's ready room. The pressure in my chest has turned into a dull ache, and every second I replay the look on his face makes it worse.

I press a shaky hand against my forehead.

I wish this was my time. I wish I could stay. Or, I wish I could at least tell him and explain.

I wish.

Chapter Thirty-One

The hangar bay feels crammed.

The walls are too close, the ceiling too low, the window too small—and that's saying something considering the size of the bay Also, the air is too thin.

I don't feel well. Useless. Yes. Like an idiot. That too.

But not well at all.

I should though. I should feel great that I'm taking a step in the right direction. Fantastic. Splendid. Yet, ever since I came back to the *Odysseus* today, I feel like it's the wrong thing do to.

Deep breath.

It's not.

I need to get off the *Pioneer*. Stat.

I scan once more over the part of the engine I fixed—and when I say *fixed* I mean brought-to-a-state-where-it won't-break-down-right-away-again. I'm never ever going to complain about Admiral Conolly's schematics taking up space on any of my devices again. Without them on PADdy I wouldn't have known where to start, and with them I have turned the *smoking heap of scrap metal* into a close-to-usable shuttle again. The last three hours made a huge difference. Right now I'd say the *Odysseus* has one jump and minimum propulsion power. That's about it, but better than nothing. And if Chase or the Chief Engineer give me a hand with the secondary systems, I should be able to make her more spaceworthy yet again without unveiling the *Odysseus'* secrets.

Alas, that may take longer than I'd like. Everybody is busy at their stations. Yes, we've cancelled Red Alert, but still. If this was my time, I should be helping, doing my part. The thought that I may never return home to get to this point, never get to be an active member of the USEF and do what I was trained to be… I don't know what it is about today, but right now it makes me nauseous. As if only in the last hour I had understood all the implications to my life, and I can't say it's making me happy.

It's so, so tempting to think about revenge. Payback. Grazer is somewhere in this time. I have forty years. Boy, how I want to get back at him for stranding me here, for setting me up to fail. Of course I'm not going to do it, I'm not *that* stupid, but it would be satisfying on a whole new level.

Huh.

I stand still for a second. Imagine I got back at Grazer in this time and that was what made him dislike me when I came to the academy. I huff. Interesting predestination paradox theory, but nope. Didn't and won't happen. Grazer dislikes me because of Dad. That one day during my very first week at the academy when I overheard him and Dad fighting… It wasn't pretty, and a few threats were flung at my dad, if I remember correctly.

Maybe in retrospect, I was a bit naive, wanting to join D-2.

Guess I paid for it.

I wipe my hands on my thighs and throw one more cursory glance out the hangar bay's window. The Quaneez cruiser still hangs in a haphazard orbit around some planet with clouds, I.e., an atmosphere.

I rub a palm across my eyes and stand up from my crouch next to the shuttle's engine block. Seriously, since I left Kieran's ready room, I feel drained. Kind of pathetic what impact our quote-unquote fallout has on me. Nothing happened between us but that one kiss—

A pang of longing slices through me, bringing my whole body to a shiver.

But what a kiss it was. I suck in my lower lip. The kind of kiss that begged for more. The kind that was the perfect opener for—

No.

No, no, no. Fixating on my feelings for Kieran won't help, like, at all. It's a lost cause, just like me in total. Get it together, Thorburn, and fix your shuttle. Get your butt in gear!

I sigh once and throw another glance out the window. I wonder—

Smoke and debris shoots out of the Quaneez cruiser's aft part.

Wait—

I tilt my head. Their orbit *is* funny, indeed. Like they couldn't keep it stable. But—

Holy cow. My stomach twists into a figure eight, pushing bile up my throat.

"*Pioneer*, what's the date today?"

"*Today is Monday, May 12th, 2255,*" the *Pioneer*'s female voice reports, completely unaware of the significance of her words.

"May 12th, "I whisper. This down there is Ursus 31! This is the day the Quaneez fake their distress to capture one of us—

The day they capture *Kieran*.

I swallow hard and look out of the window. It's been over three hours since I left the ready room.

He should've dematted down already, offering them our help.

He—damn it, thinking this hurts—but he should've been captured already.

My heart seizes and then shatters as nausea pushes the bile higher up my throat. Right now, Kieran is down there. Undergoing Quaneez' mind torture—

I slap one hand across my mouth to keep myself from throwing up.

"Kieran." It comes out as a hoarse, raw whisper against my hand as the other one reaches out toward the window, as if it would bring me closer to him. Quaneez torture… I wish I didn't know what that meant. I wish I didn't know that's what's happening to him right now. Imagining it's him… "I'm sorry, Kieran." The pain he must be going through right now… unimaginable. The clock is ticking until the *Pioneer* gets him out—

Wait.

I lean over with my hands on my knees, gasping for breath like sucker punched into the gut. No. I got this wrong, but… We're off Red Alert. Why the heck are we off Red Alert, when our captain is held captive on the planet? We should be blasting those sirens, working on our *stroke of genius* that helped the *Pioneer* crew free their captain!

Instead, the *Pioneer* is as peaceful and quiet as can be.

Without straightening up, I tap my wrist PAD, then put my hands back on my knees, angling PADdy so I can see it. "History *Pioneer*, May 12th, 2255. Flow of events, audio only."

"On May 12th 2255, the USEF Pioneer *picked up on an emergency—"*

Sun and Stars, who cares! "Specify actions on board the *Pioneer*. Focus on rescuing Captain Wildason." My words end on a wheeze.

"Commanders Chase Conolly and Zio Upinga are credited with the plan to rescue their commanding officer. For their genius, teamwork, and ability to come up with a solution they have been decorated with the Golden Star of Combat in 2255. Together, they created the antidote to Quaneez toxins and what became known as the Conolly Field Stabilizer, allowing dematting despite the Quaneez' distortions."

I know that part. Another wheezy breath forces its way through my narrow throat. "Specify names, officers, civilians, and anybody involved in rescuing Captain Wildason."

"Commander Chase Conolly, First Officer. Commander Zio Upinga, CMO." The PAD falls silent.

Zio and Chase. Nobody else.

And yet… "Specify flow of events, starting at—" I glance at the display. "Fourteen hundred hours." That's over one hour ago.

"Fourteen hundred hours. Captain Wildason's check-ins come regular. Approaching entrance to underground structure. Fourteen hundred hours and thirty minutes. Captain Wildason's communication from inside the underground structure is scrambled. Fourteen hundred hours and forty-five minutes. Bridge crew notices inconsistencies in Captain Wildason's check-ins. Fifteen hundred hours. Commanders Conolly and Upinga verify worst-case-scenario. Ship-wide Red Alert is called. Fifteen hundred hours and fifteen minutes. The commanders develop a rescue plan. Fifteen hundred hours and thirty minutes. Rescue plan gets set into motion. Fifteen hundred hours and fifty minutes. Captain Wildason is rescued in critical condition. Fifteen—"

"PAD, stop." I blow a slow puff of air through pursed lips. I was right. Sirens should be blasting, and they're not. Something is not right.

In fact, something is very, very wrong.

Chapter Thirty-Two

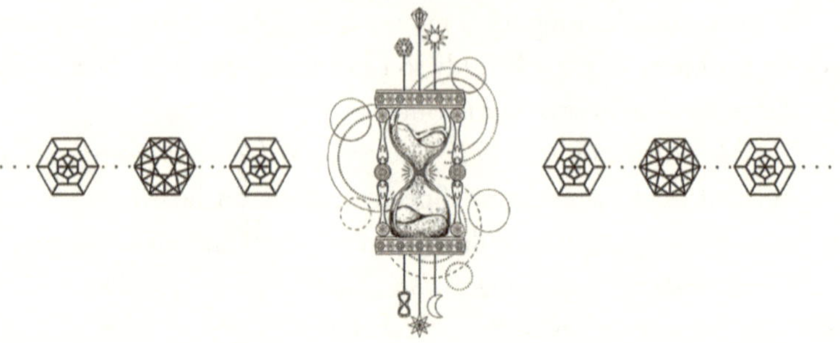

race through the Pioneer's hallways, for the first time ever truly not caring who sees me.

Something is wrong.

A junior lieutenant barely jumps out of my way. "What the—"

I ignore him. No time. Whatever is wrong needs fixing as fast as possible, or else Kieran—

The bridge. I skid to a halt, sucking in one hungry breath after another. Focus. Think. Don't give yourself away. Focus!

I straighten my shirt, then place a palm on the door's reader. What if they're busy and won't let me—

The doors slide apart, granting me access to the *Pioneer*'s bridge.

I dart forward—

And stop.

Peace.

Quiet.

Normal routine.

My head swivels left to right, taking in the surreal scene. Ops, Helm, Science, Communication—everybody is focused on their work, but in a quiet, relaxed way. The junior officers manning the nonessential stations chat quietly with each other, one of them laughing under his breath.

I blink.

Something is wrong for reals.

In the left corner, Zio looks up from his combined science- and medical station. He tilts his head and pops one eyebrow up. "Nonie."

That gets Chase's attention off the exec PAD on the right of the command chair and on to me. "Nonie. Chose a busy day coming up here." The smile I get is quicker than normal, the only indication that he hasn't forgotten something isn't right between me and Kieran.

Kieran.

My mouth opens and drops. "I… I was just wondering… I saw smoke and stuff come out of that ship's aft and—"

"Yes, we saw that, thank you." Chase focuses onto his pad again. "Was there anything else?" I know a dismissal when I hear one. One should think Kieran didn't have time to fill him in about what happened, and maybe he hasn't—but then kudos to Chase for picking up on the fact that I'm the bad guy here.

I work on a dry swallow. "Have we… I mean, are we helping them?"

This time I get a raised eye brow from Chase. "Yes. Of course." He looks back at his pad.

"And… everything's fine?" From the corner of my eye I can see Zio step closer, a curious expression on his face, as Chase sighs.

"Yes, Nonie, everything is fine. Nothing to worry about. Feel free to ask Alyssa to help with your shuttle, if that's why you're here." With that he turns away from me for good, which is why he doesn't see my face lose color, or how I have to hold on to the railing to keep myself from stumbling.

Everything's fine.

No, it's not, I want to scream. How can everything be fine if Kieran is down there—

Another try. "Where's K—where's the captain?"

Chase takes a visible deep breath before turning his attention back to me. "Took a shuttle to the planet on potentially one of the most sensitive political missions of the last decades."

Keeping my face straight is hard. Hard. "Oh. When did he leave?"

He gives me an annoyed glance. "A bit more than an hour ago."

A bit more than an hour. More than an hour. A freakin' *hour.* Way too long. My stomach cramps up. I might be pushing it here, but…

"Has he reported back? Needs help?"

The commander's fingers drum a rhythm onto the chair's arm rest. "Not that it's any of your business, but things are going well."

I doubt that very much. "You could hail him and check." And that's the moment I know I overreached. Chase narrows his eyes, as muscle in his jaw ticking.

"Once you have completed academy training you're welcome to offer suggestions, but in the meantime, I would appreciate a civilian staying out of my business. You may leave." He points at the door, and I take a stumbling step back. Crap. That did not go well. I—

From the corner of my eye, I see Zio type something into his station and look up at Chase when his colleague's exec PAD chimes. Chase gives me one more hard look, then reads the message, as if the matter was done and taken care of, but—

Nothing is taken care of. Despair and disbelief flare up. Who sends their commanding officer, their *captain*, into the unknown? Unprotected and unprepared? I get he wanted to help, I get it we're the good guys, but *this, today,* is one of the reasons USEF changed their protocols. Yet here we are: the current commander of the *Pioneer* is not concerned, while his captain has left the ship alone and is being tortured by the enemy.

Where is the help that's going to demat down and free him? If nobody is even realizing help is needed, where is the *stroke of genius* the *Pioneer* came up with—

Oh.

My throat is tight, like, so tight every single breath wheezes and hurts, but that could be because my heart hurts and cramps with every beat.

What if—It's impossible, but what if…

What if *I'm* the *stroke of genius*? Obviously nothing is happening, because *everything's fine.* I'm the only one who knows the trouble Kieran is in.

What if *I'm* supposed to be rescuing him?

Nausea threatens to overwhelm me and weakens my knees as my mind scrambles to make sense of that possibility: The academy has over one thousand practice scenarios stored, and the one I practiced the most was this very hostage retrieval—because my two mentors insisted I'd be perfect at it.

My two mentors: Conolly. Upinga.

The breath leaving my throat feels way too loud, yet I don't hear it. My gaze searches for and finds them both, Chase concentrating on whatever on his PAD, Zio watching me with his head cocked to the side—but both blissfully ignorant to the light bulb going nuclear inside my head.

What if *I'm the freakin' stroke of genius*? Then this—everything—has happened before. A predetermination paradox. Then it wouldn't have been an accident I ended up here, but… I blink hard. I mean, yes, it would've been an accident, but it would've been supposed to happen. Which also means, *Admirals* Conolly and Upinga knew I was going to be swept into the past. They knew what was going to happen, slash, what had happened already.

Doubt crosses my mind, dark as a shadow. Way too unrealistic. Yes, they trained me well in this scenario, but it's the USEF's most common one. Plus, if they knew I was supposed to free Kieran, wouldn't they have trained me even more? Even better? Especially given the fact how I ended the last training scenario?

Maybe I should check my ego and egocentric world view and consider other options, namely that my presence here on board disrupted and messed with the natural flow of events: Chase took time away from studying the Quaneez data to help with my shuttle. Zio the same. If it wasn't for me, they'd be on top of things, but because I distracted them, they're not.

And Kieran is paying for it as we speak.

Kieran.

Priorities.

I close my eyes for a way too short moment and blow out a soft breath through pursed lips. Does it matter why the rescue mission is late? No. It matters that Kieran is down there and needs to get up here, preferably soon and alive.

And at the moment I'm the only one capable of saving him.

I need to get Kieran out of there, like, now.

Because that's what they trained me for, no matter if it was predetermined or not.

"Commander, another automated hail from the captain. It says…" Chocho pauses as he adjusts the readings. "I'm sorry, something must be interfering with the signal, it's partially scrambled and there's a repeating loop in it, must be some kind of interference. It says *position stay, time, stay.* Sorry, that's all I can get out of it." He shrugs apologetically.

"Thank you, Lieutenant." Chase enters commands into his exec console attached to the flexible metal arm on the right side of the command chair. "Boy, does he take long down there."

Adrenaline spikes through my veins, bringing a rush of fear. Don't waste time, Thorburn. Don't waste time. The proof is right there—history says, the Quaneez faked Captain Wildason's communication. This is all they got from copying what he reported in before. They still don't speak our language, forty years later, but to be fair, the same is true in reverse.

The clock is ticking, and let's put it this way: according to history the *Pioneer* is late in rescuing Kieran. Maybe I'm supposed to get him out, maybe not—or maybe my presence here changed something vital. In the end the *why* doesn't matter. Kieran's survival does. It's an easy equation, and right now I'm the solution to it.

I can only hope I'm not suffering from a severe case of grandeur—or idiocy, for that matter.

My decision is made, and funnily enough it comes with surge of confidence, because predetermination or not, I *have* trained for this. With three steps, I'm next to Chase and lay a shaking hand on his arm. Nothing but utmost attention to detail and precaution will make this go right, this much is clear. I lower my voice. "Chase. We need to talk."

He stays focused on his exec console, but that ticking muscle is working overtime. "No, we don't. I'll be off duty whenever Kieran is back—"

I lower my voice even more, so only he can hear me. "He won't be back if you don't listen to me."

That gets his attention. His whole body tenses as his head whips around to look at me, blue eyes piercing. "Come again?"

"You heard me. Please do me a favor and listen to me. You and Zio, captain's office. Now." I nod my chin to the room next to the bridge. I want as much of this under wraps as possible. Hint: PADdys' data did not mention any civilians or people other than Conolly and Upinga rescuing Kieran.

For a moment I think I've played it wrong. Chase stares at me, eyes wide, an expression of disbelief on his face that morphs more and more into distrust.

I suck in a deep breath. Time is of the essence. "Please. For Kieran, Chase."

The muscles in his temple truly get a work out. His eyes narrow at me—

"Commander Upinga. Nonie. Office." He jumps out of the chair and strides ahead without looking back at me, shoulders square and tense.

Zio cocks his head, but follows stat.

Good.

The sensation following Chase to the captain's office is strange. On the one hand, it's a pretty realistic option I might faint. What I'm doing… If I'm wrong, it's a major interference with the timeline, so my heart has decided pumping blood is not important and focuses instead on fluttering and skipping beats. On the other hand I'm calm. Collected. I know what I'm supposed to be doing, because I've done it a trillion-billion times.

The office doors close behind us. Chase doesn't even sit down, but spins on his heels, one finger pointed at me, fire in his eyes. "Was that a threat?"

"Whoa!" I lift both hands. "No threat. Let me explain."

"Explain what?" Zio gives one pointed glance at Chase, one at me. "Several things are in need of an explanation, I fear."

Chase glares at me. "Better ask *her*, Commander."

Deep breath. There is a reason I was youngest in the academy and best of my year. I *can* do this. I've got it down. Never mind the small shake to my hands when I think of how exactly that scenario played out for me the last time. I can do this. "Chase. Zio. Let's focus on the important. Sit, both of you." Funny how the command tone comes through, the same as Dad's.

Zio takes a seat in the chair across Kieran's desk. "Well, this should be interesting." He looks me over with his no-BS-radar-glance.

"Are you trying to give me an order on our ship—"

"Chase. Sit." Something in Zio's tone snaps Conolly out of his rage. His mouth opens and closes, but he sits himself half onto the desk. A start at least.

I let go of a slow, deliberate exhale. Progress. "Thank you. I would like you to listen to me and hear me out. This is going to be a tough pill to swallow, but please give me the benefit of the doubt. You have nothing to lose and everything to gain."

Chase crosses his arms in front of his chest, but at least he stays quiet. Zio nods. "We're listening."

Okay then. "At this very moment I can guarantee you Kieran is not on that planet bonding with the Quaneez you have been following for the last days, but he's being held hostage by them."

Silence.

Both men stare at me, one with horror in his eyes, the other with… interest.

"Carry on," Zio says.

Okay, how much do I tell them… "Time is of the essence. The longer the captain is in their hands, the less likely it is he will not make it out alive."

"What?" Chase catapults off the desk, right into my face. "I've had enough with your threats! What the hell—"

"Chase." Zio reaches for his colleague. "Sit." He says it completely calm, not as if I just dropped a bomb on them.

Chase's mouth snaps shut. "Zee—"

"Really, Chase. Trust me."

Something passes between them, and whatever it is, it works. Conolly blows out a harsh puff of air. "Fine. Continue."

I stand up straighter, as if it conveyed more professionalism. "Taro Magona was correct. The people holding Kieran are called the Quaneez. They are extremely hostile and are currently extracting information from Kieran—or are at least trying to do so. Problem is that their way of doing that will damage his brain permanently, if not kill him." My voice breaks with the last words and I swallow hard. Can't let emotions affect me.

Chase jaw drops. "You're kidding me."

"I wish I was."

"How the hell are you coming up with this? What the—"

I hold up a hand. "Stop. That's not important—"

"Not important? *Not important?* It ranks pretty much top of my list of importance if you tell me our captain is held hostage and potentially going to be killed!" He points an angry finger out the window. "If you want me to take you seriously, you better have proof!"

"Proof?" I throw my arms up. "How am I supposed to—" *Click.* Got it. "Zio. Compare the audio file of the captain's last hail with the previous ones. Check for consistencies, run comparisons. You should find—"

Zio's fingers dance over his PAD. "… that the message is puzzled together from the previous ones." He whistles through his teeth and looks up at Chase. "Not a new message. A construction with bits and pieces taken from the hails he sent earlier."

The apple in Conolly's throat moves up and down. "Are you sure?"

"Very."

I lift both hands in a calming gesture. "Look, we need to get Kieran out of there. Think about it. Like I said before, you have nothing to lose, and everything to gain."

"I have a lot to lose! If you are wrong and we start firing, I'm starting a war that didn't need starting! This is insa—"

"Trip." Zio leans forward, eyes boring into me. "What do you suggest, Nonie?"

I take a calming breath in. "A low-risk-high-gain scenario for you. I need two minutes in your weapon's arsenal to get ready, two more minutes in sick bay. You demat me—"

Zio gives a short shake of his head. "We can't use the demat, their shields—"

"Never mind the shields. Just demat me down—"

"Never mind the shields? What exactly does that mean?" Fire sparks in Chase's eyes.

I ball my hands into fists and take another deep, calming breath. It's to keep the timeline intact. To rescue Kieran. "I might have a way through the shields."

"You might have—" His mouth drops open. "Are you kidding me? You are kidding me, right? There's no way—"

"There is, and you're wasting time."

Zio cocks an eyebrow at his colleague. "Agreed, Commander. Let her finish."

I blow out a puff of air and ignore Chase. "Thank you. Anyway, you demat me down, I do what I can, you bring us back up and get us out of here."

Chase throws his hands up. "This is getting better and better, and don't you dare shush me again!" He points a finger at Zio. "*You* want to go down? *Alone?* If what you say is true, I should send a whole unit down to rescue the captain! What the heck are *you* going to accomplish *alone?*"

I see his problem, because he doesn't know what I know. Barring other alternatives, this is my mission. I can't bring the *Pioneer*'s security officers up to speed on how to fight the Quaneez and stay alive within a few minutes. Forty years later, we're still having difficulties with that one. No, this is a one-woman-mission, the way they trained me to do it, be it on purpose or coincidental. *Who says you're not going to be alone in the most important mission of your life?* "If you sent a unit down, you're sending them into a fight they can't win. Believe me when I say I was trained by the best people for this job. I—"

"Trained? For *this?*" Chase spews at me.

I sigh and flinch. Let's not go into details I can't disclose anyway. "Yes. And at the moment, it really doesn't matter. You have no proof the opposite of what I'm saying is true—"

"But also no proof what you're saying is true." He regards me with smug superiority. "In fact, I'm worried about this sudden involvement. If you truly know how to get through their shields, for one, how would you know, for another, why didn't you—"

Sun and Stars! "Chase, every minute we spend debating here, the risk of Kieran dying increases! He's been down there over a freakin' hour, and if we want to get him back alive and without brain damage, we have less than thirty minutes! You have literally nothing to lose! I'm not a crew member, and if Command comes down on you, you can always claim I acted on my own without your approval!" Don't I know how that works. Thanks for the lesson in deception, Admiral Grazer. "Listen, here are your options: I'm right and you let me go—I rescue Kieran, you risk my life at most. I'm wrong and you let me go, you blame the political fallout on me, the rogue civilian. But if you don't let me go at all, you risk Kieran's life. It should be a no-brainer."

Silence.

I swallow dry. "Please. Nothing is more important than getting him back."

A muscle twitches in Conolly's jaw. He chews on his lower lip, the pulse in his neck jumping at an unhealthy speed.

After what feels like an eternity, he gives Upinga's ankle a slight kick. "Zee?"

Without hesitation Zio nods. "Yes."

Chase pushes off the desk and runs a hand through his hair. "Okay. *Okay.* Have it your way. Under one condition."

"Shoot." At this point I don't care about conditions as long as he lets me go to do my job.

"One, if you're not back within twenty minutes, I'm sending a unit after you. Two, when you're back—when both of you are back—we get more than this ominous stuff. Because I have questions for you. Lots. And I won't take no for an answer, or you're going to find yourself in the brig for a very long time."

Chapter Thirty-Three

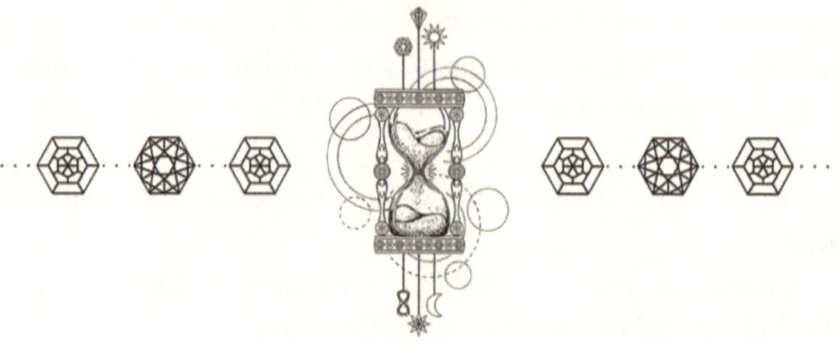

USEF Academy, Main Campus, Year Four, 2 days prior to day 0

The lights in the Sim Room turn back on, their bright, white shine piercing my closed eyelids and shooting right into my brain.

I groan and drape an arm over my eyes. Turn 'em back off. I want to lie here some more and wallow in my misery. Or, give me my mask so I can hide behind it.

Ten seconds ago, my patient was here in the very same spot on the ground, fighting for her life after I got her out of Quaneez captivity. Now she's gone, her photons sucked back into the projector, leaving only me and my permanent failure to man up and tackle the demons of my past. Hint: if I had, she may have survived to glow another day.

Behind me, the doors swoosh open and two heavy sets of footsteps enter. "Now, that was a disaster." The steps stop, one set on my left, one on my right. Great, they've got me surrounded.

I wave a hand. "Leave me alone. That sucked."

"Indeed it did, Cadet." I don't need to look to know what kind of worried glance Admiral Upinga is giving Admiral Conolly right now. I feel it. I feel it like my failure deep down inside my core, eating at me.

"Shit," I whisper-curse. I *knew* both scenarios. I freakin' knew them. By heart. How hard can it be to combine them?

Very hard, apparently. At least when one is nervous and lets that get to her. Thanks, fate of humanity resting on my shoulders.

Conolly sighs, and, judging from the rustling sounds, sits down on the ground next to me. A second later, Upinga does the same.

Oh, cool. It was *that* bad. If they had anything positive to say, they'd kick my butt to get up and into the debrief room. Them sitting down and letting me throw my tantrum… My stomach cramps. I hate disappointing them.

Admiral Upinga gives it to me straight. "You panicked. You pulled out your patient too early without medical stabilization. That's why she crashed."

"I know."

"And because you didn't counteract the poison, you weren't fast enough delivering care once you were out."

"I know."

An almost silent sigh comes from him. "You *must* incapacitate all enemy soldiers. You need to buy yourself the time to start treating the victim in the bunker, or else he or she might not survive demat. What if it's you, Nonie? Only you? No back up. What if you are the one this person's life hinges on? You have to do this right. You know that, Nonie."

"I know." I know that I know that. "I didn't think."

Pause. "No, you didn't."

I feel a finger tapping me onto the shoulder. "Nonie. What happened?" Conolly's voice is worried. Calm. At least not angry. I'll take it. "That's not you, the way it fell apart in there."

I take it back. I'd like him to be angry. Very angry. Then I could get angry in return and not have my eyes flood with tears, how 'bout that. "I don't know," I say in a hoarse whisper. *Lie.* I do know. In my layman's self-psych eval, I blame it on stress lowering my mental defenses. Or rather, blasting them into nothingness. I haven't freaked in combat drills like this since the first few months after the kidnapping when I just started Krav Maga.

Conolly pauses, then squeezes my shoulder. "Come on, sit up."

"Nu-uh."

"Sit up, Cadet!"

I jackknife up to sitting. "Yes, sir." Sniff.

Captain Upinga hands me a tissue. From where, I don't know. "Do you know what your mistakes were?"

"Everything?" I take the tissue and blow my nose like an elephant with flu. Ouch. Not the best comparison.

"Not quite. You definitely tried to regain control, but I fear matters had gotten out of hand too far to be reined in again."

"No kidding." I was one step behind the enemy at all times. Correction: A mile behind 'em.

Conolly draws his legs in closer. "Before we download the details from your recordings, tell me what you need to do better."

Again: "Everything?" Should've forgotten to turn the recording on. At least it would reduce the embarrassment to not-quite-deadly.

He harrumphs. "I want specifics, Cadet. I want you to list what to do better next time, so that it sticks to your brain and you remember. Hear me? Remember!" He gently knocks two knuckles against my temple.

"Yes, sir." I tear the tissue into little pieces. "But I don't know where to start." That's how bad I was. An embarrassment for a graduating student.

Admiral Upinga picks up some of the destroyed tissue. Eww. Here's to the Magellans' immunity to human germs. "Why don't you pick out two main things to correct and focus on those?"

"Two?" I still wouldn't know where to start.

"Two." He nods, his large eyes shining even darker than normal.

I chew on my lower lip. "One, don't let anything distract me from my mission." Because today was about that. If I hadn't thought about Grazer and his task for me, I would've done way better. That was the beginning of my downward slope.

"Good. No matter whom you end up working for, sometimes you're it, and distraction can be deadly. You were off your game today, and it showed."

Admiral Conolly forms a gun with his fingers. "You have to kill the enemy, Nonie. You have to."

I cringe. "I know. I know I have to, but…"

"It's hard." He nods once.

"Yes," I whisper. It's me or them—me and the hostage or them—but pulling that trigger, knowing it will kill a person, enemy or not…

"You've been doing fine during your last scenarios."

I pull my knees in, wrap my arms around them and lay my head down. The only reason why I did well during the last scenarios was because I told myself with every single time I shot my weapon that this was a simulation. A game. Not real.

Today… Like I said, my shields were down. Everything was hyper-realistic. And when they attacked me…

Yeah.

I sniffle and look back up. "I can't shoot them."

"You must." Conolly points over to the corner where I was overwhelmed by the enemy during the situation. "If you don't kill them, they will kill you. The last forty years have shown that. You're not acting as a single individual, but are executing the USEF's orders and acting by their guidelines. You have to kill the enemy, Nonie. As hard as it is and as much as I wished there were, but there is no way around it. Especially in a scenario like this."

Never have I felt less prepared, less trained, and less worthy or my mentors' guidance than right in this very moment. Where's the Nonie who completed this drill in under ten minutes? *Poof.* Gone. I bite on my lower lip to keep it from trembling. "Okay," I breathe.

Admiral Upinga looks at me with serious eyes. "Two. Give me the second thing you need to focus and improve on."

I shrug, and tear more pieces off the tissue. Sorry, Admiral. "I guess two falls in the same category, only differently so."

"Why?"

"Because I can't have the past distract me either." I lower my gaze too late to overlook the worry lighting up in Conolly's face. I know it's been almost a decade. I know I should be over it—and yet I'm not. Not always, at least.

Silence hovers, and it's heavy, full of my guilt and their disappointment, until Upinga sighs. "The past has a way to sneak up on us, Cadet." He stands up and holds out a hand for me. "And sometimes it has a very strong pull."

I take Upinga's outstretched hand. The moment we touch a chill snakes around my insides and *something* flickers across his face for the shortest moment—relief? But—

Captain Upinga lets go of me as soon as I stand. "The next time she'll do all right, Trip. She'll do all right."

Conolly claps my shoulder once again. "We knew that, Zee. Always did."

And as much as their optimism is appreciated, I can't help but feel like a ginormous failure. The fate of humanity rests on my performance, and I can't even save some assembled photons.

All I can do is hope tomorrow is better, and that I'll never ever ever have to deal with this scenario again.

Chapter Thirty-Four

"Anything else?" Chase hands me another weapon.

"No, thank you." I take it and attach it to my belt next to the other two guns and the additional power cells. "Got three weapons, two more power packs. Don't want to be carrying too heavy. Let's go." During most of my training exercises, one weapon was enough, but I'm not about to play with fate.

One short nod and Chase leads the way out of the weapons' arsenal. He stops once the doors open and checks the hallway left and right. "Clear."

Good. The crew has orders to stay in quarters or at their stations during red alert, but then, you never know. As secret as I thought I needed to be, this—me arming up to free Kieran—is at a whole new level.

"Time?" He looks back at me when I check PADdy.

"Fifteen minutes and thirty-three seconds." My rough guesstimating until when the chances of Kieran recovering are bleak.

The apple in Chase's throat moves up and down. "Not much time."

"No."

"If what you say is true."

I sigh. Ever the skeptic. "For now, let's assume it is. And FYI, I can get him out of there in under ten minutes." *If* I get my *beep* together. *If* I don't freeze. *If* I pull this off like I was trained to. Lots of *ifs*, and I don't need to look to feel his scrutinizing gaze on me.

"At this point, I sure hope so. And I'm beyond curious to hear your explanation for all this."

And I also don't need to have studied psychology to hear both, the underlying threat and the distrust in his words.

"We'll get there." Or not. Because as it is, I have absolutely no intention to contaminate the timeline any further, possible predestination paradox or not. As soon as I'm back on board, I intend to hop into my barbecued shuttle and put as much distance between me and the *Pioneer* as I can, no matter the danger that puts me in. Better me than the timeline.

Probably should have done that a while ago, and things might be different now.

"Yeah, *we'll get there*. In about twelve minutes, since you only need ten." Sarcasm drips from his voice, and my heart stumbles over a couple of beats. Maybe I did neglect to mention that those ten minutes applied to either the medical or the tactical part, and that I completely messed up the last combined drill. But given the fact that I don't think Chase ranks me very high in regard to trust right now it might be wiser to keep that piece of information to myself.

Today's not the day to dwell on the past.

I speed up to walk next to Chase. "Where's Zio?"

"Should bring everything you requested to the demat room." His voice carries a whole motherlode of grumpiness, but hey, at least we're executing my plan.

My heart thumps wildly in my chest. The last time I went through this scenario, I didn't exactly ace it. Today not acing it is not an option. Today it's about Kieran. I check my PAD again. At this point, it's a compulsory motion. "I need about nine minutes and thirty seconds down there. We're good so far." I hope. I'm going down there, jitters and the failure to complete the exercise stuck in my bones.

All I can do is make it better.

I crank my neck as the doors to the demat room open. Zio is already standing at the console. "Nonie. Show me." He steps away from the console, then points at the medical pouch. "Everything you requested is in there. I'm not quite sure what the synthesized medications are supposed to do—"

I fasten the kit to my utility belt. "We'll talk later." Or not. And just in case my last practice scenario was any indication how this mission might go, I drop a datachip onto the console. *What if you are the one this person's life hinges on?* Yeah, nope. We're coming up with a plan B. "If for whatever reason I don't come back, this here will give you all the information you need to treat Kieran." He will be back, that much is clear—unless I've already changed the course of history. But if this is a predestination paradox, he will survive. Me? Unclear. A shudder runs down my back.

I got this.

I got this.

Zio takes the chip and turns it over. "Coded?"

"A combination of Kieran's DNA together with a thumbprint and active pulse in it unlocks it." Because I'm still not willingly contaminating the timeline, but I'm also not willing to risk Kieran's life.

The commanders exchange a glance.

"I'll add it to the list of questions for later," Chase growls.

Oh, the ones I will never answer? "Of course. But for now, watch." *Pioneer,* i.e., Conolly, has been credited with coming up with a way to counteract the Quaneez' disruption of our sensors and scanners, but on second thought… might have been me, because so far Chase hasn't figured it out yet.

But then I distracted him with my shuttle. Or it could be a predestination paradox.

Or I could be getting a headache, because he taught the technique to us students forty years later.

Anyway.

My fingers dance over the console's keys, entering the modifications that will allow us to demat down to the periphery of the bunker—never the well-protected center, unless we have enhancers helping from the inside.

Chase whistles through his teeth. "You weren't lying. This should work to demat through the shields."

I look up at him. "It will. You got it? Because if not, both of us are going to be stuck down there." Kieran's shuttle is a loss at this point already, taken apart to be studied.

"I do. Ready?"

"Been trying to get there for the last four years." I step onto the platform, wipe my hands on my thighs, then activate PADdy's controlling function I tethered to the guns. Going into a Quaneez bunker without a stabilizing system is suicide. I let go of a slow and controlled breath. Assess the situation. Fire at the enemy. Kill the enemy. Don't be distracted. *Don't be distracted.*

One more look at the two men who will give me payback—pay forward?—for this for years when they meet me again. "Remember, you won't be able to demat us out before I'm at Kieran's side with the enhancer. Once you get the signal, get us out. And if you don't get my signal…" I'll have screwed up yet again. "If you don't get my signal in the next ten minutes, I suggest you start firing on the coordinates we discussed to get their attention. But try to wait for me. That's a last ditch effort. Got it?"

"Got it." Zio nods while Chase stays silent, arms crossed in front of his chest.

"Then engage."

Chase nods, hands flying over the controls. Last thing I see before the tingling sensation and blurriness kick in is his worried glance to his colleague—

—and then the world has turned to near-complete darkness. Adrenaline surges through my veins. I'm in an actual Quaneez bunker. Not a simulation. This is the real thing. I'm holding my breath in and my weapon at the ready, but like in the virtual scenario, nobody but me is in this narrow and dark-ish hallway. Thank the Universe for that. A ball of nervous energy forms in my stomach. Okay. Showtime. I suck in a harsh breath—

And cough. "Sheesh," I hiss-whisper, gagging. The air is so sweet, I would think they had a whole flower bed next to where I'm standing. With one quick tap, a reflex born from years of training, I activate PADdy's standard mission protocol to record and time me, then sneak forward, as close to the wall as possible. It's not quite light in here, not quite dark, more like something in between, as if they set their ambiance controls to dusk. Noises I can't identify come from somewhere, a metallic screech, some shuffling, but no voices at least. The gun stays aimed forward—

From around the corner, a Quaneez steps into my line of fire.

He has no time to react. My mental indoctrination pays off and I fire before even the slightest twitch of a limb gave away he saw me, faster than his nervous system could process the shock of seeing an intruder in his home. I'd like to imagine surprise flickers across his face when my red beam lights up the darkness around us and burrows into his chest armor, but then, I wouldn't know what a surprised Quaneez looked like under his mask. Thanks to tethering the weapons to PADdy, the beam stays stable, and—

The Quaneez collapses, limp. One second later, his armor begins to glow, bright, brighter—and he's gone, only a whiff of something spicy left in the air.

"Holy crap," I whisper. I just… I just killed a Quaneez. My hand holding the gun begins to shake as realization dawns. I killed a Quaneez. Not a simulation. A real person.

Which brings my score to several million and one, and yet… this *one* feels different.

There are soldiers who count how many they shot. Who tell stories of their heroic acts.

I doubt I'm going to be part of that crowd, if the wave of nausea assaulting me is any indication.

My PAD vibrates. Two minutes gone. *Distraction can be deadly.* Admiral Upinga's words echo through my brain. Focus, Thorburn.

I raise my gun and continue down the hallway.

Commotion around the corner—no voices, but steps so loud, they can't yet know I'm here, or else they'd be sneakier. I press my back against the wall and prepare myself to ambush them, the nervous energy bouncing in the pit of my stomach, devouring my soul bit by bit.

The second Quaneez entering my line of vision doesn't stand a chance. My aim is spot on thanks to my PAD's stabilization hooked into the weapon's firing mechanism, and within a few seconds, his armor does the same glowing-and-vanishing-thing the other one's did. Number three gets hit before he can make sense of what's going on, and number four fumbles for his weapon, but comes up empty.

Ten seconds after they turned around the corner, all are gone, only the nauseating spicy smell left in the air.

I gag and gasp for air.

Several millions and four.

Vomit pushes up my throat.

For Kieran. For the timeline. Suck it up, Thorburn. They're the enemy. They will kill billions of humans without mercy. They're torturing Kieran right now. Two minutes and thirty. Go!

Holding my breath to escape the stench, I charge forward and around a corner, my steps the only sounds. The whole bunker is like a maze, but I know it like the back of my hand. Conolly locked me inside the simulation for a whole night after I lost my way to the victim once. Needless to say it never happened again.

Adrenaline and a faster-than-normal heart rate make it impossible to hold my breath any longer. With a slight wheeze, I let go of the air I held and suck in the new—

Eww. Stinks even worse. I wrinkle my nose and gag. *Reeks.*

And it's not important.

Suck it up, Thorburn. Or rather, don't. But anyway.

The silence is eery in here as I creep forward. Controlling my breathing and keeping it quiet is harder than I thou—

ZZZING!

I scream and jump back, barely evading the yellow beam slicing down from the ceiling.

ZZZING! Another one. And another one, singeing the ground on my right.

"Shit!" I duck and fire at the automated weapons system. With a rain of sparks, it dissolves into nothingness.

"Holy cow," I breathe. Close call—and it means they have picked up on me.

Change of tactics. No need to be silent anymore.

I charge forward, gaze darting all over the place, searching for soldiers or automated weapons. My aim is spot on hitting the first three before they can adjust to shoot at me. Thank you, Admiral Conolly, for every single one one of my precision drills.

The automated weapons mean business. They fire, fire, fire, trying to predict my movements, but I'm faster. They don't hit me—but I do hit them, each and everyone of them showering me in sparks when I take them out. Here's to training this a trillion-billion times.

I'm lightning on my feet, powered by the self confidence that I can do this. That I *have done* this before. That there is no room for failure.

More steps—

With one large jump I make it behind the next corner—

ZZING! ZZZING! Yellow beams whizz at me—

I fire twice at the ceiling—done.

My chest heaves up and down with every harsh breath, but my body is on autopilot. Recharge weapon. Stay ready. The steps are coming closer, fast, running, probably about to attack me. They're coming, coming, coming—

I sidestep out of their blind spot into the hallway, gun up and index finger curling around the trigger—

Two Quaneez freeze in mid-run less than three meters in front of me.

Yet I don't shoot.

For four very long seconds neither of us moves.

Not me, with my gun.

Not the Quaneez soldier—and neither does the hip-heigh Quaneez child holding on to the adult's hand.

I don't think either of us three expected the other one. For the shortest part of a second, I wonder if this is a female Quaneez, since in many species females take care of the young, and the males take care of the fighting.

The adult reacts first. He—or she, who knows with their armor— shoves the child behind them, and with this simple protective movement my paralysis is broken and my decision made.

Like a madwoman I charge forward, a scream on my lips and determination in my heart. The second the Quaneez realizes this fight just turned from long-range to close combat, I'm already up in their personal space.

Boom!

Kick to the midsection—he or she doubles over—*boom!*—another one to the head. The Quaneez' head snaps back, and he/she collapses to the ground.

The kid behind him, wearing the same kind of whole-body armor as the adult, cowers against the wall, covering his head with his arms, shaking, the embodiment of fear, no matter the species. The energy inside my stomach turns into lead. "Sorry, dude," I whisper, ready my weapon and sprint past him, ignoring the horrific stench that hangs around him.

Another vibration comes from the PAD. Five minutes gone. Crap. I need to speed it up. Every second I waste is a second subtracted from Kieran's chance of survival.

That thought gives me fuel. I will be in time, and he will survive. History needs him. I dash forward, shooting at the automated weapons before they can shoot at me, keeping my eyes open—

Four Quaneez soldiers step out of an opening about ten meters ahead and to the left of me, and all five aim their weapons right at me.

Instinct and training command me to take aim and fire—

I ignore it. With one quick swipe, I dial fire frequency to the max while choosing dispersion mode, then throw the weapon in their direction and press my back against the wall, flattening my body as much as possible and squeezing my eyes shut.

Please, fate, be on my side. I need them to not see me for a short five or ten seconds. *Please.*

A bright white glare penetrates my eyelids for a good three seconds—three seconds that I hear no other sounds but that of... bodies collapsing to the ground?

Yes! I snap my eyes open, and whoa: all Quaneez soldiers are lying in a heap on the ground, not moving. Breathing? Yes, breathing. That worked way better than expected, but what in the name of the Universe is that flash doing to their integrated systems?

Doesn't matter. It worked! Euphoria runs high. I draw my replacement gun, jump over them and run, run, run. The stench in these corridors is hardly bearable at this point. I swear it's getting worse, not that it mattered, because I just crossed the finish line.

Quaneez bunkers don't have doors. All they are is a connection of hallways and rooms, mostly bare ones at that—and this is the room I need to be in.

Unfortunately for me, about six Quaneez soldiers came to the same conclusion. They're lined up in front of the opening to the room—to Kieran—and who knows how many more are in there with him.

Only one way to find out.

With the same swipe-and-adjust motion, I charge the second gun and throw it forward. Wash, rinse, repeat—when I open my eyes, all six of them are stunned on the ground. My fingers itch to take a look under their armor, to find out more—but it's literally not in my job description for today. Plus, how annoying would it be if they disintegrated right into my face, killing me and taking Kieran's only chance of survival?

I draw my very last gun. At this rate I'll be out of weapons in no time, and that can't happen.

Energy pulsates through me, electrifying each and every cell in my body, strengthening every fiber of every muscle as I jump over the bodies sprawled on the ground. I'm almost there.

I dash into the room—

And right into another group of four Quaneez. Granted, all four are busy with Kieran, but three of them don't waste time and turn right at me.

There's no time to think, no time to panic, no time for anything else but to react.

The Quaneez charge me like they had everything to lose, but they're wrong. That would be me.

And it gives me powers.

I lash out at the first one with a kick to the groin, moving his armor a good ten centimeters up into his body. That can't be fun, no matter which organ system is down there in Quaneez anatomy. And while my shin stings like crazy, it's the Quaneez soldier who sinks to his knees and keels over forward.

One out of the equation for now. Three more to go.

They attack at the same time. I block the first series of swings, but punching back is not an option, or I'll break my fists on their amor, if my shin is any indication. And here's where Admiral Conolly's teaching comes in: use their disadvantages to your advantage. The armor makes them slow. Heavy.

So I play them. I'm fast, kicking, hitting my targets, then spinning out of the way. The closer I am, the less I can breathe. The stench in here is overwhelmingly strong. Like rotten flesh for one second, then more like dirty gym socks. Bad breath. Decay. It's all there.

My next kick flies up to one of the *few* vulnerable spots—straight into the windpipe. I think. A gurgling sound leaves the Quaneez' throat, and then he's down too.

The last two Quaneez decide it's time to help their buddies.

And I'm fine with that.

Now, I've been trained to shoot. To hold my fire on that one spot on their armor until the enemy disintegrates. And while I could very much do that, I won't.

Instead I draw them away from Kieran until they're all like a wall of armor between me and him. I fumble for my power back and throw it at their feet, then aim the gun at it and fire.

To their credit, they realize what's about to happen.

Only it's too late.

The power pack explodes with a painful flash of light and a brush of heat across my body.

Now!

Thank evolution for my insensitive human eyes. While I do see stars, I do at least see—the same cannot be said of the Quaneez.

I dash forward to the device Kieran is strapped to—

And skid to a halt.

How many scenarios have I been through? A trillion-billion, at least.

None of the victims looked good, by any meaning of the word.

But none of them looked as bad as Kieran.

It's not that he was bleeding, no—there is not a single bruise on his skin, not a drop of blood that I can see.

But he looks like they sucked him empty. His skin is white, almost translucent, every vein on his face popping out like drawn with a blue marker. His eyes are sunken in and half closed, only the white visible under his lids, crisscrossed by red blood vessels. To be honest, he looks more dead than alive.

Hell.

It hurts to see him like this, it freakin' *hurts*.

I shake my head to clear it. Don't waste time then, dammit!

I rush over to him and check his pulse. Weak, fluttering, but there. I blow out a puff of air. "Thank whomever."

I take out the autoinjector and ram it into his thigh. PADdy vibrates. Nine minutes. The next breath comes out harsh. Almost there. "Hold on, Kieran. Hold on—"

Rustling behind me.

I spin—

ZZZING!

The yellow beam of a Quaneez disruptor hits the ground in front of me. What the—

One of the Quaneez I stunned produced a gun from somewhere, aiming it right at—

Kieran.

No!

I jump into the line of fire, his index finger curls, a yellow beam shoots out—

And hits me square into the stomach.

I yell out and stumble—

Another shot, this one missing me, missing Kieran by a hair's breadth.

No! No, no, no! Too close to lose now, too close to be defeated.

Blurry. Can't see clear. Pain—breathing hurts—no, can't. Must get enhancer. Get Kieran. Enhancer's hard to engage. Vision blurs. Am one big ball of pain. I fumble for the hablamate. Missing it. Again. *Again.* Got the button!

Quaneez takes aim. Life flashes in front of my eyes. But won't move away from Kieran, won't—

Points at me. Curls his finger—

Cool dizziness engulfs me, blackens out my vision…

… replaced by the *Pioneer*'s bright white demat room.

Collapse on top of Kieran.

Second time in two weeks.

Chapter Thirty-Six

Waking up hurts.

Body functions I've always taken for granted—simple stuff, like breathing, having a heartbeat—have turned against me. *Ow.* A groan comes from someone, possibly me, but who knows. Everything's swaying, and I haven't even opened my eyes yet.

"Easy. I'm glad you're still in one piece, but don't overdo it." A cool hand pushes mine down when I'm trying to sit up. Admiral Upinga— my mission! The plants! Did I get them? No, wait, explosion, destruction of—

I force my heavy eyelids open. Bright. Too bright—

"Hey." Big, dark eyes, hair that shimmers like an oil spill—and not a single wrinkle.

"Commander," I breathe. Not *Admiral* Upinga. Right. The past. *Pioneer.* At lightning speed, my memory returns. "Kieran?" I push the hand off me and sit up. Whoa. Shoot. Dizzy. "How's Kiera—"

Zio supports my back. "I tell you to take it easy and you sit up. Really?" He sighs. "Kieran is fine, Nonie. Thanks to your data chip— which, by the way, also saved you. The stuff they shoot with… unbelievable. Unlike anything I've ever seen before, the way it attacks the nervous system…"

Relief of a magnitude I never thought possible overcomes me. For a moment, I let myself lean against Zio's hold, eyes closed, and enjoy the feeling of the future's weight lifted off my shoulders. To some degree, at least. "He's fine." It comes out jittery, shaky, as I cover my face with my hands. I did it. He made it out—*we* made it out. Whatever else I will do in life, I did the one thing Admirals Conolly and Upinga trained me for, and I did it well. I didn't fail. I didn't let my past throw me off course.

And, more importantly, I stopped killing the Quaneez. There's been too much killing for my taste.

An image of the Quaneez kid down in the bunker pops up in front of my inner eye. He looked so scared. *She* looked so scared? Not that that part mattered, but I feel like it matters the Quaneez are even dressing their children in whole-body armor. Now, if only I knew whether that's part of their culture as a violent race, or born out of necessity. Both are sad, but for different reasons.

Zio rubs my upper back. "Yes, I assure you, Kieran's fine. No lasting damage."

Sun and Stars, thank you. History—at least this part—is saved. I draw in a big breath—and wince. "Ow."

"You'll be sore for another few days," Zio says, then regards me with a strange sincerity. "The treatment almost didn't work for you."

I look up at him, hands dropping to the area above my liver, where the breath hurt like a stab with a knife. "Why? It should've—"

"That's what I wondered as well. So I looked at you a bit closer and found this." He points at something on the display of his scanner, something very small and very well hidden between a tendon and my humerus. Something that could be a glitch in the image, but designed on purpose to give that impression.

My genetic scrambler.

Heat surges through me. "Oh."

"Yes. *Oh.*" He pauses, then wets his lips. "It's time to come clean, don't you think?"

"Come clean?" I squeak. The way he says it, like he *knew*... "I don't know what—"

"You do, Nonie. You do. And at this point, it's what needs to happen—"

The doors at the end of the room swoosh open, Chase's annoyed voice coming in first. "He said to rest, not to—"

"I don't care."

Kieran.

My body reacts on its own accord: Heartbeat? Up. Breathing? Ragged. Hands? Shaking.

Zio cocks one eyebrow at the readout above my head, then sighs. "Well, I don't need to worry about your blood pressure, it appears."

That depends on the point of view, because judging by the way I feel, it's skyrocketing. But then, I brought this on myself. Nobody else's fault than mine.

Chase has Kieran's arm wrapped around his neck and one arm around his waist, supporting him. Neither man looks happy, although if I had the choice I'd rather face Chase a million times than Kieran once. Chase I can handle—his suspicion, anger at what I did, and dislike of being played. Kieran on the other hand… I can't handle.

With every step he shleps himself closer, I want to sink deeper into the ground. Or vanish. Actually, I'd prefer the latter, coming to think about it. A myriad of emotions cross his face, and none of them are good: Anger. Frustration. Sadness. Regret. Disappointment. The choice is plentiful, and no matter which emotion it is, they all chip away the good that was between us, little by little, until only a skeleton of it is left.

Kieran holds himself as straight as he can, yet it's clear it takes him a great deal of strength. And while he does look better than down on the planet, he doesn't look well in general at all.

But he's alive, and that's all that counts.

I force myself to not drop my gaze, but to keep it up. I might be a fake in this timeline, but I have enough integrity to face him for what I did.

I think.

As soon as the pair has made it close to my bed, Zio turns toward Kieran. "You should've—"

"Not a word, Commander." Kieran shoots him a warning look, and Zio snaps his mouth closed. The order doesn't keep him from exchanging a glance with Chase though, and that glance, it speaks volumes.

Chase fishes for a chair with his foot and pulls it closer. "Here." He transfers Kieran's arm from around his neck to the back of the chair, making sure his friend can support himself on it before he lets go of his waist.

Tense silence lingers. Kieran clenches and unclenches his hands twice around the back of the chair, and I'm not kidding, his fury is palpable. Yet he keeps his face straight, although it does nothing to mask the anger rolling off of him in waves.

"Leave us alone." No please, no nothing. An order.

"Yes, sir." Zio throws one more worried look at my readouts and his captain, then follows Chase out of the room. As soon as they're out of earshot, they put their heads together, probably wondering if they're going to see me alive again or if Kieran will rip my head off after the stunt I pulled on them over the last days.

Great.

Kieran inches around the back of the chair and sits down with a suppressed grunt. For one short second I have a deja vu—Kieran at my bedside—only this is deja vu, the alternate reality version. His jaw is clenched, hands purposefully spread out on his thighs, as if he needed to make sure they didn't betray him and, I don't know, wrap themselves around my throat and squeeze.

His eyes bore into mine. "Care to elaborate?"

I flinch from the coldness in his voice. "I—"

"You're not a star hopper."

I deflate. "No." No matter what I'm going to use as an excuse, that much is clear.

"Who are you?"

"Nonie," I whisper.

"Not what I meant." He crosses his arms in front of his chest, jaw set tight.

Now, I could continue playing that game. Evasive answers. Half truths. But we'd both know I was lying. A wasted effort. So instead I shrug, like a petulant child. "I don't want to talk about it."

Kieran huffs. "Really. That's a tad disappointing, because I was hoping to get a few answers. Like, how you knew what was happening to me. How you knew how to handle the situation. Could penetrate their shields. Knew the antidote to their... methods." I don't miss the flash of pain crossing his face, gone as fast as it came. "At this point, I have more questions than answers."

He drops his voice lower, and for the first time a bit of the old Kieran, my Kieran, shines through, but his face is still tense and hard. "This is your one chance, Nonie. I advise you take it."

Tears prick at my eyes, but I refuse to blink and let them fall. "I have nothing to say." Because I can't. Fear wraps around my throat and squeezes tight. What have I done? Yes, I saved Kieran—but what have I done to my future? Maybe that's it—I'm going to live out my life trapped in the past, locked away somewhere. Will they ever connect the dots? Warn future-Nonie?

Silence hovers.

"So that's it? Nothing. All this—and… nothing." Anger flashes behind his dark eyes. Disappointment. What exactly are we talking about? My betrayal? Us— No. There is no us. Never has been, never will be.

"I'm sorry." It's a pitiful whisper, because what else am I going to say? I *am* sorry. So, so sorry—

"Me too." His voice is hard. Uncaring.

Crap. I close my eyes. How am I going to get out of this? There's only one option, one route to go. Throwing everything I have into the game I look him straight in the eye. "Let me go, Kieran. Please. Give me my shuttle and I'll be gone. I promise, you won't see me again, you won't hear from me. Just… let me go. Please." My hands are folded like in prayer, but looking at the disgust in Kieran's face I need more than that to get me out of the mess I'm in.

"Let you go?" He sounds incredulous. "After the wool you pulled over all of our eyes for the last days? For all I know, you committed treason—and you want me to let you leave? Are you crazy? Actually, never mind. Don't answer that one." Kieran works himself to standing, keeping his gaze glued to mine, eyes cold. "You have until Commander Upinga declares you fit. Then you will answer my questions, and if you don't, you will find yourself in the brig." He hesitates. "Although if I were you, I wouldn't expect to not spend the rest of our journey in the brig."

Kieran taps the hablamate on his shoulder. "Wildason to Conolly.

One security detail to sickbay."

"Acknowledged, sir," Chase's voice comes through the speaker.

Kieran lowers his voice to a growl. "You will stay under constant supervision. Security will be ordered to use deadly force should you try to escape. As of now, you are no longer a guest on board my ship." His eyes bore into mine and his nostrils flare. "I would have thought better of you. I would have thought better."

And with that, he turns around and limps away from me, unaware of the fissure cracking through my heart and soul, cutting me in half and making me gasp. A hot rush of tears clouds my vision. Damn it, I—

I screwed up.

That's all I do these days, screw up. Maybe I protected the time line, but I didn't protect Kieran. Not the way I should've.

My gaze clings to his strong frame. That one moment in the gym, when everything seemed so right... the way his skin felt, his lips on mine, his—

PADdy vibrates on my wrist. Out of reflex my gaze drops to the display—

Holy—

My next breath gets stuck in my throat as my brain scrambles to make sense of the words popping up on screen I have to read and re-read again.

I gulp in air. This—

This changes *everything.*

Chapter Thirty-Five

USEF Academy, Year Four, around midterms

The lights turn on in the sim room and the projection of the shuttle and space around me vanish. I really, really want to swipe a sleeve over my forehead to get rid of the sweat, but that would look like relief and totally give the wrong impression. I'm not relieved my test is over. I'm thrilled, because I'm pretty sure I nailed it.

"Cadet Thorburn, please exit the simulator." Admiral Grazer's voice sounds even at best. Huh. I mean, even is better than disappointed, annoyed, or mad, but after my performance I was hoping for a bit more enthusiasm. Oh well. If I've learned one thing over the last years at the academy, it's to keep my expectations for praise to a minimum. Especially when it comes to Grazer.

I exit the simulator into the small, dimly lit prep room and greet the instructors at the desk stretching from one end of the room to the other, seating three of the people deciding my fate—or rather, my grade—today. "Admiral. Captains."

Admiral Grazer nods curtly. His fingers drum an annoyed rhythm onto the desk—not what I'm expecting. Grr. I'm expecting smiles—or at least not annoyance. I think it went too well for annoyance.

He lifts his gaze from the read-out of my simulation. "Why did you do that?"

I snap to attention. "I assume you are asking why I completed the scan, sir?"

"Yes," he growls. "You could have left orbit right after you evacuated those soldiers. Why did you stay?"

"Sir, because my initial order was to bring home a tactical assessment of the planet. Once the SOS came in, obviously my priorities shifted." Which was the whole point of the exercise—reacting to the unexpected. "But once I had the officers on board, I still had time—"

"There was a Quaneez cruiser in orbit, Cadet!"

"And I was hiding from it, sir. They never saw me—"

"But they could have! You jeopardized your life and the life of the crew you just rescued!" He glowers at me, and I blink. Keep your composure, Cadet.

"Sir, I felt comfortable with the risk and comfortable I could pull it off and complete the initial mission as well. As you can see, my scan was executed in less than ten seconds before I initiated the jump and got us all to safety. Ten seconds to get us all the tactical information on this planet and its Quaneez colonies, *and* I got the crew home safe." Seriously, I went for a minimal risk with maximal gain.

Grazer's drumming speeds up. "I would've expected you to—"

"Admiral." The voice cutting Grazer off is warm and authoritative at the same time and belongs to a man stepping out of the shadows in the back of the room—Admiral Mashaule, the president of USEF.

That moment where I thought about wiping the sweat off my forehead? Should've taken the chance when I had it, because now my sweat glands are turning into faucets. How long has he been there? What has he seen? What has he heard? Please tell me I did not just make a fool out of myself in front of the most important man in the USEF, a man who probably hates my guts since Dad is running against him for the USEF presidency.

Mashaule moves out of the shadows at the end of the room and into the light. Honestly, sometimes he and Grazer look like twins: white-haired white men in their early sixties, both with a full, white beard… I'm looking at Santa, times two.

But only one Santa looks at me like I was a good girl.

Mashaule stops behind Grazer and scans over the readouts on his screen. "Impressive time, Cadet."

Impressive time. I grow about two inches right there and then.

"Thank you, sir."

He gives me a quick smile before he points at something for Grazer. "So why downgrade her to a B?"

A *B*? Grazer is giving me a *freakin' B*? I nailed this! Aced it! I did everything he asked me to do! This B would significantly reduce my chances to enter D-2—

Grazer grumbles. "The time wasn't bad. It's her obsession with following orders."

"Since when is that a bad thing?"

I barely refrain from crossing my arms in front of my chest and nodding. Exactly. Thank you, Admiral.

Grazer rubs his eyes. "It's not, but I would expect a student of her caliber to be able to prioritize."

Mashaule scans through the readout of my performance. "I think she did very well. One of the best performances I've ever seen. Fast. Life before data—but I like officers who can think under pressure. I must say I agree with the cadet. Ten seconds for that tactical data are well spent." Mashaule gives me a smile that makes me grow another two inches. At this rate, I'll be a giant in no time, and I'm already pretty tall.

"Agreed, not bad. Anyway, I'd rather move on to the next—"

"Why don't we focus a bit on Cadet… Thorburn, it is?" asks Mashaule.

"Yes, sir." I salute.

I could be mistaken, but I think I see Grazer do a quick annoyed eye-roll. "We don't focus on her a bit more, because the cadet has done her part. I wouldn't want to give her more of my time than I give anybody else."

Sigh. It feels like a rejection, but I know it isn't. Grazer is fair with stuff like that. I just wish he'd acknowledge me a bit more, you know, him being the head for D-2…

Admiral Mashaule cocks his head. "*Thorburn*, eh?"

Translation: Tom Thorburn's kid.

I keep my face blank as if I didn't understand the implication of his question. "Correct, sir." Fingers crossed he can separate my dad's agenda from mine.

"Mentored by Admiral Conolly and the String Bean, if I recall correctly."

Here's to professionalism, because I don't flinch, I don't move, I don't do anything that could be interpreted as a reaction to the slur he used. "Admiral Conolly and *Admiral Upinga* are my mentors, yes, sir." Okay, maybe I did emphasize Admiral Upinga's name a bit more. Sue me.

Mashaule chuckles and something lights up in his eyes. "Very well. You have potential, my dear. Great potential. I'm sure you're going to be a fine officer very soon—and we always have use for those. Don't we, Bas?" He claps Grazer's shoulder.

"We do, sir."

I take my chance before the window for it closes. "Admirals, if I may—I would love to go into Division Two. My grades support—"

Grazer cuts me off with a flick of his wrist. "Not now, Cadet! Speaking out of turn—"

"Admiral, easy. It's an informal conversation, the cadet did not ignore protocol." He gives me a curious glance. "D-2, eh?"

"Yes, sir." I stand ramrod straight, my heart hammering away like it was on a mission. If I get Mashaule on my good side—and looks like that's happening—my chances go up exponentially.

Admiral Mashaule's face lights up, and I'm not lying: he beams at me. Repeat: beams. At me. The admiral and current USEF president. "Cadet, I'm very glad to hear that. D-2 needs good people like you, who can think on their feet. Especially with that virus spreading throughout our colonies and most resources being diverted there. I'm very sure something can be done about your career choice." He lays one hand on Grazer's shoulder again. "Correct, Admiral?"

"Yes, sir," Grazer says, getting the hint. "I will take a closer look at the cadet's performance over the years."

My heart and soul high-five each other. Yes! That's the biggest step forward since, like, forever! This might be the one moment I can think back to that got me into D-2—my performance here and wowing Admiral Mashaule despite my last name. "Thank you so much, sir. I promise you won't regret it."

Grazer grunts and hides a quick roll of his eyes. "Too late for that, Cadet. Way too late."

Chapter Thirty-Seven

Peace is fragile, so please don't break it.

The admiral's words have haunted me since he said them two days ago, and how couldn't they? If I don't complete this mission, we're down to zero when it comes to ideas how to cure the reptilian flu, and I would very much like humanity to not go extinct because of my inability to get those plants.

A sharp spike of failure shoots through my veins. Happens when one majorly tanks their last practice scenario just yesterday. Maybe I should've taken that as a sign and bowed out. Bad omen or something. And while usually I'm all about challenges and rising to them, this feels like disaster in the making. None of this mission is exactly what they teach in year four, or at anytime, at the academy. Add the strict timing and protocol the admiral ordered me to adhere to during the mission and no wonder I've developed a nervous twitch.

A shiver runs down my spine and I pull my jacket tighter around my body. First time I'm liking that annoying face mask. Keeps the wind out to a degree. Who knew it was this cold on campus at three in the morning? I didn't. Alas, according to yesterday's briefing and the info on the data-stick Grazer wants me in the shuttle, in my civilian outfit and on the way in less than one hour, before the USEF shuttle harbor gets busy and people see me. I get it, but besides cold I still feel weird in civilian clothing. I'm the type-A personality who'd wear their uniform even on a day off. Once a USEF cadet, always a USEF cadet.

Well, USEF *lieutenant.* Secret lieutenant. I roll my eyes at myself. Great—a secret lieutenant. And if I'm unlucky, one with a very short-lived promotion, if the Quaneez truly have upped their game in the last ten months since the ceasefire began, as the admiral said during the briefing.

I really hope they didn't. Classified intelligence will only get me so far. At one point, it comes down to me and my training, and I can only hope it was enough. I sigh. Well, no way around it now. Won't withdraw, because I won't let my people down. I *can* tackle that mission. "Exactly. I can do it," I whisper to myself, shake out my hands and crank my neck as I enter the shuttle harbor building.

"Can do what, exactly?"

My gaze flies up and to the lean figures sitting in a reading alcove on the left. All color drains from my face as I snap to attention. Busted. So, so busted. "Admiral Upinga. Admiral Conolly. Sirs." Great job, Nonie. Here's a radical thought: why don't you check the lobby first, before you enter?

Easy, because the shuttle harbor is closed to regular flights until 6:00 a.m., and nobody should freakin' be here, least of all two of my two mentors—even worse, the one person with the auditory system to hear my little whispered self-motivator. And while I love Conolly and Upinga, I wish it wasn't them catching me sneaking into the Shuttle Harbor in the middle of the night. I don't like lying to them, and now I don't have a choice. "I was talking about graduating first in class, sir. That's what I was mumbling about." Of course. What else would one talk to herself about?

Admiral Upinga peels himself out of the reading alcove. Definitely not made for tall Magellans, but for human-sized people. "I doubt that is going to be a problem for you, Cadet."

Cadet. Can't help the slight blush. Not a cadet anymore, but he doesn't know it. Yet. Kind of a pity, because all I want to do is scream it out loud. Both admirals would be proud of my accomplishment, I know that. "Thank you, sir. I hope so, sir."

"You're up early, Thorburn." Admiral Conolly rises from the couch. "And it's surprisingly busy here this morning. Admiral Grazer came in a minute ago. He didn't even see us."

I fake surprise. "Really? I thought sleeping in came with the job description of being an admiral."

Conolly chuckles. "I was surprised too. But speaking of." He gives me the once over. "Couldn't sleep? Civilian outfit?"

Dang it, dang it. Heat invades my cheeks. Evasive answer coming up in three, two… "Figured could get some more training in. Before the others get up. Early bird, you know? And after yesterday's debacle…" I shrug and hope they think my blush comes courtesy of my butchered exercise, not of my lie.

Conolly cringes, his mask moving up on his face, accommodating to the movement. "Ouch. Yeah, that one. I assume you recovered from it?" His eyes take on a warmer, more empathic shine.

"K-kind of." I step from my left foot onto my right and back. To be honest, yesterday's messed up exercise has done its part keeping me from sleep. It's one thing to be sent on a mission way above my pay grade, it's another feeling very much not ready. And usually I'm OCD enough to be ready, thank you very much, PTSD, but yesterday…

I shrug. "I hate failing things." It comes out as a grumble. I hate lying to them just as much though. Really, these two are my mentors, maybe even my friends. I should be telling them what I'm about to do, not keep it from them—alas, I can't. I'm off to a top-secret mission I probably shouldn't be on, if we weren't so desperate.

Admiral Conolly laughs out once. "I know you hate failing. *We* know. Still not a reason to be out here at *three* in the morning, like Admiral Grazer."

Sweat breaks out and tickles down my neck. I don't like him mentioning mine and Grazer's name in the same sentence. Not good. Not good at all. *Nobody can know*, Grazer said. *Peace depends on it*. On *me*. I force the corners of my mouth up into the resemblance of a smile. "I'm glad I can still surprise you. But you're also up early, sirs." Best to turn the table around and the attention away from me.

Admiral Conolly nods. "Traveling. Remember?"

Right, they said something about that, but then they're always traveling. "For OUTREACH, I assume? Didn't you say that?" If memory serves right, that's why they gave me my graduation gift early.

"Am just surprised to see you leave at *three* in the morning." Because, who does that?

Conolly's bright blue eyes shine with humor and something else, something… more aware as he winks at me. "In the broadest sense, for OUTREACH, yes. And maybe Uncle Zio here likes to watch the sun rise."

Uncle Zio gives his friend an annoyed glance. "Or maybe Admiral Conolly is tempting fate today." Yup, as always not a fan of the nickname.

Conolly chuckles. He likes to ruffle Upinga's feathers with this one, and it works every time. And speaking of time: Time to get out of here.

"Right." I scratch the back of my neck. "Okay, then… I'll see you when you get back?" My voice rises unnaturally high at the end.

"Definitely." Conolly gives me a thumbs up. "Probably sooner then you'd like." He chuckles once more, like he was up to something.

Huh?

Admiral Upinga steps closer and rests a hand on my shoulder. "Don't stress too much, Cadet. A failed exercise does not mean anything in the grand scheme of things." For a moment his eyes gloss over before a wistful smile lifts the corners of his mouth. "I've said it before—I'm not worried. I know you will make a very fine officer, very soon." He says it with such conviction, it tugs on a heart string—the same one that's been bleeding with self-doubt since Grazer gave me this *vital* mission.

I couldn't have anybody better supporting me than these two. "Thank you, sir. That's—"

"The truth." He smiles for real, and in that moment, he looks more human than any of the idiots who scream and whine about *Humanity First*.

Conolly straightens his uniform. "I'm afraid we've got to get going. The clock is ticking. Fourteen-hundred hours at Outpost Twelve. Let's go, Uncle Zio." He taps the wrist PAD on his left.

Upinga sighs silently with the use of his nickname and takes his hand from my shoulder. "Of course." For a second, he hesitates. "We'll see you soon, Cadet. May your First Sense always lead you back."

"Th-thank you," I stutter.

Admiral Conolly claps my back. "Last piece of advice for your finals, or any critical situation, really. You can do it, Nonie. There's absolutely no doubt in my mind."

I close my eyes. At least that makes one of us.

He gives me one more clap. "We'll see you on the other side, Thorburn. And when we do, it'll feel like yesterday."

And with that they walk through the sliding doors toward the Senior Officers' Launching Pad, leaving me looking after them, wondering if this might've been the last time I saw my two favorite instructors.

Because somehow it feels like an era came to an end.

Chapter Thirty-Eight

The security officer's grip around my biceps pinches my skin. I give him an annoyed glance. "You can let go, you know? There's literally nowhere I could run, and newsflash, I don't have a weapon either." The muscles in the officer's temple twitch once, the only sign he heard me. And nope, he isn't relaxing his grip on me. At all.

I sigh.

Guess I deserve it. Or rather, I don't, but that's going to come as a surprise. Definitely came as one to me. Doesn't negate what Grazer tried to do, but puts it in a different light.

We stop in front of a conference room. Can't help the subconscious tuck at my shirt to straighten it. I feel much more like the USEF officer I was supposed to become now than I have since I got thrown into this time.

And boy, does it feel good.

As soon as the reader identifies the security officer the doors open to a standard conference room. Well, the interior is standard: white and light-grey walls, the *Pioneer*'s typical dark-grey carpet, the floor-to-ceiling windows at the far wall, and a large table for ten in the middle of the room. So far, so good. The only thing non-standard in here are the people: Kieran. Chase. Zio. Alyssa Lopez, the chief engineer. Two others, who I think are head of security and science. So yeah, it's a party, and all of the *Pioneer*'s senior officers have been invited.

Without a single word, the security officer guides me to the table, then steps back to take position next to the door. My chaperone-slash-babysitter-slash-guard.

Kieran nods once in acknowledgement, then gestures at the chair. "Sit." It does come out like an order, not that I anticipated him being all warm and cuddly. This is an interrogation after all—one that's going to decide not just my fate, but humanity's as well. Apparently that never gets old.

Feels super hot in here, by the way.

I straighten and fold my arms behind my back. "I'd like to stand for now. Sir," I tag on, because… well, because. It's not a social call, and like I said. I'm a USEF officer now more than ever.

A muscle in his temple pops with my last word. "Sit. That's an—"

"I'm asking for a hearing under paragraph fourteen, subsection nine."

Kieran and Chase simultaneously suck in deep breaths. Zio pops one eyebrow, and the others don't get it. At all—and why would they? This is command-only, as I have learned since yesterday.

Kieran's lips press into a thin line. "Paragraph fourteen, subsection nine. You're sure you want to pull USEF regulations on us?"

"Yes, sir."

For a moment he considers, fingers drumming a harsh rhythm onto the table. "Commanders, you stay. Everybody else, out."

Alyssa and the other two get up, not a trace of annoyance or any emotion on their faces. They're USEF. They're used to the chain of command and need-to-know basis, even though they might have never heard of subsection nine.

The security officer lets everybody pass, then throws one questioning look at Kieran.

"You too, Svenson. Thank you."

The doors close behind him and finally I am alone with the three people who'll hold fate in their hands. "Thank you, sir."

"Don't thank me yet. I'm willing to hear what you have to say as USEF regulations state, but it doesn't mean any of us will go easy on you. Understood?"

"Understood, sir." I pull my shoulders back and straight. The civilian clothing feels wrong, but if I ignore that for a second I can almost feel my lieutenant's pips on my collar. Almost. "Gentlemen, as a reminder, under paragraph fourteen, subsection nine, this conversation is to remain confidential and private. Violation of these terms is punishable with loss of rank and incarceration." I hesitate. This next part is critical. "I'm also invoking General Order twenty three—"

Kieran slams one hand onto the table. "Seriously? What kind of game are you playing—?"

I hold up a hand. "It will be clear in a moment. I'm sorry." The remorse in my voice is real. This isn't what I would call smooth. Still. I tap my wrist PAD. "For added security, I am going to activate a sound shield. Would you like to examine it first?" I hold out my wrist and PADdy toward Chase. Springing foreign technology on them unexpected is going to get me shot faster than I can say *but*.

Confusion crosses Chase's face. "A sound shield?"

I tap the PAD. "In here."

He frowns. "Come again?"

"There's an additional safety feature installed in here." *Tap-tap.* "This all applies to G.O. twenty-three, but if you feel better, I'm okay with you aiming a weapon at me until you can be sure I mean no harm."

Chase exchanges a glance with Kieran, who nods. "Do it."

Ouch. I'd be lying if I said that didn't hurt, but then… again, my fault.

Chase stands up, draws his weapon and aims it at me. "Go for it."

With an exaggerated slow move I activate the PAD. "PADdy, initialize sound shield." And *pop*, the air around the four of us shimmers and distorts slightly. No sound will break out from it, and to the cameras in the conference room the covered area will look like a white-out. Might have not mentioned that part on purpose to keep confusion to a minimum and cooperation to a maximum.

Neither of the three men expected a literal shield to pop up around them, if their glances are any indication. Chase whistles through his teeth. "Nice." He holsters his gun after a confirming look at Kieran, who focuses on me.

"I'm giving you the benefit of the doubt here, but don't stretch it."

Kieran might look calm, but the aura of coiled and barely restrained anger tells a different story.

I nod. "I will explain. Before I do, just as an FYI, you will find a schematics of the Quaneez bunker in your files. My geotagging and recording wasn't quite on point due my PAD's damage, but together with my memory, I should've gotten a pretty good schematic for future reference." Meaning, I've got to give Chase something to program future-me's training programs by, and the USEF their only somewhat detailed knowledge of the inside of a Quaneez bunker. Even added the drawing of the torture chair every student will recognize by heart in a few decades.

You're welcome.

Conolly gives a tight nod. "Appreciated."

"Of course." Anyway. Here goes nothing. I take one long look at the three people in front of me. I shouldn't be nervous. It'll be fine. I know that. Still, my heart is racing as if it wanted to make it to 2295 on its own before me. Deep breath. "First, let me apologize for the last days. I didn't intend to cause any problems, and well, here we are. Second, I'll start with the basics, so please bear with me."

My heart thuds against my chest, bruising it on impact. "My name is Nonie Thorburn. *Lieutenant* Nonie Thorburn, graduate of the USEF McGuire Academy, class of 2295."

Three pairs of eyes pop open wide. "2295?" Kieran asks, head tilted to the left. "Are you suggesting you are—"

"Not suggesting, sir. I was—will be—born in 2277, and graduated the academy in 2295."

"What the—" Chase mumbles, crossing his arms in front of his chest. "What kind of BS are you feeding us here?"

I flinch. "None, Commander. It's true—actually, most of what I told you over the last days was true, but I had to keep certain appearances in the interest of preserving the timeline."

Kieran shakes his head. "Hold on a second. Zio?"

Upinga blinks once, slowly, big eyes even darker than normally. "Alignes with my perception, Captain."

"You sure?"

"Very sure, as I said before."

Wait, what? Why would Zio know more—

Kieran waves a hand. "Carry on, *Lieutenant.*"

I barely keep from flinching again. "Yes, sir. The beginning. How I got here. What I told Commanders Conolly and Upinga was true. I don't know how I ended up at T-12—or in this time, for that matter. I was on a mission in my time when I was thrown here." The interesting question is, was it Grazer's doing sending me back in time? All things considered, I doubt it. My previous theory still stands: I was a convenient way to kill a planet full of Quaneez. I doubt he planned a foolproof way to get me killed—two ways, actually—to send me back in time.

Which nobody knows how to do.

Anyway.

"When I woke up on board the *Pioneer,* the problem became to not contaminate the timeline, and I was afraid my presence here would do exactly that."

"I doubt telling us the truth about you is helping with that," Chase remarks drily.

"Actually, it does help." I tap PADdy again. "If you wouldn't mind, Commander Upinga? Do you recognize this code?" I hold my PAD for him to see.

A small smile tugs on the corners of his lips. "Indeed. This is my personal security code, altered in the way I progress my codes, which suggests it has been added decades in the future."

"Thank you, Commander. Now, if you wouldn't mind activating your PAD so that I can transfer the file you've uploaded for yourself to read?"

Surprise flashes in his eyes. "I did what?"

"You will upload a file onto my PAD—a file I didn't know about until it got activated once I returned from the Ursus 31 with Kie—the captain. I assume its release was triggered by time and date, which would suggest—"

"A predetermination paradox." He cocks his head. "How very fascinating."

Chase's head swivels from Zio to me. "Spell it out for me, somebody? Please?"

Kieran's fingers stop their drumming onto the table. "It means the lieutenant was supposed to be here. It means it has happened before, needed to happen, and our future selfs made sure it did—as we apparently did before. A repeating loop."

"Wait, we know each other? In the future?" Chase makes a circling motion with his finger to include the four of us.

My heart skips a beat. *We* will know each other, but Kieran… My spine stiffens. Careful now, Lieutenant. I give him a shrug and wink. "Draw your own conclusions, Commander."

He huffs. "Man, the universe is weird."

I roll my eyes. "I can subscribe to that. When I arrived here, I took it as an accident. I tried to keep to myself in the interest of reducing my influence on this time, but when neither of you realized Kie—the captain had been captured…"

Zio nods. "You did what you could to have the events unfold as you knew they should."

"Yes," I whisper. "I thought my presence here had interfered with what was supposed to happen, the captain's rescue, and I needed to fix it. But when I came back and this file got activated—"

"It confirmed you were supposed to act the way you did." Commander Upinga powers up his PAD to receive the file.

Commander Conolly shakes his head. "But why this whole mess? Why not tell you right away? If our future selfs did this, and it sounds like we did—we will do—then why didn't we have this message of how it's supposed to play out pop up right away when you landed here?"

"Or why didn't you tell me all those years I knew you," I add. Biggest scam of my life, for sure.

Upinga scans over the file. "Chicken or egg, what came first? Looks like you were kept in the dark by us because that was the way it happened for us. Telling you would have altered your reactions, and therefore the timeline."

"Or maybe you tried to give me that information, but I didn't receive it. My PAD got damaged during the crash." I hold up my wrist for a quick wiggle. "Either way, it's so messed up." I sigh.

Kieran's gaze bores into mine. "Indeed it is." Pause. When he speaks again, his voice has changed. Gone is the accusatory tone, the anger.

What's left is… softer. More Kieran. Less captain. "But… it explains why you acted the way you did during certain situations—or doesn't it?" I see the pulse in his throat jump with the latter part of the question, I hear the ounce of hope in it. This isn't Captain Wildason asking about another officer's actions, this is Kieran asking Nonie why she left him hanging in the gym.

My voice drops to barely a whisper. "It was all about the timeline. I couldn't risk altering it—and I still can't. But it's only that, about the timeline. No matter how right it feels." I swallow dry. This is as close as I can come to serving my heart on a silver platter.

Kieran closes his eyes, a silent, deep breath escaping him. When he opens them again, my heart pitter-patters from the relief shining in them. "Thank you, Nonie."

Nonie.

Not lieutenant. My pitter-pattering heart pumps extra fast, now that the chains around it are gone.

Commander Upinga sucks in a sharp breath between his teeth. "How right it feels—interesting you should say that." He looks up from his PAD. "Do you mind if I turn this off?" He points at my right biceps area.

"My genetic scrambler?" I guess that cat is out of the bag now, too.

"Genetic scrambler?" Kieran's brows turn into a V.

I sigh. "My dad is protective of me."

Upinga pauses typing. "May I go ahead?"

"Well, *can* you turn it off?" It's double- and triple-secured thanks to my paranoid father and his ongoing fear of yet another abduction.

"Future-me can."

Of course. Meaning, Dad must've told my mentors I'm wearing a scrambler, and Admiral Upinga made sure to include the information. So much for privacy.

I turn to have my right shoulder face him. "Then by all means, if you need to, go for it."

Zio taps into his pad. "Thank you." The PAD beeps, and I swear the commander freezes. Rechecks something. Again. *Again.* "I didn't want to believe my future self, but… I was right. Future-me was right." He lifts his gaze off the PAD straight at me, and the way he looks at me…

"Uhh, anything I should know about? Because you're pretty close to freaking me out, Commander."

"Call me Zio, Nonie. We've talked about that. It's Zio—now more than ever there's no need for formalities."

Uh— "There isn't?"

He keeps his eyes glued to mine, unblinking. "Not between family."

"Fam—"

He nods. "Correct. Family. After all, you are my sister's daughter. I am your uncle."

Chapter Thirty-Nine

Y ou're making life a tad more complicated for me, you know that. Right, Dad?"

He swipes a finger along the edge of his desk as if checking for dust. "You have no idea," he mumbles under his breath.

I narrow my eyes. Not the answer I was expecting. "Huh?"

Dad shakes his head and plasters a smile on his face so fake it's obvious. "I'm saying that you have no idea. You chose a school where your father works. How did you think that'd go for you?"

"I was referring to your political stance, Dad, not to you parenting me in front of everybody else."

"Oh." He flinches, but even that looks fake. "Sorry. But you know—"

"I know. And believe me, from my point of view, you're the one who's right, but I can't say it's making life easier for me." I take off my backpack and turn the front for him to see.

Dad's jaw drops, then snaps closed again as his lips press into a thin line. "Who. Did. This."

"This time?" I drop the backpack on the floor, making sure the egg-stained side of it lands sunny side up.

"*This time?*"

I shrug. "Well, it has happened before."

Dad balls a slow fist, then releases his fingers again. Exactly ten seconds after my last sentence, he pushes out two single words, more a grunt than anything else. "How. Often."

Falling into the chair in front of his desk, I lift both palms to the ceiling. "Who cares? It's happened before, and it will happen again. You wouldn't even know about it if you hadn't asked to see me today." The last three times this or something similar happened, he was away visiting Mag-2. The time before that I managed to avoid him, and before that… I don't even remember.

"But now I do know, and I also want to know whom I need to expel for this."

I give him a frustrated glance. "Really, Dad? One, I'm holding up well on my own. I can ignore them. For every idiot out there, there's at least two good guys." I don't say *for now*, but I know we're both thinking it. "If you want to blame anybody, blame Humanity First and stupid Travis Roodt, or else none of them would be brave enough to do any of this in broad daylight and at the academy, of all places." But alas, you build a climate where it's okay to say or do the bad stuff, and people will do it, and will do it without regrets.

Dad flattens both palms on his desk, the picturebook example of self control. "Oh, I'm going to make them regret it."

"No, you're not." I shake my head at him. "I have many issues with my fellow cadets, but I won't have Daddy sweep in and fix my problems. It'll get better. As they say, time will teach the fools."

Dad jerks back as if slapped. "What?"

"What what?"

Dad comes up with a quick smile, the kind that's pro forma and doesn't reach his eyes. "Sorry, honey. You caught me off-guard with that Magellan proverb."

I blink twice. Caught off guard by a proverb. That can happen?

Dad sighs once and draws an invisible pattern onto the desk's shiny surface. "Your mom… your mom likes—liked—to say that a lot." He keeps his eyes glued to the desk, and I don't dare to breathe.

My mom. Dad never talks about her. Never. I know the bare basics—name, that she was tall, that she died right after my birth—but that's about it. I know next to nothing besides that. *This,* him saying she liked this proverb, is the most I've gotten in terms of personal information. And to imply we're alike, kind of… it warms my soul and lights it up.

I swallow dry. Proceed with caution. "Dad?" I keep my voice low and soft. "I want to know more about Mom. Please," I add, not quite in a begging tone, but close enough.

Dad closes his eyes, his fingers still their movement. The way he scrunches up his face, like he was in pain—I know the answer before he says it.

"Nonie, I… I can't." He opens his eyes, regret and pain shining from them—the perfect fire for my anger. How dare he look at me like a tortured puppy! This is my mom we're talking about—or rather, *not* talking about!

I wrap my fingers around the armrest of the chair I'm in. Deep breath in, deep breath out. Yelling at my dad has never and will never lead to results. "You can't, or you won't, Dad?" I shoot him an icy glance. "I'm sixteen years old. I'm going to graduate the academy next year. And all I have is a name on a birth certificate—nothing else. No knowledge about the woman who gave birth to me. No stories about her. No pictures—"

"You know I don't have any!"

Sure. I roll my eyes. "Yeah, yeah, far-off colony, all data destroyed when the Quaneez attacked." *Right.* Like my dad would never take a picture himself. Like that wouldn't be backed up and stored for all eternity. Like that Quaneez attack and destruction of my mother's home colony was the reason why I can't find anything about her in our databases.

Dad presses his lips into a thin line. "Watch your tone, Fräulein."

I roll my eyes *again*, for emphasis. "Of course. I apologize, *sir*."

My dad takes a barely controlled breath in. "What was between me and your mother is exactly that, between me and your mother. All you need to know is that your mother was and is the one for me. There will never be anybody else. And I can tell you, the pain that comes with that is greater than anything you can imagine. So I recommend you dial it down a notch and exercise some patience, and when both of us are ready, I will talk to you. But not a day before, and surely not when you're behaving like a petulant child." He levels me with an even gaze. "Dismissed."

Chapter Forty

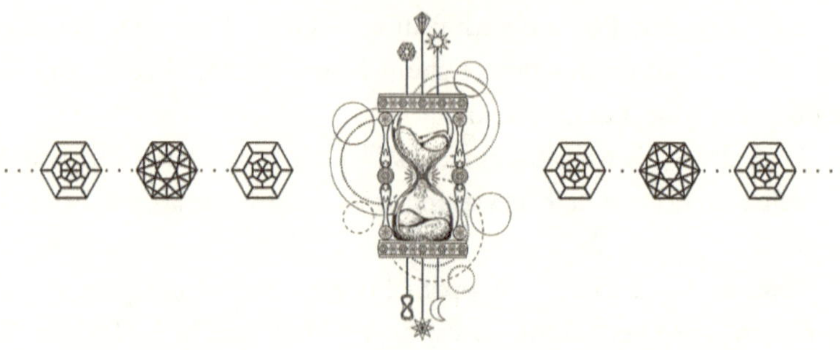

Holy Guacamoley.

I lift the glass with fake-Lubbeck's to my mouth with shaking hands. Across from me in Kieran's comfy, wide leather chair, Chase has gulped down a whole bottle already, but judging by the way he looks, he'd probably prefer something stronger.

I guess we all could do with that—besides Zio, maybe. *Uncle Zio.* He's been Mr. Calm since the revelation that turned my life upside down, although I can't shake the sensation that there's more to the story. But until I get that info, I'll take the liberty of silently freaking out over what I missed all my life.

Half Magellan.

Uncle Zio.

Uncle Zio. All the times Admiral Conolly teased Upinga, calling him Uncle Zio…

I groan.

Time travel gives me a headache.

Out of all of us, Kieran is still taking it the best, maybe that's why he's the captain. Dealing with the unexpected comes with that territory. That being said, I feel like I should get some credit as well, because going from thinking I had a quote-unquote regular human mom to knowing Dad bonded with a Magellan woman who became my mom… That's one heck of a one-eighty change. Never mind that Dad violated about a dozen USEF laws, come to think about it.

Worse: Never mind that she died—will die—in childbirth, and that I can't even tell Zio that piece of information. Although I think that ship might've sailed together with my cover story and my obvious surprise when he revealed I was half-Magellan.

Time travel sucks.

"Anybody anything else?" Kieran sets down some snacks onto his coffee table. "Nonie, you look pale, eat. Trip, stop drinking that stuff by the gallon. It tastes good, but I'm sure it's not that good for you. Zio, I think at this point we're ready for some more explanations, if you have them." With an *oomph* he lets himself fall into the couch next to me, keeping a little more distance than true friends would, but less than a captain would keep with his officers. I'll take it.

Zio gives his friend a long, evaluating glance. "You look like crap, Kieran."

Kieran chuckles once and rubs his eyes. "Is that your professional medical opinion, Doctor?"

"To a degree."

"Huh." Kieran drops his hand from his eyes over the backrest of the couch, so that it's even closer to me. "My nightmares have been cranking it up, not that it mattered. Nothing a good night's sleep couldn't fix. Or good news. Or some good, old, logical explanation to this confusing mess. Bring it on, Zee."

Zio nods and takes a seat in the second leather chair. "Okay then. I can go by the notes my future-self left and I can offer an opinion, but I don't have the answer to all your questions." I'm not sure whether he means mine or Kieran's, but either or, better than nothing.

"Please," I wave a hand, "just gimme what you got." At this point, I'd like to stop feeling like fate played me all my life, although I doubt that's going to happen.

Zio activates his PAD. "Very well then. Let's cover the basics first." He smiles when he realizes he quoted my intro from a mere hour ago. "To get everybody up to speed, Nonie's father is—or rather, will be— Ensign Tom Thorburn." He holds up the PAD, showing an old… well, *current,* photo of my dad.

Kieran startles and leans forward. "Wait, *that* Ensign Thorburn?"

His gaze bounces from the picture to me and back. "Tom is your father? We worked together on Alpha Rubrum."

I know, I want to say. Dad didn't tell me much about that mission, but that much I know. "That's my dad," I say instead.

Kieran chuckles. "Tom is your father. I really didn't see that coming. Thinking back to Alpha Rubrum..." He shakes his head, a surprised smile on his face. "Well, I guess it makes sense. Still, so odd thinking back knowing what I know now how I interacted with him."

He'd be surprised. Going with my gut I go for it. "You know, he still talks about when you put him in charge of that northern part of the Magellan Colony there. In fact, it's part of why he went into embassy duties." Add the newly minted Captain Wildason officially congratulating him in front of the assembled high brass for his achievements with the Magellans after Alpha Rubrum was evacuated, and he was set on that path.

"He did?" Kieran scratches behind his ear. "Wow. Okay. Didn't see that happen either." His cheeks take on a slight reddish hue. "But it's cool he took so much from that assignment. He was so very motivated."

"And he credits you with his career."

"Really?" His eyes widen. "Man, my influence reaches far."

"Indeed it does," Zio chimes in. "One could say if you didn't set up Ensign Thorburn with this task, he would have never met Nonie's mother."

My entire body tenses. "He— They— They met on Alpha Rubrum?" All that time ago? And right now-right now, my dad and my mom are actually an item already?

Chase whistles through his teeth. "So you're saying Bas isn't the only one who found himself some love down there?"

"But Ensign Thorburn's the only one neither found out nor prosecuted," Zio states.

"Bas wasn't prosecuted either." Chase shrugs. "Don't get me wrong, I think prosecution for love of any kind is idiotic, but Bas had Mashey's protection, and Tom Thorburn didn't. I assume he hid it better?"

My mind's in a daze. "Yeah." I nod in slow-mo. "Nobody knows. Nobody."

"Until now." Zio changes the displayed picture to one of a tall

Magellan female. "My sister Kelia. Nonie's mom."

I wish I could've met her, now more then ever, and I'd be lying if my heart didn't cramp seeing her. All Magellans are beautiful from my point of view. I always thought so. Tall, slender, dark hair with that oil-shimmer, large dark eyes… But my mom, Kelia, she is special. Maybe I'm biased already after twenty minutes of knowing I have a Magellan mom, but whatever: with her even features, soft smile, but a little spark of mischief in her eyes I feel connected to her right away.

"Now I know where I've got that from," I whisper, touching my hair. Mystery of the reflecting hair solved.

Kieran turns in his place. "It suits you." He reaches out and brushes one hand over my ponytail, then drops it as if burned. "I mean— Like— Never mind." He straightens away from me again and clears his throat. "You were saying, Zee?"

"I was going to say that Nonie's DNA comes with a number of features thanks to the Magellan input, some a surprise to me, some not."

"Surprise?" I sit up straight. "Why would—?"

As if we were twins, Kieran mimics my movement. "The same as yours?"

Something passes between them before Zio nods once. "Partially. We'll have to see. I've had about twenty minutes to make sense of this, so excuse me if I'm not as precise as usual."

I scoot forward. "What is there to make sense of? I've got two sets of genes, one human, one Magellan, what's the big deal?"

Chase lifts his glass up in mock salute. "Oh, dear. Brace yourself. You're in for a treat."

I let myself fall back into the cushions. "All right. Bring it on." Can't really be much more of a biggie than what I've heard already, predestination paradox and Magellan moms, etc.

Zio cocks his head. "For one, it gives you a natural hachimoji DNA with eight nucleobases instead of four. Which is why your scrambler comes in handy to hide that little fact."

No kidding. Now I know why Dad really wanted me to wear that scrambler. "But I'm guessing that's not the surprise you're referring to."

He hesitates. "No. The surprise would be something less obvious and more impactful. As you know, us Magellans stay separated from other species. Not just yours here in this area of space, but even before we fled our home. We never mingle—or we keep it to a minimum."

I nod. "So I've learned."

"The reason for that is different from what you might think though. We stay to ourselves because we prefer to minimize interference. All Magellans are able to… feel right from wrong. Differentiate what's supposed to happen from what shouldn't." He pauses. "Do you understand what I'm saying?"

"Uhh, not really. An ethics radar?" Good for them. Us humans could benefit from that as well.

Kieran turns toward me again, pulling his knee onto the couch and brushing it past my leg. *Butterflies.* "Kind of. What he means is that Magellans have a very strong intuition for lies. They can feel deceit—" He stops himself mid-sentence. "Speaking of: Why didn't the alarm bells ring for Nonie?" Kieran gives Zio a questioning look.

"They did. Remember, Chase? The day we brought Nonie on board, I told you something felt odd."

Chase nods. "True, he did say that. We assessed her as a security risk, couldn't find anything besides her genes not being registered in our databank. And as we discussed, that could be normal, depending on who she is and where she's from."

Kieran scratches his neck. "True, but—"

"I assume since she was supposed to be here it didn't register the way it otherwise would have."

"Huh?" Chase scratches his neck as well. Something must be itchy around here.

Zio stands ramrod straight, reminding me of myself when I'm addressing an admiral. Looks like we're related for real. "To be honest, the intuition for lies… isn't really an intuition for lies."

"Oo-kay…?" Kieran drapes the hand that worked his neck over the couch's backrest, where it comes to lie so close to me I feel its warmth like I was sitting in the sun.

"It is something about us Magellans nobody outside our world knows about." Like a cadet he looks at a spot above Kieran's head, the personification of being uncomfortable.

"Really?" Kieran sits up straighter, which means unfortunately that hand drops off the backrest. "I thought you told us your species' secret already."

"I told the version of my species' biggest secret I was allowed to tell you."

Kieran groans. "Then give me details, Zio. And please relax, you're making me nervous."

Zio sighs and deflates. "We never discuss this with outsiders—our reason why we stay alone and separated from the spacefaring community." He hesitates and presses his lips together.

Chase puts his glass down, attention a hundred percent on his friend. "Come on, Zee. It's us and we're protected by Nonie's spy shield-thingy. It doesn't get much safer than that."

"I know, but it's difficult." He sucks in a deep breath. Then huffs once. "But the path is clear. Anyway. You all know the greeting *may your First Sense guide you well.* It sounds like a nice salutation, but there is more to it. It refers to our first sense, a temporal radar of sorts."

Wait—*temporal* what? I lean forward even more, and so does Kieran. "Explain."

Zio paces between the kitchen and sitting area. "It is hard to explain for somebody without that sense, like you would have a hard time explaining vision to a blind person. To us time registers differently. It's not strictly linear, but immersive. We don't only feel its passing, like everybody else, but we feel the regular flow and changes in it, including changes to the past or future."

"Like what?" Kieran supports his upper body with his arms on his knees, completely focused.

"Like when I focus on my First Sense, I can get an idea of what is most likely going to happen in the near future if all things stay at an equilibrium. Or rather, an idea of what *should* happen—what has happened, is predetermined to happen—according to the flow of the timeline."

Kieran shakes his head. "Like a sophisticated fortune teller? Sorry, Zee, but you're making no sense."

But he does. He does! To me at least. I *think*—because if I'm right it explains that weird feeling I've had all my life in certain situations! I swallow hastily. "You mean, it feels right to do one thing, but not another?"

All heads whip over to me.

"Exactly," Zio says. "That is the natural progression of the timeline you're feeling—am I right in assuming that's what you're referring to?"

"I think so." I nod like a crazy person. Holy whatever, I can't believe it. That sixth sense I've had all my life—not a sixth sense at all, but rather a First Sense. Look at that. I swipe a non-existing strand of hair out of my face. "Sometimes I have a feeling, for the lack of a better term. For example, a few minutes ago. I know I'm not allowed to tell you about the future, but I told you my dad went into embassy services as a direct result of your influence, because it felt right to tell you." My heart skips a couple of beats. If that intuition is actually genetic… how weird and cool at the same time!

Zio nods. "That's what I'm talking about. You subconsciously felt the timeline's need for that information to be passed down. Maybe because of it Kieran is going to encourage your father even more when he meets him the next time, who knows. Fact is, it needed to happen."

Oy. I blush. Yeah, it needed to happen. That would be Kieran's official letter of recommendation that got my dad accepted into the embassy services. Sheesh. The timeline means business, it appears.

Kieran blows a big puff of air through pursed lips as he lets himself fall back into the couch. "You're not kidding, right? Neither of you?" I get a quick check with that question. "Because it does sound a tad far-fetched."

Zio resumes his pacing. "It does, but it isn't. Centuries ago—actually, millennia ago—our species was known for their accuracy in predicting time's master plan. People from all over our galaxy came for advice. All it took us is to focus our First Sense, maybe add some touch,"—he mimics laying a hand onto somebody—"and we could help them make a decision what to do. Now, would they've come to the same destination on their own? Most likely. Time is good at keeping its major line intact. But sometimes…" His eyes take on a distant quality.

"Sometimes what?" Kieran asks.

"Sometimes people want to alter it. My species was hunted, captured, and used as biological detectors either against attempts to alter the timeline or to actively alter the timeline in somebody's favor." He stops his pacing, head lowered, gaze unfocused on the ground. "We were nearly extinct at one point. Every race, every power-hungry or paranoid person knowing about us wanted a Magellan. After all, if they knew what the future held, they could try to change it or prepare for it."

Kieran rubs his forehead. "This is giving me a headache. Correct me if I'm wrong, but doesn't them knowing already influence their decisions, which could then alter the outcome?"

A sad smile appears on Zio's face. "Correct. Which is why we don't do custom-order fortune telling, to stick to your comparison. We've always seen ourselves more as keepers of the timeline, not influencers."

"Why would you need somebody to keep the timeline? Things happen, time flows in one direction—"

I tug Kieran's sleeve and wave. "You gotta keep the timeline intact, 'cause, you know, some people swim in the wrong direction."

He pauses mid-sentence, then rolls his eyes at himself. "Never mind. Apparently, time is more complicated than we thought."

"In many ways," Zio huffs. "Since Magellans have begun to record their history, seventeen attempts have been made to alter the timeline. Sixteen from a point in the future. One from a point in the past."

"Sun and Stars," Chase gasps and refills his glass, taking one ginormous gulp that empties half of the glass. "You're saying somebody time-traveled to change the past—or future?"

"Correct. And our operatives took care of them and protected the timeline."

"Who? Do we know them? Give me details." Kieran has dropped the massaging hands, leaving a red mark on his forehead that does nothing to distract him from assessing this potential danger.

Zio shakes his head. "Irrelevant at this point. The species involved have—will—self-destruct. Unless there are more attempts from other points in time, they won't have an impact on us."

A muscle thrums in Kieran's neck. "I assume the admiralty doesn't know?"

"Of course not. Instead of keeping us at an arm's length, I'm positive they'd be more *motivated* to cooperate with us."

"No kidding," Kieran says with a gloomy undertone. "So, time travel is real, and Nonie has been here before, so to speak." He glances over his shoulder at me, and for the first time since I messed up with him, I feel like the walls are completely down. "Which brings me to the point of how she got here. If going back in time was easy, we'd have it figured out already. Ideas, anybody? Nonie?"

"Not a clue." I shrug. "I didn't do anything out of the ordinary, really. And my story was true, what I told Chase and Zio. I mean, I scan that planet—*flash*—wake up here. That's it. And right now, my biggest problem is that while we now know I was supposed to be here, we don't know whether I am supposed to return." Or how. That part of my future is unwritten for myself and Admirals Upinga and Conolly. They could be quote-unquote *waiting* for me in the future, or they could be in my dad's office at this very moment with condolences and flowers.

All I know is that clearly my *Admirals* Conolly and Upinga have met me in their past: the Uncle-jokes. The PAD they gave me… little hints that make sense in retrospect.

Kieran nods, then looks at his colleague. "Zio?"

Zio pauses and tilts his head. "I have a theory I need to prove."

I cock my head to the side. "You do?" That's hope right there, as in way more than I dared to wish for.

"I do. Obviously I cannot promise anything, but… I am cautiously optimistic." He ends with a soft smile that releases the weight of at least two mountains from my shoulders. "And I would like to get to work on it, if you don't mind." That last sentence is directed at Kieran, but Chase takes that as his cue to get up and stretch.

"I think that's a great idea. Don't know about you guys, but I've had enough excitement for one day. Zio, if you want to dig into whatever it is you need to dig into, why don't you do that and we figure out the details tomorrow, when I'm not feeling like I've been through a wringer?"

Kieran chuckles, and that one sound bridges the distance between us like no other. He stands up, like Chase. "Agreed. Oh-seven-hundred hours, sharp. Conference room. Nonie, bring your… things." He nods at my wrist PAD. "We're not taking any chances."

"Will do." I nod and get up, but before I can maneuver myself out of the tight space between the couch, table and past Kieran, Zio holds up a hand. He gives first Kieran then me a long look.

"I suggest Nonie you stay for a while longer. Now that you know who you are, I have one piece of advice for you. Follow your First Sense." His gaze drifts over to Kieran, then back to me. "Interestingly, since we have been talking about a predestination paradox... I found my older counterpart left this for you on your PAD. From the *Pioneer's* surveillance cameras. Taken during Red Alert, apparently." He sighs and taps something on the screen, then nods at it. "You're welcome."

At the same time Kieran's PAD springs to life, Kieran and I suck in a deep breath.

"Holy cow," I breathe, staring at the picture.

Holy. Cow.

Chapter Forty-One

The door closes behind Zio, and I don't dare to move.

This picture… It… It…

Kieran takes a step closer to the PAD on the table, as if that in any way would change or confirm what has been staring us in the face. "That's… us." He looks over his shoulder at me, then back at the picture. "That's us."

"No doubt about it," I whisper. Absolutely none.

It's us—in an embrace. The picture must have been taken—or rather, will be taken—somewhere in the hangar bay. The lights are dimmed and reddish, and the only reason why I know it's us is because the picture is taken against the incoming light, clearly showing our two silhouettes. I can't unsee it. It's us.

It's definitely us.

Kieran and me, in an embrace, our foreheads leaned against another, one of his hands in my hair. It's such a private moment, filled with so much emotion, it brings goosebumps to my skin.

Follow your First Sense.

I swallow dry. Funny how one can feel so insecure when for a change the path is clear—when for a change I can believe my intuition. I drop my gaze to meet his, and—

Whoa. A surge flashes through me, a wave of warmth coupled with the definite certainty of what's to come. It leaves my senses tingling and brings goosebumps to my spine—or the latter could be from the way Kieran's lips part slightly and his eyes widen. Because this is Kieran, I'm looking at. Not the captain. *Kieran.*

On wobbly legs, I take a step forward closer to him then he backs up. "Kieran—"

His knees hit the couch and buckle, and he sits himself down, never taking his eyes off me.

"Are you sure?" Kieran's voice is hoarse.

"It's been right in front of our eyes." I stop in front of him, my knees a hair's breadth from touching his. "I thought I was stupid, a figment of my imagination, or wishful thinking. Turns out it wasn't." That picture proves it. Somewhere in the depth of my mind, I wonder what it means, if it meant I stayed in this time, but it's not important now. Kieran is. My breathing is way too fast and shallow, but I can't slow it down for the life of me.

The apple in his throat moves up and down. "So we're sure. We're not disturbing the natural flow of events." Kieran's gaze bores into my eyes—no, correction: not just into my eyes. His gaze bores into *me.* Those beautiful, soft eyes of his delve deep, into my core, my soul, seeing me for who I am behind all of my disguises.

Slowly, I inch forward, lowering my right knee onto the couch next to his left thigh. "We're not," I whisper. Him and me, whatever it may lead to, feels more natural than anything in my life before, including breathing.

I bring my other knee to rest next to his other thigh and scoot closer, until my knees hit the backrest's cushion. "The First Sense I never knew I had has been trying to tell me that, only I was too afraid to listen." I lower my weight and come to sit straddling Kieran's lap.

For the shortest moment, I see his eyes roll back as his lips part with a soft sigh—then his hands come to lay on my hips.

Yowza.

My heart's beating too fast, but barely fast enough to support all those butterflies. They need their oxygen.

"You and me?" His question comes out as a growl.

"Yes."

A muscle in his jaw pops—and he leans forward, connecting our fronts.

His sudden proximity makes me dizzy. The scent of his hair, his body, it calls to me.

For a moment, neither of us moves, but then he stretches up his chin—and I follow my First Sense and bring my lips to his.

The first touch of our lips is testing. Calm. Gentle. A mere probe if we're still on the same page, but when I give him a small lick, a throaty groan leaves his throat—and that sound, it undoes all the restraint I might've had. Within a second the kiss turns heated. Hands begin to travel: his up and down my back, mine delving into his hair. We're grabbing each other, gasping for air, yet neither of us dares to break the kiss. It feels too good, too powerful, too addicting to ever stop.

Kieran wraps his arms around my waist, pulling me in tighter, *tighter,* deepening the kiss, the hard ripples of his stomach muscles pressing against my front. Every little inch of skin we're touching is burned by the lightning crashing through it. *Burned.* He sneaks one hand under my shirt, and that brush of his palm over my back, it makes me grind my hips into him.

The breath he sucks in and sighs out through our kiss… extra-fuel for those butterflies. His touch stays light as he explores my body, fingertips grazing down my flank. Everything inside me contracts, every muscle, every fiber, every nerve. My body is on fire head to toe and in-between. Definitely in-between.

And I want more.

I break the kiss. "Wait."

Alarm flares up in his eyes as he pulls back, lips swollen and red. "Too fast?" Worry clouds his expression, and how could I blame him? We've been here before. Making out. Me stopping it.

Only this time I shake my head. "No. Not too fast. Not fast enough." I grab the hem of my shirt, pull it over my head and discard it to somewhere behind me.

A strangulated gasp leaves his throat as his eyes pop wide.

Thank you. Exactly the reaction I was going for with my goods on display at eye level.

His fingers dig into my sides so hard it's close to painful—in a good way. "Nonie," he whispers. "You're sure?"

I tilt my pelvis forward. "More than I ever was for anything." And I want more. I need more.

Slowly, so, so slowly, Kieran lifts his gaze up to meet mine. The pulse in his neck beats feverishly, every single beat calling my name. For a moment we're both frozen, trapped in the same spell, but then the apple in his throat bobs with a hard swallow—and he trails his fingers up my sides, every brush heaven and hell. Fast, yet not fast enough. He moves them high, higher—until they graze the bra at the sides of my breasts.

Oh, dear Sun and Stars.

My back arches into his touch like drawn in by a magnet. "Kieran," I breathe, and something mischievous lights up in his eyes. Ever so slowly, he moves forward and licks over my neck.

Whoa—

A soft moan breaks free, one I had no chance to control, absolutely none. He licks again, then gives the side of my neck a soft suck. That's when I lose control and rock my hips harder into his. It's a need I can't fight—I don't want to fight. It's a need for more of him. More of his touch, his—

Kieran's entire body jerks, the same shockwave crashing through him as through me. If this is normal for others, congratulations, because it is one heck of an upgrade to me. I never knew sensations could be this strong, this powerful and overwhelming, without causing a heart attack.

One of his hands shoots out and cups my butt, pressing me harder against him. Not a single sheet of paper would fit between our lower halves, and I feel *everything*. Every long inch of him, hard, pressing through his pants into the softest parts of me. My senses are hyperaware, yet completely blind to anything apart of Kieran. Everything revolves around him, and to be honest, has been for a while now. Warmth floods my chest, and it has nothing to do with what he's doing to my body, but everything with what he's doing to my soul.

For the first time in ages, I'm at peace.

Chapter Forty-Two

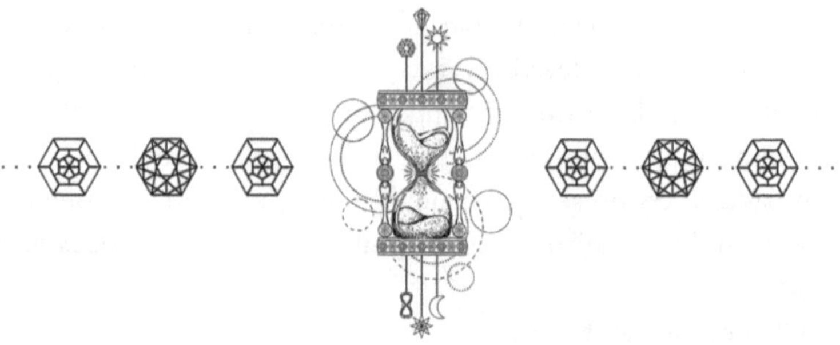

"Ten HUT!"

As one, the entire group of cadets snap to attention. Hundreds of arms slap against thighs, hundreds of booted heels crash together into a forty-five degree angle, and hundreds of chins dip down the slightest bit to keep the line of sight parallel to the ground.

We are one well-oiled machinery that is the McGuire USEF Academy.

"Faculty and students, welcome." Admiral Grazer's voice carries over all seven hundred of us, powered by the hidden speakers in our assembly hall. I've only been here once, when I got sworn in as a USEF cadet. The second time I expected to be here was my swearing in as a full-fledged officer next year. But then, there is only one forty-year anniversary of the Quaneez wars. Only one day to commemorate and pay tribute to the fallen soldiers and civilians.

The Admiral lets his gaze drift over the rows and rows of cadets. "Today, we assemble here to pay our respects to forty years of history. On this very day, forty years ago, the *USEF Pioneer* was forced to retaliate against a Quaneez attack. As you all know, this incident sparked years of wars, billions of deaths on both sides and has deeply affected each and every one of us. There isn't a single human being alive today who has not lost somebody to the horrible crimes of the Quaneez people."

He pauses, and the image of the *Pioneer* hovering in space opposite of five Quaneez battle cruisers pops up, projected into the air every ten meters throughout the assembly hall. "To this day, we hail the crew's reactions as exemplary. Attempt to establish contact. Seek peaceful means of communication. But when that fails…"

The image changes to a battle picture, probably taken by a drone, like the first one. The Quaneez cruisers' fire is so rapid, the shutter speed and light weren't sufficient, turning the single shots into one continuous line of fire. It looks like straight lightning rods shooting out of their weapons, trying to pierce the *Pioneer.*

Grazer sighs, and it carries over the mike like a wave of sorrow. "The *Pioneer* didn't run. The *Pioneer* stood her ground. The crew turned around what could have been a devastating loss for humanity and what experts think would have led to the extinction of the human race."

At this point, a picture of the Hotshot Trio pops up. "Thanks to the brilliance of these three men, we are standing here today. Thanks to them, we found a way to retaliate against Quaneez attacks. Thanks to them, a swift loss and surrender was avoided."

The image changes again, this time to space filled with debris, the *Pioneer* hovering at the outskirts of it. Charred black marks are scattered across its hull and the starboard side shows some quite impressive hull damage with a blue-glowing patch in the middle, like a plasma leak had been hastily sealed and nobody bothered or had the time to fix the hull breach. This is the most famous picture of the Battle of Balthar—the *Pioneer's* victory. The details and tactics of said victory are super-secret, which of course has nourished speculations for the last forty years, but it stayed a secret. Neither Admiral Upinga nor Conolly gave me a hint. Every time I've asked about this day—Day Zero—their faces darkened, and to say I haven't gotten much in terms of information would be an understatement. They don't like to talk about it. At all. Which scares me. What did they do? What is so bad they can't talk about it? So bad it was made Top Secret?

Grazer lowers his voice. "Those brilliant men taught us that even in the face of adversity we do not lose hope. We do not give up. We carry on." A line like taken from a textbook. He swallows, then jabs a finger at the image. "*This* is what USEF is all about. Not accepting the odds, but turning them around. Not resigning to a loss, but reinventing the battle. Not succumbing to an outcome, but trying to change it. These men did all of us a favor."

Somewhere behind us cadets the faculty, and therefore Admirals Upinga and Conolly are standing. I wonder how they're feeling, seeing what they did up there, them and Captain Wildason. Knowing that they started the war, because that's what happened: On that day, on May 15th, 2255, their actions started the Quaneez wars. Did they have a choice? No. Did they, all things considered, do a quote-unquote good job during the Battle of Balthar? Yes.

Does it make them feel better? I bet not.

That's one heck of a way to go down in history, and I don't think it was—is—easy.

"So today, on this fortieth anniversary, we remember the heroic acts of the *USEF Pioneer*, who saved us from sure extinction. We remember every soldier, every civilian, every being killed by the enemy. And we swear to bring an end to the murder of our species. We stand united as humanity, fighting for our freedom until each and every last suppressor is gone and until we can walk in peace."

Ouch. While I appreciate the sentiment, that little speech strikes me as wrong, or at least as not complete. He could have mentioned the Magellans. They might not have helped with manpower, but they did help with technology. He could have mentioned any of the other four species we discovered since then, three of which have offered to help, only we shut them down because… good question. Officially, we don't want to drag them into a war that's not their's. Unofficially, I bet we don't trust them. We're not letting the Magellans in, and we know them really well. Why would we trust a species we've known for even shorter time?

Grazer pulls his uniform straight and folds his hands behind his back. "May each of you contribute to this fight, may each of you contribute to our win, or die trying."

The cadet in front of me twitches. Strong words to say to a group of mostly underage students, but this, the Quaneez wars, is our reality. I know my two mentors are working on something regarding the Quaneez, but who knows if it's going to be working.

We're safer assuming it won't.

Grazer lets his gaze drift over the assembled masses. "Dismissed."

A collective exhale follows his last word, like a sigh of relief from hundreds of people. The fact that we're all trained for this war doesn't change how painful it is to see those images, to read the stats, and to imagine the unspeakable sorrow the war has brought us.

The other cadets around me fall into groups of two or three and make it out of the assembly hall. The rest of the afternoon is off—it is Quaneez War Memorial Day, after all. I sigh and tug my uniform straight. Maybe I can find Dad. I weave through the masses of students looking for him, which is moderately easy as one of the taller cadets. Ah, there he is—standing in front of the Quaneez Wars Memorial outside, a crowd of reporters around him. Must be at least fifteen, judging by how many camera drones are hovering between them and Dad. Of course they would interview him on a day like this. He's the admiral with the most experience with other cultures, i.e., the Magellans, and one of the few promoting team work and unification over sticking to everybody's own affairs. Admiral Mashaule stands a couple of meters over to the left, even more reporters around him. I sneak in closer to Dad, but stay out of sight, not wanting to distract him.

One of the reporters raises her hand. "Admiral Thorburn, are you not afraid the aliens will take over our culture? Our planet? Change who we are?"

Dad tugs his uniform straight, a habit I've unfortunately inherited. "Oh, by all means, I want them to change who we are. I want them to make us better, to help us evolve, and in return, we will do the same for them. Throughout humanity's history, there's always been migration followed by integration, and the mixing of knowledge has always advanced us and made us stronger. Smarter. The time for brutal territorial battles is over—or at least I dare to think that we have moved beyond such unnecessary violence. We have the intellect to see what everybody can bring to the table and to see that joining forces will ultimately make us stronger, and not weaker."

Another reporter isn't too happy with that reply. He wrinkles his nose. "But what if you're wrong? What if the aliens don't share your high opinion on integration, but try to conquer humanity? We are standing here on the fortieth anniversary of the Quaneez wars. You must admit that worry is valid."

My dad levels him with an even stare. "If I had to bet, I would say the chance of any of the races we encountered *conquering humanity*, as you said, equals zero. In fact, I would push it further and say that personally I'm more afraid of narrow-minded humans and the damage they can do to our society, than I am of any of the alien species we have discovered."

Some other reporter raises her hand. "A growing number of citizens is siding with you on that topic, Admiral. What do you say to those polls that have you up and coming?"

Dad gives her a nod. "I'm saying that I'm more than happy humanity is seeing the advantage of teamwork. Together we can be stronger—"

"Strong enough to defeat the Quaneez?"

Dad shrugs. "Maybe. But we won't know if we don't give teamwork a chance."

"There's news about a new viral strain infection of our colonies— are you talking about teamwork with the Magellans?"

"I'm not limiting team work to the Magellans, although they are an obvious choice. I know about the virus, and USEF is keeping a close eye on it." Dad nods at the next reporter, giving the non-verbal go-ahead.

"With the election coming up next year, will you run for president against Admiral Mashaule?"

I twitch. Sheesh! My dad, running? That thought hadn't even crossed my mind.

He chuckles. "We will see. It's still early. If the USEF would like a leader with more insight into alien mindsets, then I would be more than happy to serve them." He points at some other reporter, but he doesn't get a word out, because every single one of them steps forward, calling my dad's name for attention.

"Admiral! Would you—"

"Admiral Thorburn—"

"Sir, what about—"

"Admiral, can you confirm you're running—"

"Did we hear that right? Are you—"

The flock of reporters swallows my dad, and even the ones who interviewed Admiral Mashaule leave him standing, watching with a sour face as my dad becomes the center of attention of the combined assembled press.

And if I'm not mistaken, I think... I think I just heard him announce he's going to run for President.

Holy cow.

Chapter Forty-Three

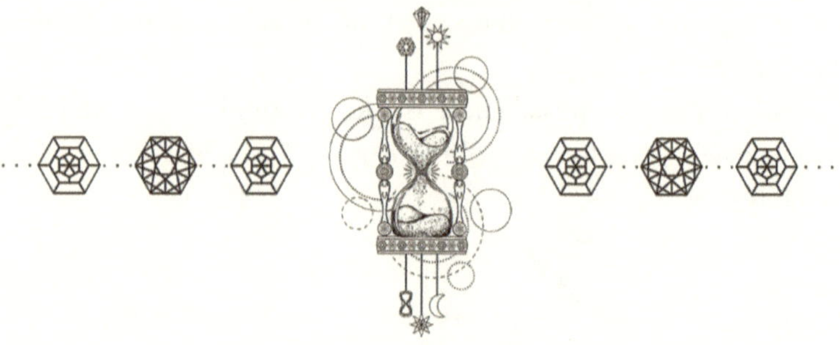

Waking up is a dream, and for once since I arrived in this time, a good dream. Not a nightmare.

So not a nightmare.

Kieran is snuggled into me, one arm draped over my chest, his nose buried deep into that corner where my neck and the pillow meet. Every single one of his breaths warms me up and brings goosebumps to my skin, which is saying something considering that breathing down my neck isn't really up in the top ten of things we did last night that brought goosebumps to my skin.

I suck in my lower lip and blink hard. I'm positive this is real, right? Just making sure, because waking up from a fever dream and discovering it wasn't would be quite the downer.

Kieran twitches in his sleep, the leg he wrapped over mine jerking up closer to my mid-thighs.

Ah. Nope, not a dream. No way those butterflies can be dreamed up. I angle my head the slightest bit and press a kiss to his hair.

A low, comfy growling sound comes from Kieran's throat. "More."

I chuckle, then oblige and kiss him again. "Good morning."

"Morning." He purses his lips and kisses my neck. "I'm usually not a morning person, but today I am." He pulls me closer into his body. "Wonder why."

I snuggle into his hold. Funny how being with Kieran can feel completely routine, like we'd been doing it forever, and at the same time exciting and thrilling and new. "Yeah, can't think of a reason." I use the arm not trapped under his body to wrap around his back, then drag a finger down his spine.

He shudders in my arms. "That would do it," Kieran whispers.

For a moment we lie silent, my fingers dancing over his skin, finding new areas I haven't touched, I haven't caressed, new muscles I haven't brushed over. This is what *content* feels like.

Kieran does the same soft growling sound again. "I don't care whether I have Magellan fortune-teller genes or not—not, obviously, but this," he squeezes me once, "feels right."

"Agreed," I whisper.

"Hah! I knew it!" In one quick motion he rolls himself onto his back and pulls me with him, reversing our positions and cuddling me into his chest. "You probably fell for me the minute you saw me." He pokes a finger into my ribs and I giggle.

"Down on that planet with all that mud on you? You stank!"

He protests. "Hey! That wasn't me! It's the Quaneez! They don't quite smell like roses!"

That rings a bell. "Actually, they do."

"Huh?"

"In the bunker, when I was coming for you. I dematted down, and it smelled like a flower bouquet in there."

"Really?" He looks at me in disbelief. "That's odd."

"That's what I thought too. But didn't last long. Two hallways farther down it smelled like rotten whatever sewage stuff."

His chest wobbles from a chuckle. "Rotten whatever sewage stuff?"

"For a lack of a better term." I was focused on other things, like saving Kieran. Doesn't mean I don't remember the details: The silence. That stench. Should have put that in my report for Chase, how it changed from flowery to disgusting. A shudder runs down my spine. Need to update that report. That Quaneez child, whose scent changed from okay to—

Kieran's finger poking into my ribs pokes harder. "Well, if you're describing it as that disgusting, no wonder you thought I was perfect when you met me all smelling normal and covered in beautiful mud."

I hide my grin in his chest. "Puh-lease. You're overestimating your cuteness and attraction."

"Oh no, I'm not." He digs that finger in deeper until I laugh full out and curl up more into his side to protect my flank. His hands still, and his tone loses the playfulness. "Because for me… that's how it was."

I hear him swallow and lift my head to look at him. Kieran drops his gaze onto my hand splayed out on his chest. "The moment I saw you you were like my angel, coming to rescue me. And… okay, maybe that's ridiculous, but I swear, when you checked me for injuries and you touched me—"

I remember. "Like an electric current. *Zzzing.*" I zigzag my finger down his back with a lift-off at the end, like a bolt of lightning, and drop my voice to a whisper. "Same for me." There was this one split second where nothing else existed but him. Granted, it was overruled in a heartbeat by the sheer fight for survival, but still. It was there. *Is* there.

A small smile tugs on his lips. "Told ya. It's my undeniable attraction."

"Right." I pinch his back, and he laughs, then sobers up, takes a breath and holds it, splaying his hand on my flank and holding me tight.

"But… but how is it going to play out? How are *we* going to play out?"

That question kicks my heart in the butt, right into a bucket of ice water. "I… I don't know." I have no idea. *We* came out of nowhere for me. My quote-unquote research showed Kieran single.

He holds me tighter. "Call me crazy, because we've only been together since last night—"

Together! He said we're together! My heart pulls itself out of that ice water with three strong, excited beats.

"—but I feel already like… like…" He sighs. "Like being without you would break me. And I know that's not normal and probably just hormones—or gee, finally a night without nightmares talking, but still. I don't want to lose you. I don't want to give you up."

A slight bout of dizziness comes over me, brought on by Kieran's emotions open on display for me. "Same for me," I whisper. Talking about feelings of this magnitude is scary. "It's like we belong together. Quite cliché, eh?"

He chuckles slightly into my neck. "I'm okay with cliché if this is what it feels like. I'm just worried because…" Both his hands glide down my back and up again. "Time is not on our side. We're not the typical couple. I'm what, forty years older than you?" A bit of humor colors his voice, relieving some of the somberness of the conversation.

I push myself up into a push up to look at him. "Forty-four, actually. Wow, I'm really into older men, it seems."

We both grin for a moment, before reality takes over and Kieran's smile fades. "What I was trying to say is, our tomorrow differs from everybody else's. Tomorrow you might be back in your time, and me stuck here, to age naturally through it. The problem is, that's probably the way it should be. And I don't like it one bit, but… who am I to deny you your life? Your place in the universe? Your own way? If some kind of time-vortex opened tomorrow and swept you back to the future, I should be happy that you're back where you belong, but…" He reaches up and cups my cheek, the warmth of his touch lighting me up on the inside, but it does nothing against my stomach twisting into a figure eight.

"Yeah," I press out hoarsely. "Same here." No need to say it out loud. I get it. It mirrors exactly what I'm feeling. We're stuck between a rock and a hard place, between past and future, and to think we're not going to break from it is probably naive.

I let myself sink down again onto his chest, listening to each strong heart beat, to each deep breath sucked in.

For a moment, silence lingers, but a different kind, more nervous. Kieran opens his mouth and closes it. Again. And again. Finally he bites his lower lip, and when he lets go of it he sucks a big breath in. "But I still like to play with that thought: What if… what if you stayed?" He plays with my hair, wrapping a strand around his fingers and releasing it again.

"Stayed?"

"Here. Not just in this time, but also on board. What if we can't get you back? I mean, time travel, come on. So, I guess I'm just asking… what if you stayed?" His fingers draw random patterns across my skin as I splay my fingers wider on his chest.

If I stayed. What a tempting, yet impossible mind game. Part of me would love to stay, mainly the part that's been falling for Kieran since I met him. The other part, the responsible part, is screaming at a deafening volume that I have to try everything in my power to return.

Which is why my stomach is cramping even harder.

I close my eyes and take a deep breath in. Kieran's scent floods my senses and brings the butterflies inside my stomach to flutter up like magic. "I don't know what's going to happen," I whisper. "But I must at least try to get back home. I have… I have a job to do." Or rather, I have to own up to failing it and to kick some butt for being set up. "And even if I had to stay in this time, it couldn't be with you on the *Pioneer*." Nonie Magnetta doesn't belong to this crew, neither now nor ever. "We won't work out like a traditional couple, Kieran." It's a wonder we're even here, together in one bed, anyway. The future could be short for us.

He stills his fingers, then resumes to play with my hair. "I know. I just feel I want to mess with fate because she messed with us. Ignore her. Ignore predestination. What if we re-wrote the stars, Nonie? Changed history? Made our own?" He twists a little so that he can get a better look at me. "It's tempting, but I know we can't. What needs to happen needs to happen, and…" He places a kiss onto my temple. "If we can get you back, I will do everything in my power to do so, because that's where you belong. If we can't, then I'll do everything in my power to help you live your life here." I get another kiss, and this one lingers. "Here's my promise to you: The timeline comes first. I'll do my very best to support you, no matter how I may feel about it." His voice holds a mix of resignation and determination—and that would be part of the reason why Kieran was promoted to captain at such a young age. He sees the bigger picture and puts duty and doing what's right before personal gain.

My voice comes out hoarse with my next sentence. "I wish I belonged here." In this time. On this ship. With this crew.

"So do I. I don't know what it is, but since I met you… I feel you, all the way in here." He presses my palm harder into his chest. "And the thought that you're leaving—and in a way where I will have absolutely no chance to ever see you again until decades in the future—it makes me physically nauseous."

I pale and lift my head to look up at him. "Decades in the—"

He flicks my shoulder, a sly expression on his face "Aww, come on, don't pretend. I heard it through the grapevine. You know us when we're older. Zio. Chase. Me. I'd say the academy, or else it wouldn't make sense."

Oh, in the name of all that's holy. "The—"

"I understand you can't confirm it, timeline, etc, but the hints you dropped—totally accidental, I might add—tell me that we all know each other in the future. Zio left a message for us, and the way you look at us… You know us."

I bury my face in his chest. Must try to not let him see what his words are doing to my soul, how they're tearing it apart bit by bit, every aspect of this crappy situation deepening the wound. *You know us.* No. I will know Chase. Zio.

But Kieran…

Kieran will be long dead in my time.

Chapter Forty-Four

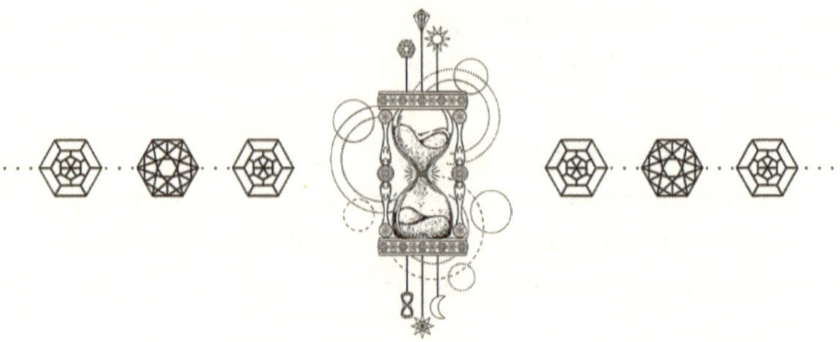

The nurse pulls away my blanket without a warning and reaches for my leg. "Time for your dressing cha—"

Flash!

As if I'd been transported back to two days ago, I'm not in the hospital anymore: Dirty, chipped off walls replace the pristine white ones around me, the stench of a human body in dire need of showering overpowers the scent of disinfectant, and sheer panic overrules everything else.

"No!" I scream and try to back away. "Let me go! Don't touch me! No!" Must scoot away, must get away—

But can't. Railing up, nowhere to go. Must climb—

The man talks. His voice is nicer than I remember. "Nonie, hey, it's Yossi, your nurse. It's all right—"

No. Nothing's all right. He hurts me, he—

The hand reaches for my face. "Calm down. It's fine—"

I slap it away and scream. Scream, scream, scream, scream, scream—

The door gets pushed open so hard it hits the wall behind it. "Nonie!" Fast steps approach—

Arms around me. Arms I know. A scent I know. A voice. "I'm here, honey. I'm here. It's all good. Daddy's here."

I'm being rocked back and forth, back and forth, back and—

My internal compass adjusts. Slowly. "Dad?" I whisper. My voice shakes, and so do I. Cold. Scared. *Cold.*

"I'm here. You're safe." His voice breaks with the last word, and that, hearing the emotion in it, opens the flood gates.

Tears stream down my face. "I'm sorry. I'm so, so sorry. I thought I was *there*, I—"

"It's all right, honey. You've been through a lot. Your mind is processing it. But you're safe." He lets go of me and cups my cheek. "Nothing like that will ever happen to you again. You. Are. Safe. You hear me?" Dad's thumb brushes across my cheek.

Safe.

I thought I was safe, and I wasn't. I don't think I'll ever be safe again. How could I?

Dad stops caressing my cheek. "Hey. I promise, you're safe, Nonie. And you will be. Always. I won't let anything happen to you ever again. Do you understand?"

I know what he expects, so I nod. Easiest way out.

The nurse clears his throat. "Okay, I'll go ahead and change the dressing then."

Dad whirls around. "I don't think so. Obviously, we need to work on your bedside manner."

The nurse blushes. "But Mr. Thor—"

"It's *Admiral* Thorburn, and you may leave."

"But—"

"Leave. And see to it that nobody disturbs us for the next half hour." Dad focuses back on me as the nurse sighs and does as he was told. That's what Dad's command tone does, even to non-military people on some small colony outpost. Don't I know it.

Dad's eyes soften as he pats my cheek and then drops his hand. "They can change the dressing later. How is your leg, by the way?"

I suck in my lower lip. "I don't know." I haven't looked at it at all after the Magellans fixed it. It's too scary. All I can think of is how the men took that heavy thing and rammed it onto my knee. My shin. Again and again until blood was everywhere and bone, I think, and the pain—

A shudder runs down my spine as nausea rises. "I don't want to go back home, Dad," I whisper. Because that's where they took me. On my way to school. I'm not safe there. Maybe I'm not safe anywhere.

Dad presses his lips into a thin line. I know what happened hurt him too, but differently than me. "Nonie, honey. We got the bad guys. They won't hurt you again."

My voice drops even lower. "But what if there are others?"

He reaches for my hand and holds it. "There are no othe—"

The door opens without a knock. "Admiral Thorburn. A word, please? Ironically, I don't have much time."

A muscle in Dad's jaw ticks, a dead giveaway he's trying to keep his temper in check, which would be why he's looking down at my hand in his, and not at the incoming person. I know his tricks for self control.

"What's so difficult to understand about do not disturb?" There's a bite in his words I also only know too well.

The visitor closes the door and comes closer. She's dressed in all black, like a Division Two uniform. I blink. Is it— Could it be— Everything's blurry from *that* night, but—

She halts a few feet in front of my bed. "It's not difficult to understand at all. But I'm overruling your authority in this case."

Overruling his authority? Nobody overrules my dad's—

Dad's entire body tenses as he whirls around—

And freezes.

Surprise flickers across his face, turning into disbelief and maybe even—

That's when I recognize her. "It's you!" I try to sit up straighter, but can't. Still too weak. Doesn't matter. She came, like she said she would!

"Hey, Nonie." She winks and me and gives me a little wave. "Can't tell you how good it is to see you feeling a tad better."

I nod like a bobble head figure. "Much better. Thanks to you!" And true, all of a sudden I do feel much better. She's my lifeline. If she hadn't gotten me out, I'd be dead. I know that.

Dad's head swivels left to right, from me to her. He's pale as a sheet. "You... That... Nonie—"

The soldier laughs once. It lights up her face. She must be high ranked, or else she'd be more afraid of my dad. People usually are. "Admiral. I know. We better talk. And, Nonie?" She steps closer to my bed and squeezes my left foot. The ring on her hand shimmers like a rainbow in the artificial light, kind of matching the rainbow on her shoulder patch. "You'll get better. I know that. One day, you'll be as strong and fast as me. Don't let what happened determine who you are. You can and you will do whatever you want, you hear me? You're stronger than the fear."

I nod. My heart hammers like crazy, as if it wanted to agree with what she said. "Yes, Ma'am."

She grins. "Way too formal. Call me Star Hopper."

Funny name, but I like it. It must be a code name for Division Two, secrecy and all. "Okay." I blush. Military brat, as Dad says. Not used to first name basis with any officers.

Dad slides off the bed and pulls himself up to standing. "*You* saved…" He looks from her to me and back. The apple in his throat moves up and down twice. "You. Are…"

I'm not used to speechless Dad. It's a tad embarrassing. "Yes, Dad. It was her. She got me out." I roll my eyes at Star Hopper, who chuckles.

"Admiral, I know it's a lot to take in. But if you don't mind, you and I also have a lot to discuss. In private." She gives me an apologetic smile. "Sorry."

Dad rakes a hand through his hair. "Yeah. Yeah. Sure. We should… an office, maybe—"

"I'll take care of things." She taps her watch twice. "Let's go."

Dad throws one more look at me, then at her as he follows her to the door. "Be back in a sec, okay?"

I know why he says it: so I don't worry. So I'm not afraid when he's gone. But something… something changed. Star Hopper is right. What happened doesn't define me. Maybe one day I really can be as good as her. As in control. As tough.

Maybe one day I'm going to be just like her.

Chapter Forty-Five

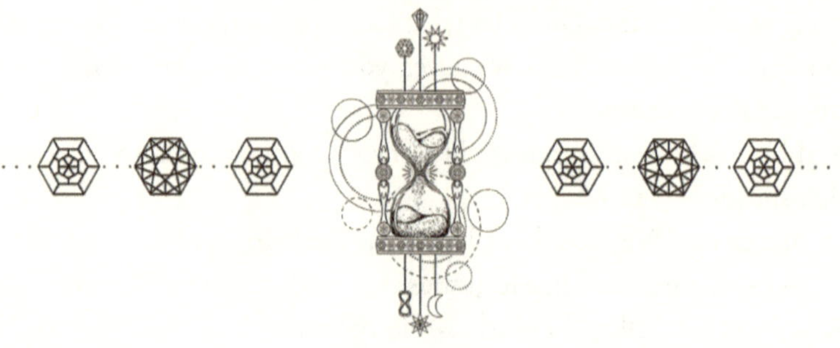

This is a historic moment. For me at least. I'm part of my first-ever Senior Officer meeting. Okay, maybe that's exaggerating a bit, but hey, we're in the conference room, which makes this official. Doesn't matter it's only Kieran, Chase, and Zio together with me, it still feels official and therefore counts. Yay me!

Kieran nods at Zio, the last to arrive, as soon as he pulls a chair out from the oval table in front of the window. "What'cha got, Zee?"

Upinga gracefully folds himself into the chair clearly modified for his physical attributes. "Some more of the data that was salvaged from the *Odysseus*. And a new theory that might help us send Nonie back." He nods at me seated to the right of him.

Like a punch to the gut, his words make me blow out a puff of air. To send me back— "You're not messing with me, are you?"

Zio's brows pull together into a V. "Not in the least." He pauses. "Although there are a couple of drawbacks to the implementation of my theory you might not like."

I'm about to groan, but Kieran beats me to the punch. "Define drawbacks." He leans forward at the head of the table, hands folded in front of him, the picture book example of one hundred percent attentive, but I see the worry in his eyes that mirrors mine: are we over before we even began?

"I'll get to the drawbacks once I have established the basics, Captain.

First, there have been reports about the possibility of time travel with a certain gene mutation in Magellans. I assume—and mind you, this is a theory and nothing more—that said mutation is in Nonie's genome. From what I gathered when looking at Nonie's DNA, her unique make up of human and Magellan attributes enhance the Magellan genes responsible for our… *sensitivity* to the timeline. They also seem to be the reason why she ended up in the past, with us."

I lift both palms up. "Why didn't it happen before then?" The whole thing seems implausible, impossible, and a whole motherlode of other "im-" adjectives. "Did Magellan puberty hit or something, and suddenly I can time travel? *How* did it happen?" It's not as if I'd clicked my heels twice and *zzzip* I was here.

Zio raises one eyebrow at me. "That brings me to my second point of the basics to establish. You said what brought you here was an explosion of sorts when you scanned a planet, correct?"

"Correct." He better not tell me my genes were responsible for triggering that as well, or else I might just jump out of the nearest air lock.

He types something into his PAD, and a clear, transparent view screen rises out of the middle of the table. Ah, the good old days before we invented holographic displays. "Going through the *Odysseus'* scanner log, I did find a high spike of Setayashi radiation, like Chase said before. Unfortunately, much of the collected data from that planet was lost in the fire or is unaccessible to me right now. Other than that, our scan of the *Odysseus* shows some odd tau-particles, but that's most likely negligible for now."

"Tau-particles?" Kieran's brows scrunch up. "If my science one-oh-one isn't completely off, isn't that used for terraforming?"

Zio gives him a thumbs up. "A-plus, Captain. Yes, tau-particles, while used in engineering for plasma recovery and repairs, are used on a grand scale for terra forming. But this spike is low, so I can only assume it occurred naturally, since Nonie said the planet was uninhabited." I get an odd glance from him, the same as before when this topic came up. Maybe he knows I'm lying, but in the end, does it matter? He also knows that if I am, I have reasons to do so. Nicely enough, Zio doesn't dig into my fake story, but instead switches the displayed image to a simulation of a planet.

"Now, the only reason for a destruction of this scale is if the planet contained a Marmelite core."

"Marmelite? Is that a thing?" Chase scratches his nose.

Good question. "I never heard about it either." And my academy training is fresh and forty years more up to date.

Upinga points to the simulation on screen. "Neither the USEF nor the Magellans have much research on it. In fact, the USEF has nothing, while I found a few articles about Marmelite in the Magellan database. From what I could gather, a Marmelite core is a very rare planetary core. As far as we know, it stabilizes a planet's rotation and therefore optimizes its orbit around a star, which in return is beneficial for the development of life."

"Sounds like Marmelite is da bomb." Chase gives a fake-excited thumbs-up.

"Ironically, quite correct, Commander." Upinga moves his finger in a circle, representing the core. "That is in fact the problem with Marmelite. It's highly volatile to many things, including high-intensity radiation bursts. So I imagine this happened: A high-powered scan hits the planet. Penetrates the core. Activates the Marmelite in it."

The simulation shows a rendering of my shuttle, a beam shooting out of it and penetrating the planet's core.

"Then, the Setayashi radiation is released a split second before the explosion, triggering Nonie's genes and sensitizing the time-space continuum." A wave of blue radiates off the planet and hits my shuttle. "Lastly, the following explosion as the Marmelite turns unstable, combined with the previous damage to the time fabric, rips the stability of the time line and transports Nonie here."

Silence.

The understanding of what happened sits like lead in my stomach. Did Grazer know about this Marmelite? Or was he just quote-unquote lucky it would've killed me, if the Quaneez didn't?

Well, let's find out. I turn my wrist over and activate PADdy. Nice I don't have to hide it anymore.

Neither of the guys minds me while they keep discussing science.

I type into PADdy.

> Search Request: Marmelite
> Access Denied.
> Admiralty override required.

That means—
Yeah. All doubts, erased.

> Search Request: H-155
> Access Denied.
> Admiralty override required.

A tickle of disgust paired with horror rises in my chest. Here it is, all official. Restricted access can only mean one thing: We, as in the USEF, know about Marmelite. We also knew about the unstable Marmelite core in H-155.

Grazer knew.

As an admiral, he would be privy to this kind of information. He wants to send me to H-155, he enters that into the database and *this* pops up? He better read it.

At this point, it's clear he used me as an accessory to mass murder. The full horrific, revolting magnitude of his betrayal washes over me. This is proof Grazer purposefully instructed me to do a Level-Six-Scan—a *modified* level-six scan—fully knowing it would trigger the Marmelite, destroy the planet, and with it, its entire Quaneez population.

Of course I wouldn't be suspicious with the task. We scan planets all the time, and as a general rule, they don't blow up. My systems were… *changed*, as Chase found out when he checked my shuttle, which probably gave my scan some extra *oomph*, and I destroyed H-155.

Anger floods my veins. What kind of disgusting, repulsive being do you have to be to come up with this plan? How could I have misread Grazer so much? *Peace is fragile, don't break it*—I believed him! His worries!

I ball my hands into fists at my sides. Oh, the perfect plan. It all makes sense: Get little Nonie, she is so motivated and naive, she'll believe the BS about the special assignment. Set her up to follow orders, because we all know she will, let her kill five million of our enemies and herself—how convenient—and then we can still deny all knowledge or involvement and pretend our hands are clean. Rogue human.

Dark rage fills me and rushes through my system.

Five million people.

A setup to kill *five million* people.

I'm gritting my teeth almost to the point of breaking.

The image of the destroyed planet hovers frozen in mid-explosion between us. It feels wrong, and it is. This should never have happened—and yet it did. I caused this destruction, and with it the death of millions of sentient beings.

Can't look at the image anymore. Can't. I get up and walk to the synthesizer. My throat is parched.

"Nonie?" Zio raises his voice.

"Huh? Sorry, I… I was distracted." By the sheer evil of human nature.

Zio acknowledges my excuse with a raised eyebrow. "Nonetheless, I'm quite confident that if it took the explosion of a Marmelite core to get you here, I assume that is also what it will take to get you back."

My blood pressure drops so fast I have to support myself against the wall next to the synthesizer. "Another planetary destruction," I whisper. That's the *drawback* he mentioned and what I feared since I got here.

"Correct." Zio nods.

I blow out a harsh puff of air. Not what I wanted to hear. I—

"Can we synthesize Setayashi radiation?" Kieran asks.

"Not at this moment. It only occurs naturally. With the explosion of Marmelite."

Kieran's lips press into a thin line. "What size of a planet?"

"Any size of planet with a Marmelite core will do."

"I don't even know if we have any in our database." Chase types into the screen lighting up in the table in front of him, then grunts with displeasure. "Nothing. Very helpful."

Actually, it's very helpful.

It makes my decision easier.

No known planets with Marmelite cores only means one thing: I'm not going to return home. And even if we knew a planet fitting the bill, the price would be too high. "I won't be sacrificing a planet for my return. No, no, and no. No." Nauseating flutters churn inside my gut. Can't say the prospect of living with the destruction of a Quaneez planet and failure of my first mission for the next forty years sounded appealing in any way, but the alternative is unacceptable.

Hiding my face away from them I turn to the synthesizer and begin to program it. "I'm not willing to blow up a planet. If there is no other option, I stay in this time. And wait it out." I'm saying it as if it's no big deal, but it is. It's a ginormously big deal committing to staying, and the tremor of my hand is giving it away. My life—everything that was me—will be gone, and I'll be damned to inactivity until young Nonie vanishes into the past forty years in the future. I'll have to watch history unfold without interfering until my time has come.

A tingling runs down my back and I turn to catch Chase staring a my every move programming the synthesizer. My hands freeze, hovering over the controls. "What?"

He blushes and looks away. "Nothing."

Liar. I suppress a sigh and double the volume of my soda. At this point, I fear it's safe to say I was the one addicting Admiral Conolly to Lubbeck's. Wordlessly, I put a glass of fake-Lubbeck's in front of him, ignoring Commander Upinga's disapproving glance. Hey, all I'm doing is catering to the self-fulfilling loop.

Chase blushes and mouthes a silent *thank you*. Any time. Whatever I can do to keep the timeline intact, right? Seems to be my job these days.

Once he sets the soda down, his fingers drum a fast rhythm onto the table. "Maybe we don't have to and there's another way. Does it say anything else that might be helpful in the file we left ourselves in the future?" He nods his chin at my wrist PAD.

"No." Zio shakes his head. "All I have is rudimentary data after the damage Nonie's PAD and shuttle sustained during the travels here. There are hints that our future selves did leave more information for us, but it's nothing I can put back together."

"Of course." Chase rolls his eyes. "Would've been too convenient to get enough information on this. But that means as well we don't know what's *supposed* to happen, do we?" He puts *supposed* in air quotes.

Zio stares at me for a few seconds, eyes wide, with that spaced-out expression I know only too well. I guess it's him accessing his first sense and trying to figure out what comes next. Too funny that Admiral Upinga has been doing this to me for years and I never knew what it was.

He blinks a few times. "It's hard to read at the moment. Nothing is dominant, from what I'm seeing, which is odd. Right now, I can't guarantee Nonie is making it back home."

I suck in a sharp breath. Thinking it to myself is one thing, hearing Zio say it out loud another.

Kieran blows out a big puff of air, the look he gives me loaded with raw emotion. "You think she might be… trapped here?" He drums his fingers on the table, matching Chase's rhythm. I don't think either of them notices. I do. I notice everything in this moment, as if reality had cranked it up to super-HD status, hyperrealism for every sound, color, or scent. *I might be trapped here:* Trapped between a rock and a hard place, between past and future.

Chase points at the PAD. "Gotta say, I'm moderately positive Nonie does make it back somehow though, or else our future selves wouldn't have prepped her the way we did back in her time."

"Not necessarily so." Zio takes a seat. "Even if we knew we didn't get Nonie to her time, but we knew young Nonie was going to be thrown back, we'd still be prepping her to save Kieran. We'd still be giving her as much data on her PAD as we could."

Kieran claps his hands together twice. "We'll find a way, Nonie. There must be a Marmelite-containing planet somewhere. We can help you search for an uninhabited one that fits the bill." I hear the strain in his voice, almost completely hidden under professionalism. "The *Pioneer* has the most up-to-date long-range sensors—"

Aww, man. I stop and turn, both hands up, palms toward the men seated at the table. "No. Thank you, but no. I can't have the *Pioneer* do that, I really can't." Literally, can *not*. The *Pioneer* has more important jobs to do than to look for a planet for me to blow up. And if that strands me in the here and now, because obviously I can't find another ship to search for a way to bring me back forward in time, so be it.

Suck it up, Thorburn.

Kieran tries again. "I'm not saying to make it an official mission,

I'm saying to scan along the way as we continue our exploration of space according to our mission parameters. Best of both worlds. You stay—for now—and we do our best to find a way home for you." He sounds hopeful, and I can't fault him for it. In the grand scheme of things that sounds phenomenal. Never have I felt more at home than on the *Pioneer*, with these men. With Kieran. It's easy to get lured into that fantasy. What are a couple more weeks? Months? Years? Let me stay here for a while, while we search. What does it matter when I leave the past to return to my time?

Yeah. It's a fun mind game, only it makes me hurt inside even more.

As I sit down with my soda, I feel Chase's expectant eyes on me. "We'll find you one little unimportant planet—"

Find me? No. I'm not going to be responsible for the *Pioneer* veering off the path laid out for her. She's the single most important vessel of the next few years. Now imagine the crew being distracted by searching for a stupid Marmelite core for little Nonie to go home. Not going to happen. My guilt weighs enough already, I'm not going to add any more, even if that means stranding myself.

I slam my soda down on the table so hard, half of it spills. "No. No, *we* can't *find me* a planet. And even if we did, could somebody please address the elephant in the room? Namely, the fact that I wouldn't even know how to get quote-unquote home? Even if we replicated the exact same scenario, I wouldn't know how to get back to my time! Who is to say—"

Zio cuts me off. "Once such a Setayashi energy spike would hit you, I would assume you should be able to control the flow of time, knowing that it's coming."

My eyes pop wide. "Control it? How the heck am I supposed to do that?" Controlling being thrown through time—right. I missed that class during academy one-oh-one.

"That's where your First Sense comes in," Zio says, tapping his heart twice. "Don't underestimate it."

"So all we need is one gigantic energy discharge, then I try to not get blown to pieces while navigating myself back into the future and trying to make it a perfect landing on the day I left. Did I get that right?" Sarcasm comes naturally at this point.

"Indeed you did."

I huff out loud. "Sure, easy-peasy! Control me being thrown through time—just like this! Who is to say I don't end up another few decades, or worse, centuries in the past? What then? Now at least I can handle staying here. Compared to how bad it could be, this is actually good!" At least to some small degree I'd have Kieran. Chase and Zio. The *Pioneer.* "And if I wait it out, I'll eventually be back where I started and—and— Damn it." My voice breaks, and with that my eyes fill with tears. Damn it. First official senior officer meeting, and the lieutenant starts to cry. Fabulous.

"Nonie." Kieran leans forward and reaches for my hand, his dark eyes locking onto mine. "Clearly, this is a complicated and multi-faceted topic. We don't have to decide anything right now. *You* don't have to decide anything right now. All I'm asking you—and us—is to consider all options. The timeline comes first, as much as we may hate it." The way he emphasizes the *we*, I know he means *us*.

I give his hand a squeeze. "Thank you." For the reassurance. For understanding.

"We have your back either way," Chase says, and winks. "And—"

The intercom squeaks once. *"Captain to the Bridge. Five Quaneez ships just popped up out of nowhere!"*

For one half second, everybody is frozen.

Five Quaneez ships.

The puzzle pieces of history fall into place. Oh, in the name of all that's holy—

Kieran jumps up. "Acknowledged. On my way." With two quick strides he crosses the ready room toward the entrance to the bridge. "Red Alert!"

Sirens begin to howl and the lights dim.

Five Quaneez ships.

Nausea rises.

How could I be so short sighted? How could I not remember? How could I be so distracted with my own emotions I forgot the most important day in recent history, the Battle of Balthar?

Because, war with the Quaneez starts today.

Or rather, it starts *now.*

Chapter Forty-Six

Earth, 2291, Nonie's Home

The last week has been unbelievably long.

Long, hard, exhausting, demoralizing and plain ol' annoying—and that was only the first week.

Welcome to life at the academy.

Guess the difference between acing my entrance exams and acing my academy performance is as big as the difference between a eukaryotic cell and a higher evolved organism: gigantic. That's not to say I was naive and figured I'd be the king—queen—of the castle there, but I thought I would have a leg up. Pun intended. News flash, everybody else here aced their exams as well. I joined a club of overachievers and became one of many, a small fish in a deep pond amongst a million others.

Which means, this fish better learn to swim—and to do so faster and better than the others. Let's put it this way: I need outstanding grades in as many subjects as I can, because once we go into physical stuff... Yeah. I doubt I'm ever going to be good or even comfortable at self defense, fighting, or anything even remotely in that direction.

I let go of a deep sigh and rub a palm over my eyes. So, so happy it's Friday. So happy Dad is home and not on assignment, and I get to spend the weekend with him and to sleep in my room, not in the dorm. I get weird stares there, and for what? Pick a reason. Would've thought being the youngest, I was the least mature, but with all the ogling I'd pass that baton to half my class. Yes, I am the youngest cadet ever, but I don't look like a kid.

Anyway. Whatever.

I place my palm against the reader to open our gate. Never has returning home felt so relieving. The smell of the flower beds, the silence of the suburbs, the darkness of the night. Great combo.

I palm open our entrance door—and freeze one foot in the house, the other on the door mat: Yelling. Two voices. My dad. Another male.

"—can't be serious!"

Pause. They must be in the living room, but I can hear Dad's heavy breathing all the way to the front door. He's mad—but the other person sounds equally unhappy. "I don't need to spell it out for you, do I? Mashaule finds out, what do you think is going to happen? Let me enlighten you. He's going to call it *silent infiltration*, a threat, and it will play right into his hands. Is that what you want? Besides the obvious implications of stripping of rank and jail for everybody involved? Are you ready to carry that burden?"

Somebody slams a hand down onto our tabletop. I know *that* sound. "Are you threatening me?" Dad growls.

For a moment silence hovers. Uhh… Clearly I shouldn't be here, but… I mean, do I sneak out and pretend I never came in? Do I walk in and apologize for interrupting? Maybe—

The other person sighs. "This isn't about threatening you. This is about doing what's best, and clearly you haven't gotten the memo."

"What do you want me to do? Revoke admission—?"

"That would be best. Or a transfer. Europe. Asia. Actually, off-world would be best."

Dad gasps. "If you're expecting me to—"

"I'm expecting you to do what we agreed upon! This is my ass on the line as much as yours—"

"I know that! But you can't let him drag you down with him. You—"

"Please," the other person huffs. "As if I had a choice. I owe my career to him. If you—"

"It's out of my hands. Was from the moment—"

"Really? Then I'm telling you the consequences are going to be grave if you don't watch yourself! Mashaule will be on your case if I don't do it first. My hands are tied, Tom! He won't let it stand, you know that. And with your ambitions, you're making yourself a target. And not just yourself, if you get my hint. My protection only goes so far."

Somebody—probably Dad—sucks in a sharp breath through their teeth. "I think we're done here."

"You're right. There's nothing more for me to do. You're digging your own grave." A chair slides back, but no steps follow.

Two or three seconds later, the other voice speaks again. Calmer, this time. More resigned. "You know, Tom… Sometimes I'm still angry you got to keep what I couldn't. But are you still sure it's worth it?"

Dad sighs. "Every day of my life. Without a doubt."

"That's what I thought." That person turns on his heels, boots scratching over our wooden floors.

Oh, crap. I push down the door handle and throw the door wide open, so it rams into the wall behind it. Dad hates it when I do that. "Dad! I'm home!"

The person who comes around the corner falters in mid-step, but so do I, because—

"Admiral." I snap to attention a mili-second later.

"Cadet." He barely spares me a glance when he walks past me and out of our house, the cool air of his hasty retreat brushing my face and giving me goosebumps. Dad was fighting with *Admiral freakin' Grazer?* What the what?

"Nonie." Dad walks into the hallway, and if I didn't know he just yelled at his colleague, I wouldn't think anything was off. He looks genuinely happy to see me—which I know he is, but there's not a trace of what went down written on his face.

I cock my head to the side as I close the door. "Admiral Grazer? What's he doing here?"

Dad shrugs. "We had something work-related to discuss."

Discuss. Right.

I cross my arms in front of my chest, giving him my best impression of himself when he calls BS on me. "I thought you guys didn't agree on much."

Dad huffs. "Honey, Bas and I haven't agreed on anything since our mission to Alpha Rubrum when I was a junior officer, and I doubt we ever will. But listen and learn, *Cadet*, even with a difference of opinion, progress can be made and discussion can be had."

"Yes, Admiral." I salute, because *discussion and progress*, when clearly neither happened here.

Silent infiltration, stripping rank, jail time, making yourself a target, you got to keep what I couldn't—the words swirl through my mind, burying themself deeper and deeper into the folds and grooves of my brain. What is Grazer talking to Dad about? Unease spreads through my veins, bringing a harrowing sensation with it.

Dad rolls his eyes at my salute. "Stop mocking me, take off your uniform, put on comfy clothes, and get your butt to the kitchen. I haven't been slaving in there for two hours only to have the food get cold or dinner be ruined by Grazer. That man…" He shakes his head. "You'd do well to stay away from him as much as possible. I don't trust him."

I chew on my lower lip. *That man* is unfortunately the head of the division I want to join, but that's not a Pandora's box I plan on opening tonight, so all I do is smile and salute again. "Consider it done, sir."

Am going to leave that battle for another day.

Chapter Forty-Seven

"Captain! Five enemy ships, same design and configuration as the ones we encountered before!"

"Weapons?" Kieran slides into the captain's chair.

"As far as I can tell not charged, sir." Hayes focuses on his console.

Not charged? What the—

"Well, that's at least something. What else are you reading?" Kieran leans forward, eyes fixed on the screen as if he could see through it and right into the mind of the Quaneez.

"No shields yet either, Captain. But I'm assuming they're lined up in formation in front of us to protect the third planet in this system, sir. I'm reading several thousand life signs similar to theirs, most on the northern hemisphere."

I suck in a sharp breath. There was a Quaneez colony? That's not mentioned anywhere—

Chocho turns around to face Kieran. "Captain, would you like me to hail them?"

Kieran chews on his lower lip. "Actually, no. Let's take it easy and for once match them. We have always initiated contact when we met them, maybe that's what got them on the edge, who knows? For now, if their weapons are offline, so are ours. They're silent, so are we. Watchful waiting. In the meantime, give me as much data as you can, Hayes. And Chocho, notify Command we found them."

"Understood, sir."

"Yes, sir."

Chase steps closer to the captain's chair. "You sure? No hails? They could perceive that as a provocation."

I all but roll my eyes. Everything is a provocation to the Quaneez. In my time, systems are set to automatically blast our message of peace in all languages as soon as Quaneez ships are within hailing range. Has it ever helped? Nope.

Kieran lifts both hands, palms to the ceiling. "Well, so far, they've perceived hailing them as a provocation, so it's not like I'm risking anything." Good point.

Conolly shrugs. "True. Still, I'd prefer getting ready."

"Do it." Kieran keeps his eyes straight up front, glued to the view screen and the display of the five Quaneez ships blocking our way.

"Conolly to Lopez. Get ready to give us as much power as you can. Things are about to get dicey up here."

"Understood, Commander." Lopez' voice comes back distorted through the hablamate.

"Manazari, get ready with those shields and to return fire. Don't charge the weapons yet, but keep a finger close to those systems. Understood?" Chase points at the weapon's station.

"Crystal clear, sir."

Kieran supports his chin with his hand. "What are they playing at? Why shoot at us every time, and now, with their colony down below, not? Why, why, why?" With the last why, he glances over his shoulder at me, but I only shrug.

I don't know. This is even more confusing for me than for him. Quaneez *always* fire first. Why they're not, I don't know.

"Let's try something." Kieran jumps out of his chair. "Helm, quarter speed backwards. Bring us to a stationary point three clicks back. I want to see their reaction."

"Aye, sir."

"But, Captain, retreating—"

Kieran cuts Chase off. "Sign of weakness? I don't know. Is it? I want to see what this is about. Understand what's going on in their mind. Do they follow us? Do they not? It makes a difference."

Thaler turns in her seat. "Stationary position achieved, sir."

"And?" Kieran looks at the screen. "They're not following. I would interpret that as them not wanting to fight. They flexed their muscles when we entered their territory, but they didn't initiate aggression. They're not chasing us away. I'd say this is progress."

My heart hammers like crazy. Progress, yes—but not for long. This won't end well for the Quaneez, although I'm amazed at how this is playing out so far. I'm assuming minor details like this got lost during time, not that it's important. The outcome is disastrous, period.

Kieran continues. "I'm willing to let them take the next step. Everybody, watch them like a hawk. I want to know about everything and anything that could be perceived as communication. Hails, morse, binary, heck, even smoke signals. Anything. We're waiting for them, so get comfy, we might be here for a while."

No, we won't.

A deafening, high-pitched and distorted screeching sound breaks through the speakers. Ugh—

My hands fly to my ears, and so do everybody else's.

"Chocho, what—"

Chocho lifts one hand up, like in school, yelling over the noise. "Apologies, Captain. Command is getting back to us, their communique overloaded our bandwidth. I've got it—" He enters a couple more commands, and the noise stops. A collective sigh of relief goes through the bridge crew.

Chocho clears his throat. "Anyway, they're ordering us to hail them and to broadcast on all frequencies."

Kieran flinches. "Send the communique to my chair." He sits back down and types into the interface, with every passing second frowning more and more.

Chase bends lower, talking quietly to Kieran. Only because my ears are sensi— Oh, right: only because my ears are *half-Magellan* can I pick up on what he's saying. "Let me guess. Command has a different tactical approach."

"Clearly," Kieran grumbles. "But it's out of my hands, apparently. Chocho, hail them on all frequencies. Don't give'm one of those feedback noises we just had. We want to make friends. Let's see what they give us this time."

"Aye, sir, getting ready to hail on all freque—"

"Sir! I'm reading a power surge—they're charging weapons! All five ships!" Manazari turns to face the captain, wide eyed and pale.

Kieran curses under his breath. "*Now* they change their mind? Shields up, Battle Alert. Stations, everybody!"

Chocho defends himself, an ounce of panic in his voice. "Wasn't me, Captain! Hail isn't even out ye—"

Sirens howl, and while nobody on the bridge needs to ready themselves for battle, I know what's going on all over the other parts of *Pioneer* right now: hundreds of men and women scrambling to reach their assigned stations, from weapons to engine to medical. Some will have been woken from sleep, others were already at their post for hours. But all of them will be wide awake and full of adrenaline just about now.

This is it. The Battle of Balthar, the beginning of the Quaneez wars, playing out right in front of me. *Dizzy.*

"They're firing!"

"Everybody brace for impact—*ugh!*" Kieran and everybody else gets thrown forward and rattled around as the first salve of torpedos hits the *Pioneer*'s shields. If it wasn't for the automatic grav-bumpers springing to life and keeping every occupant restrained wherever they stand or sit, we all would have been shaken off our butts like fruit from a tree.

"Shields holding, sir! Ninety-eight percent!"

"Acknowledged. Tactical display up front, give me readouts!"

The display up front changes to an overview of the five ships lined up between us and the planet below them.

"Evasive maneuvers, Thaler! Get us out of here! Hayes, I want you to scan their ships with all we've got! We know next to nothing about them and that has to change. Chocho, keep transmitting the usual, and make sure they're hearing it!" Kieran claps his hands. "Let's go, people! Not a drill!"

Chase flies his fingers over the tactical display. "I'm getting the same configuration as the ship we encountered before. Difficult to penetrate their shields, unless I'm using…." He throws one glance at me from under his lashes. "Got it, I can penetrate. Over five hundred life signs per ship, sir, and odd readings—*ugh!*" The next impact throws him against the instrument panel and me into a stumble, despite the grav-bumpers.

Shoot.

"Thaler! What happened to those evasive maneuvers?" Kieran barks.

"Too many, sir! They know what they're doing!" Thaler's entering commands into the controls so fast, she must be breaking some kind of speed record.

"Incoming!"

Boom! Another hit.

"Shields holding, but down to eighty-one percent!"

I pant, every breath coming in wheezing. This is scary, no matter I know the outcome. Or, maybe because I do.

"Captain, should I return fire?"

"No! As long as we can evade, we'll do so! We won't be dragged into a war here. Lieutenant, bring her behind those vessels, but away from the planet. I don't care how you do it, but get us out of the line of fire!" Kieran digs his fingers into the armrests of the captain's chair. "Chocho, how 'bout them hails?"

"No response, sir. I'm cycling all frequencies and blasting their ears off."

"Acknowledged. Thaler, go, go go! Get us behind them, shields stay up! It's one thing to fire on a perceived aggressor, another to hunt down a retreating ship that doesn't return fire."

Unfortunately though, the Quaneez don't have any qualms with that. Never did.

"Continuing their fire, sir, shields at sixty-three percent and holding."

For now. Every impact rattles us, every impact draws from their power, and we all know we can't sustain this kind of attack for much longer.

Kieran slaps the armrest twice. "Ideas, people. Brainstorm!"

"Incoming!" Chase shouts a mere second before the next hit lands.

Hayes on the station behind Kieran recovers first. "We run! This is not a race the USEF would want to be friends with."

Chase waves him off. "So we're teaching them they can scare us away like this and invite them to come knocking at our home door? Still not a message I want to send, especially now. Different when nobody is firing, but the game has changed when they did."

No kidding.

Boom—another impact. Somebody yelps out in pain.

"Go for a full attack, sir. They're trying to demonstrate strength, we can do the same!" Thaler throws in from her console in the front, never taking her eyes off the screen and display, fingers flying over the controls and keeping us out of harm's way—more or less, if the steady bumps and rattles from the impact against the shields is any indication. Outflying five ships and getting behind them is nearly impossible if the other pilots know what they're doing.

On the other hand, I know how it's going to end, cue the famous image of the *Pioneer* hovering in space, surrounded by a field of debris.

Nausea rises.

Yeah. It's different being here than reading about it.

Kieran grimaces. "Full attack? I think it sends the wrong message, like a complete retreat would. We're neither cowards nor aggressors, and we don't know how they'll react to either or. Communications?" He turns and looks at Choco.

"Nothing, sir. Not even confirmation they're receiving our hails."

Kieran makes a slashing gesture across his throat. "Stop hails. Focus on getting that distance, Thaler!"

"Aye, sir!"

"Once we're in position—"

"Sir, weapons' fire has ceased!"

"Confirmed, weapons hot, but not discharging!" Chase double-checks the read-outs. "For now, at least."

"Captain, their ships—"

The image on the view screen changes—and none for the better. "They have us surrounded, sir." Or as surrounded as one can be by five enemy ships and one planet. No wonder they stopped firing. They've got the upper hand.

"Do you want me to hail them?" Chocho's fingers hover over the console.

"No." Kieran gives a slow shake of his head. "Holding still worked before, let's hope it does again. What are they doing?"

"No hails. Not firing, obviously. Nothing, basically."

Nothing. That together with something in Kieran's words strikes a chord in me: *Holding still worked before.*

Holding still and *nothing.*

Holding still, like he did on Alpha Rubrum.

Nothing, as in, the Quaneez never hail. And from what I've seen since I arrived here, they don't like to receive them either. Not in this time at least—or am I mixing that up? Am I imagining things? Could it be this simple? Could the Quaneez perceive our hails as an attack?

It sounds impossible—they're hails, for crying out loud—but given that we know next to nothing about the Quaneez it's a possibility. What if *something* in our hails triggered *something* in the Quaneez? Maybe it hurts their ears, maybe they have a different organ that's sensitive to it— but isn't it too much of a coincidence that they don't hail themselves, and react with retribution as soon as we do?

Manazari breaks the tense silence. "Their shields are still up, sir. Their weapons are hot."

"But they're not firing." Kieran pushes himself out of his command chair. "What's their game? On, off. On, off. Which one is it?" he whispers to himself. "Chase, Zio. You're with me. You, too." I get a nod. "Manazari, you have the bridge. Any movement, any change out there, and you get me. Understood?"

"Understood, sir." Manazari takes over the seat, signing into the data pad and taking over command with his palm print.

Kieran leads the way through the sliding door on the port side of the bridge to his ready room. As soon as the doors hiss closed behind him he whirls around. "Options, guys? Nonie?"

I shrug and drop my eyes. "Not my place." Not my time, either, nor do I have a brilliant idea. A theory. Maybe. If at all.

He sighs. "Figured. Chase, Zio. What's your point of view?"

Chase looks out the window at the ships hovering in space. "I don't get them. That drive of theirs is the most imperfect design for space flight ever. I mean, I'm surprised nothing has blown up yet! A ship, a planet, *space...* Your choice." He shakes his head. "And I can't make sense of them. They don't answer hails. We didn't provoke—"

Zio cuts him off. "They have a colony with about seven thousand lives on that planet. Our mere presence here could be—or probably is—considered a threat."

"But we didn't do anything!" Chase throws his arms up, which earns him an eye roll by Zio.

"That's what we think, but again, there are cultures who will start a war over somebody desecrating their holy grounds. This could be similar."

"Good point, Zee." Kieran rubs his chin and paces back and forth in front of his desk. "And we've been chasing them for the past days, which is probably not making them feel any warmer toward us. Maybe they needed time to make up their mind whether they wanted to attack or not. Maybe they had to—have to—wait for orders. So hopefully by retreating, we're showing deference and are removing the threat. Let's keep our fingers crossed they'll take the hint and back down as well." He looks up at us. "Question is what to do if they don't?"

Chase's hands ball into fists at his side. "Fire back. We have to fight, Kieran. It's not our style, but we have a crew to think about."

"Five ships against one… we have a great crew, but the odds are not in our favor." Kieran nods his chin toward the window and the Quaneez battle cruisers hanging in space.

Zio clears his throat. "There is one option. Not a good one, but one that is the last resort. The very last resort, actually."

Chase makes an impatient hand gesture. "Talk, Zio!"

The Magellan levels him with an even stare. "My scans have shown one interesting fact about the planet they're protecting. It posseses a Marmelite core."

What the what?

Zio's words hang in the air, charging it.

Chase blinks hard. "Are you saying what I think you're—"

"No. All I'm doing is giving you information of tactical advantage. If not a high-powered scan, one well-focused shot or a few torpedos strategically placed should activate the Marmelite and cause an explosion. I'm not saying we use—"

Chase ignores him. "If the shit hit the fan, that could be our way out."

Kieran blows out a harsh puff of air. "Seven thousand people? And maybe their holy grounds? I'm not sure I'm willing—"

"It could be our way out *and* it could get Nonie home."

Oh, hell to the no! "You're not going to blow up a planet because of me!" I stomp my foot. Please don't tell me they did this—will do this—because of me. Please, no. There must be another way. "In no way was I ever okay with blowing up a planet *and its population* for me!"

Kieran sucks in his lower lip. "And neither am I, sorry, Nonie. I guess all Zio is saying, that if—if—push came to shove and this was our last resort, to have you ready as well."

Chase stays infuriatingly calm. "Playing devil's advocate here. The question becomes, if we don't use this option, what else do we have—against five battle cruisers." He gives me a pointed look, but I won't have it.

"I don't know! The details of the battle are top secret." The *Pioneer* comes out victorious, but how, I have no idea.

"Top secret—are you sure?" Kieran exchanges a look with Chase.

"Yes, top secret. We all know the outcome, but how it happened, we don't know."

Chase points at my wrist pad. "Okay, might be top secret, but obviously we survived, or else you wouldn't know us in the future. And if the battle tactics are top secret… That's a good sign." He scratches his neck, then frowns. "Or rather, not. The only reason to make the details of a battle top secret would be to protect sensitive information in regards to tactics or weapons, which makes me think… Using a Marmelite core for planetary destruction—if that knowledge leaked, the USEF would be in trouble. Imagine what that information in the wrong hands could do…" He looks first at Zio, then Kieran. "Honestly, knowing that the battle is top secret, I think this is what we did—will do. It makes sense. It's a valid theory."

All three of the men pale.

Kieran swallows hard, then rakes a hand through his hair and lets go of a big puff of air. "I agree it makes sense, but there must be something else. I cannot believe we would sacrifice seven thousand beings to keep our three hundred alive—and I'm not saying we waste our lives, I'd never do that, you know that. But—"

"But what if the stakes are higher? What if this is not only about this battle? If we lose here, what will happen to Earth and our colonies? Will that be the signal that we're weak and easily defeated? With all due respect, Captain, but we've got to think big here." Chase breathes heavily.

I swallow hard. Am really hoping history plays out as it should at this point. Without a planetary destruction.

Kieran rubs his eyes. Those dark circles, I don't think they were there before. "Point taken, and I will take it under advice. I want to conserve life, not destroy it, so here's my two cents. Resume communication. Find a peaceful way out of here. But if we can't, we begin to defend ourselves, and that would mean firing so that it penetrates their shields. Think you can do that, Chase?"

"Yes, sir. Their shields are not quite so impenetrable anymore, thanks to Nonie."

"Anytime." I add a little bow. Fate, the timeline, and me, we're besties at this point. I'm obliging to their every little quirk and whim.

"Okay then, complying with Command, the adjusted version. Wildason to Chocho." He taps his hablamate. "Resume hails. Broadcast on all frequencies and all languages including binary data that we are retreating and will not come back."

Chocho's voice comes through the speaker, slightly distorted. "Understood, Captain. Part of my systems are down, so it's manual work. The message will go live in about a minute."

In real life, meaning, in my time, I would speak up right about now. It's only a theory I have, but the way I was trained a theory needs to proven or disproven before it can be dismissed.

Only now is not the time, quite literally.

"Wonderful, Chocho. Wildason out." Kieran gives us a resolute glance. "They let us go, we red tape this area. They don't—"

"Then we'll have a plan set up." Chase gives him thumbs up. "And thinking ahead, it makes sense. We should keep that whole Marmelite-thing under wraps. Nobody needs to know the dangers of such a core. Marmelite is too dangerous for common knowledge, I'm afraid."

Kieran raps his knuckles on the table. "Agreed. I'd prefer not having to mention it, but if we have to for whatever reason, I'll make sure it'll be top secret. We'll make this need-to-know and admirals only. If it became common knowledge what can happen and that knowledge fell into the wrong hands… Not good."

"We'll mess up future-Nonie though." Chase grins at me. "Sorry, you're still gonna end up in your past with us, when this becomes top secret."

Not secret enough for Grazer not to find and use the information. I fake a smile. "Do what you have to. It—"

Boom!

The *Pioneer* jolts and shakes, throwing Kieran against the table and Chase into a stumble.

Boom!

BoomBoom!

"Wildason to Bridge! What—"

"We're under fire again, sir! All five ships—continuous fire!"

Chapter Forty-Eight

Kieran is already out the door and storming onto the bridge. Manazari jumps out of the command chair. "Chocho had just sent the message, and *boom*! They don't care about peace!"

I mentally file that information for later. Maybe there's something to my theory. For right now, *and boom* is definitely right. On screen all five ships can be seen firing upon us, and every single blow to our shields shakes us like cheerleaders their pom-poms.

"Evasive, Thaler!" Kieran barks from his command chair.

"Way ahead of you, sir!" Thaler yells back.

"Shields holding, ninety-three percent! Return fire, Captain?" Chase takes over tactical from a lieutenant.

"Not yet! Evasive! Can you jump us out of here, Thaler?"

"Negative, sir! I need more room, or else the jump drive won't engage!"

Kieran nods crisply. "Get us that room. Maneuver us out until we can jump. We're getting out of here! Manazari, keep the shields up."

"Sir!"

BoomBoom!

"Direct hit, aft shields down to eighty-eight percent and falling!"

"They're fast, sir! I can't get us away from them!" Thaler shakes her head, eyes darting over the readouts in front of her, fingers moving so fast they become a blur.

"Keep trying, Lieutenant. We have to get out of here! Chocho, send emergency signal and recording to Command. Deploy drones. We—"

Boom!

Everybody gets jostled forward with a grunt.

Kieran pulls himself up again. "We need to—"

BoomBoomBoom!

Somebody falls out of their chair with a heavy thud.

"Report!" Kieran yells. "Shields?"

"All shields down to seventy-nine percent! At this rate, we won't make it long!"

"Thaler, come on!" Kieran claps his hands. "I know you can do it!"

"Thank you, sir, but they're purposefully keeping us close! They know we need the room, if I had to guess."

And that guess would be correct. The only data the Quaneez seem to have read after hacking into the *Pioneer*'s systems were the technical specs, that much is clear, even forty years later.

BOOOM!

This hit is different than the others. I'm thrown off my feet onto my knees, and so are most of the others.

"Full hit starboard side, Captain! We're leaking—ugh!" Hayes can barely hold on during the next salvo hitting the Pioneer.

"We're getting our ass kicked!" Chase calls out. "Captain!"

"Damn it!" Kieran slaps the hand rest. "Return fire! All weapons! Aim to disable—"

Boom!

He rocks back and forth, hair falling into his face. "Aim to disable, but if you destroy them, so be it!"

Chase on tactical nods, more or less hammering commands into the console in front of him. "Returning fi—"

"Captain, we're leaking plasma from the drive coils!" Hayes projects a smaller picture onto the main view screen. "Big leak. It's affecting our ability to jump and maneuver. We can't—"

"Incoming!" Chase yells.

I grab on to the railing—*boom!*

"Shields at forty-three percent, falling! It's like every hit overloads and drains them at the same time!"

"Sir, one direct hit into that plasma and we'll—"

"Blow up, I know!" Kieran calls over his shoulder. "Thaler, evasive, keep our injured side away from—"

"Trying, sir! Limited maneuverability with the leak!" An ounce of stress creeps into Thaler's voice.

"Got it, Lieutenant. Do what you can! Chase, I want nobody close enough to light us up. Hayes, can we fix it from inside?" He points at the smaller image showing the *Pioneer*'s outside hull, starboard side, a glowing, glittering flux of plasma oozing from a man-sized ragged tear in her hull.

My next breath gets stuck in my throat as history aligns with the current present inside my mind. That's why the *Pioneer* looked patched up in the pictures after the battle: hull breach, plasma leak!

Hayes checks his readings, then turns toward Kieran. "Negative, sir! The damage is too big. We can only repair it from the outside!"

Kieran gives him a short acknowledging nod. "Got it. Wildason to Lopez, ready all three shuttles for repairs from space. We've got to get that leak fixed!"

I let go of the breath I held. I mean, yes, I know they're going to fix it, I've seen the pictures, but still. Good to know we're on the same page here.

"On it." Lopez doesn't waste time with pleasantries.

A messy, icky lump forms in my chest, making every heart beat heavy and painful. It doesn't look good right now. Anybody can see that. We're supposed to win—but how? Outnumbered, outflown, outwhitted—and leaking plasma. We're sitting ducks. We—

"All three shuttles deployed, sir!" The image Hayes projected before zooms back a bit, bringing the three *Pioneer* shuttles into view.

The lead shuttle stays close to the *Pioneer* as it dives under its belly, and—

A salvo of yellow fire hits its shields.

"Wildason to *Rhine*, enforce your—"

Within two seconds the shields begin to glow bright, brighter, brighter—

"*Rhine*, recalibrate—"

Right idea, but too late. The *Rhine* explodes into a fireball, rocking the *Pioneer* worse than the incoming fire. Somebody cries out, several people grunt from the impact—

I blink twice. The *Rhine*… It's gone. Gone.

Kieran jumps out of the captain's chair. "What happened? They have the same shields as we do! One hit shouldn't do that! Answers, people! It's not looking good right now!"

No, it's not. Agreed. My heart hammers as if it hadn't read the history books. Adrenaline floods my veins, replacing every ounce of blood I have. This is war. The beginning of it. I knew what to expect, yet being here… is different. Even though I know the *Pioneer* will prevail, adrenaline is taking over, readying me for a fight I know the outcome of and won't participate in. The shuttles will fix the leak, the *Pioneer* will win.

Hayes voice breaks as he yells his findings through the cacophony of alarms and noise. "Sir, the shuttle's shields… I mean, same for us, but we're bigger, we're compensating better. The weapon's fire is overloading the shuttle's system! It's as if the energy was sucked right into the shuttle's circuits and—"

"And it exploded. Damnit!" Kieran punches the air. "Meaning, they're easy bait. Chase, can you extend our shields to protect them?"

"For a while, yes, but I'm rerouting power from secondary systems already, so it won't be for long!"

It took us years to figure out how to mostly compensate for the energy dispersion from their weapons. Years and many, many casualties.

"Has to be enough. Do it! Chocho, hail all shuttles. I want them within our shields!!

"On it, sir!"

Another explosion rocks the *Pioneer*. Someone screams as hot air hisses from a busted pipe somewhere in the back of the bridge.

"Captain! Two Quaneez ships attacking the *Danube* and the *Moselle*!"

"Helm! Bring us between the shuttles and the Qua—"

Boom!

The *Danube* explodes in a ball of white light—

"They're firing agai—"

Boom!

A third explosion—

And the *Moselle* is gone.

Silence hovers on the bridge. Desperate, disbelieving silence. Three shuttles. Gone. Three people. Gone.

That… can't be.

Can't.

They're supposed to fix it. The leak. It needs to be gone, or else we can't jump. We can't maneuver. It's supposed to be fixed—I saw it fixed! I gulp in air that bring no oxygen.

Chase looks up from his console. "All shuttles…" He clears his throat. "All shuttles destroyed by the enemy, Captain."

Kieran closes his eyes for the shortest moments, hands balling to fists at his side, then relaxing again. He nods crisp, once, more to himself than anybody else. "Tactical. Aim to destroy. At this point it's them or us, and I prefer it to be them. Thaler, attack pattern epsilon-three, mix it up with beta-four. Confuse them."

"Yes, sir! I'll give you as much as *Pioneer's* still got!"

"Aye, Captain."

Boom! Boom! Boom!

Everybody stumbles forward, barely catching themselves.

"Shields at twenty-seven percent, sir! Whatever happened to the shuttles is happening to us, only slower. Assume because of the higher-powered shield generators, but—"

"But it won't be for long, understood, Hayes." Kieran sits down slow, like an old man. "Lopez, any way we can get jump capability?" His fingers cramp around the arm rests.

"Negative, sir. As long as that leak is there—"

"Understood. Keep the *Pioneer's* shields working as long as you can, I'll take care of the rest."

He lowers his head and rubs his forehead, muscles in his jaw tight.

Boom! Boom!

Boo—

Super-bright white light bursts through the screen—

"We got them! One battle ship down, Captain!" Chase pumps a fist. "Four more to go!"

Elation flares up, only to die down the second everybody realizes what they just did—that they killed five hundred sentient beings.

It's nothing against my five million, but I know the feeling.

Boom! Boom! BoomBoomBoom!

A cacophony of reports fills the air:

"Sir, fire increasing, shields—"

"Damage to hull decks nineteen and twenty-three, starboard! Damn, close to the leak—"

"—won't be able to support them much longer! At nineteen percent!"

"Returning fire! They're getting reckless—"

Ka-boom!

This time I know as soon as the bright, disorienting light blinds me what it means.

"Second ship destroyed, sir! They're focusing on attack over safety! We can—"

Kieran stands up. "Chocho, hail the planet and their colony! Tell them in all languages if they stop firing, we will! I'm not killing anybody else unless it is absolutely necessary!"

"Aye, Captain!" Chocho busies himself with the com. "No response, sir. Same as alwa—"

"Incoming! They're not turning—" Chase yells, but Kieran is faster. One glance to the view screen, and the danger is clear.

"Thaler! Evasive, now!"

The image of a Quaneez battlecruiser takes up most of the view screen, getting larger, larger, larger—

"Oh, hell," I whisper under my breath. "They're trying to ram us!" Sweat forms and rivulets along my brow. What the heck is happening here?

Thaler pulls the *Pioneer* into a yaw so tight, the ship groans under the forces working against it. Kieran steps forward, arm extended, pointing at the screen.

"Chase! Underbelly, seven o'clock, fire!"

Without a second between the order and the execution, Chase fires—

Ka-BOOM!

A collective grunt and gasp bursts from the bridge crew as the third battle cruiser explodes, its shrapnel and debris hitting the *Pioneer's* shields and deflecting off of them.

At this point, recovery is swift.

"Shields at fifteen percent, Captain! We can't sustain this much longer! A few more hits—"

"Both remaining ships on continuous fire, sir!"

"*Pioneer's* reacting sloppy, sir! Can't keep us out of the line of fire much longer! She—"

Kieran rubs his forehead, lost in thought. He chews on his lower lip, then whirls around, looking straight at me. "Commander Conolly, you have the bridge, I'll be working on that leak!"

"But—"

"I need two minutes if we want to come out of this alive!" Kieran rushes over to me with long strides, as Chase's gaze darts from him to me and back, then widen.

"Oh. Got it. Aye, sir! I'll keep us in one piece." He sits down in the command chair and signs into the PAD with his palm print. "Manazari, continue fire like I did. Aim for the shield generators on their underbelly!"

"Sir!" Manazari takes over swiftly, as Kieran pulls me off the bridge by the hand.

As soon as the doors to the bridge have closed on us, Kieran turns to me, eyes wide, both hands on my shoulders, squeezing. "Nonie. The shields in your shuttle, will they hold better than ours?"

I shake my head so hard my brain hurts. I can't tell him the details, he knows that.

"Nonie." Kieran's grip gets stronger. "I'm out of options, and I need to get back on the bridge. I'm sorry, but—" He inhales deeply and it comes out in an unsteady rush. "But if you don't fix that leak, we're all going to die."

Chapter Forty-Nine

I empty my glass of Lubbeck's and set it back onto the coffee table. "And then Captain Rivera gives me the shuttle and orders me—*me* of all people—to repair that stupid leak! I mean, I would like to say I was doing an outstanding job with tactical, so why take me? What about the cadets majoring in engineering, maybe? Why me? I thought Rivera—Captain Rivera, sorry—was not on Team Against Nonie." I let myself fall back into the chair. Seriously. Another case of my dad's reputation messing with my Academy performance.

Admiral Upinga exchanges a glance with Conolly. "How did you do?"

I give him the eye. "What do you think? I got it done, I got back inside, and took over tactical again." I blow onto my cuticles like it's no biggie. "One hundred out of one hundred points. Thank you very much." I fake a bow, which is pretty hard when you're sitting down. Looks probably more like I've got stomach pain, but oh, well.

Conolly gives me a slow clap. "Hundred percent. Nicely done, Cadet! Now you can check external repairs off your to-do list."

"Admiral, it wasn't even *on* my to-do list."

"But nonetheless, it's good to have this performed during a live exercise at least once. It's different when you do it as a simulation."

"Yeah, but—" Wait a minute. "Why are the two of you grinning like, I don't know, Rumpelstiltskin? What am I missing?"

"Nothing, Cadet. Absolutely nothing." Conolly grins wider, and even Upinga cracks a smile.

A groan escapes me. "You did that. You asked Captain Ramirez to have me repair the leak." Of course. That's why he made this unreasonable choice instead of sending the cadets actually training in this kind of thing.

Upinga keeps a neutral expression. "We may or we may not have, but in the end, you came out of this exercise smarter than you went in."

"But—"

Conolly ignores me and holds up a hand for Upinga. "And we're getting her there, one day at a time."

Upinga meets his colleague's hand in a slapping high five. "One day at a time is all we ask."

Chapter Fifty

'm running after Kieran through the hallways of the *Pioneer*. "But I can't get involved—"

"We survive this, or you wouldn't know us! And right now the only way we can make it is if we're maneuverable and that leak is gone," Kieran calls out over his shoulder. "I see no other option!"

I sprint after him, every breath short—too short to bring in oxygen. He's got a point, but—

No, actually. He might be right: One, I know the leak gets fixed. Two, we're out of shuttles. So the only solution is… me.

I yank on his hand. "Kieran! What if that's why the battle details are top secret? Because I—"

He stops in mid-run, face lighting up. "Because it's you who fixed the leak! Yes! That makes sense!"

It does, it really does. Even more so if I think back to who made me do this exercise during my third year at the academy. I straighten my shirt. "Okay. Okay. I can do it. You're right, my shields should hold better." We lost so, so many until we found a way to reinforce them. Both sides have learned way too much about killing the other one and not getting killed themselves. The underbelly trick Kieran used? Will stop working within a few weeks, once they upgrade their shield generators. It's a constant race of adjustment, and so far I wouldn't say we're winning it.

Kieran yanks me forward into an embrace. "Thank you, Nonie." As fast as he hugged me, he lets go. "We have no time to lose. Thaler is a fantastic pilot, but she can only outfly them for so long." Meaning, he'd better be back on the bridge when they engage the enemy. "How spacefaring is your shuttle?" We start jogging down the hallway again, toward the shuttle bay.

"It flies. Limited jump capability, not that I'd need that. Most secondary systems offline, but I won't need those either."

"Got it." He taps his hablamate hard. "Wildason to Upinga. Meet me in Shuttle Bay Three!"

"Acknowledged, sir."

Another hit throws the *Pioneer* left and right.

"Bridge to Captain—we're having trouble with the evasive up here! Whatever you're planning, speed it up!" Both of us hear what Chase is really saying: get Nonie out there. *Now.*

"Acknowledged! Keep us out of the line as fire as much as you can and give me two minutes!" He speeds up, the doors of the shuttle bay barely opening in time to keep him from running into them. "Ready your shuttle!"

I sprint over to the *Odysseus* and press my palm into the reader on its outer hull next to the hatch. The red lights from the alert system are throwing odd shadows all over the place. "When I'm out, you don't have to protect me with your shields," I call over my shoulder to Kieran. "Keep favoring the leak, I'll stay glued to your flank!" Autopilot is online to some degree—it's gotta be enough to stick to the *Pioneer* like peanut butter to jelly.

The doors hiss apart for Zio jogging in. "What do you need, Captain?"

Kieran is already elbow-deep in some conduit on the backbord-side of my shuttle. "I want you to double-check me. Chase is busy up on the bridge."

"What's the plan?"

"Nonie takes the *Odysseus* and fixes the leak. Her shuttle should be able to handle a couple of shots. Check my work—we need her to emit a low-level tau-particle stream and direct it at the leaking plasma conduits. That should seal it for now. Am I right?"

Zio bends down and inspects Kieran's work, then reaches in and wiggles a few connections. "Correct. You're sure you—" He looks up at me.

"I'm fine. I can do it." In fact, I have done it. Thanks, future Conolly and Upinga…!

Upinga sticks his head deeper into the bowels of the shuttle. "Not much is working besides the bare necessities. Minimal weapons. I wouldn't recommend flying this shuttle under normal circumstances."

"Good, because they're anything but normal." Says time-traveling, potential history-saving Nonie. "And from my repairs, I'd say I have one good jump in it, if push came to shove. Some weapons and no more than that one jump, but still…" I shrug. So be it. Hopefully, the Quaneez will focus on the *Pioneer*, no hard feelings.

As Upinga crawls out and stands back up, Kieran shoots me a worried glance. "We *will* have your back, Nonie. We'll keep you protected." He says it with a hundred percent conviction behind it, not only like a promise, but a fact.

Zio brushes his palms off his pants. "Not like other people, huh? What rhymes with asshole, as Chase would say?"

Kieran gives a tight smile at Upinga's attempt to lighten the mood and seals the panel back into place. "Yeah, this isn't Alpha Rubrum." What the what? *What rhymes with asshole?* "Mashaule?" I crunch my brows. "What's he got—"

His gaze whips up to me. "You know Mashey?"

My eyes pop wide. "Your Captain Mashey is Mashaule?" *Admiral Mashaule* is the captain who abandoned his crew? Who potentially altered his ship's systems? Who—

"Yeah. He was our Captain, and Bas—"

Duh! *Of course!* "Grazer," I whisper. *Se*bas*tian Grazer: Bas.

"—was the first officer. Why?"

My legs are rooted to the floor. Somewhere in the the depth of my mind, a connection is being made, a very fine, insecure string of thought coming together, and it changes things and makes my knees wobbly. If I'm right… If I'm right…!

Holy Sun and Stars. It all makes sense, only differently than I thought! This is one gigantic, mind-blowing set-up, if I'm correct. And not only for me. I suck in a harsh breath to slow myself down. "I think I might've been wro—"

Somewhere sirens are howling.

"Another hull breach!" Kieran swallows hard. "I've got to go—"

No kidding. Not that I mind Kieran with me, knowing the *Pioneer* will come out in one piece, more or less, but the whole captain leaving the bridge during red alert or leading ground missions is *so* pre-Quaneez spacefaring years.

"Go." I wave a hand as my priorities shift. "I'll get it done. See you in five." Or six. But no longer.

"Yeah." A small smile tucks at his lips as he turns away.

I exhale roughly. Man, usually the past preps one for the future, but in my case… I shake my head, about to step into the *Odysseus*—

"Nonie!" Kieran all but runs me over in the biggest embrace ever. He wraps his arms around me so tight, I feel like I'm being attacked by a desperate octopus. He glides his fingers through my hair as he draws me closer for the shortest moment before he sighs and breaks the hug, keeping his forehead leaned into mine and his hands on my upper arms. "Watch out for yourself out there, will ya?" he whispers, his breath feathering across my skin.

A short sense of deja-vu flares up—a screenshot of us, red alert, in the exact same embrace. "I will," I breathe back. Gosh, I want to stay here, right here, in this very moment with Kieran. Without the *Pioneer* about to be shot down, preferably.

The intercom buzzes. "Captain to the bridge! We're losing main power!"

Kieran grimaces. "On my way!"

One more squeeze for my arms, one more promising glance at me, one more second where it's just us, and then he's gone.

And I don't know why, but somehow, it feels final.

Chapter Fifty-One

It takes me exactly ten seconds to realize flying through quiet space and flying through a war zone are two completely different animals.

"*Odysseus*, evasive! Automatic setting, keep us within fifty meters of the *Pioneer*'s starboard sid—*ugh!*" I grunt as the shuttle dips into a nose dive of epic proportions following the *Pioneer*.

"*Acknowledged. Keeping distance steady at fifty meters.*"

All I need. If I can stay in my seat, that is.

Like a maniac, I enter the commands to patch up the *Pioneer*. "*Odysseus*, initiate tau-particles to these coordinates." I ram my index finger down onto the control button.

"*Acknowledged. Tau-particles initiated.*"

A red beam shoots from the *Odysseus* into the damaged flank of the *Pioneer*. As soon as it hits its target, the leaking plasma begins to glow blue. It's working!

"*Odysseus*, open channel to *Pioneer*."

"*Unable to comply. System down.*"

Blech. Great.

"Display tactical information of battle on main screen."

"*Unable to comply. System down.*"

Seriously? I enter the commands to open the front windows completely for a better overview. Where are those battle cruisers? I lean forward and to the left—gotcha, one is firing at the *Pioneer* from the other side. The other one—

My heart drops to my knees. "Crap! Shields to maximum, evasive alpha-two! *Now!*" The *Odysseus'* engines howl as she follows my command a millisecond before the second Quaneez cruiser fills my view screen to the max.

"What the—?" Sweat breaks out and runs down my brows and back. Are they trying to ram me? Yes, I'm smaller, but that could still be a suicide mission!

"*Odysseus*, lock weapons onto—"

"*Unable to comply. System down.*"

Of course it is! "Crap," I yell and ram my fist onto my thigh. I thought I fixed that!

Pioneer's maneuvers come so fast, internal gravity lags behind and throws me around, and while it brings me away from that suicidal cruiser—thank you, Kieran—I'm a freakin' sitting duck here! I can't leave, I can't defend myself, I can't even call for help! And while the future tells me the *Pioneer* will make it… it didn't tell me whether *I* will make it. Fear creeps in, silent as a ninja, spreading like wildfire. I don't want to die here. Not out here. Not in this time. Not now.

Pressure builds in my chest, making it hard to breathe, hard to think. It takes all the willpower I have to not let that fear consume me. Focus, Lieutenant!

"*Odysseus*, announce progress with the leak and keep track!" Come on, come on, tell me it's almost done, so I can get back to the *Pioneer*!

"*Leak contained by eighty-seven percent.*"

Damn it—

The Quaneez battle cruiser makes a tight turn… and heads straight for me again. Of course. From a tactical point of view, it makes sense. I'm fixing the one damage that is detrimental to their enemy, ergo, they need to take me out.

"*Leak contained by ninety percent.*"

The cruiser dives under the *Pioneer,* and I swear I see its weapons array light up and glow.

"*Leak contained by ninety-one percent.*"

The weapons glow brighter, brighter—

KA-BOOM!

The cruiser vanishes in an explosion so bright, the automatic light filters can't keep it all at bay. I scream out and cover my eyes with my arms—

"—contained by ninety-four percent."

Another ship gone.

Four battle ships gone. It's nothing in the grand scale of the war, but right here, right now… It's too much. When does *better them than me* not apply anymore? When—

The *Pioneer* moves in a tight downward spiral to get into a better position between the last remaining Quaneez cruiser and the planet, pulling me with her, thanks to the *Odysseus* complying with the programmed settings.

"Leak contained by ninety-seven percent."

Almost there!

The *Pioneer* fires as the cruiser flies directly at her—fires, fires, fires—holy cow, they can't try to ram them again, what—

At the very last second, the cruiser veers aside and passes the *Pioneer*, continuing on a straight course toward the planet.

"—by ninety-eight percent."

Pioneer speeds up, trying to catch them. We're so close, all I see is the planet in my view screen. What are they doing? They're heading straight for the colony and—

They can't be—

Realization feels like a punch to the gut. *They are.* My heart is jackhammering inside my chest. I think I'm going to be sick. "No, no, no!" I yell and jump out of my chair. The cruiser fires at the planet, not at the colony, I *think*, and races down to the planet, faster, faster, faster—

Pioneer fires, trying to keep them from doing the unimaginable—

And the cruiser rams itself into the planet's surface, exploding in a fireball of white and yellow.

"—tained at one hundred percent. Tau-particle stream can be discontin—"

For one blissful, quite moment nothing happens.

But we shouldn't be so lucky.

With resounding *BOOM* a wave of pure bright light hits my

shuttle—

"*Warning. Core explosion imminent. Core explosion imminent.*"

"No!" I yell. How can they—

Oh, shit!

"Marmelite core," I breathe. An unstable Marmelite core, triggered by the shots or the exploding cruiser—

They knew what they were doing. And instead of giving up, of surrendering, they made sure we didn't take any prisoners. True Quaneez fashion.

"*Core explosion in ten seconds. Safe distance not reached. Seven—*"

No, no, no, no—

Pioneer pulls back at maximum speed, yanking me with her, my tau-beam jarring its hull plates in a zigzag pattern.

A second wave of light, this time even brighter—

"*…five—*"

My skin begins to tingle, to burn, to buzz like I was set on fire and touched a live wire, both at the same time. The laws of physics must be broken, because I see… nothing. Everything. Nothing *and* everything. Planets. Galaxies. People. Aliens. Suns. Moons. Past. Future. Alternate realities.

I see everything and it tears me apart one atom at a time,

A scream tears from my throat, so hoarse—

Space contracts around me—and all that's left is one thought: *Home.*

Chapter Fifty-Two

Waking up *hurts.*

Like, for real.

Ow, ow, ow—heartheartheart*everything!*

I groan and lift one hand to my chest.

Ow.

"Warning. Core explosion imminent in ten seconds—"

What the what—

I jolt upright, ignoring the pain—did *Pioneer* reach a safe distance—

There's no *Pioneer* in front of my window.

No Balthar System.

"... seven... six..."

Another freakin' countdown! My heart cramps, adding to the pain. Maybe that's why I need one second longer to process what I'm seeing. Holy cow, this is H-155 and I'm right above it!

Something flashes to my right, like a ship initializing a jump—

"Odysseus, get me out—"

"Unable to comply while particle stream in action. Core explosion in three... two..."

"No!" I yell. I just made it back—I can't die now! My fingers dig into the armrests of my chair. I suck in one desperate, painful last breath before the planet—

Wait a second.

Wait *another* second.

It's not exploding.

It's *not*—

"Core stabilized. Tau-particle stream can be discontinued."

What the what? My heart is pumping hard enough to punch a hole into my aching chest, each beat stinging and cramping like it was stabbed—but pumping. Alive.

The freakin' core stabilized. But how—

The breath I held comes out shaky and with a sigh at the end. Nausea swamps my systems, and even though I should feel better, I'm not.

Core stabilized. Could the tau-particles have done that…? I shake my head, a small laugh bubbling up. That's for the scientists to figure out. All I know is that no planet is going to blow up today. Nobody is going to die today! No millions and millions' deaths on my shoulders! Never has anybody been happier than me to hear a whole planet of Quaneez is going to be alive.

"Warning. Three Quaneez Battle Cruisers approaching."

Oh, crap. Adrenaline surges. I'm right back where I left off what feels like ages ago—in the middle of my invasion of Quaneez space. I take it back. Nobody on the planet is going to die today, but the jury is still out on me. I blink quickly, aligning my brain with the here and now.

Right. Mission. Plants. Unforeseen complications.

"Odysseus, shield status!"

"Shields are up and at sixty-three percent. Cruisers in weapons' range in twenty seconds." Once their silent propulsion drive has caught them up with me and they feel safe enough to fire without risking damage to their planet's atmosphere.

"Odysseus, can you reroute power to the weap—" I snap my mouth shut. No. Wait. It doesn't… *feel* right. In fact, my gut is telling me the opposite. Could it be… I mean, is that my first sense, as Zio said it was? Feeling what is right? Or is it… I mean, there is a pattern emerging when it comes to the Quaneez. Only we've all been too blind to see it.

I make an executive decision. *"Odysseus,* take weapons completely offline. Are any communication channels open?" Not that I thought they fixed themselves…

"Communication is still offline."

Good.

I check my readouts of the work I started a lifetime ago as fast as I can. Just because I'm not firing doesn't mean I don't still have a mission to complete, no matter I was set up to fail, and no matter I'm not sure anymore it ever was a true mission. Won't risk the lives of billions of humans on suspicions.

"Weapons' range in ten seconds."

Hurry up! I ram my finger onto the enter button. "Demat from this location, max speed, add containment field!" There's *something* there that looks like it could be what we need.

Not that I have time to check or look for anything else.

"Acknowledged." The *Odysseus* pauses for six long seconds. *"Demat completed. Weapons' range reached—"*

Crap. "*Odysseus*, can we jump?" I'm not risking my life on a wobbly theory if I can avoid it.

"Jump capability still limited to one jump. All vessels within weapon's range."

Within weapons' range—but not firing.

One-Mississippi.

Two-Mississippi.

Three-Mississippi.

That's enough. "*Odysseus,* jump!" I slam my palm down onto the controls—

Space contorts around me, buckles—and stretches out into a beautiful canvas dotted with a myriad of stars in front of me.

Hello, USEF space. Looking spiffy today.

No H-155.

No Quaneez cruisers.

I look over my shoulder to the mid-section of my shuttle: I do have several plants we need in my hastily erected containment field.

Holy Sun and Stars. No way. Seriously, no way. "I did it," I whisper and glide a shaky hand through my hair. They didn't plan on me succeeding. Quite the opposite—they set me up to fail. And yet I did it. I kept H-155 from exploding, returned alive, brought the plants that—

hopefully—have the potential to safe humanity, *and* I might've discovered the secret behind the Quaneez wars. *Might* have. "Unbelievable. All this time, and nobody figured—"

"Warning. Incoming Battle Ship. Weapons locked onto our position."

What the freakin'—

Gone is the elation of a successful mission. "*Odysseus*, identify!"

"Vessel identified as the USEF Guardian."

The *Guardian*? The *Odysseus* picked up on them on the way into Quaneez territory in what feels another lifetime, if I remember correctly. I was a bit preoccupied at that point. Why are they so far out and close to the border—and more importantly, why on earth are they locking their freakin' weapons on me?

"*Odysseus*, hail—Dang it," I curse. Communications are down. "Belay that. Use all external lights, morse code, SOS, continuous emission."

My fingers fly over the control board—

"Ow." I flinch and press one hand to my heart. This burning, stabbing pain, like something had been ripped out from underneath my sternum, hurts to the point of nausea.

Alas, priorities. Dropping my second hand back down to the controls, I work like a maniac, accessing the systems. Maybe I can fix communications, maybe—

An alarm goes off, accompanied by a red light in the lower corner of the console—and I swear my heart stops for a moment. "*Odysseus*, confirm *Guardian*'s weapon status."

"Weapons are charging. Locked onto our position."

They can't be firing onto their own! Are they blind? I'm in a freakin' USEF shuttle, and even though I'm not responding to hails, which I presume they're sending out, no reason to fire! Protocol says to—

"Weapons completely charged."

I stare out the window, and there they are, maybe two kilometers off my starboard side. Never has a USEF ship looked more dangerous to me. Their weapons' array begins to glow, and—

Boom! BoomBoom!

Three shots hit my shields, their impact knocking the *Odysseus* off course and me half off my seat. I scream out. "I'm one of you guys, you idiots! *Odysseus*, evasive pattern theta four! Shields?"

"*Pattern initialized. One shield generator destroyed. Shields at twenty-one percent and holding.*"

For now, I mentally add, and curse again. Shows how much more effective modern weapons are compared to what the Quaneez shot at me at Balthar.

Boom! Boom!

"*Shields down to fourteen percent. Aft shields about to fail.*"

"Begin irregular zig-zag pattern evasive maneuvers, keep aft away from them! And idiots, stop firing at me!" I can't take this kind of damage much longer, and I have no freakin' way of defending myself or communicating! This is an execution!

Boom!

"*—shields have fail—*"

A warm, tingling sensation engulfs my chest, relieving the pain I felt since I woke up back in my time. My vision blurs. It's a demat—

Chapter Fifty-Three

Somewhere, 5 seconds later

••• **a**nd when my eyes come back online, I don't believe them: I'm on board a USEF ship, a *modern* USEF ship, grey and white and sleek and spiffy. But that's not what brings my pulse up to a good two hundred bpm and my adrenaline to spike. That would be the man standing in front of me, an angry expression on his face no face mask can hide.

"You," I breathe. Not what—or whom—I expected.

"You, *Admiral*," Admiral Mashaule's glare shoots daggers at me. "What was *that*, Lieutenant?" He points a furious finger at somewhere behind me. "You never struck me as somebody to disregard orders, but I guess there's a first for everything!"

I blink. "What the what?" Only now do I notice the two security officers behind Mashaule, and the tiny, but crucial fact that they have their weapons out and aimed at me.

Oh, and no name tags or any identification visible.

The admiral snarls under his breath. "You had one job to do. One job, Lieutenant. Scan the planet and get those plants to help humanity survive the flu! And here you are, without your mandatory face covering and without the plants!"

My brain has to shift gears with his show. Are we really keeping the pretense up? "But sir—"

"And you have failed spectacularly, not to mention that you have brought the Quaneez against us again! Quite an accomplishment for a few minutes' work! This is going to get you courtmartialed! The implications of what you did are disastrous!" It's a good performance, the all-angry and righteous admiral.

He really wants to play that game?

By all means then, let's. I have more than one ace up my sleeve, I think. "Admiral, I did bring the plants."

Surprise flickers over Mashaule's face. "Y-you did?"

I stand up straighter with my hands folded behind my back. One quick double-tap onto PADdy, and I'm set. "Of course, sir. As I was ordered to."

The admiral recovers like a pro, the surprised look gone, replaced by a rather arrogant one. "Please, Lieutenant. You obviously didn't scan the planet. How could you have brought the plants?"

I step down the demat platform so that I'm no more than a good arm's length away from Mashaule and give him my most innocent face. "But why would you think I didn't scan the planet? Sir?" Placing one hand over my heart, I continue my charade, sucking in a theatrical breath. "Or… were you thinking I didn't scan the planet because… it didn't explode?" I put steel behind my last words, and it cuts. For a moment the admiral's arrogant and angry features give way to the shock of realizing that I know.

Oh yeah, I know all right.

Have suspected it for a while, but it was too grande a scale to be believable. Worse than Grazer being responsible.

Silence hovers, although I could swear my sensitive half-Magellan ears are picking up on Mashaule grinding his teeth.

Without taking his eyes off me, he waves a hand. "Jergens, Nguyen. Dismissed."

The two security officers give a short acknowledging nod as they holster their weapons. Within ten seconds, they have cleared the room, leaving me alone with the unarmed admiral.

Unarmed—but at this point I wouldn't say he has a friendly attitude toward me.

"What exactly are you insinuating, Lieutenant?"

I relax my stance, a move I wouldn't have dared before. But well, I have forty years more experience, so to speak. "Admiral, please. We both know you set me up." From the get-go, the very moment he backed me up in front of Grazer about joining Division Two, from the moment he knew I was a Thorburn. How convenient for him. The daughter of his political enemy. If only there was a way to use her against her father and advance Mashaule's own political agenda...

Keeping my voice level and cool, I glare at Mashaule. "You manipulated the *Odysseus*, so that the level six-scan would ignite the planet's Marmelite core and destroy it." The same setup—the same odd particles—found on the *Odysseus* as on the *Eclipse* at Alpha Rubrum. Only connecting puzzle piece? Mashaule. Not Grazer. Grazer was down on the surface with the rest of the *Eclipse's* crew, so he couldn't have manipulated the systems. Mashaule, *Captain Mashey,* was on board, so logic concludes he did it. Also, we found the same traces on the *Odysseus'* scanners, after Grazer said Admiral Mashaule personally oversaw the adjustments to my ship. One and one equals two, doesn't it?

Plus, I genuinely believe Grazer wants peace. Just a feeling I have, but I'm learning to trust them. He wouldn't want me to kill five million Quaneez when finally we had some sort of armistice, even though he doesn't understand said armistice. Mashaule on the other hand... He has a motive. All he ever wanted is win this war, and winning from his point of view means dominating the Quaneez. Defeating them.

There's a small part inside my soul that still hopes I'm wrong. That nobody could be this cunning, deceiving, or cruel, but that little bit of hope is snuffed out when the admiral chuckles and rubs two fingers over his chin.

"Oh, well then. I'm surprised you figured it out. I specifically chose you because of Grazer's criticism of you—your obsession with following orders. I would've thought better of you, Lieutenant. If you had complied with your instructions, we wouldn't be having this discussion now."

Duh. "Because I'd be dead." Killed in a planetary destruction.

"Precisely."

Ouch. "Sorry to disappoint, Admiral, but I try to avoid genocide whenever I can." I push this out through my teeth. What an appaling plan. Two birds, one stone. How convenient. "And after using me for mass-murder, you wanted my dad to take the fall. No Admiral Thorburn, no contender during the election." Because my dad's career would've been over after his daughter made the Quaneez wars flare up. Daughter dead, the war raging… A perfect storm to hit my dad—a perfect storm prevented by my Magellan genes sending me back in time. How ironic for Mashaule.

The admiral regards me with silent disgust. "A bonus of choosing you. Of course you would be the same peace-loving fool like your father. *Integration instead of separation.* Never have I heard more idiotic ideas. Your father poses a threat to humanity, and people need to recognize that. Peace is an illusion. It can only be kept if we're in control, and with your father as president, that would never have happened. We'd probably have Magellans and who knows which species running around freely on Earth, mixing with humanity." He spits it out like he had a bad taste in his mouth.

Anger rises. "Believe me, once my dad wins—"

"Oh, but he won't."

The *Guardian* shakes once, making both of us take a step to the side, or else we'd be falling.

Mashaule ignores it and adjusts his stance. "Because my plan still works, Lieutenant. You were just caught returning from Quaneez space. I'm sure it won't be much longer and the Quaneez will come knocking after you shook them up. And then—"

Another quake of the *Guardian*, but this one comes after a resounding *boom*. The lights dim and turn reddish as the sirens for red alert spring to live.

Boom, another shake, this one heavier.

I stumble, but catch myself. Graviton waves? An attack? Are the Quaneez—

A muscle in Mashaule's jaw twitches. "As I was saying, the Quaneez will be retaliating because of what Tom Thorburn's stupid daughter did, invading their space—"

My hands ball into fists at my side. Never have I wanted to fight somebody more than I do at this very moment. "I'm not going to stay silent—"

"Oh, but you will." Mashaule reaches behind his back and pulls a weapon on me.

Damn it—

A gasp breaks free as realization strikes. "You're going to kill me."

"Lieutenant." He says it with a hint of disappointment in his voice. "Of course I'm going to kill you. After all, you attacked me after we dematted you over. I had to defend myself."

He raises the gun, and in this very moment something shifts inside my brain, something that has been in the making since I was nine years old.

I shoot my left hand up from underneath the weapon, and before Mashaule can pull it back, I have my fingers wrapped around the muzzle, redirecting the line of fire away from me. With more power than I thought possible, I burst forward, pushing the gun into his abdomen to keep it away from me, and deliver the most powerful punch I've ever given straight into the admiral's face.

His self-sealing mask goes flying as he stumbles back from the unexpected impact, taking me with him, because I won't let go of that gun. The hold I have of it is the difference between life and death.

I use my second hand to cup the weapon and break it from his fingers—

With a roar, Mashaule punches me in the jaw with his free hand, the impact throwing my head back and bringing stars to dance in front of my eyes.

But I don't loosen my grip on the gun.

Instead, I force-twist the weapon back into his hold, against the resistance of his index finger in the trigger guard—

Mashaule screams out at the same time I hear an odd cracking sound and feel the resistance give. Maybe it's the pain of a broken finger, maybe it's the mind of a crazy man, but the admiral throws himself forward into me. I grunt from the impact as I collapse under his full bodyweight. We hit the ground with a thud, me on the bottom, Mashaule on top of me, my legs wrapped around his waist, taking him in my guard to at least control him to some degree.

Memories assault me, but for once in my life, they don't stop me.

They fuel me.

I won't let him kill me, not after everything I've been through, not with what he's threatening to do with my dad. I won't.

Mashaule is trying to keep me from yanking that gun off his broken finger by putting all his weight on me, keeping the gun squished between our stomachs.

My problem is, I have both hands on the weapon.

His advantage is, he doesn't.

Mashaule swings his left arm as much as he can without taking his weight off me and the weapon, and rams his fist against my right temple. "You won't survive this time, you won—*ugh*." He grunts in anger, when I avoid his punch by crunching up closer to him, cheek to cheek.

It makes him even madder. Every word he says is accentuated with a left-handed punch of some kind. "You. Are. Dead. *Dead.* Stupid. Bi—"

My right temple is nothing but pain. Making my vision blurry, my brain slow. Must get that gun. Can't get knocked out.

"I. Will. Kill. You. And it'll even look better, now that you broke my finger. Kill. Yo—"

I can't take that much longer. Dizzy. He's too heavy on top of me. Can't move.

Only one way left to fight back.

I let myself fall backwards to the ground, as if the last punch did me in. Cruel pleasure lights up in Mashaule's face as he readies himself for the final strike.

Pride comes before the fall, right?

With all the strength I have left, I crunch up and forward in the fastest sit up I have ever done and slam the strongest part of my forehead smack into the middle of the admiral's face.

Something crunches, something pops—

A short, cut-off grunt breaks from his throat and is snuffed out the moment Mashaule's eyes roll back and he collapses on me, unconscious dead weight.

"Holy crap," I wheeze. Heavy.

This wasn't just a headbutt, it was the mother of all headbutts, powered by determination and sheer, raw anger.

Keeping both hands on the gun—because I wouldn't put it past Mashaule to fake this—I roll him over, grunting in the progress. Whale, stranded. Once I end up on top of him, I pull the weapon out of his limp hands as fast as I can and scramble up and back, away from the man who wants me dead. Every breath comes heavy and hard, but hey, I'm breathing, that's not something I would have expected a few weeks ago had you told me I'd fight an admiral. Or anybody, really.

Question is, what now? How do I get off the ship—

The doors straight ahead of me slide open. I raise my weapon—

And let it sink when I recognize the two men leading the group of security officers into the demat room.

"You," I breathe, my heart filling with a warmth that counteracts at least some of the pain lodged in there since I arrived back in this time.

They came.

Admiral Chase Conolly and Admiral Zio Upinga.

My mentors.

My friends.

Chapter Fifty-Four

Admiral Chase Conolly and Admiral Zio Upinga make room to let the security team storm in and go to town on Mashaule. For the first time, I notice red alert is cancelled and the lights are back to normal. No idea when that happened.

Chase—*Admiral* Conolly—raises a hand, a faint, wistful smile on his slightly wrinkled face visible behind the mask. When he speaks, he sounds shy. Tentative. "Hey, Nonie." He takes a hesitant step toward me, but then his eyes fall onto the security team placing the unconscious admiral in handcuffs, and he stays where he is. He clears his throat, and his next sentence sounds like an admiral addressing a student. "What happened here, Cadet?"

I get it. Pretense. Oh, haven't I become a master at it.

Ignoring the throbbing pain in my chest and head I snap to attention as much as I can. "Sir, Admiral Mashaule attacked me and tried to kill me. He's the one who ordered Admiral Grazer to give me this mission. He tampered with my shuttle, so that it would destabilize the core of H-155, causing the entire planet to explode. I…" …*had forty years to figure it out and luck on my side…* "…I countered the beginning planetary core rupture with tau-particles and stabilized the core—"

"Of course." Upinga slaps his forehead. "That would make sense! If it worked as a phi-stabilizer—"

"Admiral." Chase gives him one of *those* glances. "Boring science details later. What else, Cadet?"

The security team shoves an anti-grad-sled under Mashaule's limp body. I wouldn't wanna carry him either.

"Sir, Admiral Mashaule admitted to planning the destruction of H-155 to restart the war and to take my father out of the race for the USEF presidency. And I do have proof." I lift my wrist with PADdy on it up and give it a wiggle before I tap it to stop the recording.

A wide grin spreads over Conolly's face. "That's our favorite student. Now, what exactly—"

Upinga cuts him off. "Chase. Wait. Nonie, are you… are you okay?" He places one hand over his heart, mirroring the exact spot that feels like somebody took a hot iron stake and stabbed me with it.

Am I okay? That simple question, it unleashes something in me, a pain that goes so deep, it roots in the bottom of my soul. It brings a yearning, a restlessness and aching with it unlike anything I've ever felt before. Yes, my head hurts. My body. But the dominant pain is different from that. Never-experienced. Like my soul was ripped in two.

A chopped breath leaves my throat. "I don't know. I… I don't think so." One hand creeps up to cover my heart, like Upinga's did, because, yes, he's right: *That's* where the pain is. Like somebody used a butcher's knife to cut out my heart.

Chase smacks Zio over the back of the head. Lightly. "Stupid question. You got eyes in your head, Doctor?" he asks with a pronounced glance down at the handcuffed Mashaule, who is being transported out of the room by the security team.

"Not what I meant, Trip." Upinga gives his colleague a pronounced glance.

"Oh. *Oh.*" Chase flinches. "I'm sorry. Of course it would be reciprocal." He looks like he wanted to say something else, but snaps his mouth shut, keeping an eye on the security team until the doors close behind them and Mashaule, leaving us alone.

Silence hovers, heavy with a past that's new, yet old to us.

The admirals' gazes soften once we're alone.

"Forty years," Conolly whispers. "Forty years." And, as if they'd rehearsed the moment, they both open their arms for me at the same time.

I all but throw myself forward and into their embrace. As soon as they wrap their arms around me, I'm overwhelmed by familiarity—a very confusing familiarity. I smell Admiral Conolly's aftershave I've known him to wear for the last years. I pick up on a faint whiff of Magellan tea from Admiral Upinga. That's all *now*. But the feeling of belonging, the words they whisper, they're not.

They're from *before*.

"When your shuttle vanished that day, we thought we lost you." Chase's voice breaks at the end. "We thought the explosion killed you. To say Kieran took it hard would be an understatement."

Kieran.

A silent tear sneaks out and runs down my cheek, only to be soaked up by Zio's uniform. Just thinking Kieran's name makes the pain in my chest worse, intensifying the cramping and suffocating sensation. A small *oomph*-sound escapes my throat.

Tears blur my vision as I look up at Zio. "I can't believe… I can't believe he's dead." I hugged him less than an hour ago. Talked to him. And now… Kieran is gone. Has been gone, for decades. Grief wraps around my heart and squeezes with its icy tentacles.

He's gone.

There's no goodbye for me, no last words, no nothing.

It's all in the past, buried under years and impossible to reach.

Zio squeezes my shoulder. "It's been nearly four decades, and I still can't believe he's dead. You'll need time to adjust. Your body and your mind. Your soul."

I move back and out of the group hug, then wrap my arms around myself. Gotta keep it together somehow. It's so unfair—leaving like this. Being torn out of that life on the *Pioneer* without the chance for a last word. "I didn't expect to not come back to the *Pioneer*, or I would've said good bye. I didn't want to leave like this," I whisper. Didn't want for him—them—to think I was dead.

Chase expression turns pained at the same time nausea cranks it up for me. "It took us months until we found out your ship wasn't destroyed, and when we did, it was quite the shocker." He huffs out a laugh and wiggles his hands. "Surprise. We—"

A beep comes through the com system. *"Zetumer to Admiral*

Conolly."

Chase cocks an eyebrow and taps his hablamate. "Conolly here."

"Admiral, I have good news and interesting news for you."

Conolly huffs. "Gee, go ahead, Captain."

"First, the Guardian *is under our control. Resistance was minimal."*

"Fantastic. What's the interesting news?"

"Well…" The captain stretches that word. *"That would be the USEF ship that just pulled up on our starboard side, sir. We're getting a code three request for you, Admiral Upinga, and Cadet Thorburn to demat over."*

Zio and Chase exchange a glance. "A code three? That's quite unusual, but—

"That's not it, sir." Zetumer pauses. *"It's the ship requesting your presence, sir. It's the* USEF Pioneer. *"*

Chapter Fifty-Five

"**S**o much for being a museum ship," Chase growls as we step off the demat platform, then blows out a puff of air as he takes in his environment. "Man… It's been too long."

Actually, just a few mere hours for me. Plus forty years, but you know, who's counting these days anyway.

Just sayin', because I do realize my life has become surreal. Completely surreal, thank you very much. From the very moment I was called in to Admiral Grazer's office and conditionally promoted to lieutenant to this very moment every new day has outdone the last.

And I doubt the surprises are over.

For one long moment, the admirals take in the *Pioneer*—the now fully automated demat console, the colors of the room that looked so modern and new once and now somehow feel… dated.

Conolly smacks his lips. "She's still the best ship ever, no matter what."

"Agreed. She held the hopes of a generation." Zio steps next to his friend. "Ours, too."

"And I can't wait to find out who orders us over here via code three. Conference room, Zetumer said." He nods his chin toward the doors. "Let's go."

Chase leads the way, with Zio next to him and me trailing behind. I'm glad they're in front of me, I don't feel a hundred percent on top of my game, and not just because my head hurts from Mashaule's assault. More… overall. Like I was drained, and as if every drop of energy that left was replaced with a dull, ever-present ache. Time travel seems to be a pain.

Chase leads us in the direction toward the bridge and main conference room. Walking down the hallways of the *Pioneer* is strange. Like I'm walking over somebody's grave, and it feels wrong, somehow. Empty. Too quiet. Too… dead, no matter our steps echoing through the hallway.

Everything *looks* the same as I remember it from, well, a few hours ago. Forty years ago. Whatever. Maybe the floors are marked more when before they were spotless, maybe the color of the walls has dulled a tad, but it's the *Pioneer* all right, only now, she's been through years of fighting the Quaneez.

It just doesn't *feel* the same.

"Creepy," Chase whispers under his breath. Good to know I'm not the only one feeling like this.

I keep my hands pressed into my abdomen while I walk. It helps with the ache, to a degree. With every step closer to the command area it changes. Oh, it still hurts, but there's also this… longing. A pull. Like a string was attached to my soul, pulling me along to—

I stop dead in my tracks.

Kieran's quarters.

I swallow so loud, there's probably an echo in the empty hallway.

"Nonie?"

Zio and Chase have stopped, both looking at me with this mix of pity and worry.

I shrug. "I… I dunno. I feel… weird, for a lack of a better term." I shrug again. This overall sense of… *something* is there, now more than ever, that I'm in front of Kieran's quarters.

The admirals exchange one of those glances, then Chase points at the door. "Well, whoever ordered us here can't expect us to not do a wee bit of sightseeing, can they? Let's say hi to the past."

Rather, *say hi to Kieran's past.* To be honest, I'm afraid to enter. Not quite sure exactly of what—that it's not the same, or worse, that it is the same. But no, it can't be the same. Not without him.

I place my palm onto the reading pad. It's probably locked, but—

"Nonie Magnetta. Access granted," the *Pioneer*'s computer voice announces.

A surprised chuckle escapes me. "I'm still in the system," I whisper. Nonie *Magnetta.*

"He never revoked your access, Nonie." Chase lies a hand onto my shoulder. "Come on. Let's visit the memory of an old friend."

Kieran didn't delete me, and as risky as it is—was—for the timeline, it means the world to me.

The doors slide apart and close behind us after we enter.

Silence.

Neither of us moves. But then, I doubt any of us are in the here and now. We're all in the past, if only in our minds. I know I am.

Yes, these are Kieran's quarters. Everything looks the same, with a few new nuances, but nothing that wouldn't make me feel right at home. The air smells stale through the face mask Zio had me put on, but… I inhale slowly through my nose. I could swear the slightest hint of his scent is still here, and it patches up my soul and rips it open at the same time.

It feels so much like yesterday… and yet there is a world of time and death separating us.

"They really kept everything the way it was." Chase places a hand against the wall, his voice raw.

I swallow hard and take a few tentative steps through the room, dragging one finger over the dining table.

We just ate here for the first time together. Chase grilled me for information.

Next, the couch. Where he held my hand for the first time after that power outage.

The window, where he almost kissed me. Gosh, I wish—

A stab of barb-wired pain shoots through my core.

This is hard. So hard. Kieran is everywhere yet he hasn't been here, in this room, in decades. Letting my gaze roam through the quarters it's drawn to the desk like by a magnet. With three large strides I make it over there. Here, he showed me his secret drawer and chocolate stash. My heart hammers like crazy, as if it was reliving those memories. At that point I was head over heels for him already. There he was, the famous captain, hiding chocolate. A smile steals itself onto my face as I place my hand where he did when he showed me the secret drawer.

Pop!

With a little squeak, the wooden panel pops open, and all of a sudden, I'm assaulted by a wave of… anticipation? Like my body knew more than me. I pull the drawer out farther—

"What's that?" Zio comes over to the desk. "A hidden drawer?"

For a moment I feel bad—it's Kieran's secret chocolate hiding place. But then… yeah. Not that it matters anymore.

"Yeah," I whisper. "A secret drawer." My First Sense flares up—or at least I feel like it does, this weird fluttering nausea sensation.

And no wonder why: in the very back of the drawer lies a small envelope, sealed. And the kicker?

The letters NM written onto its front: Nonie Magnetta.

A wave of heat rolls down my body. Kieran left this for me. How long has that been there? When did he put it there? And most importantly…

"How did you know I was going to find it, Kieran?" I whisper.

"Find what?" Chase catches up with us, then sucks in a sharp breath when he sees me lift the envelope from the drawer. "Oh." He pales. "Nonie—"

"Let her." Zio lays a hand on his friend's forearm. "Let *him.*"

I fumble to open the envelope. Fine motor skills are gone. I want to rip it open to get to the letter faster, while at the same time want to keep it as pristine as possible. Kieran wrote to me. I pull out the paper and unfold it with shaking hands:

> N,
>
> It's been years since you first arrived. Years. I can't forget, and I don't want to. I always have the hope that we meet again, but the way you react when we talk about the academy… I doubt it. We won't see each other there. Time and, well, probably death, have separated us for good. Something will happen to me, and to be honest, my main regret is that I won't see you again. Or maybe it's better that way, I'd be old, you'd

still be young.

I hope that when you find these lines, you're in a good place, in more than one sense of the word. I'm sorry I won't be there for you, even if it were only as a friend and mentor. You'll have Chase and Zio though, that much is clear. I think they're getting worried about me. I've been moody lately, but in my defense, the war has taken a toll on me. Without you I'm missing a stabilizer, a balancing force in my life, and all the killing is so much harder to take. I wish we could stop it.

You know, the nightmares are getting worse. Every night I hear them, without fail. Can't even let me sleep in peace. Zio is worried I'm getting suicidal, but it's not that. I feel them in my dreams. Don't tell Zio or Chase, or they're gonna call me crazy, but I feel them. It's just all so draining.

By the way, don't ask me why after all those years I feel like I have to write this down for you. After all, I always hope you'll be back, but... I don't know. Maybe this war is affecting me more than I'd like to admit to myself. Maybe it's the lack of sleep and those nightmares taking their toll. To be honest, it feels odd leaving a message for over three decades. So much can happen, and here I am, writing on a piece of paper, of all things. Back to the basics, I guess. And in the end it doesn't matter how I leave those words as long as I leave them, because there's always the risk that this is going to be my only way of saying what needs to be said. We never had time on our side, did we?

I hope you make it here and find this letter as a sign that no matter time or death, no matter how little of said time we spent together, for me you were it.

You were it.

Love,
K

Kieran.

Kieran.

The letter turns to heavy lead in my hands. Carefully, I lay it onto the desk, then bury my face in my hands and focus on breathing. *You were it.* Reading those words in his voice is heaven and hell at the same time. It's been mere *hours* and I miss him. Terribly, like on a physical level. While the fight with Mashaule didn't help, those bruises have stopped hurting. My heart, for a lack of a better term, hasn't.

"I should've known he'd leave you something." A brief look of sorrow crosses Chase's face, replaced by a wistful smile. "It's something he'd do."

I nod once. Can't talk. There's a lump in my throat the size of a boulder. *I always have the hope that we'll meet again.* So do I. And to imagine he's gone, that he knew he might die—

Oh, Sun and Stars. I glance back down at the letter: It's dated one day before his death.

One freakin' day before he died.

My heart seizes and then shatters, broken by the sheer unfairness of life. Of fate. Of time.

Zio lays one hand on my shoulder. "Nonie, Kieran always—"

"Bridge to Admiral Conolly." Chase's Hablamate lights up once with the incoming hail.

He taps it. "Go ahead."

"Your presence is still requested in the conference room."

Translation: get moving.

A muscle in Chase's jaw ticks. "And we will be there momentarily. Conolly out." He taps the hablamate again, cutting off the other side. "Considering they're bossing around two admirals, they're quite passive-aggressive. Who the heck does that person think they are? No, for real, who the heck are they?"

"I guess we will find out in a minute. Are you ready, Nonie?" Zio squeezes my shoulder once.

Being in Kieran's quarters, reading his words, it feels so much like *before*, like forty years ago, that part of me is surprised to find the older Upinga looking at me with worry in his eyes when I turn around, and not his younger counterpart.

"I'm ready, I guess." My voice is thick. I'll need a while to come to terms with everything, and I mean *everything*. I fold the letter, put it back into the drawer and close it. It's safer here. It belongs here. With

Kieran.

"Okay then. Let's go." Chase crosses the room, and the doors open once they detect his path. "I'm sure we'll have time to come back here, Nonie." He rubs a palm across my upper back when I pass him. "In fact, I feel like before we leave, the three of us should have a little talk anyway. Kieran's quarters are perfect for that, don't you agree, Zee?"

"I do." Admiral Upinga leads us toward the conference room a few doors down the hallway. "There's a lot to be discussed." His last word is drowned out by a swooshing sound of the doors to the conference room as they open. Zio steps in, followed by Chase and me behind—

Chase stops dead in his tracks. "Oh."

That *oh*, it carries a whole motherlode of information, none of it reassuring: *Oh*, crap. *Oh, you. Oh*, no. *Oh*-oh.

I squeeze past Chase. Wait, is that—

Grazer.

My entire body tenses. "You." I narrow my eyes at the man sitting at the right of the table, just a mere two meters away from me. To say that I have mixed feelings about him would be an understatement.

"Lieutenant," the admiral replies, looking at a spot somewhere over my head.

I curl my hands into fists. Clarification: not mixed feelings. Angry feelings. "You let Mashaule—"

"Nonie." The voice coming from the left is like a homing beacon of childhood, restraining my anger and releasing a flood of happy hormones.

I whip my head over. "Dad?"

My dad all but jumps out of his chair across from Grazer and rushes over to me. "Nonie." He scoops me into an embrace bigger than any I can remember, unless I count the one after my abduction. On that day he had to be more careful because of my injuries, so today takes the cake. He makes good use of his power to squish me, not that I mind it. No matter my rank, no matter what happens, I'm always going to be his daughter first. And right now, daughter-me is ecstatic to see her dad.

He exhales harsh next to my ear, his self-sealing mask rubbing over my cheek and bumping into mine. "Almost nine years, Nonie. Waiting and seeing the inevitable happen in front of my eyes... I'm so, so happy." He swallows hard—but I'm hung up on the first part of the sentence.

"You knew since *then*?" I untangle myself the slightest bit so I can look at him. He knew since I was kidnapped?

Dad lets go of me, but keeps both hands on my shoulders. "Biggest mindfu—surprise of my life, I can tell you."

I don't get it. Isn't that *not* supposed to happen? *Keeping the future secret and the timeline intact*, etc blah blah? "Why? How? Did Star Hopper tell you? How would she have known—"

"Because she was one of my operatives," a raspy voice comments from the table inside the conference room. Wait, is that—

I look past my dad. "Taro Magona?" I blink hard. Why is the Taro on the *Pioneer*? That makes absolutely no sense.

"Good to see you again, Nonie Magnetta." The Magellan lowers her head in greeting. Forty years, and like Zio she has aged well. With her wearing a mask, I only notice a couple of more lines in her face, in addition to the few lighter streaks of hair. Otherwise, she looks like the woman I saw a few days ago—forty years in the past.

"Taro," Zio bows the slightest. "This is—"

"Don't tell me *unexpected*, Zee." Chase squeezes past the road block my dad and I are causing.

"I was going to say a pleasure." Zio takes a seat on the left, diagonally across from the Taro. "I have always considered the Magellan's involvement a distinct possibility."

He has? "Involvement in what?" I slide into the chair next to him, and this time Dad sits down across from me, next to Grazer. To be honest, I'm glad I'm sitting. I feel as if I've been hit by a truck, and not because of that ever-present ache and soul-ripping sensation since I came back from the past, but because fate keeps throwing me hook after hook. Eventually, it becomes exhausting.

The Taro lowers her head. "That is exactly what I intend to discuss with you."

"Color me intrigued after ordering us over to the *Pioneer*, of all ships." Chase takes the seat on my other side, so that I'm boxed in between him and Zio, kind of where… I swallow hard, as the ache inside my chest intensifies. Kind of where Kieran sat the last time we met the

Taro.

Which also puts me right across from Admiral Grazer.

Good.

I like to keep an eye on him, just in case.

The Taro folds her hands on the table in front of her and leans forward. "I apologize for the manner of requesting your presence, but this meeting is classified." She makes a swiping motion with her hand. As if I'd been punched in the gut, I suck in a sharp gasp. The patch on her shoulder is a rainbow-like swirl in the center of a circle. Recognition strikes, and it brings a wave of... deja vu. That patch, plus the Taro wearing a black uniform instead of the typical Magellan dark-blue makes it easy to do the math.

I lift a shaking finger to point at her patch. "That's the uniform and sign the officer who rescued me was wearing."

Magona folds her hands on the table. "Correct."

But that also means I did said math wrong all my life until now. "I always assumed the black uniform meant D-2, and it made sense—only I was wrong."

It meant *this*.

Whatever *this* is.

A faint smile pulls on the corners of her mouth. "Also correct."

Chase raises a hand. "I know I'm always a step behind when Magellans are involved, but may I ask—"

"What it stands for?"

He nods. "Assuming it will open a whole new Pandora's Box, since I'm seeing both, USEF insignia *and* Magellan. On the same uniform."

"A fact that I am quite curious about myself." Grazer narrows his brows. "Being very aware that the USEF's policy on cooperation with Magellans is limited." His glance slides over to my dad, then right back at the Magellan. "And because of that, I also wouldn't mind if you could start by explaining what it stands for, Taro."

Magona tilts her head to the side. "Of course. This is the sign of the FBTI, the Federal Bureau of Temporal Investigation."

My jaw drops. "Temporal investigation?" Holy Sun and stars, that's coming out of the blue. *Temporal* Investigations…! Not sure which part of the name makes me more nervous.

Sucking in a sharp breath, Chase reaches behind me and taps Zio on the shoulder. "This it, Zee? Does this explain it?"

Zio cocks his head. "If you all let the Taro speak, we'd know."

Temporal Investigations… not good. What did I do? My blood pressure drops as fear begins to spread. "Is it because of where I'm coming from— I mean, Taro, you know where I just came back from, right?"

"Of course I do, Lieutenant. I remember meeting you forty years ago, which for you should only have been a few days. At that time, I didn't know the details, but I felt something was different about you— after *Commander* Upinga reminded me to check my First Sense. Still appreciate that, Admiral." She bows toward him, and Zio mirrors the gesture.

"Anytime, Taro. Anytime."

Grazer swallows so hard I hear it from across the table. "Are you telling me— Am I to understand that the lieutenant traveled back in time? And you knew about it?" He looks at my dad.

The Taro answers instead. "My operative had to warn Admiral Thorburn about the dangers ahead for the lieutenant. It was imperative that she go to the academy and choose her path, no matter the obstacles."

I've got to say, hearing it like that makes the whole free will-thing look a bit shaky. The academy was all I ever wanted, but was it because *I* wanted it, or because the *timeline* needed me to be there? Or is that the same? What a headache. Again.

Grazer shakes his head ever so slightly, mouth opening and closing behind his mask, no words coming out as he tries to digest the news. Welcome to my life, sir.

Magona cocks her head. "The FBTI is a very elite and secret branch of the combined USEF and Magellan forces, and by secret, I mean top secret."

Dad sits up straighter. "So are you telling me USEF is developing common sense when it comes to working with non-humans? And why do I not know about it? I'm the Liaison to the Magellan people, for crying out loud!"

"Rest assured, Admiral, that only a mere handful of authorized officers know about our organization. And to answer the first part of your question, to a certain degree, yes. We are autonomous, off the records—"

"In other words, rogue." Grazer keeps his gaze glued to the table. The way he sits, his shoulders hunched over, head lowered… He looks beaten. Not to the point I pity the man, but still it's a noticeable difference compared to how I know him.

"We prefer the phrasing *off any official documentation or oversight*. We were founded almost fifty years ago, shortly after the first contact between our people, when the Admiralty wasn't as near-sighted as they are today."

Zio's brows scrunch together. "But pardon me, Taro. Maybe I'm just confused about a Bureau of Temporal Investigation that humanity knows about. Or maybe I'm overly sensitive, as I myself was forbidden to return to Mag-2 or to take a partner because of my decision to join USEF and the risk the Magellan High Council thought I was to our… *special talents*." The last sentence holds some bitterness I can't fault him for that, especially assuming he's referring to the Magellan's *special talents* when it comes to sensing the timeline.

Magona folds her hands on top of the table in front of her, real empathy shining from her eyes. "I regretted that decision ever since I had to make it, Admiral Upinga. It seemed unfairly cruel and unnecessary, but it needed to happen. You had to be where the timeline needed you. As for your future… we will reevaluate, for obvious reasons. As for your concern regarding sharing our *special talents* with humanity… it's also what the timeline needed. Our First Sense and its foreboding is the reason why we founded the FBTI."

Dad gasps. "The First Sense… I thought it gave you more a general idea of the future. Very rough. But it's so sensitive you founded a whole bureau around it?"

It's so sensitive? He knows about what the First Sense can do? Whoa, Dad! Didn't see that one coming. Maybe the Magellans aren't as good at keeping this secret as they thought.

Judging by the Taro's raised eyebrow, she's equally surprised. "You know about the abilities of the First Sense."

Dad squirms in his seat. "Well…" He casts a careful glance at me.

"Having a Magellan wife… you pick up certain things over the years." His cheeks redden, and he straightens his collar. "And uhh, again, I— I'm the Liaison. It's literally in my job description to know these things."

Well, he has a point. Dad is the best informed person about Magellan culture I can think of. Plus, him and Mom were together for what, over fifteen years—twenty?— before her death, and when you live that closely—

Click.

Oh.

No, of course not. "Huh. But you didn't live with Mom," I say. It's obvious. She's Magellan, he's an officer with USEF. I look at the man who's much better at keeping secrets than I am. "You saw her whenever you went to Mag-2." A minor epiphany in the grand scheme of things, yet still an epiphany. I always imagined my parents as, well, the classic couple until Mom died. Didn't question it, and why would I? Dad didn't tell me much anyway, and while now I know why, I didn't think about the day-to-day as a human-Magellan couple once I found out Mom was Magellan.

Dad and I, we *so* need to talk.

He grimaces. "Yes. No. We didn't live together. How could we have with all human and several Magellan laws against us. All laws… but at least not all people." A wistful look softens his expression. "I couldn't have kept seeing your mom if Captain Wildason hadn't suggested me as the liaison. I don't think you'd ever been born then."

Oh. I blush hearing Kieran's name coming from my dad. There's so much to talk about, so many details. So much heartbreak, for both of us.

Dad smacks his lips and leans forward. "And he wasn't the only help I had, as you all know. I was incredibly lucky to have colleagues and friends who stood by me and supported me." He looks from Zio to Chase, then over to Grazer, his voice heavy with emotion when he carries on. "You all knew about Kelia and me from one point in time, and you all did your part to help and support us. And while we never talk about it, please do know that I appreciate it from the bottom of my heart. I wouldn't have Nonie without all of your protection. And I wouldn't have her safe here without it either." Warmth shines from his eyes as he makes it a point to look at every single person seated at the table. "Thank you all, from the bottom of my heart. You made the impossible possible and you kept us safe."

Aw, Dad. I clear my throat from the lump clogging it while Chase rubs his neck, the slightest pink coloring his cheeks. "I think I speak for all of us when I say it wasn't a big deal, Tom. You've known our point of view in these things. We—"

"I didn't see it. I should've, probably, but I didn't." Grazer's words, spoken so softly, yet in such a beaten tone, cut Chase right off.

"See what?" Dad sounds as confused as everybody else looks.

Grazer takes a long, controlled breath in. "What Mashaule had planned for Nonie. I didn't know the mission to retrieve the plants was a setup. The only red flag was that planetary core, but nothing else. I… I understand the planet was inhabited by Quaneez?" True embarrassment shines in his eyes—no, *remorse*. Grazer is *sorry*.

I lower my chin in a nod. "Yes. And Mashaule's adjustments to the shuttle's systems were designed to destabilize the core and destroy the planet." And with it the Quaneez. And, well, me.

Dad cramps his fingers into a fist hearing that, while Grazer turns even whiter. "From what I knew, the planet was uninhabited. I—I don't want to make an excuse, but maybe he manipulated…?" He glances over to Zio.

"I'll check for traces of tampering within our database." Zio makes a note on his PAD.

"Thank you. But, either way, all information he gave me… The data looked good, and…" He releases the rest of his breath in one puff into his mask, not raising his gaze from the table. "And yes, knowing him, I was worried he might plan something, but then, I couldn't find anything or fault him. He was right picking Nonie. It was out of left field, but reasonable picking her. She's good, despite her youth."

My eyes pop so wide, they must be bulging out of my skull. Grazer actually thinks I'm good! Holy Sun and stars—it shouldn't matter to me, not at this point, but hearing it feels fantastic. Actually, it fills up all those deprived ego storage cells that had to survive on a strict diet whenever Grazer was involved.

Dad twists in his seat to face his colleague. "Bas. It's okay. You had my back all those years and Mashaule has always been cunning. I don't fault you for any of this."

Finally Grazer looks up, face tense, meeting Dad's gaze. "Still, I'm sorry. For all her academy time I tried to keep your daughter away from me with a ten-foot pole, but she still caught Mashaule's eye, despite my efforts to the contrary. There's only so much one can do rejecting a top student over and over again without raising suspicion."

Oh. Double-oh. I squirm on my chair. How blissfully unaware was I, thinking my biggest problem was him not liking me. Reality check. I was so wrong, in so many ways.

Dad chuckles. "Tell me about it. You know, no offense, but I tried to keep her away from you, too. That worked out well." He gives me the paternal look of disapproval, but it comes with a loving, proud gleam in his eyes.

Grazer lifts a corner of his mouth in a sad approximation of a smile. "We didn't stand a chance, Tom. Remember I tried to warn you admitting her to the academy would be a mistake? You're just lucky Mashaule didn't find out about Kelia, or else you would be in jail or possibly dead right now, and so would Nonie. This way at least he only saw the potential in her to bring you down." Grazer deflates and sighs, then looks at me. "Lieutenant. I'm sorry. I tried to keep you away from D-2, but…"

For the first time since I started at the academy, I think I understand Admiral Grazer and why he acted the way he did. Not because he didn't like me, not because he didn't want me for his division, but because he was trying to protect Dad and me. What a reversal. I literally didn't see that coming.

I give him a smile that hopefully conveys I'm not holding a grudge. "Yeah, you couldn't have kept me away from D-2." All I wanted was to join, be that because of my own free will or because the flow of time demanded it. Who knows these days? And go figure that I had it all wrong. Not D-2, but the FBTI is where I want to be.

Which brings me back to the obvious elephant in the room and the noose around my neck since the Taro mentioned the FBTI. "Taro, with all that being said, since you're from the Bureau of Temporal Investigation, and here I am, I can't help but assume I did something wrong on the *Pioneer*." My insides cramp, adding another layer of discomfort to the existing ache. "What did I do? What did I mess up in the past?" I was so careful, so damn careful, but fate kept throwing me in for a loop. What did I do wrong? How bad is it? Everything seems normal on first glance.

The Taro shakes her head. "Lieutenant, you needn't worry. The reason why the admirals and you are here is not because you did something wrong, but because we need you."

Huh? "Whom?"

"You, Lieutenant. We need you to travel back in time and protect Captain Kieran Wildason from an assassination that could kill him before his official death on June 8th, 2257."

Chapter Fifty-Six

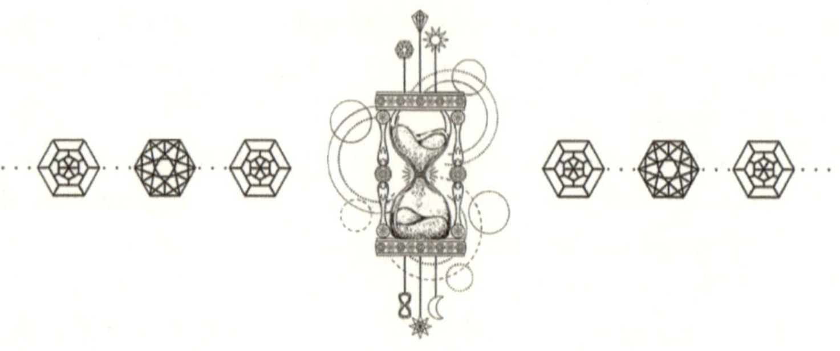

USEF Pioneer, Conference Room, Day 0

ilence.

Stunned, all-encompassing silence hovers, heavy as a lead blanket. I blink and pinch myself under the table, but it doesn't change a thing. "You want me to travel back in time and save Kieran from an assassination?" I heard her words, but they make no sense.

"I believe that's what I just said." The Taro activates the conference table's display. "Now. If I may explain myself—"

"Oh, please." Chase leans back into his chair and waves a hand. "Don't stop on our account."

"Thank you. Admirals, Lieutenant. There is an urgency behind this meeting I cannot stress enough." She pauses and looks at each of us in turn before she continues. "Over the last weeks it has become increasingly clear that we are at the brink of a temporal war."

"A temporal war?" Grazer leans forward, adjusting his face mask with one hand, surprise and disbelief flickering across his face. "Are you kidding—?"

A slicing hand motion from the Taro cuts him right off. Talk about authority. Magona oozes it from every pore, and even Grazer is affected by it. "You will learn that I do not kid about matters of time, Admiral. It may come as a surprise to you, but we are living in an altered timeline already—modified with help by your old friend Admiral Mashaule."

"What?" I blurt.

Everyone's eyes bulge as wide as mine likely are. Well, besides Zio's, maybe.

Dad is all business as he effortlessly slips into his admiral persona. No trace is left of the softie-dad who thanked everybody for keeping his daughter safe less than a minute ago. This is Admiral Thorburn, ready to take on the world: spine straight, eyes narrowed, head cocked to the side. "What do you mean? How can we be in an alternate timeline? What's the impact? How do we know?"

Before the Taro can reply, Zio cuts in. "To a degree, our genes protect us from the loss of memory that comes with alterations to the timeline. Depending on our personal ability, one Magellan's skills might be greater than another's, and I can assure you the Taro, as the head of the M-3 and our science division, is the most skilled and talented of all of us."

Something lights up in the Taro's eyes. "I didn't know you thought that way, Admiral."

"Always have, Taro. There was just no opportunity for me to express that sentiment."

For an eternal second, they look at each other, like, *really* look at each other, but before it gets too awkward for the rest of us, the Taro drops her gaze and clears her throat. "As I was about to explain, we also know about the future's interference because of the traces they left. Breadcrumbs, to use a human analogy. There were several instances during which the upstream powers tried to change the course of time, but to what desired outcome is not quite clear to us, as there were different targets with no obvious connection. I believe the initial contact occurred with Captain Mashaule at Alpha Rubrum. As far as we can tell, Admiral Mashaule has been receiving intermittent orders from the future for several decades. He has had help from the future at critical points in our past with the intention to alter them, as he has already tried on Alpha Rubrum. You noticed the odd readings on the *Eclipse*'s systems." Magona gives an acknowledging nod to Zio.

"You read my log, Taro." Appreciation rings in Zio's words. "And yes, they were odd readings indeed. On key systems on the *Eclipse*, as well as on Nonie's shuttle back on the *Pioneer*."

"They struck you as odd for a reason: both modifications were performed with tools from the future. We assume Mashaule was recruited from about two hundred years up the stream of time. We also assume their technology allows communication through time and, to a degree, travel through time, but from what we know, neither are very precise."

"Well, that's reassuring." Chase rolls his eyes. "Let's send somebody through time and make it a surprise when they pop up."

I cut him side eye. "Yeah. Who'd do that?" Because one of us was thrown to the wolves and told to follow her First Sense when nobody knew it was going to work.

Taro Magona ignores our comments. "*Two*, the second attempt to alter the flow of time: Kieran Wildason's assassination attempt as a child."

My jaw drops. Is she talking about— "The babysitter? She was from the future?"

Zio raises a surprised eyebrow at my comment, while Chase gives me a short acknowledging nod and sly grin. "See? Told you it wasn't my place to tell the story." Then, he sombers up and addresses the Taro. "Now that you mention that incident, Kieran was also at Alpha Rubrum. Do we assume their goal is to kill him? And if so, why? He died not long after Alpha Rubrum. A few years."

The Taro frowns. "Unclear. It is a possibility his death is the ultimate goal, but I feel we're unaware of another, vital, piece of information. Without wanting to undermine his accomplishments until his death, I cannot see any event that, if eliminated, would alter the course of time."

Her words sting much more than they should. Maybe because I'm hurting all over already, maybe because I left Kieran less than two hours ago, maybe because I just read a letter he wrote to me a mere day before his death—but what the Taro is saying is that Kieran didn't matter. Not enough, at least.

Magona shifts her gaze to me. "Another reason why I do not think Captain Wildason was the ultimate target is because there is a third intervention years after Captain Wildason's death and unrelated to him: your kidnapping, Lieutenant."

"What?" Dad and I shout it out in unison. His face turns red, while

I feel the color drain from mine.

"The kidnapping," I whisper. Of course. Knowing what I know now, it makes sense. I reach across the table and lay a hand on Dad's forearm. "Remember how the kidnappers vanished from the USEF jail? I bet—"

The Taro lowers her head in agreement. "You are betting correctly, Lieutenant. The two men who kidnapped you were from the future and escaped back to it after their capture."

My kidnappers were from the future. That sounds beyond unbelievable, but not because of the time travel part. I can get behind that, but… "Why would they kidnap *me* and think it would change anything?" I'm *me*. Kieran, as hard as it is to think that, is a more worthy target to take out, no matter what the Taro thinks. His impact was—is—far reaching, who knows whom he might have influenced who could change the world. I don't think Magona is seeing the full picture here, meaning, taking Kieran out of the equation would make sense in a morbid way. But me?

The Taro shakes her head. "That I don't know, Lieutenant. Their motive is unclear to me."

Dad clenches his jaw so hard, it's a wonder he can talk. "All these attempted alterations, and we still don't know what they're after? How do I know they're not going to target Nonie again?"

"You don't, Admiral. But I do trust in two things: that we can give her the training and support to thwart any additional attacks on her person, and that the timeline will correct itself to a degree, like it has done before. After all, the lieutenant has gone to the Academy and ended up in this very moment."

Agreed, I have. But I still feel like Magona might be missing something there. What if I was almost killed because of something I am destined to do and haven't done yet? Maybe going to the academy and ending up right here, right now, wasn't what the kidnappers were concerned about. And maybe now I won't do whatever great thing I was destined to do because of said kidnapping. I'm seventeen with many years ahead of me, I hope. Maybe the jury is still out whether the timeline corrected itself or not. Maybe it corrected itself, *for now*.

Dad is equally skeptical. "You're sure about that?"

"One hundred percent. That I can feel. My First Sense is quite clear about it."

That makes at least one of us.

"Excuse me." Grazer shakes his head, for the first time looking more like the admiral I'm used to. "I understand what you're saying, Taro, but why do we have to deal with this? The problem originates in the future, let them handle it."

Taro turns to face Grazer. "To a degree, we are the future handling it, as you phrased it. We have been—and we will." Her gaze brushes over to Dad, before she returns her focus to Grazer. "I can tell you that the timeline strongly prefers our interference. We do not have any other choice."

I rub my forehead. At some point, I'd just like to go home, take a bath, and think of absolutely nothing. Alas, looks like that's not going to happen anytime soon. Pun intended.

Magona reaches behind her and retrieves a black bundle. "Which brings me back to the purpose of this meeting. Lieutenant Thorburn, with your unique sensitivity to the timeline, you are of the utmost value to this mission. I hereby am offering you a position with the FBTI. You will need to be trained, your First Sense to be honed further, and we will need you to have support within USEF—and with support I mean you, Admirals." She nods at Upinga, Conolly, Dad, Grazer, then back at me. "Do you accept the invitation to join the FBTI, Lieutenant?"

I don't need time to think. Maybe it's my First Sense or good old human common sense, who knows, but accepting feels right. "With pleasure, Taro. Yes, I do. I accept." Because since I was nine years old, I wanted to be like *her*. Wanted to fight the good fight. Wanted to wear that uniform. Small errors in interpretation of said uniform's origin aside, that's what I worked hard for. And now I'm there. Am *here*.

It feels simultaneously more and less like an accomplishment compared to when Grazer promoted me to lieutenant. Today, it feels right. Right-*er*. Like I had done even more to earn the uniform. After all, I made it through eighty years of time, if you count both directions of travel. And I might've figured out a few crucial details about the Quaneez, although I'm not ready to blurt it out loud in front of everybody. *New FBTI officer? She didn't have her facts right.* Nope. It'll be a discussion between Zio, Chase, and me, for starters.

Magona pushes the neat bundle of black clothing she retrieved over to me. "Lieutenant, it is my pleasure to welcome to the FBTI. Here is your uniform."

I catch the clothing and pull it into my lap, the fabric soft against—

A sharp, unnatural sting shoots though my midsection, making me gasp. It comes with such an overwhelming nausea, such an overwhelming sense of doom I have to put both palms on the table to stabilize and convince myself the floor isn't moving. As if something yanked on my insides, shoving open a door that wasn't there before, I see things—no, I *feel* them, similar to an awareness when somebody else is in the room, this feeling grows by the second.

And it's not good.

Not at all.

"Crap," I whisper, my voice hoarse and breaking at the end. One hand pressed into my stomach I look up. Zio and the Taro, they're not doing much better than me.

The only ones unaffected are the humans. Chase looks from his friend to the Taro. "Guys. Guys? Hey. What's wrong?" He turns to his side, facing me. "Nonie?"

Dad stands so fast, his chair topples back. "Nonie? What's going on? Are you all—?"

I ignore them both. If I'm right what this means… Looking at the Taro, I ask her, "You felt it? You both?" I nod at Zio. Because if I'm not mistaken, this was my First Sense acting up. No, *screaming out*, at a deafening volume.

"Yes," Magona confirms, her face pale. "The temporal war… it's changing. But I can't see who's the key—?"

I blink. "I… I think I can." Which is weird and scary and confusing at the same time, but I really think I can.

Her pupils widen. "You see it?" She sounds as incredulous as I feel, because… yeah, I do. I see it. Feel it. Whatever.

Rubbing a palm over my stomach, I nod, my breath coming in short bursts. The sense of doom is close to overpowering. "It's not clear-clear, not like I saw a movie. It's more like a distant memory… of something that hasn't happened yet, weird as it sounds." A bit fuzzy around the edges, more black-and-white than in color, and kind of in flux. But the overall direction is quite clear. Unfortunately so.

"You're describing what your intuition from your First Sense should be like, Lieutenant. What are you seeing?"

I let go of a shaky puff of air. "Mashaule. He made a decision that's about to alter the timeline." That's the sensation I'm feeling, I'm sure of it without ever having read a First Sense one-oh-one manual. Like I know what hunger feels like, or thirst, or fear: this is the feeling of the timeline about to reshape if we don't act.

"Wait, what?" Chase looks at the Taro, then at me.

"I feel something else too, like an imbalance in the future, like something's changed...?" If old-me could hear myself, about one month ago, I'd call myself crazy, but it makes absolute sense right now.

Zio is pale, his eyes wide and dark as he nods. "I feel it too. Like there was a rift and a connection from the future to the present that wasn't there before." His gaze whips over to the Taro, her face ashen.

"We have to act." She taps her hablamate. "Magona to demat room. Prepare for demat. And get us permission for room-to-room to USEF Central Arrest."

"*Acknowledged, Taro,*" says a voice from the hablamate.

"And do what?" Dad clenches his fists. "Talk to me, somebody!" A hint of panic rings in his voice, the type that comes when somebody who's used to calling the shots feels out of the loop.

I keep my hands pressed into my stomach. "Whatever Mashaule has just decided to do will alter the past. From what I see—" I glance at the Taro. Not sure how much to trust myself yet.

"Go ahead," Taro gives me a curt nod.

"From what I see, something or somebody upstream from us has interacted with Mashaule, which has caused him to make the decision that's about to change the flow of time." And not for the better.

War. Death. Despair.

The images keep flashing in front of my inner eye, like a distant memory I can't quite grasp. It's quite weird, actually.

All color drains from Dad's face. "Oh. A new player? Or the same upstream force you've been talking about?"

Magona is all business. "That remains to be seen. Fact is, if we don't intervene, history as we know it and with it the future, is going to be rewritten. They attempted to alter time before and failed, because we corrected it—will correct it. Now somebody is trying to do so again. Lieutenant, Admirals Conolly and Upinga. The three of you will demat to USEF Central Arrest without me. Obviously, as a Magellan, my options are limited. Admirals Thorburn and Grazer, you will remain here for the time being."

Zio stands up as well. "I assume we are to interrogate Admiral Mashaule—"

"Interrogate, apprehend, and listen to your First Sense. Secure him and keep him under observation until I have contacted my USEF sources and we can transfer him to an FBTI-secured facility. This goes beyond USEF security at this point." Her expression darkens. "May your First Sense lead you well, or else the timeline might be affected beyond repair."

Chapter Fifty-Seven

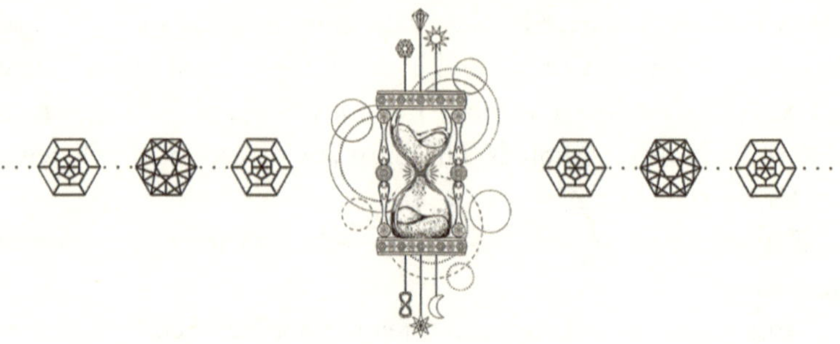

USEF Central Arrest, Earth, present time

One thing can be said about the Taro—she doesn't mess around. Within two minutes, we've dematted from the *Pioneer* to Central Arrest smack dab in Nowhere, Iowa, directly into the facility. Magona's team gets stuff *done*. Fast. No lengthy security clearance, no nothing. Appreciate that, because if the sensation in my stomach and chest is any indication, time is of the essence.

I cringe. Shouldn't really use that phrase. At all.

The second my eyes adjust to the new environment I pick up on three armed security guards in front of the door of this small demat room.

And it's not just that they're armed. It's that their weapons are trained on us.

"At ease," Chase barks at them. "Weapons down, officers."

All three snap to attention. "Yes, sir. Adhering to protocol, sir."

"Wonderful." Chase steps off the demat platform. "Let's go. Cell Z-23. Zio, you and your photographic memory lead the way."

As soon as Zio begins to move, not only Chase and me fall behind him, but the three security guards as well. Annoying, but also reassuring. I'd rather have security tight in a prison.

We hurry down the nondescript hallways, their walls white, their floors sparkling clean, their ceilings dotted with cameras, the sensors integrated into the floors sending constant information to the central AI.

Zio sets the pace as his fast walk turns into a jog, then a run, and for the last few corners, he sprints.

I'm not the only one feeling the sense of doom, of inevitability. Those nauseating flutters churning inside my gut are cranking it up with every second. I'm a jumble of anxiety, fear, and dread as Chase and I stay on Zio's heels, my legs and heart pumping like crazy. We must be on time to stop Mashaule. Must be. Must, must, must.

After we've passed about ten or fifteen more narrow hallways on the left and right, Zio stops in front of another one. "Z-23." He turns halfway to face the security guys, who probably think we're crazy sprinting here, but still kept up. "Lower the force field." He jabs a finger in the direction of where I assume is Mashaule's cell. Because USEF Central Arrest uses force fields rather than doors, it looks like I could walk straight down toward the admiral, but I ain't stupid enough to try. I don't appreciate being struck by a forcefield's electricity. At all.

The guard who spoke in the demat room steps forward. "Weapons, please. This part is high-security. No weapons allowed by anybody."

"Not going to happen. I'll keep my weapon," Chase growls, placing one protective hand over it.

"Then I cannot let you enter." He narrows his eyes.

Zio shakes his head, a wild, concerned look on his face. "Chase. Time." He rips his weapon out of the holster and slams it into the guard's palm.

Cursing once, Chase draws his and does the same. "And now lower the freakin' forcefield!"

"Yes, sir." The guard enters a command into the touch panel integrated into the wall and confirms it with his hand print. A second later, a red light flashes around hallways opening, accompanied by a warning tone. "You can pass in five seconds, once the sound and light alerts stop. The field will reengage after three. Do not touch the prisoner's forcefield. It's set to high."

The nausea, my constant companion for the last few minutes, intensifies.

The blinking stops—

And we run.

That short sprint, down the hallway for what, maybe twenty meters, feels like it takes forever. Nausea, pain, fear, they all swirl together into a suffocating mix, strangulating every breath I try to take.

We dash past several other cells, all occupied, some of the prisoners wearing a prison hood. A shudder runs down my back. Prison hoods are cruel: Complete sensory deprivation. Can't see who's underneath it, and they can't see what's in front of them. The people having to wear them must be high-profile prisoners or really bad guys.

Some tall ensign walks toward us, maybe in his thirties. He jumps aside and salutes, an odd expression on his face. "Admirals. Lieut—"

And we're past him, me in the lead, the other two following.

A few more meters and we can secure Mashaule—

I stop dead in front of his cell, panting, wheezing—

No clue what I expected, but not Mashaule sitting on his cot, a tray with food next to him and an arrogant gleam in his eyes when his gaze falls on me. He looks calm. Collected. Which is completely at odds with the urgency I'm feeling. The admiral looks comfy and at ease in his fresh prison uniform, while I'm still stuck in my forty-year old outfit from the *Pioneer*. Meaning, while I probably look like something the cat dragged in, he's all clean and spiffy, and definitely not like *he* was dragged out of the *Guardian's* demat room less than two hours ago, with a bloody face nonetheless. To my very disappointment, he's been well taken care of. Wouldn't have minded letting him bleed a bit longer.

Chase and Zio stop right next to me, both straightening out the uniforms as they do, Zio's breath coming out as short and irregular as mine.

Mashaule's eyes narrow. "Thorburn. Where's the fire?" He greets me with a lazy wave of his wrist, but doesn't spare a single glance at Zio or Chase.

I curl my fingers into fists. "Why don't you tell me?"

"Ouch, so aggressive. One could think you don't like me." He juts his lower lip forward in an arrogant fake sad expression that makes me wish somebody had slapped a prison hood, or at least a face mask, on that man. The less to be seen of him, the better.

"If one thought I don't like you, they'd be right." *Admiral.* The word is *this* close to leaving my mouth after years of obeying the hierarchy of command, but I keep it in. He doesn't deserve either, the title or my respect.

Chase steps closer to the forcefield. Anger flares in his eyes—barely controlled anger. His body is coiled, as if he could reach through the field, grab Mashaule, and shake some sense into him. "What are you planning? What's the next thing you're going to wreck?"

Mashaule wears a scowl that could kill on sight. "I never got what women saw in you, Conolly. What anybody saw in you. You're lacking the IQ to recognize when things have to change."

There—wrapped in an insult, an opening! My insides tighten. "What needs to change?"

"The future, of course. And for it, the past."

Sun and Stars. His words bring another wave of nausea. Like his plan was solidifying as we speak. My pulse kicks into an erratic overdrive.

Chase's anger becomes a tangible third party. "You son of a—"

"But why?" Here's to the new me, who dares to cut off an admiral, but cursing at Mashaule is not the way to keep him talking. I think.

Mashaule's gaze meets mine. "Because it's faulty. I'm improving it."

Oh, wow. The nerve. "Who says it's faulty?" Any bit of information is key. Anything.

He shrugs. "I have my sources."

"Right. You sure they're trustworthy?" Because I doubt it. Whoever is calling the shots from the future has their own agenda and goals in mind. Not Mashaule's, I could bet.

"Very much so. And they're also very convincing." He slides forward on his cot until both feet hit the ground. "You're young, Thorburn, but let me tell you, we've made mistakes. Grave mistakes." A shadow crosses over his face. How I could ever think him and Grazer looked like Santa, I don't know. I must've missed the cold look in Mashaule's eyes, the tight lines around his mouth, and for sure the aura of arrogance surrounding him.

Well, you live, you learn. I straighten up and cross my arms in front of my chest. I need to know whatever he has planned, or else we can't prevent it. Or, we can't *hope* to prevent it. At this very moment my First Sense is running amok, showing me bits and pieces of a dystopian future, picking at my sanity and dismantling it bit by bit.

We're losing this game we don't know how to play.

"Mistakes," I say, scrambling to keep him talking, interacting.

"What kind of mistakes?"

He huffs. "Many of them. Too many. Our biggest, though, was to not extinguish the Quaneez when we had the chance, early on. It could've prevented so many deaths." His jaw tightens.

To a degree, I have to agree. Less people dying would've been better, no doubt about it. Still, I give a slow shake of my head. "But that's not the way it happened." And how would we know we're not preventing one disaster and at the same time opening the door for another?

"No, it's not what happened. But it could've been, and even though there's a price to pay, for which I'm terribly sorry, it's a small price if we consider the grand scheme of things. The biggest pity is that history will never know the role his early death played. That it saved billions of people."

An icy arrow shoots through my heart. *His death*. "Kieran."

Chase and Zio must've done the math like me, if their simultaneous sharp intake of air is any indication.

Mashaule lifts an eyebrow. "Yes. Wildason. He was annoying before I knew what taking him out early could change, but now that I know…" He stands up, shoving both hands in his pockets. "I'm willing to risk my life to save that of countless others."

"I don't think we're going to let you." Chase is so close to the forcefield, any closer and he'd touch it.

A slow smile creeps over Mashaule's face. "And I think you don't have a single word to say in this."

A chill tiptoes over the nape of my neck and my next breath gets stuck inside my throat. Something's happening—and it's happening *now*, without a doubt. The feeling is there, announcing *something* to happen—but what? What could Mashaule do from inside a super-secured prison cell?

Mashaule steps closer to the forcefield, looking at me like a specimen in the zoo. "You're trying to figure it out, aren't you?" he whispers. "Problem is, you're so far behind the curve. About two-hundred and fifty years, my dear."

With that, he pulls his right hand out of his pocket, an egg-sized grey disk between his fingers—

A tsunami of nausea rolls over me, no—*crashes* over me, barring no mercy, threatening to sweep me away and bury me to be forgotten in

the sea of time. Can't breathe, can't breathe, can't think, can't—can't—
can't…!

"This is the key," Mashaule whispers in awe, "to unlock the past."
Staring down onto the device, mouth half open, he presses his thumb
onto it—

Zing!

The device erupts into bright light, each and every ray penetrating
each and every fiber of my being, calling to me, energizing me, priming
me—

Within a microsecond, a warm, tingling sensation engulfs my chest.
My breath comes out short, rough—

Mashaule's form begins to flicker, like he was here, yet he wasn't.
I'm being torn forward, yanked by my soul, forced by powers I don't
understand.

"Good bye, Thorburn. It's nothing personal." Mashaule becomes
more and more translucent, his outline melting away—

Pressure builds in my chest. Something hot and urgent buzzes
through my veins, begging for a release, begging me to let go, to give in,
to—

A furious outcry bursts from Chase's throat. "He's leaving— He's
actually traveling back *right now!* Zio, do something, he—"

Dizzy. Can't focus. My insides are being torn apart, called upon by
forces of nature too powerful to deny.

"What am I supposed to do? I can't stop this! He's opened a
portal—"

Chase hammers his palm against the reader. "Lower the force field!
We can still stop him!"

But he's wrong.

We can't.

But I can.

Maybe.

Instinct takes over, calming the near-overpowering sensation of
dread.

I throw one last look at my mentors desperately trying to enter the
cell, to save the future, the past, and the present.

Then, I close my eyes and give myself over to the force of time.

About the Author

Micky O'Brady is a pediatrician-turned-writer living in beautiful, dry Southern California with her husband and two critters (one son, one dog). Micky loves to write YA thrillers with a romantic twist, mainly because she wishes her life had been such an awesome mix of action and cute guys when she was a teen.

When she isn't up at around 3 a.m. (with a cup of tea, Earl Grey, hot) drafting stories she can't get out of her head, she can be found at a martial arts dojo, though maybe not at 3 a.m. She holds a 2nd degree black belt in Judo and a brown belt in Krav Maga, and is convinced every girl should know how to kick some butt.

Micky also is a firm believer in the healing powers of Nutella eaten straight from the glass and in the magic that can happen on a rainy day, as long as there are fuzzy socks and a cup of hot tea involved.

Her previous publications include a doctoral thesis and several medical articles as well as a medical book about emergency communication. None of them are as fun to read as her YA novels though. Her first YA-novel, THE PRESIDENT'S DAUGHTER, and its sequel TRIAL BY ICE, are published by Curiosity Quills and available through all major retailers, such as Amazon, B&N, Kobo, and Smashwords.

Through Snowy Wings Publishing Micky is the author of YA-sci-fi romance BETWEEN WORLDS and PLAYING WITH #FIRE. She is happy to announce more novels will be coming your way.